TWO RIVERS

For Mary Lewis Harris, my late friend,
with whom I have shared the beauty of great music and great literature,
and who understood so well "the hard earned ecstasy"
which comes with the creation of an elevated line.

Acknowledgments

Two Rivers is the fulfillment of a dream begot in childhood
but which never would have materialized without these sponsors:

First, I want to thank my dear sister, Bernice Rawls,
who first read to me and who created enchanting stories,
introducing me to the magical world of words.

Second, Lynn Mertins, my English teacher colleague,
was my mentor and critic as *Two Rivers* evolved. It was she who
read chapter by chapter and gave invaluable input.

Third, Beverley Turner, my proofreader,
was better than my computer.

Fourth, my special thanks go to my little dog, Betsy, who
waited patiently many afternoons for her dinner.

Fifth, a whole roster of friends and relatives believed
in me and *Two Rivers:* Blanche Floyd, John and Eulee Williams,
Mary Pitts, Ben and Sharon Rawls, Gilly and Beverly Simmons,
Bonnie Williams, Sarah Brown, Thomas and Sharon Weidman,
Sister Kay Purser, Robert Lamb, Beth Woodward, Vivian and Charles
Funk, Margaret Williams, Nan Haskell, Louetta Williams,
Freeda Williams, Fr. Franklin Martin, Ruth Keaton, Johnnie Crowley.

Sixth, Cathy Harris Helms, granddaughter of Mary Harris,
to whom this book is dedicated, has rendered invaluable
service in research and legal advice.

Seventh, my hundreds of former students who have held me
to the promise that one day I would write.

And last, but not least, I thank E. Randall Floyd, my publisher, who,
after my many futile attempts with literary agents and
publishers, read my manuscript and found it worthy.

Two Rivers is for all of you. I thank you.

SOUTHERN MURAL

She sits on a low bench braiding her hair
  Dark woman!
Aslant in the doorway, cleaving the air,
  Dark woman!
Though pieces of porch will limit her view
She knows that the hills are a beautiful blue
That April has walked in the night and her tears
Have tendered and sweetened the bitterest years
That earth is yearning beneath the brown crust
To capture and claim her as burnt golden dust
  Dark woman!
As she sits, light and shadow catches her hair
Her dreams and her longings, what dreams do they share
In the leaning frame house, the gray color of earth
Are they laughter and caught to the colors of mirth
  Dark woman?
As I wait in the circling of broad fields to hear
Her answer as pungent as steel in the ear
With scarcely a turn to my reference to death
She sings in a sob on a single deep breath
  "Dark children!"

Mary Harris

PROLOGUE

SPRING COMES EARLY in the Deep South. No mountain snows trickle down to swell streams. Lakes do not clack under a thaw. Frigid days are few even in January, and winter's breath is little more than icy mists collapsing hours later under the gaze of Phoebus. Activity in the Low Country of South Carolina halts when infrequent snows stroke the earth in temporary paralysis. The farmer, after a one or two day holiday, returns to his plow, the fisherman to his stream, the tradesman to his shop—all await with no surprise the bursting buds of spring even as northern neighbors shiver in the cold blasts of March.

Clement as the weather is, life in Britton's Neck, a strip of dark land bordering the Little Pee Dee River, was harsh at the turn of the century for those dependent on corn and cotton for their livelihood. Children invented their own recreation and like the older residents of the Neck welcomed the warming earth bursting with fruit and flower. In this southern clime, spring also came early for many of the young maids, their swelling breasts obvious even before their teens. The woods edging the swamp where cypress and water oak stood knee deep in water was the stage where little girls play-acted adult roles, many of them unconscious of the woes of early motherhood. On such a morning in early May, barefoot time, Liza Marion, barely ten, and her cousins, Addie and Sally, had shed their high-topped shoes and cotton stockings and walked on the cool moss, peering under stumps and fallen logs for spring's first violets. Daisies were plentiful, but a purple violet with its yellow eye was as good as a four-leaf clover and bound to bring good luck to the first finder. For Addie and Sally, flower hunting soon palled, particularly since Liza's sharp eye spotted every crevice in which flowers nestled. They were ready for a new game.

"Let's play Mama," they trilled in chorus. Unwilling to be a spoilsport, Liza dutifully followed their lead, turning her gray gingham dress buttoned down the back to the front. Addie and Sally stuffed their flat bosoms with Spanish moss, unaware of the red bugs that would plague them later. Cradling bunches of wild honeysuckle to their bulging breasts, they were nursing mothers. Liza's breasts remained flat. She had scooped up her skirt and busied herself jumping from one tussock to another. "Come on, Liza," the little

Mamas begged. "Let's play."

Liza didn't want to be a Mama even in play. Little Ida was only two, but already hiding from her when she called. Now Mama's stomach was punched above her ordinarily flat hips. Joey was only four and had cried from the day he was born. Mattie was going on seven. A regular pest. She was always hanging around and talking a mile a minute when Liza wanted to be left alone to read a book. She didn't have to play Mama. She was for real Mama. She had almost killed Joey once. Left to tend him while Mama stripped fodder, she had turned a pot over his head so his cries wouldn't be heard and engrossed herself in the magical world of the Brothers Grimm. Her Mama had saved the day when she came home unexpectedly for a pitcher of cool water. Joey was already blue in the face. No play-mama for Liza, now or ever. She was going to be an old maid like Aunt Sarah and go about staying with the sick. There was little hope now or ever of going to live with Uncle Joe and Aunt Lizzie where she could go to a real school and have plenty of books, not just the frayed volumes available on loan from the dusty shelves of Mr. Haskell's general store. Cousin Harold had moved to Charleston. Maybe he would get rheumatism and she could go cook for him when Mama stopped having babies. Charleston was another world, as fantastic as the one Alice found when she fell through the well into wonderland. Charleston had wagons and carts that didn't have to be pulled by horses. Might even have a knight in shining armor and a princess who needed rescuing from the wicked witch. Maybe she could save enough money to buy a store bought dress with lace and ribbons and tiny tucked rosebuds and a skirt billowing over gold slippers. Why in the world would anyone want to have babies? Besides, it hurt Mama awful bad to get a new one. She didn't believe for one second that Granny White brought it in her black satchel. If she had thought so, she would have filched it the night Little Ida came and put it on somebody else's doorstep like the stories of foundlings that Mama told her about in English novels.

"I'm never gonna get married. I don't want babies. They're always wet and crying." She shook back her jet black hair already reaching her waist, her dark eyes fiery with determination.

"Crazy, crazy, Liza," they chimed. "Pretty girls always get married. Only the ugly ones like Aunt Sarah can't find a husband. You don't know nothing. Why you gotta act so different? Jist cause you always reading books and your Mama come from a big house across the river ain't no cause to act biggity. Our house better and bigger than yourn."

Liza was different from the top of her smooth black head to her toes, although her second and third toe were grown together like Papa's. She felt different, way down deep inside her. There was singing inside when she found the first violet, and her heart bounced when she saw a sunrise creeping over the black waters of the Little Pee Dee, threading the reflections of cypress and willow in gold. How she wished she could duplicate such a picture in a quilt. From hand-me-downs and discarded Sunday dresses, worn from many wears, to minuscule scraps gleaned from a new dress for Easter, Liza's nimble fingers highlighted dull grays and blacks with bright colors in crazy quilt design. Mama said she spent entirely too much time piecing scraps. You can't see quilts at night Mama said. You just have to have enough to keep you warm. But even in the dark Liza could see the colors in her handiwork. No, she wouldn't play Mama, not even to please her friends who looked at her sullenly, sensing her indifference and disliking it. For now, her lean strong body gamboled across the forest

floor, her fist clutching violets centered with three white dais-
es as carefully ordered as the numerous quilts she would
make — a contradiction to the shape her life would take.

CHAPTER ONE

THE MOTHER

NORA ROCKED THE CRADLE, not rhythmically like she pedaled the treadle sewing machine. There were distinct moments when her foot was idle, and her hand paused over a dishpan of butter beans, not the fancy green ones like the town people served, but speckled with splotches of purple or colored in array of shades of pink. Cooked, they turned a slate gray. That's what life did to people. Took out all the color. Now they lay scattered at random among unshelled green hulls where they had been absently dropped as Nora's gaze strayed from the unpainted walls of her kitchen to the one window through which she could see. No more than a half-mile from her cabin lay the Little Pee Dee River, its water dark and sluggish, crawling through the forbidding gloom of dense foliage. Some said it got its name from tribal Indians; others claimed an Irish adventurer penetrating the swamp had carved his initials on the trees. The origin of its name was no real concern to Nora; yet strangely enough the Pee Dee had helped to shape her life, bringing her to this hideous shack and a baby every year. Even now her husband, George, was paddling its creeks and streams with his drinking buddies, fishing for bream and catfish — a welcome addition to supper — that is, if he came home with them, dependent entirely upon how many swigs he took from the jug of corn liquor. Eventually he would come, scaring the children with his banging on the door. George couldn't hold his liquor and though sick he would be, she wouldn't let the little ones see their father drunk. She relegated him to the front porch where he would fall into noisy slumber. The next day he would be contrite enough to chop extra wood or offer to draw the water for the family wash. Masculine pride forbade "I'm sorry." Pee Dee southern men were expected to have their little escapades that usually took place on the river or in the dense swamp where they trailed deer in season and lured wild ducks and turkeys to their twelve gauge shot guns.

Omega gave a sharp cry. Nora resumed her rocking. Her fingers found another shell, her thumbnail breaking the seam followed by the soft rumble of beans falling into the pan. It took a long time to produce enough for a family her size. No hull ever had more than four beans. "Please, God," she whispered, "this fifth child; let it be my last."

In a moment Liza would be coming back from her

cousins, her siblings trailing behind her. What would Nora do without her first born? In her heart she knew that a ten year old shouldn't have the responsibilities of caring for her little brothers and sisters. Time enough for her to take on the burdens of grown-ups. She needed to be a child, to run free, to think free, and to carry the memory into the years when the burdens of womanhood shackled her body and her spirit. Maybe Liza wouldn't let herself be squeezed into the mold which shaped Pee Dee girls. Even now Liza had a mind of her own. "If she could only escape—if she could avoid the trap I fell into. God, don't let a George come into Liza's life. Don't let my sin be visited on my child got in springtime." But the jasmine and honeysuckle had been so sweet, the green grass so soft, and George's arms so strong. "God, I don't ask for myself. Let it be different for my children, especially for Liza."

"Mama, Uncle Joe and Aunt Lizzie coming. The buggy just turned in." Liza's thin gray-clad body stood framed by the kitchen door. "Maybe you'll let me go home with them this time. They got a school near their house. They ain't got no children. Please, Mama. Papa don't care."

Nora thought, "She's just like me when I was her age, not my coloring, but my spirit." Slightly curling jet-black hair fell in abundance down her childish back. Her black eyes in that olive face were pleading, but perhaps already knowing what Nora would say.

"Oh, Liza! We've been over this before. I got to have you to help me. Who's going to look out for the babies when I chop cotton? I'm not as strong as I used to be. Omega keeps me awake half the night. She's always hungry. It looks like she doesn't get enough milk from me. I got to work. We need a new cow. Mama can't spare you right now. Maybe next year when Omega's weaned and your sister is older to help me."

Fat tears flooded her cheeks and her lips trembled in baby woe.

"That's what you always say. I ain't never gonna go live with them. I hate you. I hate Papa. I hate everybody; I hate Omega."

"Liza, God is going to strike you dead for such talk. You got no cause to talk like that to your Mama. You scared of anybody? Me? Papa? God? You are going to pay for this talk. God doesn't love ugly. You are going to get snatched away one of these dark nights. Won't be any need to cry to Uncle Joe and Aunt Lizzie then. You going to be in the bad place and the devil has pitchforks. Now, stop that sniveling. Not going to do you a piece of good. Go wash your face. You don't want your aunt and uncle to see you like that."

Liza turned blindly, headed for the basin and the well. In her rush she knocked over Joey, who let out a howl.

Nora put her hands to her ears, willing it all to go away. Knowing that it wouldn't, she placed the pan of beans by the chair and stood smoothing her apron. Her hands brushed back the straying hair which escaped the bun on her neck.

"Hush, Joey. Liza didn't mean to do it. Come here. Mama will give you a teacake." The little boy toddled toward her, sufficiently recovered to receive his reward for his injury. Behind him came two other sets of hands claiming their shares.

From the yard came the whinny of Joe's mare. Her brother was proud of that animal. Joe loved things and had things. A pity he and Lizzie had no children. Lord knows they could afford them better than his sister. It just didn't seem right. Here they had five hundred acres of bottom land, not to speak of the woods running down the big Pee Dee. That land would grow anything. Put down a corn seed in that black dirt and overnight came a green stalk soon to be loaded with bearded ears. You could actually hear corn growing on a warm night in late spring. Everything Joe touched turned into dollars, and every dollar he made Joe kept. Their Papa had left the land to Joe, the eldest, the only son. Joe had promised Papa on his deathbed that he would give Nora a home. That was before she married—had to marry George. Liza was on the way. Nora had disgraced the family name not only with a child out of wedlock but by marrying a good-for-nothing without a nickel and not a post to hang his hat on. Oddly enough, when Liza came, Lizzie and Joe took to that black-haired, blackeyed baby, named for Lizzie in hopes of mending fences. They had offered to adopt her. Only they didn't want Liza ever to know who her real parents were. Didn't want their child being called a bastard. So when Nora signed the paper, she would be signing her flesh and blood away, giving up her right ever to claim her. It was too much. Not even George would agree. "Well, you made your bed hard," Joe said. "Lie on it. Don't expect nothing from me and Lizzie."

"What about the land, Joe? You promised Papa to give me my share."

"You got any papers to prove it, girl?"

"You know I haven't. Your word doesn't need a paper."

"Till you find me a paper or a witness, don't be coming asking me for favors. Papa ain't here to prove nothing. You done shamed your name. He wouldn't give you a thin dime the way you acted up."

The subject was closed. Nora knew the futility of opening it up again. She thought that would be the last she'd see of them. To her surprise he and Lizzie came now and then, never announced. They might bring a dress for Liza, a bag of apples and oranges, a sackful of sweet potatoes, or a shoulder of cured pork cut from a smokehouse brimming with country ham and sidemeat. Once they brought fresh butterbeans, Nora's Mama's beans from seeds saved back each year for two or three generations. Nora had spread them out to dry, seed for next spring. Come summer she would have a little of her heritage even though it was no more than a colored bean. The land was never mentioned; however, occasionally she nibbled on the fruit of the family soil. That was as close as she could ever get to it. A girl who got herself in the family way before marriage wasn't welcome in Joe's house. Nora could hear Joe's voice outside.

"Well, Liza, what you crying about? Did that good-for-nothing Papa whip you?'

"No, sir. Papa ain't here. He's gone fishing." Liza brushed away tears from her red eyes.

"Jist like him. Oughta be out plowing and laying by that patch of cotton."

"He says it's too wet to plow." Liza gulped defensively.

Joe let out a horse laugh and winked at Lizzie, who had now taken the child's hands and was drawing her close. "Too wet to plow," Joe chortled. "But not too muddy to go fishing."

"Stop it, Joe," Lizzie ordered. "Don't shame him before her. It ain't right and decent."

Nora stood on the porch with Omega on her hip, forcing a smile. After all, Joe was her own brother, her nearest kin. She would be nice if it killed her, and sometime it almost did. Joe's next words sent color flaming into her pale cheeks.

"Well, Nora. You and George been busy, eh? Must come home sometime. What is it this time? Boy or gal?"

"Her name is Omega."

"Great God, Nora! Where you git such a name?"

"It's from the Bible, Joe. Course you wouldn't know that. I doubt if you been in a church since Papa died." Nora smiled inwardly. She was glad he didn't know what the name meant. It would bring just another snort.

"Church for sinners, Nora. You and George best go every Sunday."

"Hush up, Joe." Lizzie was now beside Nora. She reached out to take the baby in her arms. "I declare she got your curly hair. But them eyes is George's. Right pretty little thing. I didn't know you was expecting."

"She's three months. Came early. Seems healthy enough. Always hungry."

"Well, she's not old enough to eat this," Joe quipped. He held up a bag of candy canes. From nowhere came three pairs of hands. Little Ida screamed, "Me first."

Joey came first. "Joey, you the only man around here. Reckon one boy's the best your Papa could do." Mattie was next and Little Ida came last. She was always referred to with the diminutive prefix. Nora feared that she had marked her with that idiot Pope child, reminding her that old Jacob in the Bible had marked his father-in-law's sheep with ring streaked rods, causing the calves to be spotted. Granny Brown had warned her to stay away from crowds. A woman in the family way shouldn't see somebody afflicted or deformed. Liza stood at the well, showing no sign that she wanted to share in the goodies.

At that moment George emerged from the woods, a veritable replica of an older Huck Finn. How long it had been since clippers had shorn his blond locks was anybody's guess. Certainly a razor had not touched his cheek for days. Despite his unkempt head, there was a rugged handsomeness in his face and a merry glint in his blue eyes, unconscious of his faded muddy pants and toes sticking through his brogans. Even in his disreputable garb, any woman's eyes would have lingered on him longer than the male clad in brown suit and string tie. George was carrying his day's catch, red-bellied bream, some still flapping in protest of being strung up by the gill on wild vines. It was obvious that George had not met John Barley Corn on the river. He held up his treasures proudly.

"Well, dog gone, Nora. We got company. I betcha you ain't had a mess of these suckers since the woods was burnt. Little Pee Dee fish better'n them out of Big Pee Dee. Water too muddy. Found me a cypress log and snagged 'em in as fast as I could bait my hook. Ran out of earthworms or I coulda caught twice as much." He spoke with the pride of Izaak Walton himself. If his in-laws didn't appreciate his talents, it was no skin off his nose. Hospitable like any southern backwoodsman, he was willing to share.

"Nora, stove still hot? Tell you what. I'll build a fat light'erd fire out here," pointing to a mass of greying ash from a similar cookout. "Get the spider out and a hunk of the hog lard. You folks must be hongry. Come jist in time. Liza, you go fetch the cornmeal. Fish ain't no good without a hoecake of corn bread."

Neither Liza nor Nora moved. They knew their visitors wouldn't be staying.

Lizzie spoke first. There was real warmth in her voice. Had it been her decision, she would have stayed; she liked her sister-in-law. "Thank you, George. We done et. Stopped by my brother Richard's at the ferry. Filled us up with chicken pilau and collard greens. We jist stopped by to see how you folks was doing. Been a long time since we seen you. We got to git down the road before dark."

Joe, who still had not spoken, was busy hauling out croker sacks from the back of the buggy. It was as though he was completely unaware that his brother-in-law had arrived. He addressed his sister.

"Nora, I thought you and the younguns could use a sack of Irish potatoes. Dug them yestiddy. Roastin' ears jist come in. Here some porkbelly to bile in beans. Betcha didn't plant any cucumbers or 'maters."

He piled the sacks on the front porch and made one last trip to the buggy. In his arms was a watermelon, light green with dark green stripes, a hefty twenty-five pounder, its stem still green, and evidence of having been freshly pulled.

The children let out a whoop, Little Ida, Joey and Mattie. Omega stuck her tiny thumb in her mouth and sucked vigorously. Liza, eyes still down, disappeared behind the woodshed. She had no desire for courtesy of goodbyes — nor a taste for melon.

CHAPTER TWO

GROWING UP

LIZA WAS TWELVE. That morning something strange had happened. Blood. In her drawers. What did this mean? But it was only a few drops. Still it worried her. Liza couldn't stand the sight or smell of blood. Papa's bag of doves, little heads drooped in death, their soft white feathers matted with blood, turned her stomach and killed her appetite. Liza was puzzled. She could not reconcile what she heard in church about the dove that lit on Jesus' head declaring Him the Son of God and these defenseless little birds. Suppose Papa had been there.

Would he have killed the dove? Sometime Papa made her pluck the feathers of the little creatures. For days she could still feel the stickiness of their little bodies and imagine a stray down of feather clinging to her fingers. Now something had happened to her. What should she do? Mama had already gone to the garden—butterbean planting time. The signs in the almanac were just right. Mama didn't have time for nonsense. She could just hear her say, "Liza, for land sakes! Get the basin and wash. I told you not to climb trees. Girls don't climb trees. You probably snagged yourself on a limb of that oak I caught you in yesterday." Poor Mama! There was never playtime for her with five children, a run-down house, and a husband whose efforts sometime put food on the table but who sometime disappeared for days in the swamp of Britton's Neck. A garden was a must. Mama's industry put beans and peas in the dinner pot. Early spring brought green, tender cabbage, garden peas, and new potatoes. Even in winter there were collards and turnips cooked with backbone or sometimes just with hog lard. Cornbread always went with Mama's vegetables. It was not company fare or dinner-on-the-ground at church, where each family brought a pot, but they were not hungry. Mama saw to that. Her workload never seemed to get easier even though there had not been another baby since Omega, now three, who now busied herself beating a dishpan tom-tom. As long as she amused herself, Liza could put up with the noise. Hoping to find a teacake, Little Ida was standing tiptoe in front of the safe. At five she was half as tall as other girls her age, but just as independent. Liza, convinced that her little sisters' occupations were harmless, returned to her book. It was a copy of an old blue-back speller that had belonged to Mama. School not being accessible, with her Mama's help Liza had learned to read. Words intrigued her.

Those clusters of letters made special sounds. Liza could hear water running, birds twittering. Best of all were the colors. *Sunset* flashed with purple, yellow, pink. Strange words had a special fascination. There was a section in her speller called "common words commonly misspelled." A whole page where a word beginning with a P you didn't even hear. People died of pneumonia, but she certainly didn't know it was spelled with a P. A dictionary had all the words in the world. Liza had never seen one, but Mama said Uncle Joe had one that weighed fifteen pounds along with whole shelves of books that Mama used to read. Imagine knowing every single word in the world! You'd never get bored no matter where you were or what you were doing. You didn't blow out your thoughts with the kerosene lamp. Night was the best time. Darkness and silence opened Liza's world which she didn't have to share even with Mattie, who slept beside her.

Liza had just found a new word. *Sepulcher*. She sounded it out. What did it mean? Of course! It was what Jesus was buried in. Preacher Smith had talked about it Easter. Good Friday flooded her vision. White linen around his body. Blood seeping through white like the little doves Papa brought home but the little doves stayed dead. Jesus came back and ———-

The stool on which little Ida had been standing crashed to the floor and the blue-speckled coffee pot skittered from the wood stove across the pine boards, emptying a brown river mixed with coffee grounds. Above the clatter was little Ida's scream. She lay on the floor, her little blue gingham dress drenched in brown. Jumping up, Liza tipped over the bench on which she had been sitting. Her screams now mingled with Little Ida's. Omega ceased her drumbeat. "Little Ida sick," she squeaked. Now there was a trinity of cries. Liza grabbed Little Ida up and headed for the well—cold water. When she burned her finger, cold water stopped the pain. She hoped the bucket was full..

Mama was already at the door. Brown soil still clung to her hands. One corner of the apron tied in a knot kept the precious bean seed safe.

At one glance Nora knew what had happened. "My God, Liza! Go get Aunt Mae." Nora took the screaming child from Liza's arms.

"But, Mama, water!"

"Liza, don't argue. Go get Aunt Mae. The whisper woman. Across the branch. For God's sake, hurry!"

Liza struck out through the woods. If a bird sang, Liza did not hear it. No wild flowers bloomed; no tussocks invited hopscotch. A snake rousing himself from a winter's sleep held no threat to her bare feet. Across the footlog she ran; ignoring her childhood fear of falling into the murky swamp branch teeming with slimy life. Now she could see Aunt Mae's cabin. Thank God, she was at home. A thin line of smoke curled from her chimney.

"Aunt Mae, Aunt Mae!" Liza's fists beat the wooden door. The bolt slid out. A black woman turbaned in a brown cotton stocking stood before Liza, her voluminous body enveloped in nondescript brown. She was toothless except for one gold snag which she brandished like a jewel to match the gold earrings in her pierced ears. Folds of fat embedded her small black eyes. Hard to tell if Aunt Mae saw you.

"Aunt Mae. Little Ida bad hurt. Pulled a pot of hot coffee on her. Mama said come quick. Please Aunt Mae!"

"Lemme git mah satchel. Where mah shoes?"

"Aunt Mae, hurry!"

"Comin', chile."

With a black bag in one hand and a hickory cane

knobbed to support her hand, Aunt Mae trailed Liza.

"Caint run fast no mo, chile. Outta bref. Too old. Caint walk dat footslog. Fall in, sho nuf."

"Aunt Mae, I'll hold your hand. You won't fall. Little Ida bad off."

"Caint hep it. We goes roun de branch. Not much fudder. You ain't big nuf to hole me up. What dat I see runnin down yo legs? Yo Ma bettah look after you. Yo done fell off de roof, I spec. You sho liddle to be gittin lady."

Aunt Mae's word made no sense to Liza. "Falling off roof"——"Lady."

Liza grasped the old lady's hand, pulling her along, willing her to follow. Desperate as Liza was, she realized the futility of guiding Aunt Mae across the footlog. They would have to take the longer path.

At last the two reached the clearing of the wood. Even before Liza saw the house, she could hear the din of voices, Omega's screeches, Mama's moans. Joey and Mattie were on the porch, craning their necks toward the path down which Liza had disappeared earlier. At the first sight of Liza, both ran to meet her, their voices a jumble of woe.

Little Ida lay on a pallet on the kitchen bench. Her little body had been stripped. Mama was bending over her, dabbing wet soda to her beet red chest and stomach. Oddly enough, the child made no sound though pain glazed her blue eyes.

Aunt Mae fell to her knees. She dropped close to the scalded skin, her head moving back and forth. From her lips came a low, unintelligible chant.

"What's whisper woman saying, Mama?" Liza's words were barely audible.

"Talking out the fire. Pray Liza, Joey. Pray, Mattie."

Omega, momentarily quiet, nuzzled up to her Mama, the thumb still stuck in her mouth. Her brother and two sisters obediently knelt on the pine floor, white from innumerable lye soap scrubbings. No sound came from Liza, but Joey's and Mattie's childish trebles mixed bedtime prayers with Bible verses and Sunday school songs. "Now I lay me down to sleep: I pray the Lord my soul to keep: Yes, Jesus loves me. The Lord is my shepherd." In that rude little room petitions rose— some in childish wails; some in desperate pleading; some in silent anguish. Black and white knelt together, bonded by pain.

"Oh, merciful, Father! Relieve my baby's pain. Don't let her suffer for my sin. I made mistakes. Make me pay, not little Ida. Please! Please!"

As the sun sank down in fiery swirls behind the great swamp, Little Ida felt no pain when Mama's hands washed her for the last time, when Liza gently draped her little sister in the white dress embroidered around the collar with baby rosebuds, the work of Liza's nimble fingers. Little Ida had worn it Easter Sunday.

Neighbors came to follow the family behind the small homemade coffin overstretched with white broadcloth secured with ornamental gold tacks. They murmured: "She's better off. One less mouth to feed. Poor Nora. A body can stand so much. No doctor. Only whisper woman. George off in swamp. Got home just in time. But God is merciful."

At the graveside the preacher intoned. "God is merciful. He moves in mysterious ways his wonders to perform. God's will is done. He is merciful."

Dry-eyed, Liza stood looking into the black cavern into which the little box was being lowered. "Merciful!" She wanted to scream. "Merciful to let Little Ida die!" Merciful to give her the blame she would have to carry on her shoulders.

Mama had not said a word, but Liza could read her eyes. It would have been kinder if Mama had whipped her black and blue. The unspoken word had lacerated her spirit. It would be a long time before the wounds would begin to heal, leaving scars carried to the earth under which Little Ida now lay.

That night, after she had washed and put on fresh rags folded as Mama had directed, Liza spied the blue-back speller lying on the corner of the dresser. In swift precision she tore the leaves from its binding and shredded them. At her feet lay a mass of torn paper, but the kerosene lamp caught one word that had escaped the massacre. *Sepulcher.* For the first time Liza covered her face and sobbed.

CHAPTER THREE

OMENS

EASTER WAS A LITTLE OVER two weeks off. This year it had come late in April. Spring had been so curious. The seasons had got all mixed up. Some said the end of time was coming. The Bible had predicted strange things. Now that a new century had dawned, Jesus, after nineteen hundred years, was coming back to claim the faithful —the living and the dead. Actually spring had come in February. Peach trees spread their pink arms out to the warm skies. Birds started building nests. Overnight, dogwood sprinkled the swamp transforming it into a white studded paradise. March, however, came in like the proverbial lion and with it heavy skies that filtered the real thing — white flurries that began before daylight Saturday. It snowed on the Pee Dee, not just a few stray drops adrift from the North; the heavens poured down swirls of flying flakes. Somebody up there had emptied tons of feather bedding which proved not to be so light as it continued two whole days, collapsing sheds over milk cows and plow mules. It filtered through chinks in shingles of houses and sleeved peach and dogwood in ermine. Old and young alike caught panfuls of this strange concoction and made ice cream by adding vanilla extract and sugar. Firewood, buried under white mounds, made hissing noises when lit in fireplaces. "The time was out of joint," they would have said, but Shakespeare and Hamlet were as alien as the white stuff drifting silently from the sky. Pine limbs snapped like twigs; roosters crowed at midnight; old ones shook their gray heads and muttered "Someun bad coming. Somebody gonna die. Bad signs."

Liza did not share their qualms. She stood transfixed at the window, gazing at this manna from heaven which had turned the chicken coop into a miniature castle and black stumps into mountains. Too soon the sun broke through granite skies. In two days the white grandeur had turned into black slush. Spring blossoms had vanished and winter descended once more on the earth and on Liza's spirits. March's winds gave way to rain. The river rose and crawled over the bank. Sodden gardens supported no seed. Hopes of a spring planting vanished. The graybeards remonstrated, "God telling us. Warning us. Look out for trouble."

Nora had feared for the future of summer vegetables. The whole county was wet, dank, and mildewy. Had God not promised never again to destroy the earth by water, Nora would have been sure the second great flood had set in. Incessant rain kept the children indoors. Cramped quarters incited bickerings, even fisticuffs. Nora was tired. She couldn't seem to cope any longer. George was gone now days at a time. She suspected a liquor still hidden in the wet confines of the swamp, and now she didn't care. If it brought dollars to feed her children, God would just have to understand. "God, don't let him get caught," she prayed silently.

April moved in mercifully without showers. Spring nights warmed the earth. Around Little Ida's grave, miraculously, Sweet Williams and thrift outlined the miniature mound decorated with seashells and bits of colored glass. A small stone marker donated by Uncle Joe bore name and dates. Nora had chosen the epitaph: "Asleep in Jesus." Easter would be here soon. Graves needed to be tended. Shortly after Easter came the anniversary of Little Ida's death. Nora, equipped with rake, hoe and a bucket of chicken droppings worked on her daughter's grave. Having cleared away the debris from wind and storm, Nora, on her knees, was carefully planting seed which she had ordered from a catalog, anemones, baby's breath, phlox.. Perennials. That meant they would be here next year even if she wasn't. She wondered if perhaps she might be lying beside Little Ida. No. That just couldn't be. The children needed her. Liza was almost a woman now, putting up her hair. Boys' eyes had begun to follow her slim figure and softly rounded bosom. The others were growing up, too. Joey had already been baptized and joined the church in last summer's revival. Mattie spent her time imitating her older sister, borrowing her clothes and insisting that she was as grown as Liza. Omega, the baby, was spoiled. After Little Ida's death it was as if a double portion of maternal affection was lavished on this last child, young enough to hug and babytalk. The others, especially Joey and Mattie, watched and wondered at their Mother's effusive demonstrations. Why was she so different? Of course, wise Liza knew. Omega was now Little Ida, not lying in the cemetery, but a living, breathing little girl who could throw her chubby arms around her neck and coo, "Me love Mama." Omega to her siblings was a pest, demanding the first slice of cake, throwing tantrums at a whim, rejecting any discipline that threatened her place on the princess's throne. Nora had to do something about Omega. Better to make her learn now that the biggest plum was not hers for the demanding. Life would certainly teach her otherwise. Yes, her children needed her. George could get along. Marriage and family had posed few problems to him. A fishing pole and a jug could work magic; wife and children disappeared with a two pound bass on the end of his line and two jiggers of corn liquor in his belly. George was not unkind, just unaware. He was never brutal; his hand had never struck her nor had he wielded the whip to the backs of his children as some other more prosperous fathers had done. George was just what he was: a playboy without an allowance; a charmer who had lost a great deal of it for Nora, who was the one who worried about such trivialities as enough food for the table, adequate clothes for the winter. Yet there were nights when George reached for her, tender and slow in his advances, that Nora momentarily recaptured those spring evenings when the two moved to the same rhythm and lost themselves in the glory of first love. George would be all right if something happened to her. Would he see after the children? He loved them, but he loved his freedom more.

The real worry was Liza. If only she had given her as an infant to Joe and Lizzie. Now she would be almost ready to graduate from high school. In addition, she would own the land, Nora's heritage. Bright, she would top anybody, brainwise or lookwise, with that wavy mane of gloss, those black eyes, questioning, observing, but sometimes dreaming, that acute perception which understood the wounded rabbit or a mother grieving for a lost child. Yet Nora had never put her arms around her and whispered, "Liza, it wasn't your fault. Don't blame yourself. It was my sin. God punished me." The words wouldn't come. She could not bare her soul even to her child to whom she felt closer than anyone else on earth. How could she describe the insidious sting of guilt which followed passion unauthorized by her God and southern standards. She had been selfish. Only to herself could she admit that in her bright, beautiful firstborn could she relive her youth and her dreams. Where had she come from, this lone dark beauty among blonds?

A shadow fell across the mound. It was Liza. "Mama, you got a letter from Uncle Harold. Mr. Huck's just brought it. Been in the post office several days."

Liza handed her Mama the letter postmarked Charleston addressed in flowery cursive. Liza loved the way Uncle Harold flung his curlicued *W*, and although she had not mastered the art herself, she practiced the same style with *L*, a descending tail which looped twice and curled in a flourish downward.

Nora wiped her soiled hand on her apron. With her index finger still begrimed with Low Country mud, she unzipped the envelope. It was a single sheet of paper with a folded slip inside. Yet it took Nora, it seemed to Liza, minutes to read.

"What does it say, Mama? Bad news? Somebody dead?" Liza inquired.

"Liza, I been meaning to tell you. I got a lump in my

breast. Been there a year. Now there are knots coming down my arm. Been hurting right smart the last months. Reason I ask you to draw all the water for the wash. I don't think it's anything bad. But I thought I ought to let a doctor look at it to be sure. Harold has got me an appointment. I can stay with him. He's sent me a money order. I'll catch the ferry, then the steamboat. He'll meet me at the station."

"Mama, you going away?" Liza uncharacteristically reached for Nora and grasped her around the waist. "You should have told me. You've been hurting, and I didn't know. Did you tell Papa?"

"Papa knows. He's going to look after you while I'm gone." Her voice did not sound convincing.

"But, Mama, how long will it take? Will you be gone two weeks, a month?" Liza's voice edged with alarm ended in a sob.

"Now, Liza! None of that. You're a big girl now. Mama's counting on you to keep things going. I give you leave to spank that bad little Omega any time she sasses you. Joey and Mattie will mind you. You are their big sister. You can cook as well as me. Papa says your tater pudding puts mine to shame. You'll manage." Nora lifted Liza's chin looking deep into her eyes. "You always have managed, Liza. You always will."

For a brief second Liza had the urge to cry out. "Mama, I'm tired of being big. Tired of being mama. Tired of making things right. I didn't ask to be born. Let me go. Let me go!"

Instead Liza scotched the tears; only a few drops escaped those dark eyes. In a voice too calm and too restrained for a sixteen year old, Liza promised. "Yes, Mama, I'll manage. You can count on me."

Nora turned to the abandoned hoe and made one last

trench at the foot of the grave. Turning the handle downward, she plowed a tiny furrow into which she sowed a few seeds. Forget-me-nots.

The old ones were right. Strange things were happening. George came home that evening. He had been gone only two days. Nora heard his steady steps on the porch; no hint of unsure feet. Nora lit the lamp and moved to open the door. Not a whiff of spirits on his breath; instead there was a broad grin and a lilt in his voice.

"Nora, gal, I got a surprise for you. Jist set down here. You gonna faint."

From his pockets he began drawing out silver dollars. One, two, three, four —- they clattered in her lap. "Fifty of 'em gal. They yourn. Want you to buy you and the younguns fitten clothes for Easter."

"Oh, George," Nora whispered. She didn't ask where he got them. She didn't need to. As she bathed her hands in the mound, she could see new shoes for Joey, bonnets for the girls and even a new dress for herself. A white one. The kind she might have been married in. But not fussy. She wasn't a bride anymore. The lamplight on the table beside her fell on the letter, an icy missive dispatching warm plans.

"George, I heard from Harold. He made arrangements with a doctor, a surgeon at Roper Hospital. Sent me money for fare. I'm supposed to leave Monday after Easter. That's only a little over two weeks." Her voice had lost its early jubilation. There was just a hint of a sob in her words.

George dropped to his knees, reached out and encircled his wife's waist. "Don't worry, baby. You gonna be alright." His blue eyes misted. "Be back home in no time. Me and Liza gonna take care of the younguns. She a good cook. She one smart gal. Jist like her Mama. Everything be jist like you left it. Anything special you want me to see after, baby?"

Nora's hands touched his face. One finger traced the line of his jaw covered with three days' growth of beard. It was like old times. Nora chose her words carefully.

"George, I want to get married proper. In the church. I never felt right about the Justice of the Peace. Easter Sunday would be a good time. Omega could be the flower girl. Liza, my maid of honor."

"God Amighty, Nora! Folks think you teched in the head."

"I don't care what folks think. It's what God thinks. I could rest easy. Please, George. Do this for me. I won't ever ask anything again." This time her voice broke.

George buried his head deep in her breasts, his arms tightening. Like the child he was, he mumbled, "Okay, Mama. Easter Sunday. We do it right this time."

CHAPTER FOUR

SPRING WEDDING

LIZA AND NORA STOOD AT THE COUNTER in Mr. Haskell's general store. Before them lay bolts of cloth. The shelves beyond, rising to the height of the twelve foot ceiling, housed an assortment of dry goods—blue denim overalls, brogans, straw hats, felt hats, parasols, cotton yarn. Farm tools—plow lines and plow points, axe handles, post hole diggers, hoes, rakes, shovels. Haskell's served the Pee Dee, the one-stop trade station. Coffee beans were sold by the pound; sugar came in fifty-pound cloth sacks labeled in blue and red, "Pure

Cane Sugar." Flour and rice were packaged the same way. Those who could not afford a whole bag bought smaller portions weighed in brown paper sacks on the scales suspended from a crossbeam. A small corner near the front door was the drugstore. Castor oil and calomel for yearly purgings; Carter's Little Liver pills; Doan's pills for backache; balsam copaiba for runny noses. What nature didn't cure, Mr. Haskell's apothecary or death did. Shoppers came for miles on wagons and buggies, leaving with essentials for kitchen, wardrobe, and farm. Some sacks held sticks of licorice and gumdrops for the children. Plugs of Brown Mule chewing tobacco, a can of Prince Albert for the pipe were nonessential necessaries for Papa and Grandpapa. Some of the fair sex had a taste for Tube Rose sweet scotch snuff, which they tucked in the corner of the jaw. Not Nora. If she ever saw one of her girls with the filthy stuff in her mouth, there'd be the whip. Once she thought Mattie was guilty. Nora caught her on the porch, her two fingers of her right hand spread to frame her mouth, spitting with a crackle into the yard. "I was just seeing if I could spit as far as Miz Pope," Mattie had explained. "It's only cocoa and sugar, Mama."

"Nothing to be proud about, Mattie. Nice girls don't dip snuff."

Nice girls also had proper weddings. Nora fingered the white organdy. "How much it worth, Mr. Haskell?"

"Thirty-nine cents a yard. Good quality. Just got it in last week."

Nora made a mental calculation. "Is that the best you can do?" That was the housewife's way to dicker prices, the desperate effort to save each precious penny.

"Well, now, being it's you, Nora, you can have it at thirty. I knew your Papa and Mama. Folks don't get any better than them. Ain't seen your brother, Joe, lately. Not sick, is he? Stops by when he comes across the river."

"Joe's alright, thank you. I want five yards of the white, five yards of the pink, four yards of the purple, and two of the yellow. I need spools of thread to match. And Mr. Haskell, how much is that a yard?" She pointed to the hank of white lace on the counter.

"Five cents. You kin have the whole thing for fifty."

"I'll take it."

Mr. Haskell began unrolling the cloth, measuring it on the ruler taped to the counter. "Must be going to dress you and the girls up fine for Easter."

"That's right. This year is kinda special. I don't have much time to make four dresses. But Liza here is a wonder with a needle."

Liza stood silently, her eyes vacant and unrevealing. What was happening to Mama? She could just hear Addie and Sally laughing. "Never heared of sich a thing. Daughter sixteen years old and gittin married again to the same man. Lord, have mercy! And her younguns standing around her all dressed up like bridemaids. You and yo Mama sure different."

Liza had already rehearsed her response. "It's not like a real marriage. It's a renewal of vows. I read it in a book. Plenty people do it, specially Catholics and 'Piscopalians." She could just imagine their reply.

"Yeah, they the ones love the Virgin Mary more than they love Jesus. We heared about them."

Liza would shrug her shoulders and turn away. She herself could not see the logic in her Mama's actions. Could it be that those lumps had gone to her brain?

Nora interrupted her train of thought. "Don't you think the pink is better for you, Liza? If you rather have the purple, we can switch with Mattie. Pink seems your color. Brings out your hair and eyes."

"Pink is fine, Mama."

"Alright. How about going over there and pick out a new tie for Papa and Joey. We gotta hurry. I want us to have these dresses cut out before dark."

"Yes, Mama, but I want to check out these books." She held worn copies of *Gulliver's Travels* and *Jane Eyre.*

"You won't have much time for reading, Liza." Mama reminded her.

Laden with packages, they were home by noon. Mattie had watched the dinner pot and laid the plates face down on the oilcloth kitchen table so that flies would not get on them. They ate in a hurry. Everybody was getting a new dress. Omega could not contain herself. She loved the yellow organdy and had held it up to her chest, prancing around like the Cinderella she would be.

By dark, four neat separate piles of cloth lay ready for tomorrow's stitching. Nora would be at the sewing machine. Liza with her needle would turn up collars, hand tuck, put in hems, whip down lace, and transform each garment into a gown worthy of a couturier.

"Liza," Nora said softly, "we've done three days' work today. You tired as me?" Suddenly she pulled Liza close to her and smoothed her long black hair. "Oh, Liza! What would I do without you? I know I can count on you. Don't fret. We are going to start something. Before you know it, the Powells and Lawrimores will be doing the same thing. A wedding every Easter."

Easter Sunday dawned bright and clear. The family was up early. Eggs dyed in every color were ready to be taken to the Easter egg hunt for the children. But the wedding would come first. Papa looked spiffy in his old blue serge, shiny with past pressings. Joey's pants were a mite too short, but his hair parted down the middle was slicked down in place and the little bow tie made him look like a preacher man. The girls wore identical dresses, high Elizabethan ruffs edged in lace over a tucked yoke that fell into billowy skirts. Even Liza seemed caught up in the moment. The family had never looked so grand.

"Mama, you look so pretty," Liza offered shyly.

Nora felt pretty for the first time in years as she marched her brood to service at Shiloh Baptist Church. There they could hear once more the story of the Resurrection. No one would notice that Liza cringed at the word *sepulcher*. Someone would heist the hymn, "Jesus Rose. Up from the grave Jesus rose." Nora would smile through her tears as she looked out of the church window to the little mound surrounded by spring blooms, the only one of her little family who would not stand with her at the altar rail.

"George, do you take this woman for your wedded wife?" A hundred eyes stared in disbelief; fifty necks craned. There had never been such a thing at Shiloh before. Course Nora came from a different people cross the river. Had a rich brother. Didn't have much to do with his sister who married beneath her. George was a good old boy but didn't have two dimes to rub together until recently. Wonder if uppity Nora knew where the money come from to buy them dresses.

"With this ring I thee wed." George slipped the heavy gold band on Nora's finger. It was the only thing of value that had belonged to her Mother. She had fought Joe for it. Now she looked down on its elegant splendor. One day it would belong to Liza, who stood in front of her in a pink cloud. Around her stood the other colors of the rainbow – Mattie in purple, Omega, clutching a spray of Carolina jasmine the exact color of her yellow dress.

"I pronounce you man and wife. In the name of the Father, the Son, and the Holy Ghost."

"Amen," Nora whispered.

CHAPTER FIVE

HOME-COMING

LIZA SAT ON THE PORCH sunning her hair. She had just washed it. It fell in a glistening cascade down her back almost reaching the floor. Now and then Liza lifted the heavy tresses airing her slender neck. It was only May, but it felt like July. It hadn't rained since March. The beds of moss roses Mama had planted around the steps had yielded no blooms, and even though Liza had watered them from the well each day, they still didn't look promising. Maybe they were waiting for Mama to come home to burst into a riot of pink, purple, yellow. Liza loved them. They opened their eyes with the sun and folded their lids at night. Maybe they were tired, too, like her. It would be so good to have Mama back. She would have been gone a month tomorrow. Why hadn't she heard? Surely Mama could have dropped a line. Liza sent Joey to the post office every day. He complained about walking three miles, but when she volunteered to slop the pigs and hoe the garden Mama had started, Joey was glad enough to rid himself of his chores.

Papa was seldom home. When he was, he was no help with the others. Ever since the wedding, Mattie had got the notion that she was an upcoming bride, prancing around in her Easter frock, puffing up her hair like she was grown and actually rolling her eyes at that good-for-nothing Buddy Wright in Sunday school. Joey, always begging Papa to let him go fishing with him, dawdled at his chores, sometimes leaving them for Liza's hands. And Omega — she missed Mama so. She cried herself to sleep every night. Awake, she planted her six-year old feet on the stand that "Mama would let me!" Thwarted, she would bang her head against the safe, screaming her protests. Yesterday she operated on Raggedy Anne, which Mama had painstakingly made for her birthday. With scissors she slit the doll's torso, removing a wad of cotton. Not content with breast surgery, she yanked out her button eyes and amputated one leg. Poor Raggedy Anne! "Mama, come home," Liza whispered. Guilt hung heavy. She had taken Mama for granted. It was Mama who had curbed Omega's temper, placated Joey, set Mattie straight and though unspoken, her eyes told Liza, "I know. I understand. Hold onto your dreams." She wondered what Mama was like at sixteen. Maybe they had the same dreams, only Mama got lost in children, a husband in a four-room house scarcely out of the mud of the swamp. "When Mama comes back, I'm gonna talk to her. Really talk. Where did it go wrong for her? What happened? God, don't let me make her mistake."

"Somebody coming, Liza." It was Omega, running up the steps. "Better put on your shoes. A man." Omega was reminding her that Mama never met company barefooted, especially a man.

He stood now just at the foot of the steps, a tall young man in his early twenties. Removal of his hat in ceremonial greeting revealed light brown hair damp with spring heat over light blue eyes that seemed to smile. There was kindness about his whole demeanor. Despite his big strong fingers, Liza had the distinct feeling that those hands were gentle. His voice matched this first impression.

"Miss, your Papa at home?"

"No, sir. Left early this morning. The Martins' barn burnt. He went to the barn raising. I'm his oldest, Liza. Mama's not home, either. She's in Charleston hospital. Can I help you?" Liza made an effort to hide her feet under the hem of her dress and to right her still damp hair.

"No, Miss Liza. I have a little business with him. You expect him home by night?" There was no indication that he intended to discuss "the business" further.

"Well, mister, I don't rightly know. Sometimes he goes fishing or hunting. He may not be home until tomorrow." Liza was curious. What did this nice young man want with Papa? Was Papa in trouble? Where did Papa get all that money before Easter to buy all the dresses? Mama would know what to say. Couldn't he see that Liza was upset?

"Miss Liza, you don't know me. We distantly related. Third or fourth cousins on your Mama's side. I'm Tom Brown from Georgetown County. How far is it to the Martins?

Maybe I could catch him before he goes fishing." His words were hesitant but reassuring.

"The nearest way is to go to the Parker Landing and paddle across to Sugar Loaf. The Martins live a mile or two from there. If you walked the long way, you might miss him. You could leave word with me. I could give him the message. Save you the trouble."

"Thank you kindly, Miss Liza." There was a strange edge to his voice almost as if he might cry. He drew a blue handkerchief from his shirt pocket and wiped his forehead. Looking straight at her, taking in the anxious young woman who was completely unaware of her striking beauty, he continued. "I best be going. I'll try to see him. If I don't run into him, I'll leave a message at the post office." With that he bowed slightly, replaced his hat, and turned toward the lane, nearly bumping into Joey, running with a letter clutched in his hand.

"Got a letter from Mama, Liza. Hurry up and read it." Liza was down the steps, oblivious of her bare feet or the tear in her dress. Omega, pulling at her sister's dress screamed, "Read to me first."

Liza ripped the letter open. The young stranger had not moved but stood listening as Liza read:

> *Dear George and children,*
>
>   *The doctor is going to operate tomorrow. He thinks it may be cancer. I don't know what the outcome will be but pray that it won't be too long before I can come home. Liza, I'm depending on you. Omega, listen to what Liza tells you. Joey, you and Mattie help Liza with the work. Don't forget to water my flowers and especially around Little Ida's grave.*
>
>   *My love to all,*
>   *Mama*

When Liza looked up, she saw Papa striding up from the swamp, his clothes dripping wet, his arms outstretched toward them. Papa never greeted them this way. His first words revealed why.

He caught Omega up in his arms. In a voice not belonging to Papa, he sobbed, "Mega, your Mama's gone. Died on the operating table. You ain't got no Mama now."

Omega wrenched herself away and ran to Liza, screaming. "Papa storied. Tell him, Liza. Not so. Mama coming home. Letter said so."

Liza dropped to the ground near Mama's flower bed and gathered her little sister to her. Joey stood beside her twisting the empty envelope in his hands. No sound came from Liza's lips but her slim body shook.

"Cousin George!" It was the stranger's voice. "I come to help. I come to bring word the coffin done come to Georgetown. Her brother hired a wagon to bring it in. Be here tomorrow night. Her kinfolk's coming."

George made no answer. He, too, knelt by his children, picked up a dry twig and broke it into little pieces, dropping them one by one on the black, dry earth. Above Omega's cries and Joey's muffled sobs, Liza thought she heard her Papa mumble, "Nora, Nora, Baby."

The front room had been cleared of most of its furniture. Against the gray clapboard wall where Mama and Papa's bed had stood was the coffin skirted in purple folds and supported on each end by stools. On the lid, sealed in Charleston by the undertaker for health reasons, flickered a single candle, which sent curious shapes across the dove-gray casket cloth. Around the coffin straight chairs were arranged chapel-like for mourners. It was "setting-up" time, the wake before the funeral and interment. Neighbors and kin had come with food and drink to watch with the family and to see how they were taking it. Only one member of the family was now visible. After midnight Papa and the other children had gone to bed. Neighbors had insisted, "Go, git some rest. Tomorrow's a hard day. You'll need your strength." Liza however had not listened to their admonitions. Instead, she had pulled a chair from the row and sat close to the box, facing the head, a dark profile in black. She did not move except occasionally touching the surface of the box with her right hand. There were no flowers, but a curious perfume permeated the smoky room—artificial and sickeningly sweet. From time to time came the sound of those on the edge of sleep, while others whispered exchanges ranging from spring planting to good fishing holes. Eventually the conversation turned to death and the woman enclosed inside that mute slate box. Liza, in her own gray world, heard only a whirr of voices. They might have come from insects buzzing in the silence before a summer thunderstorm. To her they were as meaningless as this barbaric display that accompanied death. What did food, drink, talk have to do with what lay beside her? She was angry at them for intruding, angry with God for letting this happen, angry with herself for not being close to Mama, angry at the role she would have to take. She could hear Mama's voice. "Liza, I'm depending on you." Here was the trap into which she must fall. She had no other choice. Perhaps Mama's trap had been something like hers, bringing Mama to the miserable life she had led.

Liza's ears suddenly pricked to two whispering voices.

"Well, poor Nora. Proves you can't do wrong and get by. First lost her child. Now she's gone."

"Nearly broke her family's heart. No wonder Joe kicked her out. Lost her land, good name, everything."

"When you lose your good name, you done lost it all."

"They say Joe told her she'd made her bed and she'd have to lie on it. Washed his hands of her."

"Nothing but trouble since she married – had to marry – that worthless George."

"And to think she had the nerve to get married in church Easter in front of good Christian people. Standing up with that bastard youngun' as her maid of honor. Born three months after her and George got married the first time."

"God sure don't like ugly. Nora sure paid dear for her frolics."

"Didn't knock that uppity way out of her. Walking like a queen and talking proper like a edjicated fool. Teaching her younguns to read and write—-"

Liza lurched from her chair. She took one long stride toward the whispering gossips. Her right hand slapped one mouth; the left hooked the other. Her voice pierced the silence. Never before had such words been on her lips. "Bitches. Get out of here! You are not worth one hair on Mama's head. Don't you ever set foot in my Mama's house again." Liza's strident command ended in a sob. Like an avenging angel she herded them to the door and hurled them into the darkness. She spat out, "Bitches! Go to hell!"

Leaning against the closed door, she addressed the shocked stillness. Her voice was strangely calm, quiet and pleading. "Please go. All of you. I want to be with my Mama alone. I want to tell her things. Go, please."

Alone, she laid her head on the casket. Like the penitent approaching the confessional, she might have whispered, "Mama, forgive me. I have sinned, not you. I didn't know. Oh, Mama, I love you."

Whatever she said was for Mama's ears only. At the end, the candle flickered and died with a thin wreath of smoke.

CHAPTER SIX

POST-MORTEM

LIZA SAT IN SHILOH, half listening to Preacher Smith. A month ago she had heard him intone, "Now we commit Sister Nora to the dust. Ashes to ashes; dust to dust.." Today he had taken his text on the elect, those chosen by God and bound for heaven. Mama had said she didn't believe a word of such nonsense—little babies in hell because they were not numbered with the chosen few. Hardshell Baptists believed in predestination like the Presbyterians. Mama's church across the river had no truck with such teaching. They were Anglicans; people who lived the right life went to heaven. The "right life" includ-ed bringing up children in the church, and since Shiloh was the only one available in Britton's Neck, to Shiloh she would take her children.

That was the reason Liza was in church with Omega squirming on her right side and Joey and Mattie punching each other on her left. She put a restraining hand on Omega and gave the others the "stop it" look.

Election and predestination had been nothing but words to Liza. Now they took on new meaning. Choice—free will. Who would choose to be born where one mistake made you an outcast—branded like the slaves in early times? No wonder Mama had no friends. After Liza's outburst at the "set-ting-up" not even childhood playmates would speak to her. "I'm not sorry," she had told herself. "I don't care." Yet she needed someone to talk to. Last week she walked the footlog to Aunt Mae's, the whisper woman. Liza found her setting out collard plants in her tiny garden plot. Aunt Mae folded Liza in a fat embrace, mixed with sweat and cow manure. Aunt Mae didn't know nor care that Liza came early—that she had been conceived out of wedlock. Her voice was warm and motherly.

"Chile, I done heared about yo po mammy. You chill-ins 'gon miss 'er. You be Mammy now."

Tears flooded Liza's eyes. "Aunt Mae, I don't know where to turn. I can't seem to get myself together. How long does it take to get over death? You know. You lost so many. Your 'Lijah found dead in the swamp."

"Jesus help you, Chile. Jesus bes fren."

"Aunt Mae, why did Jesus take Mama? We loved her so. We miss her. We need her."

"Jesus love her, too. Dat why. She done been too tired. She resting now. She got no pain. She happy."

Aunt Mae's words should have been reassuring. She felt such a closeness to this obese black woman that she shared with no one else. Still Aunt Mae's words troubled her. Liza needed Mama more than God needed her. It didn't all make sense.

Preacher Smith's voice drew her up to the present: "God don't make mistakes. He took Sister Nora. Have mercy on her poor soul."

Liza could feel eyes on her as they had been two months ago when she stood with Mama, Papa and the others at the altar rail, the mercy seat. Maybe they secretly hoped that she would burst into another tirade so they could titter behind their straw fans. Instead, Liza looked through the window to where Mama and Little Ida were lying. This morning she had picked a bunch of Paul Scarlet roses that climbed the garden wire. Mama had brought a clipping from her Mama's bush and tended it lovingly. Now a bouquet in a fruit jar stood on Mama's breast, buried halfway in the dust so that the wind would not blow it away.

Somebody raised, "God be with you until we meet again." Liza gathered her brood and walked straight out of the church, looking neither to the right nor to the left, her head held high.

"Just like her Mama," somebody whispered.

If Liza had heard, she would have been proud; if Nora had heard, she would have been prouder still.

Shiloh was only a half-mile walk from their house. As the quartet turned into the dirt lane lined with chinaberry trees, they could see Uncle Joe's buggy and his gray mare tethered to the hitching post. Omega let out a whoop. Uncle Joe meant candy and watermelons. Uncle Joe had once meant to Liza books, freedom, pretty clothes. Now she didn't know.

This was the man who had kicked Mama out; the man who might have made Mama's short life more bearable. He had scorned her like the others. Mama had taken his quips and slurs, humble enough to accept his occasional charity, swallowing her pride for her children. Liza wondered why they had come. They were noticeably absent at Mama's funeral, although his pocket book had bought the coffin and paid the undertaker for a decent burial. Such latent generosity maybe salved his conscience.

The three were sitting on the porch. Aunt Lizzie and Uncle Joe were in the swing. Papa was in the rocker. Aunt Lizzie rose and with outstretched arms scooped up Omega, who threw her arms around her neck. She piped, "What you brung me?"

"Omega, shame on you. Mama told you it's not nice to ask." It was Liza's gentle reprimand.

"Liza, let her be. She's just a child. I bet a nickel Uncle Joe can find something in his pocket." Aunt Lizzie turned now to hug the others. Liza could see her aunt's eyes well with tears.

Papa now spoke. "Liza, the Kentucky Wonders from your Mama's garden done. Kept the fire going. Made the cornbread myself. Joe here brought us all kinds of vittles. We can heat up the stove and fry a few slices of his ham, and your Aunt Lizzie done brung a nut cake. They gonna eat dinner with us. Ain't that nice?"

Here was a change indeed. Never before had they graced George Marion's table with their presence. Liza was troubled. Uncle Joe was up to something. She was soon to find out.

It was company fare. Beans, tomatoes, cornbread, and ham washed down with cool milk which had been lowered in fruit jars tied with strings into the well. Aunt Lizzie's cake speckled with black walnuts and blended with sugar, country butter, eggs, and flour ground fresh from Uncle Joe's mill had been reduced to half its size. However, Liza had taken only one bite. The walnuts had stuck in her throat like pebbles. There had been no talk of Nora, except a side remark on the crispness of the beans planted before she went to the hospital. The meal ended, and Uncle Joe cleared his throat.

"George, me and Lizzie want to talk to you and Liza. Why don't we set out on the porch a spell? Cooler out there. Joey, why don't you see that Omega and Mattie clean up the table real good?" Uncle Joe was letting the younger ones know they were not to be included in the talk.

Settled on the porch, the grown-ups took their former seats. Liza sat on the steps, her arms clasping her knees. At first there was no sound except the creaking of the swing as Joe's foot rocked it back and forth.

Again he cleared his throat. "Well, George, Nora's gone now. You left with four motherless younguns'. Provisions got to be made. You're gone most of the time. It ain't right or safe leaving them alone. Some crazy nigger might come along one night. No telling what he'd do. Best to make plans. Best to look ahead."

"Joe, I 'preciate your kindness. Me and Liza here gonna manage. She grown now. Keep house like her Mama. I'm gonna stick close. Been plowing over at the Lawrimore place. Home by dark most every night. We gonna do alright."

"George, that is tom-foolishness. You ain't no home-body. We may as well get down to brass tacks. You cain't expect a sixteen-year-old gal to be mama and papa to three younguns. She ain't more'n a youngun herself. Pretty soon boys gonna be coming round. Liza's already a looker.

Womenfolk need protection."

"Joe, you right. I cain't help myself right now. We doing the best we can. Things gonna look up. I ain't got no choice 'cept to do what I'm doing."

"You got a choice, George Marion. Me and Lizzie figured it all out. They got a good orphan home in Georgetown. You could put the three young ones there. I can get them in. They'd be together. I give the home money every year. Willing to increase it. Me and Lizzie willing to take Liza here. Send her to school. Give her our name. Make something out of her. She ain't got a dead dog's chance in the sunshine in this God-forsaken swamp. You'd be a free man. Go and come as you please."

Now Aunt Lizzie spoke, directing her remarks to Liza. "We'd be proud to have you as a daughter. Pretty and smart as you are, no telling what might happen. You could be a teacher – marry some rich man. Your Mama's done a fine job with you so far. Me and Joe here could put on the finishing touches. Even send you to college where your Mama was headed before—-"

George interrupted her. "Fore she messed herself up with me. A pore boy with nothing—no larning, no land, no prospects. I give her something you didn't give her. I loved her. Me and Nora didn't have much. What we had was good. These younguns we got together. Proud of 'em. Nora was proud of 'em. We'd a made it somehow if—-" his voice cracked. He dropped his head in his hands.

Liza's spine tingled. Words should be tumbling out, but they were stopped inside her. There was anger at her aunt and uncle, grief for her Mama, and pride for her Papa. Papa had just given his valedictory. If only Mama could hear him. Something wonderful, and good, and shining, and pure had come out of this union. She moved quickly to Papa and gathered him in her young arms, her slender fingers caressing his hair. She found her voice. "Papa, we loved her, too. We love you, Papa. Mama would be so proud."

George spoke haltingly. "Liza, I don't wanta cut you out of what your uncle got. Plenty going for you. Jist like your Mama. Hard as it is, I do what you say." His voice teetered.

"Well, Liza, it's up to you. Use your head, gal. Don't let this little scene make you lose your common sense. You won't ever want for nothing again. We gonna start calling you Elizabeth to go along with your new last name."

Liza stared out into the yard. The little moss roses were in full bloom. The colors of their Easter dresses. White, pink, purple, yellow. Their little faces seemed to be listening. What were they saying? "Don't uproot us. Water us. We'll grow." Now she could see the roses, transforming the hog wire fence around the garden into a floral wall. Beyond stood Mama's Kentucky Wonders, reaching to the top of the sweet gum poles shorn of their leaves. Something was happening that was a wonder. Fancy dresses, books, jewels faded. She twisted the heavy gold wedding band, wrapped in thread so it would fit her slender finger. Mama's gift to her. Rings went with promises. Her voice was clear and solemn with never a quaver.

"I promised Mama I would manage. She's depending on me."

With that, she walked into the house.

CHAPTER SEVEN

VISITORS

TIME STANDS STILL in flat country.   Rivers run lazily through dark swamps; days crawl into endless nights. Even the inhabitants of the Neck move sluggishly. There is nowhere to go and little reason to hurry. Liza, bent over her sewing, glanced at the clock on the mantelpiece. Had she forgotten to wind it? The hands pointing to midnight had scarcely moved since she looked at them last. Still it was late and time to join Mattie in their shared bed. Omega slept on a cot beside them. Now and then Liza could hear baby mumbles. She was in her sleep calling for Mama, gone now over a year. Her absence had torn a hole in the texture of their lives that Liza's nimble fingers could not mend. The months had not lessened the grief much, but Liza's tired back felt the increase of toil. She must finish this dress tonight. Mattie's calico, too small for her burgeoning bosom, was being altered for Omega. It was to be Omega's school dress. Progress had come slow to the Neck, but at last there was now a one-room schoolhouse for children seven to thirteen. Liza was determined that Omega should go. She and Joey would take turns walking her to the Post Office, where Miss Parsons, an eccentric old maid with a yen for philanthropy, opened the door to alphabets and numbers. Unlike the slow pace of the Neck, rumors had been flying about niggers lurking in the swamp watching for white girls. Liza didn't believe a word of them; still she couldn't risk another blame if something happened to Omega. Actually she felt closer to Aunt Mae than to the white Christians at Shiloh, who reared their superior heads and staunchly and complacently accepted that slavery had been ordained by God in the Old Testament. Of course, they felt superior to Liza, too, whose Mama disgraced herself and passed on her sinful ways to a daughter with a filthy mouth. Liza had found kinship with her black neighbors. Both were in bonds; one shackled to a race; the other, to class and tradition. As poor as Liza's family was, they were better off than the blacks. Whenever Liza had extra venison from Papa's and now Joey's guns or pork from a hog killing, she shared. At first their brown eyes were suspicious of her meager offerings. One day a can of huckleberries appeared on her steps. Another day a row of beans in the garden had been neatly weeded. There were no formal thank-yous, but a tacit understanding emerged.

Liza pulled the basting thread that gathered the little

skirt for Omega's tiny waist. From the swamp came the bay of hounds. "Papa's out with his cronies coon hunting," Liza mused. Now came the galloping of horses. They were coming up the chinaberry lane. The dress slid to the floor as Liza rushed toward the window. "My God," she whispered. Each rider, robed in white from head to toe, brandished a flaming cross. Across the front yard they sped, headed toward the swamp and the river. It was as if the Neck had suddenly come alive after a slow time—alive with horse, rider, and flaming cross. Where was Papa? Was he one of those riders? What were they up to? There was no doubt in Liza's mind now who they were. She had never seen them before, but their trappings identified them. The next thought terrorized her. When they finished their work, would they pause to punish "the nigger lover"? Liza had made no bones about her friendships. One Sunday after church, Sally's Mama had said, "Liza, I hear niggers hanging around your place. You jist remember they got thick skulls. Ain't like us. Kill you in a minute. Animals! Know your Papa gone most of the time. Know you a hardhead. Better listen. I heared a whole family across the river cut to pieces by niggers."

"Yes, 'em," was Liza's reply. Secretly she wondered who had cut whom. Shiloh had done a good job cutting Liza and her family to pieces. So Liza nodded and continued to accept gratefully any help black hands would give.

But now cold fear stabbed her ribs and pushed her heart into her throat. She must rouse Joey and Mattie and get Omega. The tater bank. A circular wooden frame supported a pyramid of straw and dirt which kept sweet potatoes from freezing in winter. They could hide there. Fire wouldn't get to them.

"Joey, Mattie! Wake up!" Sleeping Omega bundled in

her arms, Liza whispered, "The Klan. They are down by the river. Follow me."

Not questioning their sister, they trailed her to the backdoor. Just beyond the garden, the potato bin housed the fall crop. Liza tore open the wooden gate just large enough for a body to crawl through. At that moment the galloping horses returned – pale horses and pale riders. Liza clasped her brother and sisters close. There was no time to pray. Prayer hadn't done much good in the past anyway. Instead, Liza addressed Mama. "You said I could manage. Help me, Mama."

Miraculously the cavalry passed down the lane onto the road that wound circuitously to the village post office. Liza folded the three of them closer. Her voice was surprisingly calm. "It's all right. Let's go back to bed." Omega, now awake, screeched, "Liza, where we?"

"Omega, just a bad dream. Go back to bed. We safe."

Into the house she marshaled her charges. She tucked Omega into her bed and crawled in beside Mattie. As hard as she tried, she could not help from shaking.

The sun rose calmly over the swamp – over the black man lying across a log, a paddle in his hand and a bullet through his skull. He had never reached his boat, which rocked peacefully in the black waters of the Little Pee Dee. The same sun fell across Liza's face and a loud knocking at the door jarred her.

"Miss Liza! Miss Liza! You all right? It's me. Your cousin, Tom."

Liza having slept fully dressed, swung her feet to the floor. "Just a minute." She sloshed a few drops of water from the pitcher into the basin on the dresser and bathed her face. She reached for the comb to tame the wild strands of her black hair. Slipping her feet into her shoes, she guided them to the door.

"Morning." It was Tom Brown. Their first meeting flooded her memory. He had been too kind to tell her that Mama had died and had lingered, offering his help when Papa broke the terrible news. Vaguely she remembered his face at the funeral, but she was sure that it was his strong arms and hands she had seen on the ropes that lowered Mama into the black earth. Now he stood before her, his clear blue eyes intent upon her, his voice, steady now that he saw her whole and unharmed.

"Miss Eliza, I heard about the Klan. I spent the night down with the Lawrimores, Sally's parents. I see there's been no harm."

Tom's eyes moved appreciatively over Liza. The morning sun caught the red luster in her dark hair carelessly falling down her slim body. Black eyes penetrated the man in front of her. Not only did they see uncombed hair and shirt that in his haste had escaped his pants but also they were examining his thoughts, sorting them out and deciding which ones were acceptable – which, unacceptable. A blush crept into his face. His whole body felt suddenly warm. What he wanted to do was gather her in his arms. What he would say he hadn't the faintest notion.

Liza spoke softly. "You need not worry. We are fine. There's no trouble here." Her eyes strayed in the direction of the swamp. Fear rose in her chest. "You heard any news?"

"No Ma'am. I mean, I know about the Klan." What he did not say was that Abe Lawrimore had come home at daybreak in high spirits, breathing corn liquor and bragging. "Won't have no trouble from them niggers for a spell. No, siree. Sons of bitches. Britton Neck men know how to shet them up. Yes, siree. No sass about wages no more. Be glad to work for twenty-five cents a day."

Liza chose her words carefully. After all, she did not know whether a Klan advocate stood in front of her. "Lots of men round here probably belong to it. Only thing I know they passed by here last night heading for the swamp and came back this way."

"You never know what'll happen," Tom commented, "when a bunch of hotheads get together. Maybe in the beginning they done some good. After the war and all. Don't see much use of 'em now. You have to let people be. Treat people right. That's what I say. Christian thing to do."

His words gave her courage. "Terrible! Running around at night scaring people. Cowards! The last one of them. Hiding their faces behind sheets with holes punched out for eyes."

From the swamp emerged four black men. They were bearing a crude litter constructed of undressed lumber. Stretched on it was the body of a black man, his body partially covered by a faded, ragged quilt, his feet encased in rubber boots sticking out. The party skirted the edge of Liza's yard toward the lane leading to the road. Looking neither to the right nor the left, they moved in sepulchral silence. Liza covered her face with her hand. "Oh, God!" she moaned.

In a split second Tom was at her side. He put his arm around her waist and guided her toward the door. "Don't look, Liza." This time he had discarded the salutory prefix. Let's go in. I'll fire up the stove and make coffee." He led her inside, past Mattie and Joey in their nightclothes, staring at the solemn procession disappearing down the lane. Tom pushed the door shut with his foot and eased Liza into a chair. On the floor lay Omega's unfinished dress abandoned so quickly the night before. He stooped to pick up the little garment, folding it awkwardly and placing it in the sewing box on the table.

"You just set there, Liza. Me and Joey gonna get the fire going. Have coffee ready in a jiffy. Mattie here can get out the cups."

Strange, Liza thought, that he knew her brother's and sisters' names. Stranger still that she was willing to relinquish family reins, feeling them safe in the strength of his kind strong hands.

The four sat around the kitchen table. Mattie had brought out Mama's best cups. Already she was calling Tom by his first name. Moreover, she had donned her Sunday dress and at every moment flounced back and forth to the table — here offering Tom extra coffee — there remembering the tea-cakes in the earthenware cookie jar. What had passed through their front yard seemed not remotely interesting to Mattie, who saw in this blue-eyed young man an audience for her feminine charms. No doubt about it. Mattie was a born flirt. Liza, though embarrassed by her sister's ostentatious lack of modesty, had other worries more pressing. She had recognized Aunt Mae's grandson among the party. Joey was oddly quiet but animated. Did he know something? And why had she permitted this distant cousin, the second time she had seen him, to come into Mama's house and take over? What had happened to her heart when he had slipped his arm around her? Where was Papa? "Don't let him have his hand in this awful thing," she prayed silently.

There came an immediate answer to the last question. The front door swung open and Papa stood in the kitchen doorway carrying a cardboard suitcase held together by cords. Beside him stood a young woman in her early twenties whom Liza had seen once or twice at the post office. A new family, the Ports, had moved into the Neck. Two heavy plaits of red hair crowned her small head, which seemed not quite to fit her short stout body. There was a suspicious swelling around her waist and distended stomach. Her sharp green eyes surveyed the group at the table.

Papa spoke first. "Well, chillun, you done got you a new Mama. This is Jane. Got hitched last night. Liza, Jane here gonna take some of the work off you. Joey, you and Mattie come shake hands with you new Mama."

Neither of them moved. At that moment Omega appeared, rubbing sleepy eyes. At seven she still sucked her thumb. When she saw the red-haired stranger, she thrust herself between the newlyweds and ran to Liza's lap. Now she turned on them, her little face in a scowl.

Papa held out his arms. "Come on, Mega. Meet your new Mama."

Omega twined her arms around Liza's neck and buried her face.

"Omega, Papa called you." Liza could not remember ever hearing such sternness in his voice before. He took a step toward Liza and wrenched the child from her arms. Omega's fists beat against his face.

"Not my Mama. Mama's in a big hole. In the graveyard." Her high-pitched scream rattled Mama's china.

There was a sharp crack as Papa's hand descended on Omega's bottom.

Liza was on her feet, black eyes blazing. She grabbed Omega from him. "I dare you to touch her again. You got no right." Now Liza was sobbing. "Mama left me in charge. No red-headed slut can make me break my promise."

Papa slapped her smartly across the mouth. "Now, you jist hesh up, gal. Long as you under my roof, you mind me. Me and Jane here gonna make it better for all you younguns." His voice was softer now. "Besides, you all gon have a new sister or brother before long, eh Jane?"

Tom had risen from his place at the table. As much as he wanted to interfere, he had the wisdom to hold his tongue. He walked to Liza's side and took her hand. "Miss Liza, I best be going. I'll be seeing you around." With that he moved toward the front porch. Liza stared at his retreating figure. She had the urge to rush after him.

"George," the new Mama reported, "I see I got my work cut out. Leave it to me. They be buckling under in a week."

CHAPTER EIGHT

CHRISTMAS

THE BOOKS ALL TALK ABOUT CHRISTMAS in the same way: snow falling like petals adrift from angel wings, reindeer prancing tunes on their silver bells, Santa's sleigh bulging with presents that never ran out, children laughing, snug in Yuletide bliss. Liza recognized this as fiction, an unreal world as fragile as happy dreams spun in airy nothingness. The Neck was non-fiction, the real world with a new Mama and a Christmas that would be an ordinary day. Last year at least they had had a little pine tree strung with popcorn and festooned with bright scraps starched stiff and cut into stars, bells, and fruit. They had made their snow with flour sprinkled on the branches. Mama's handiwork, the stockings with candy cane appliques and each name embroidered in different colors, hung over the chimney that heaved up sparkles from oak logs. Christmas morning each stocking held Brazil nuts (called nigger toes in the Deep South), an apple, an orange and stick candy. Mattie had a pretty handkerchief edged with tatting, her initials embroidered in the corner; Joey had a pair of knit socks, and Omega a new rag doll to replace the Raggedy Anne she had mutilated. Of course, Mama's stocking was empty except somebody had scrawled on a piece of tablet paper, "We miss you." Dinner was baked wild turkey, Papa's contribution from the swamp, cornbread dressing, greens from the garden, and sweet potatoes. Dessert was cake brimming with hickory nuts painstakingly gleaned from the fall crop and watermelon rind preserves, sticky and sweet in the medley. Despite Mama's absence the kitchen table, centered with holly and cedar, rang occasionally with laughter. Joey swore he had seen thirteen squirrels up one tree and had bagged four of them with one shot. Papa told the story of the old woman who lost her pipe and after having searched the house, looked into the well. She spied it in the water, but then it dropped from her mouth. Omega outdid them all when after stuffing herself, she poked out her little tummy and chirped, "Going to have a baby like Cousin Addie." That was Christmas last year.

These were Liza's musings as she rethreaded her needle and rocked the cradle of her half-sister, little Clara, two months old. Her sewing did not include such nonsense as ornaments and stocking surprises. Every scrap, every thread, and every button had to be utilized. Jane had three maxims: "A penny saved is a penny earned"; "Idleness is the devil's workshop"; and "Spare the rod and spoil the child." The last one she was ready to implement daily with Papa's razor strop. Mattie's and Joey's backs bore proof to the precision with which she administered punishment. She would have liked to direct her chastisement to Liza more than to anyone else, but she did not quite dare. Dark eyes flashed the unmistakable message to green ones. "I'm bigger and stronger." Still Liza had been forced to yield authority over the household. Papa had made that quite clear. So Liza complied with Jane's directives and said little until Jane moved into Liza's sacred territory. Then war broke out. One battle began with Omega.

Liza realized that Mama had spoiled Omega and had been derelict in giving her correction. Bereft of her champion, Omega, willful and determined to hold her ground, was first to experience Jane's belief in not "sparing the rod." Liza said nothing so long as the weapon was a hand or a peach tree switch. But the morning came when Omega had wet the bed three nights in a row. Jane, exhilarated over the discovery, waddled into the kitchen from the back porch where Papa usually shaved, with the razor strop in tow. "Wet the bed again, you little idget!" With that the strop fell across Omega's shoulder as she sat in front of her breakfast bowl of grits.

Liza caught the strop in mid air. With a quick twist of Jane's wrist, it fell to the floor. The two measured each other. "If you ever touch Omega again, I'll kill you. You are the idiot. You got rocks in your head. The pigs we kill got more brains."

With that she scooped up Omega and rushed to the woodyard where Papa and Joey were splitting logs for winter. Jane's woodbox would be full, cut to size for stove and chimney.

Liza met Papa head on. "Papa, I can't take it anymore. Jane's whipping Omega for something she can't help. She never wet the bed until you brought that woman in here. I'm warning you and her. So help me God I'm gonna get the law on her —- you, too, if you don't stop it."

Papa knew he was whipped. He could, in fact, see the injustice. Still he felt obliged to defend his position.

"Liza, you and the younguns never give her half a chance. From the first day. You got to mind her."

"Mind her? Who does the work around here while Fatso bellows orders from her rocker. Mama would roll over in her grave." Now Liza was sobbing. "You made promises to Mama. You let a skirt make you back down on your word." Liza had touched a sore spot.

"I'll talk to Jane. Baby be here now 'fore long. A woman in family way be cantankerous. Jist try to git along. I'll talk to Jane."

After that, silence had hung over the house. Words were exchanged rarely. Even Omega seldom talked. The welt on her back had healed over raw skin, but her spirit lay bare. She still wet the bed at night. Every morning Liza wordlessly removed the bedclothes, washed them in lye soap which Jane made in the back yard in the black iron wash pot. A paddle in her hand for stirring, Jane sat by the boiling cauldron filled with every sliver of fat and laced with Red Devil Lye on a can labeled POISON. Eventually the mixture would harden and be cut into squares. Liza's hands became as red as the figure on the can, but the face of Satan with a pitchfork penetrated her dreams. Sometimes she was after Mama who had abandoned her, sometimes Shiloh, sometimes Papa, but mostly she chased red-headed Jane, whom she had refused to address as Mama, though her siblings used it when Papa was around.

One day she sneaked away to the swamp and the familiar footlog which led to Aunt Mae's. She was sure that she had a glimpse of Aunt Mae in the garden pulling a mess of turnips. But as Liza drew near, she had disappeared. Pounding on the door did not produce her either. "Aunt Mae," she called. "It's me, Liza." No answer. "Talk to me. Thing are bad for me, too. Papa had nothing to do with it. I'm so sorry. I know you miss Moses." Now her voice broke. "I miss Mama, too."

There was no sound from Aunt Mae's. Liza knew she was inside. She could almost see her face, her lips mumbling unintelligible sounds, verses from the book in which black and white alike took comfort. But a grandson dead from a white man's bullet had closed the door, and the warm brown arms that might have comforted her were now locked in their own grief and frozen in anger against Liza's kind.

Liza said softly, "Aunt Mae, I didn't do it. I don't blame you. I feel the same way. God doesn't seem to hang around the Neck these days. For you. For me. You still think he loves us? Oh, Aunt Mae!"

Liza moved toward the swamp. The wooden door did not open. Aunt Mae answered her, but Liza did not hear. If she had, the words would have been meaningless like Preacher Smith's. "Chile, Jesus know bes'."

In November Clara had come. Liza at eighteen was part midwife and nurse. As angry as she was at Jane, when she first wrapped little Clara up in the blanket, she wished she could keep her warm and protected against the Janes and Klans of the world.

A firecracker popped in the front yard. Clara stirred in her slumber. Liza went to the front door. Joey, with a handful of swamp buddies, was sending red sparks into the night sky. That was the way he was spending his pay working for Mr. Haskell down at the General Store.

"Joey," Liza called. "Where's Mattie? You are both supposed to be home. The get-together at Shiloh is long past."

"Mattie ain't coming home. She spending the night at the Lawrimores. Told me to tell you." He let out a giggle.

"What do you mean, Joey? Not coming home? What will Papa say?"

"Not much," Joey laughed. Last time I seen him and Jane they was shaking a leg at Abe Lawrimore's fiddle. Don't ' spect them home either. Papa's legs pretty wobbly."

"Joey, where is Mattie?" There was no nonsense in her voice.

"Well, Liza. I spec by now her and Buddy Wright warmed up in hay."

"Joey, what do you mean?"

"I mean Mattie done got herself hitched. Preacher married 'em tonight. Papa done give consent."

Liza leaned against the door. What was it she had read? "Amen. So be it." Buddy Wright, like Papa, had no property, no learning, no prospects. But what did Mattie have here? A sharp-tongued stepmother willing to crack the whip at the slightest provocation. If Buddy loved her, that would be something. "One less mouth to feed." Liza had heard that before. One less for Liza to worry about. Joey at twelve stood on the brink of independence, already following Papa in the swamp, already earning money from nocturnal labors. But there was Omega. These days she ate so little. Night after night she cried in her sleep. At least now she could leave the cot and sleep with Liza. "So be it," Liza whispered.

Christmas morning dawned bright, clear, warm, and unthreatening. During the night Jane and Papa had come home. Awake at six, Clara cried for her feeding. Half-asleep Jane put the nipple in her child's mouth and was soon snoring. Liza had not slept at all. She felt the covers around Omega, whom she had put in bed in Mattie's place. There was no dampness. "Merry Christmas, Omega."

Omega yawned and opened Papa's blue eyes. "Mama." Her eyes widened. "Where Mattie?"

"It's all right. Don't worry about Mattie. Santa Claus came. Just for you."

From under the bed she drew a sugar sack that had escaped Jane's miserly eye. "Open it, Omega. It's from Santa."

Omega smiled and hugged Liza. "From Liza," she corrected.

There was a candy cane, a red apple, and two dresses. One was a miniature red gingham dress with drawstring to fit Raggedy Anne the second, now quite soiled with dirty hands. The other was for Omega. Liza had cut down her pink organdy wedding dress and had magically made it into a tucked yoke and bouffant skirt. From a scrap she had fashioned a bow for Omega's blond curls. A white starched petticoat with lace edging was underneath. The smile that wreathed Omega's face was ample pay for the stolen hours after midnight with her needle.

"Oh, Liza!" She stripped off her little night gown. In a moment she stood gowned in her finery. "How I look, Liza?'

"You look beautiful. Just like Cinderella in the book going to the ball."

"Your dress, Liza."

" It is your dress, Omega. Let's go wake Joey. Santa left something for him, too."

"You Santa, Liza."

For the first time in weeks there was peace at the table. Joey, proud of his box of gun shells that Liza had begged Papa to buy for him, sat drinking his coffee, weakened with milk and sweetened with sugar. Liza cooked breakfast. With Papa at home Jane could do little about the missing eggs and flour that made the biscuits Joey and Omega were now sopping in ribbon cane syrup. Mattie's place was vacant, but in the glow of good food and presents on Christmas morning, the three tacitly accepted her absence.

There was a knock on the front door. Liza rose swiftly. She didn't want anyone to waken Jane and Papa. She eased it open. Tom Brown, hat in hand, stood in the morning sunshine.

"Liza." His words came haltingly, almost as if what he was going to say had not been determined by his brain. "I'm on my way to the Lawrimores. Thought you could use a little Christmas goodies." He handed her a square box tied in a red bow. Whitman's chocolates. Liza had never seen them before.

"Good gracious, Tom," Liza's cheeks colored. "You shouldn't have gone to this trouble." A smile stole across her face. "But I thank you kindly. It was real thoughtful."

"Nothing to it. Going to be over at the Lawrimores for the next week or so. Abe wants me to help him build a room onto his house. I'd be mighty proud to come over Sunday and walk you to church."

"Why, Tom, I can't see any reason why not. Shiloh's not the friendliest church, but I suppose it's better than no church at all. Mama always took us. You're welcome to go with Omega and me." Already she had dropped Mattie from the company, and Joey had stopped going ever since Preacher Smith had scolded him for talking during the sermon. "I'd ask you to come in, but Papa and Jane are still asleep."

"That's alright, Liza. Got to be on my way. I'll see you Sunday." There was a broad grin on his face. That candy was worth a day's pay at the sawmill.

CHAPTER NINE

THE RIVER

LIZA SAT ON A STUMP of what had once been a cypress tree overlooking Parker Landing. She wondered idly where the rest of it was now. Did it prop some cabin teeming with children? Was some wild rose bush curling around its knobby knees, or had its hollowed out body become the escape of a lone fisherman paddling the dark waters of the Little Pee Dee. She had never been on the river. It was forbidden territory for a woman, who had been relegated to the shore, where she bore children each year, where she waited for her husband to return at will from the sacred precincts reserved for men only. Of course Mama had traveled that river once—down the Little Pee Dee to its big brother, Big Pee Dee which joined another sibling, the Waccamaw. It had taken her on the first leg of her journey to death and the watery grave of the church cemetery in the heart of Britton's Neck. How frightened Mama must have been to make that trip alone. She had always been afraid of the water; she couldn't swim and had not been brave enough to steal away to battle the Big Pee Dee, her childhood home. Liza, however, with cousins Addie and Sally, had dared on summer afternoons to doff their shoes and hike their dresses to wade into the murky shallows, their girlish screams blasting their delight in the tingling chill against bare legs and the squishy sand between clenched toes. Liza had always ventured farther than her playmates but not quite enough to see what was around the curve of the river as it widened and drifted downward, its water losing blackness and giving way to the lighter colors of Big Pee Dee. "Someday," Liza thought, "someday, I'll get away, too. Like Papa. Only it won't be for a day or a week."

  The soft swish of a paddle stirred the smooth surface directing a small boat to the landing. The man in command of the vessel was neither fisherman nor scout. Dressed in Sunday best, Tom waved one hand as he neared the shore. Somewhere in the boat was the work garb exchanged at some point down river for "courting clothes." Liza smiled as she imagined the scene. He would have shed his sweaty habiliments, diving naked into the water. Afterward he would redress, slickening down his thick brown hair, using the river mirror. Liza rose slowly, watching him anchor his craft to a cypress knee. He turned now toward her, smiling sheepishly. She knew exactly what he would say, what he had been saying since Christmas week now almost a year and a half ago. "Well, now, Liza, pretty as ever." Deficient in the language of gallantry and suffering from shyness, he found difficulty, particularly upon arrival, to find words. It amused Liza to watch his discomfiture, but at the same time she was flattered. He approached her now with the same diffidence, a subject with a petition, making her feel regal, queenly. She knew he loved her, could read the message in his blue eyes, could feel it in his touch as those big hands helping her in and out of the buggy lingered a bit longer than necessary. On his last trip he had risked drawing her to him as he said goodbye, his lips just brushing her cheek as she turned her head to avoid his kiss. She knew she had hurt him. Had told him she was sorry. The truth was she really didn't know what she felt for Tom. He was kind, gentle, understanding. Those big hands would never strike her, would slave for her, but would carry her like Mama to a house and motherhood. Still he would take her away from Papa and Jane, whose ill temper and demands became more oppressive daily. But Omega. What would become of her defenseless little sister? Separated from Liza's protective eye, Jane would crush what little spirit the once imperious Omega had left. There was still another troubling question. What would Tom say if he knew how she really felt about church and the inanities that fell so freely from the preacher and his flock. "God knows best. He don't make mistakes." Every nerve in her body bristled at such platitudes. It wasn't that she didn't believe in God. She could sense a Presence in a sunset, even in a creative design of a quilt pattern. But a God who engineered suffering and death, who advocated laws that ostracized people like Mama who had found young love in the wrong place and the wrong time – a God who from his throne delegated certain unfortunate souls to a burning hell. Was this the same God that she imagined breathed on a bare tree, the mist turning into spring blossoms?

What would Tom say if she aired such thoughts? It had never occurred to him to question providence, and although there was not a hint of sanctimony in his nature, there was simple acceptance grounded in unquestioning faith. Could such different people share a life? Would it be fair to Tom?

"Well, now, Liza. Pretty as ever." His blue eyes stole a quick look before dropping downward to study his shuffling feet.

Deviltry flashed in Liza's dark eyes. What would he say to this. On impulse she encased his cheeks in her hands and planted a firm kiss on his mouth. He stood like a man turned to stone. For a moment Liza thought he was going to topple over into the water behind him. He recovered himself and gulped, "Well, Liza. I'm real glad to see you, too. My, My, Liza!" He reached for her, but she slipped mischievously out of his reach.

"Tom, let's do something different. Take me for a ride on the river."

"Why, Liza, it's not fitten' to take a lady on the river. You can't swim. What would happen if the boat hit a snag?"

"You can swim. You could rescue me," she challenged impishly. "Besides, Papa says the Little Pee Dee's not more than three or four feet deep. Hasn't rained in a month." She reached out and took his hands. "Will you, Tom? Just for me?"

"Liza, what would your Papa say? 'Spose he met us on the river?"

"Papa. Are you afraid of Papa, Tom?" The unspoken words questioned his manhood. "Papa's too busy with a new wife and new swamp business to care about me. I can't see that he ever troubled himself about what's 'fittin'.'"

"Okay. Just for a little way. Never forgive myself if something happened to you. I," now he was groping for words, "care about you, Liza. A whole heap. I—-"

Liza stopped him midsentence. "Then let's go." With both hands she steered him down to the boat lazily rocking in the water.

Liza sat on the crossbeam facing Tom, who was moving the paddle from one side to the other, steering the small craft around the bend. There was animation in her face that Tom had never seen. Her black eyes flitted from the half circle to search out the route ahead and the one behind. In breathless silence she beheld for the first time the real river, meandering and widening. Gaunt willows bearded in Spanish moss rippled the black velvet waves. Occasionally random glints of sunlight played on the ebony surface while cypress knees edging the swamp stood motionless in watery silence. This was a different kind of beauty — the kind that etched itself on the soul — the kind that had the power to charge memory in flashes of light and dark — the kind that Liza could not verbalize now or ever — the kind that made her bow her head to its forbidding grandeur and made her feel at one with the river. Raising her dark eyes to meet Tom's blue ones, she whispered, "It's fitten'." Tears welled and slid down her smooth olive cheeks. Liza did not know whether what gushed from her being was love either for the man facing her or the watery road on which she rode for the first time. Her strong hand, reddened with lye soap washings, grasped his free hand. "Tom, it's taking us away; let's never go back."

What was she saying? This was not the Liza on the shore. At this moment she was more beautiful than he had ever seen her; yet the wild excitement in her eyes frightened him. Even as he wanted to possess this creature, to claim her body and soul, he knew that she belonged to something apart from him – a place he could not enter, that even if he could, he would not understand, would be afraid to attempt to understand. The water wobbled his dreams of Liza patterned in the age-old designs of husband, wife, father, mother, children. The woman before him was a thing apart, not anchored to the shore but moving in and out of mysterious coves before striking out to the open sea. Yet he had no choice except to follow her. He knew that to leave her was as impossible as changing the current of the river.

"Liza, will you be my wife?" The words were clear, spontaneous, rising on the wind now whipping the black tendrils of her hair escaping the confines of the coiled roll framing her face.

"Tom, I'm not fitten'. You don't know me. You are so good. There are things about me that won't make for a good wife."

"I love you, Liza. Loved you from the first day I seen you drying your hair on the front porch waiting for a letter from your Mama you didn't know was dead. I can't get you a fine house like you deserve, not right away. But together. Someday we can own the land around this river. We can maybe go on a steamboat to Charleston, to Savannah – whatever you say." He cupped her chin in his hand, looking into the depths of her eyes. His voice rose just above the sound of the paddle plowing the water. "Fore God, I'll take care of you. Long as I live."

"Oh, Tom!" This time her lips lingered on his and the paddle, forgotten for the moment, allowed them to drift wherever the current took them.

CHAPTER TEN

JUNE WEDDING

"LIZA, WHATCHA MAKING? Me a new dress out of Mama's?"

Omega stood at Liza's knee. In her lap lay the voluminous folds of white organdy Mama had worn at Easter three years ago. With the sharp end of a needle Liza tediously removed stitch after stitch, dropping now a sleeve, now a bodice into the sewing basket beside her. She could almost see Mama standing with Papa at Shiloh. Mama had loved the dress; it had made her beautiful. Now Liza was taking it apart,

reducing it to pieces of a pattern never again to be re-assem-
bled. Liza's heart lurched. Her fingers were slowly ripping out
the past. Mama was gone forever even as the dress she had
worn so proudly.

"No, Omega, not yours. It's mine. My wedding dress.
I'm getting married. But you're going to wear the pink, my old
dress. Remember? I gave it to you Christmas."

Omega's mouth primped. She dropped her head, her
childish treble tremulous. "What does it mean, *married*, Liza? It
mean leaving? Leaving like Mama? Coming back in a box?"

Liza drew her little sister into her arms and tilted her
head. Gazing into the depths of teary-blue eyes, Liza whispered reassuringly. "No, no, Omega! It means going. You're
going to have a big, kind, sweet brother. We're going away
with him. Across the rivers."

"Will Papa and Mama Jane and Joey and little Clara
go?"

"No, Honey. Just you and me and Tom. Papa said you
could go with me. You'll be my little girl and my little sister."

How hard it had been to wring Papa's consent. It
would have been easy had it not been for Jane, who saw in
Omega a potential nursemaid, servant, slave.

"George," she had accused, "you let that Liza tell you, a
growed up man, what to do? Who wears the britches in this
house?. You or your first wife's younguns? Ain't right for younguns to boss they Papa. 'Sides," she whined, "Mega gittin big
enough to help me with Clara. No telling how long I be down
when the other one come."

Liza bristled. "Listen to her, Papa. It's not me bossing
you that is worrying her. She's losing one slave, me. She
intends to make Omega take my place, if she doesn't beat her
to death first. Papa, have you forgotten what you promised

Mama? Use your head. Can't you see what's behind all this talk?"

"Now, Liza, cool down. You got to respect Jane here. She your new Mama now. Jane's right. She needs Mega. Ain't right neither to give my flesh and blood away."

"Your flesh and blood!" Her voice was scathing. "You love your flesh and blood so much you willing to see this——" she caught herself before she said the word. "This woman kill a little child who still cries for Mama every night, who shakes like a leaf when (pointing to Jane) that thing comes near her?"

"You hesh up, Liza. You done gone fur enough."

"Papa, I'm going further. You let Omega go with me or I'm going to tell the Magistrate, Mr. Tindall, what kind of business you got in the swamp. That's my promise, Papa. You better think twice."

Papa kicked the stool across the kitchen floor, its clatter waking Omega. "Mama," she called.

Papa knew he was whipped. The question was closed. Not even Jane dared to open it again. She knew what side her bread was buttered on.

The next few days the silence was even heavier, responses limited to grunts and gestures. Liza felt something brewing. There was a sly gleam in Jane's eyes. So when Liza opened the small box secured with a ribbon, Mama's wedding ring had disappeared from its bed of cotton. Liza stood in the shed room just off the kitchen shaking like the aspens in Colorado she had read about. Had her reading extended to Shakespeare, she might have thought of Hamlet, who prayed that he would not, like Nero, get so angry that he would murder his mother. Two fears struck Liza simultaneously. One, that she would not retrieve the ring. Two, that she would hurt Jane. Naked hatred gleamed in Liza's eyes. Still she measured her steps to the kitchen where Jane sat hunched over a bowl of hopping johns, her hand grasping the fork shovel fashion. Even Omega knew the proper way to eat. Mama was poor, but she never forgot table manners.

"Jane, I want Mama's ring. Don't deny it. You took it. I just want it back."

"Don't know nothin' 'bout no ring."

"Jane, I'm giving you a chance. Give it back and I won't even tell Papa."

"Tell 'im. I ain't seen no ring. Wouldn't have that big-gity woman's ring if somebody give it to me."

"Suppose I tell Papa something else? Papa has never been able to count. It seems to me he said he met you at Jess Paul's barn raising. That was the end of March. I wrote it down. Little Clara came last of October. Count your fingers, Jane. You are smart enough for that."

Jane reached in her bosom and drew out the ring and threw it at Liza's feet. Liza stooped to pick it up, flashed a smug smile in Jane's direction and walked out. Now she looked down at the wide gold band encircling the third finger of her right hand. In less than two weeks Tom would place it on the third finger of her left hand.

Omega brought her back to the present. "Liza, will it be like Mama at Shiloh? Will Mattie come? Will Papa wear his suit? Will I hold your flowers? Like you did at Mama's?"

"Hey, little one! One question at a time. No, it won't be at Shiloh. We're going to be married outdoors at Parker Landing. No, Mattie can't come. She lives too far away. I don't know about Papa. Yes, you're going to hold my flowers. Mama's roses will be in full bloom then. Then we'll get in the boat, you, me, Tom. We'll float down the river."

"Will we ever come back, Liza? I'm scared."

Liza picked up a sleeve and measured it to her arm. "You know, Mega, I'll tell you a secret. Promise you won't tell?"

"I promise."

"I'm scared, too."

Gray light of morning was spreading over the Neck. Liza stood in front of the dresser, looking in the beveled mirror. Not even age splotches on its surface could mar the reflection. Liza had scooped out Mama's wedding dress to a sweetheart neckline, and although the fullness of the skirt had been sacrificed for puff sleeves, it fell regally from an empire waistline ballooning out over starched petticoats. Liza had copied the dress from a picture she had seen in a magazine on Mr. Haskell's counter. Nobody in Britton's Neck had ever seen such a dress. They would be talking about it forever, along with how she wore her hair. Instead of a coil around her head, Liza had drawn it straight back, secured it with a white ribbon at her neck and let it fall over her left breast. A ruffle of organdy resembling a chapel cap topped her head. She was a portrait in black and white. What she saw in the mirror pleased her. Omega, standing just behind, piped, "Oh, Liza! Pretty Liza!" A new word had been added to her vocabulary recently. She tested it out, "beautiful bride."

"You're beautiful, too." Liza had curled Omega's blond locks and tied them with a pink ribbon to match her dress. There was a sparkle in Omega's eyes that had not been there since Mama had left. Taking her little sister by the hand, she walked out of the gray log house into the early morning. Something else the Neck would be talking about. Liza was getting married, not only at Parker Landing but at sunrise. "Jist like her old Mama. Thinks she's bettern than us. Sich fancy notions. Married at daybust on the riverbank. Didn't even ask Preacher Smith. Gonna have Tindall, Justice of the Peace." These would be the sentiments of the Neck, who had not been invited. Still they would come. They wouldn't have missed such a spectacle for a pass into the Golden Gate of Heaven.

Tom was waiting for her with his friend, Neil. As Liza and Omega descended the steps, both men gasped. "Great Jumping Jehosaphat, Tom," Neil whispered. "I'd give a gold guinea to be in your shoes. Prettiest woman I ever seen."

Tom, in black suit and bow tie reached out for his bride. "Well, now, Liza, pretty as ever. You, too, Omega." His voice choked with pride. How could he, Tom Brown, a blacksmith's son with a Mama who could not recognize her name in the Bible have won this woman before him. Not only pretty — smart in the head, too. Book learning. Not in dreams, not in pictures, had he seen such a creature.

The four reached the landing just as the sun rose, shimmering in the dark water. Parker was lined with Shiloh, who had tittered behind their fans at Mama. Liza smiled. There was fresh fodder for Shiloh Sunday. She had managed to bring a little excitement into their dull, drab lives. But she had not planned her wedding to create gossip or bring diversion for them. She was starting out on a new journey. It needed to be at sunrise near the river which would carry her into another world. She said softly to herself, "It's fitting."

Mr. Tindall stood on the cypress stump where Liza had sat two months earlier, where with Tom she had drifted down the river, where he had declared his love, where, for better or worse, she had given her consent to become his wife. Now she stood with Tom on one side, Omega on the other. She looked down at the bouquet of Paul Scarlet roses, each thorn having been snipped carefully the night before and now centered with a bit of white organdy. "Oh, Mama! You would be so proud," she whispered. Leaning against a scarlet maple was Papa. She could have sworn there were tears in his blue eyes. By his side stood Jane, holding Clara over her bulging stomach. At that moment a peculiar sensation moved over her. Suddenly there was no anger against Papa, Shiloh, not even Jane, brutal, hard, fighting to maintain a place in the aimless circle, stealing what morsels she could to feed her loveless being. There was another planet for Liza, looming over that river before her. It had to be different from the Neck. She and Tom would make it different.

"Dearly beloved, we are gathered together to join this man and this woman in holy matrimony in the presence of God and these witnesses."

From the swamp came the three sharp notes of a bobwhite, seeking out his lady. Liza smiled.

"If any man can show just cause why this man and this woman cannot be lawfully joined, let him now speak or forever hold his peace." The only sound was the splash of a fish passing on his way down the river.

Liza handed her bouquet to Omega, and Tom slipped Mama's wedding band on her finger. His voice had an unexpected lilt to it as he repeated, "With this ring I thee wed."

"By the power invested in me by the State of South Carolina, I pronounce you man and wife."

A short whistle was the bobwhite's answer to her mate.

"It's fitting," Liza repeated. Tom's lips stopped her words.

CHAPTER ELEVEN

LANDING

THE FLAT-BOTTOMED BOAT carrying the bridal couple neared Peter's Landing. Tom at the oars furrowed the muddy waters with his strong brown arms. His gaze was not on the water but on Liza, who sat by Omega facing him. The sun caught the reddish glints in her jet-black hair, now bound neatly on top of her small head. Liza's eyes, however, scouted the swamp and shallows to which Tom was directing the craft. The rapid rise and fall of her rounded bosom conveyed her excitement.

Somehow the roles had been switched. Tom remembered that April afternoon when he had first held her in his arms, when those dark dreamy eyes had locked his as she murmured, "Oh, Tom. Let's never go back." Today he might have echoed her words. More than anything in the world would he have liked to turn around and steer toward Georgetown and the little inn where his hand, calloused with labor of carpentry, farm and sawmill, had caressed her smooth skin tenderly, not wishing to bruise her with his rough touch. This girl facing him with her arm around her little sister, his wife now, one body one flesh like the Bible said, was not looking backward but ahead to the new life – to new people, his family. The determined set of her mouth and the squareness of her shoulders showed no fear. But he was afraid. He was afraid of Ma's tongue when this strange creature whose head was not only beautiful but also packed with strange notions, alien to women like Ma — afraid of Liza's eyes when she saw the four-room cabin he had hurriedly raised for her after she had said yes on that river cruise down the Little Pee Dee. A curious regret stole over him. Gone now was the black magic of its dark waters that matched the magic when he first tasted the sweetness of her lips and listened to the plans already formed in her busy head. But he knew, as he slowly maneuvered the boat to prepare for anchoring it to the shore, that there was no turning back. Here was a woman whom he loved with all his being, for whom at this moment he would die, protecting her with his very life. His greatest fear was that he would not be able to measure up – that he would see the disappointment in her eyes and that she would shut the door of her world, because he was not strong enough, brave enough, smart enough to live in it with her.

Omega's voice rang out. "We here, Liza! This where

we live?"

"No, no, Omega!" Tom replied as he lifted her from the rocking boat and planted her little feet on the shore. "The horse and wagon up there apiece."

Liza, standing erect in the boat, was ready to throw the rope to him, coiling it as she had seen Papa do so often. She called out, "Ready, Tom? Catch." Her voice was bright with excitement with a bit of mischief as she twirled the rope in preparation. She deliberately did not aim it for Tom's waiting hands. He had to jump for it, catching it in midair. Liza's laughter rippled.

"Oh, Liza, you can do better than that." Liza lifted her red gingham skirt and started to the bow. The boat heaved.

"Stop it, Liza! You'll fall. Wait 'till I tie her up."

"I'm not afraid". One flying leap took her over the shallows to Tom's arms.

"You won't do. Just won't do." There was pride in his voice. Her hands joined his on the rope.

"I'll help pull her in."

Tom looked down into her eyes and said mischievously, "It ain't fittin."

"It's fitten." Together they tugged the boat around and tied it to a sweet gum. Tom caught her in a quick hug.

"Come on, Liza. The horse and wagon right down there." Omega pointed to the winding path she had just explored. "I'm hungry."

"It won't be long now, Omega. We'll eat at our new house. Miss Brinkley, you know where we spent last night, gave me a jar of soup and a slice of pound cake to bring along."

Tom interposed. "Liza, that's mighty nice. But Ma 'specting us for dinner. We can save it for supper."

"Oh, Tom. Kinda looked forward to our first meal in

our house." The sparkle had gone out of her voice. She saw the troubled furrow on Tom's brow. She added quickly, "Of course, I didn't know you had made plans. Course I want to meet your folks. Wouldn't miss it for the world." Her words were not entirely convincing.

"Ma's put the big pot in the little one, as the saying goes. Pa's anxious to see you. Asked me a million times if you look like your Mama. Couldn't tell him. Never seen her. Think Pa mighta been sweet on your Mama when she was a gal. Wouldn't blame him if she looked like you. Wouldn't blame him atall."

Liza's thoughts swerved to that Sunday afternoon after Shiloh and the wedding. Mama had been still in her white dress, that was now lying in a pillowcase in Tom's boat. The two in their finery were sharing the front porch swing.

"Mama, did you have many boyfriends before Papa?"

"A few. I was not pretty as you. There was one. I could have married him. A cousin. Good, hardworking man."

"Did he love you, Mama?" Liza was now ready to explore Mama's girlhood — curious about other romances more glamorous than she could imagine was Mama's and Papa's.

"He loved me."

"Did you love him, Mama?"

"Oh, I don't know, Liza. It's been so long ago. I left to go off to high school. Then I met your Papa. That ended that." Her voice also indicated the end of the discussion.

Now Liza mused. Could it be possible that Tom's Papa had been —— Liza's voice suddenly regained its animation. "Yes, Tom, I want to meet your family. 'Specially your Papa."

By this time Tom had lifted the suitcases from the boat to the shoreline along with several sacks. One housed a clipping from the Paul Scarlet rosebush and a stocking tied up to hold butter bean seeds. Somewhere there was a bundle of dried herbs which Aunt Mae had brought the day before the wedding. "Heared you tying the knot. Keep dis unner you pillow. Keep your man from runnin round." Liza had embraced her. It was the most treasured present she would get. Aunt Mae had braved the swamp alone to tell her goodbye. Now came the pillow case and hers and Mama's wedding dress. Liza twisted the gold band on her finger. "I didn't leave you back there, Mama," she mumbled.

"What's that you saying, Honey?"

"I was saying let's load up and get going. The sun is getting hotter. We don't want to hold up your Ma's dinner." Liza hadn't decided yet what she would call Tom's Mama. For the moment she would use the address by which Tom referred to her.

Shortly the wagon pulled out of the swamp and turned left on a dirt road. "Where does the other end go, Tom?" Liza questioned.

"Down to Port Hill. Ain't much of a Port. It's just another landing. Pa's got a farm down there. Raises cotton. You'll see it soon enough."

"Uncle Joe raises cotton, too," Omega informed him. "And big watermelons." Her growling stomach yearned for the red juicy sweetness of the heart of a melon cooled in the well water.

"We got a patch of melons, Omega. Won't be ready yet. By the Fourth. Always got one ripe by Fourth of July if the season's been right. Only two weeks off. I'll give you the first piece out of the first one we cut." He looked down at her, a twinkle in his eyes.

Omega clapped her hands and hugged Tom's arm horizontal with the reins on Old Blue, the family transportation that doubled as the plow.

There was another dead end. Tom pulled on the reins and old Blue clopped to the left. They could now see the small white washed frame church squatting on cypress blocks and topped with a spire. Graves, mute guardians, marked with marble, others with pointed wooden slabs from the heart of an oak, stood around the structure, appearing sturdier and certainly more imposing. In the yard anchored to a pole was a cowbell from which dangled a gray rope. Across the way was a house that seemed out of place. A small picket fence divided it from the road. It was a two-story dwelling looming above the church and graveyard, seeming to declare its superiority and independence of its neighbor. To the left of the house was a one-room office over which a signboard revealed its identity: "Brown Hill Post Office, S.C." Liza examined her new address. She doubted that any letter would be coming to her, Mrs. Tom Brown, nor would she be writing any right away.

"Who lives there, Tom?"

"Uncle John and Aunt Mary MacDonald. Not really my aunt and uncle. Call 'em that out of respect. They maybe distant cousins. Everybody's kin around Brown Hill. Uncle John's the Postmaster. Also school teacher in that there house just across the branch." He pointed to a building behind the church barely visible through the long leaf pines. "Uncle John's the only man I know been to college. He's got a whole room full of books. Calls it his liberry. Mystery why he wanted to settle here in Brown Hill."

"Where's the hill, Tom?" Liza laughed as she surveyed the flat land before her.

"Dog if I know. Musta got washed down in the river. Mighta been leveled in the Great Earthquake in 1886. Got no idea. Been Brown's Hill 'fore I was born. Be here I 'spect after I'm gone," he added philosophically. "We home, Liza."

The wagon turned to the left just beyond the church where a small newly built log cabin stood, its tin roof glistening in the sun. On the small porch was a lone rocker cushioned in blue mattress ticking, looking almost an afterthought on the bare little house. To the left of the top wooden step leading to the porch was a banister extending the length of the house and turning to join the wall. Liza smiled as she surveyed the unfinished structure waiting patiently for its completion. Already she could see morning glory vines climbing on the strings from eaves to banister.

"Didn't quite have time to get the other side up. Got the wood all sawed and ready though. Do it tomorrow."

Liza reached her arms around his neck and drew his face down to hers. For the first time she whispered, "I love you, Tom."

CHAPTER TWELVE

BRIDAL RECEPTION

TO LIZA, the four-room house was a palace. The living room running the length of the house facing the road gave way to a small hall that divided two bedrooms. Beyond was a small covered breezeway connecting the kitchen. Tom had put every nickel he had saved into the building; therefore, the furnishings were sparse —two iron bedsteads, one with a straw mattress, a squat little iron stove, a knotty pine table and two benches. Liza's quick eye was already transforming it with a quilt there, curtains here — flowers on the table. Here would be no querulous Jane. She would be mistress of her household and together she and Tom would make it home. She could already see stockings hanging over the hearth in the fireplace standing on the east side of the living room. She ran from room to room, mentally decorating.

"Is it all right, Liza?" Tom asked hopefully. "Best I could do. Not much time. Not much money neither."

"Oh, Tom, it's fine. You just wait. It won't look like this next year."

"Liza," his voice was earnest now. "I ain't got no cash now. Times going to be hard. We have to put up with pretty much what you see 'less folks give us something. There might be a house warming by neighbors, but I don't want to borrow money — get in debt. Don't know what's down the road. We have to manage with what we got for awhile."

His troubled financial admissions did not quell her enthusiasm. She'd find a way. She could feel it in her bones. "Course, we'll manage, Tom. I'm strong. I can work. I bet I can pick more cotton than two my size. I bet Uncle John could use me at the Post Office sometime. I might even help out at the school house." Now she giggled and batted her dark eyes, flirting outrageously. She deliberately lapsed into country jargon. "You ain't seen nothing yet. Done bought yourself a woman and a half. Don't want to take her back, do you?"

"Liza, Liza!" He was about to scoop her up when a voice called from the front porch. "Come on out, Bud. Lemme see your woman. Ma's got dinner on the table. Pilau gittin cold. Ma'll be as mad as a wet settin hen."

Liza took his hand and led him to the porch. The young man standing there leaning against the banister post had to be Tom's younger brother. He had the same blue eyes and brown mop except with a cowlick that needed no slickening to keep his hair from his face. Evidently he had already made friends with Omega, who was busy unwrapping a piece of chewing gum. One look told Liza that here was a friend, an ally if she ever needed one. His eyes moved admiringly over her.

With hands outstretched, Liza moved toward him. "You must be Jess. Good looking like Tom said. Maybe I married the wrong man."

A blush suffused his face. "Well, Ma'am, you ain't so bad looking yourself. Tom's done right good." The red deepened as he added, "Couldna done better myself."

"She's a looker, eh Jess? Told you so. Don't be getting any notions. I saw her first."

"Stop it, you two," Liza commanded. "My head is already swollen twice its size with all those compliments. Folks will be calling me big-headed."

"Ma's gonna be calling us pig-headed if we don't get going," Tom said. With that he ushered the four to the road and the short stroll to the Brown house.

The porch and part of the yard was full. Liza wondered if she would remember all those names. Her eyes searched for Tom's father and found him standing beneath an oak. He was taller than either of his two sons, thinner —his angular face reminded her of pictures she had seen of Abe Lincoln. His hair, darker than his sons', fell in a hint of a curl over one eye. When her eyes looked into his gray ones, she knew beyond the shadow of a doubt that this was the man who had loved Mama, had wanted to marry her. His eyes swept over her almost as if he were searching for some resemblance that could connect with the past. Did she imagine sadness about him, or was it restlessness —the kind that came when you felt hemmed in like she did in the Neck. His voice was deep, resonant, welcoming.

"So this is Nora's girl."

"Is she the one who got in the family way 'fore she got married, Gideon?" The question came from an old woman on the porch bonneted and dressed in black.

Tom's father came to life. He whirled around to face the questioner. His voice was stern and commanding. "Aunt Sue, you ought to be ashamed of yourself. You apologize to Liza right now. You don't insult a guest in my house, specially my new daughter."

"Didn't mean no harm, Gideon." Her mouth puckered like a child about to be spanked. Tears slid down the brown creases of her cheek.

Liza addressed her soothingly. "It's all right, Aunt Sue. I know you meant no harm. You're right. I'm Nora's daughter, Liza. Her oldest." She lifted her head proudly almost as if she were about to deliver a proclamation. "I am proud of it. I just hope I can be half the woman my mother was."

"Amen!" It was Aunt Lizzie who had broken from the group where she had been standing with Uncle Joe. What in the world was Uncle Joe doing here, Liza thought. In a moment Aunt Lizzie had swept both Liza and Omega in her arms. Even Uncle Joe came forward, picked up Omega who wrapped her arms around his neck.

"You bring a watermelon?" Omega quipped. The crowd laughed. The awkward moment had gone. Every eye seemed to be focused on Liza. This pert little woman could take care of herself, they had no doubt. The men eyed her beauty, delighted in her upstart behavior; the women looked at her jealously, knowing that not one of them would be a match for her in looks, brains, or courage. Only Aunt Sue, who had been roundly scolded, entertained kind feelings for this little stranger who faced her foes and was ready to defend her territory.

A small woman in a white flour sack apron holding a fan of turkey feathers stood in the doorway. Thin brown hair in a ball sprinkled with gray topped her head. Her face was plain, but she had that solid look of pioneer women following their men. Her eyes measured every inch of Liza's person, but it was to her husband she spoke.

"Gideon, if you don't git these folks in here, dinner gon' be stone cold. Been waitin for you long enough, Tom. Rations been ready two hours."

Liza flinched at the reprimand. Here was the enemy, the Jane who had followed her across two rivers. Nevertheless, she mounted the steps and headed straight for her. "Miss Minnie, I'm Liza." She held out her hand. All eyes turned to her mother-in-law, who had no choice but to take her hand grudgingly. Omega had inched her way to Liza's side. "And this is my little sister, Omega. Say howdy to Miss Minnie, Omega."

Omega responded with a half-curtsy that she had used when she played storyland with Liza. "How do, Miss Minnie. Glad to meet you."

There was a softening in Minnie's face. Her girls had turned out to be boys. This child in front of her could have been her own. The midwife had told her after Jess was born there wouldn't be anymore. All her love went to her sons, but especially to Tom, her eldest. Now this black-haired girl had taken him away from her, like her Mama before her had taken Gideon. Minnie stooped to take Omega's little hand. "You come on in. Got to be hongry, too."

Liza paused, waiting for Tom. He took her hand and led her into the house. Behind them came the others — Gideon, Jess, Aunt Susie, Aunt Lizzie and Uncle Joe. Spectators in the yard, uninvited guests, ambled off. They had come to see the bride, to watch the fun when Tom's Ma put her daughter-in-law in her place. It had been worth the trip, but it held a big surprise. Liza Brown was nobody's fool. Not even Minnie Brown would buckle her. Minnie had met her match. They had been waiting a long time for excitement. No one knew that it would come in the form of a little lass from Britton's Neck who had an indomitable spirit that could stop the tongue of Minnie Brown. Brown Hill had suddenly come out of lethargy of a hundred years.

Gideon, who sat at the head of the table, seated Liza on his right. Had Minnie known that this position was the place of prominence, she would have been furious. Gideon served the pilau – chicken and rice cooked together in a savory bog and generously sprinkled with black pepper and herbs – sweet potato pone, black-eyed peas, mustard greens, cornbread, corn on the cob. Liza's plate was filled first, but while the others, including Tom, began eating immediately, Liza waited for her host and hostess, a nicety that escaped Minnie completely. Gideon, however, noted her table etiquette appreciatively. She even held her fork in the same dainty way Nora had. His thoughts strayed to that afternoon when he had seen her last. He had floated logs from Port Hill down the river to Georgetown but had returned by way of Plantersville, where his wealthy cousins lived. Joe and Lizzie were not at home, but Nora was sitting on the porch, a suitcase at her feet. It turned out she was waiting for George. Gideon remembered her exact words.

"Gideon, we both made a mistake. I made the worst one. You have Minnie and two little boys. George will be coming soon to take me to Britton's Neck. We're going to get married. Going to be a mother, Gideon." Her head dropped down; her hands were clenched in her lap. "Lost my head,

Gideon. I'd rather tell you myself before somebody else."

"Nora!" His voice filled with anguish. "What's going to happen to you? George Marion can't support you hunting and fishing. Listen! I don't have much. What I got, I'll help you. I can mortgage a piece of land. Send you to the Door of Hope. Put the baby up for adoption."

"No, no, Gideon. I wouldn't let you do that. I couldn't give up my child, George's and mine. Besides" she looked him squarely in the eye, "I love George. Joe says I've made my bed hard. Well, I'll lie on it."

Now this child she had been carrying was sitting at his elbow; she was his son's wife—would bear his son's children, his grandchildren. It was almost as though Nora had returned to him, younger, prettier, more spirited. This strange elation made him feel warmth for Minnie, who now sat at the end of the table, frequently waving flies with a turkey feather fan. She had been a good wife, hardworking, loyal, frugal. Together they had raised two good boys. Yet there had been something missing. Something he couldn't share—the way he felt when he saw a newborn calf jumping, a field of waving wheat, the sound of his hammer on pine as he fashioned a coffin in his blacksmith shop. Such diverse sensations — life and death. Nora would have known. He would even have been able to verbalize, and what he couldn't articulate she would have understood. It would have been registered in her deep blue eyes which saw, whose lips knew when to be silent. It might have been different. Maybe this was the way that God placed his signature on the Nora chapter—closed but uncannily reopened with this beautiful dark little being at his side. He had already glimpsed the malicious sparkle in Minnie's eyes. Granted she could neither read nor write, but Minnie's womanly intuition sensed the chasm between him and her, and although she knew it was there, she could do nothing to bridge it. These thoughts prompted him to say,

"Minnie, best pilau I ever tasted. Not too greasy. How many chickens you kill?"

Minnie did not answer. Instead, she rose swiftly from the table and bustled to the stove busying herself with bringing out extra helpings. No one saw the tears gleaming in her eyes.

Dinner had ended with a four layer caramel cake. Liza had to admit it was better than what she made. Somehow she could never get the sugar for the caramel browned just right— it always came out burned and hard or soft and sticky. She was about to ask Minnie to share her secret, when Minnie abruptly stood up. Her voice held no warmth of hospitality.

"You folks help yourself. Jess, spread the cloth on the table so the flies won't get to it. I got to git out to feed my old hen; jist come out of the woods with a dozen biddies."

She left the kitchen, still not having acknowledged Liza. With the exception of senile Aunt Sue, all at the table recognized the cut. Even Uncle Joe seemed embarrassed. Tom looked down at his plate and squeezed Liza's hand under the table. Gideon pushed back his chair.

"Well, folks, kinda warm in here. There's a breeze out on the porch. Let's set a spell until Minnie's vittles settle. She'll be along in a little bit. She's crazy about raising chickens. Course that's what went into the dinner pot." It was as near as Gideon could come to apologizing for his wife's behavior.

Tom spoke. "Pa, Liza hardly seen her new house. We best be gittin down the road. We got a heap of things to do."

"Gideon," Uncle Joe said, patting his stomach, "Mighty good fare. Lizzie and me'll chaw the rag awhile, but we best be going soon. We want to stop by to see Liza here. Brought her a few things for a wedding present."

Omega's eyes widened. "You bring me something, Uncle Joe?"

"Wait and see. Might find a doll hiding in the buggy," he teased.

Joe Brown was after something. Liza had been watching his tricks for as long as she could remember. His gifts carried price tags paid not by the giver but the receiver.

Omega could hardly contain herself. She grabbed Uncle Joe by the hand and propelled him to the door. Minutes later screams of delight came from the blacksmith shop, where Joe's mare waited hitched to a brand new buggy. Liza, now in the yard with Tom, watched her little sister fly into Aunt Lizzie's arms. She clutched a doll with real hair and china face. Aunt Lizzie took the doll from Omega, turned it on its stomach. From its back emanated an eerie sound. "See, Omega; she cries. She goes to sleep, too." Heavily lashed eyelids that could open and close had replaced the ever staring button eyes of Omega's rag doll. Omega was enchanted. She had entered in the storyland where Liza had so often led her.

Omega caressed the folds of the doll's yellow lace dress. "I'm gonna call her Cinderella." Her index finger wagged in the face of the doll now sitting in blue-eyed awakeness on Aunt Lizzie's lap. "You better be good and don't cry or you won't go to the ball."

Silence fell on the group. Liza felt the searing tears that she tried to control. "Come on, Omega. Let's go home now. Thank Uncle Joe and Aunt Lizzie."

Aunt Lizzie spoke. "Let her stay with us. We'll drop by in a little while."

Omega crawled into Aunt Lizzie's lap, Cinderella in her arms. Icy fear clutched Liza's heart. She knew now what Uncle Joe's price tag would be. Omega.

CHAPTER THIRTEEN

THE BARGAIN MADE

SCARCELY HAD LIZA HAD TIME to bathe her face in the basin that Tom had fetched from Uncle John's, before they were there—Uncle Joe, Aunt Lizzie, and Omega. Uncle Joe, having toured the house, turned to Tom on the front porch. "Well, Son, you done right good for starting out. It's gonna take some doings to make living tolerable. Me and Lizzie brought you a few things. Liza's gonna need a bunch of stuff to set up housekeeping. You jist step out here with me to the buggy and hep me bring in Christmas in June."

How they had managed to pack in the buggy all they had brought Liza would never know. But when she saw the outlay – pots, pans, skillet, dishes for the kitchen – bolts of cloth, scissors, sheets, pillows, she could not believe her eyes. There was even a fancy quilt in the Star of Bethlehem pattern. Already she could see the little house turned into a real home.

"Liza," it was Tom grinning appreciatively over the haul, "I see I not only got me the prettiest wife in Georgetown County but the best uncle and aunt. Can't tell you how much me and Liza 'preciate all this. Tell you one thing. You done got you a nephew who won't forget what you done."

"Aw, Tom, it ain't that much," Aunt Lizzie assured him. "Liza always been like a youngun the Lord didn't see fit to give us. Nora even named her for me. We couldna done no less. Me and Joe wanta hep his sister's younguns anyhow we kin. We are willing to lend a hand with Omega, too. She even looks more like her Mama than Liza."

Omega, still carrying Cinderella, sidled up to Aunt Lizzie and tugged her skirt. "Ask her, Aunt Lizzie." Her little voice was full of excitement.

It was Joe who spoke. "Me and Lizzie kinda thought you two lovebirds might need a little time alone. Omega's been asking to go home with us. Give you time to git settled."

Omega turned to her sister pleadingly. "Can I, Liza? Pretty please? Aunt Lizzie says she's got lotsa dolls at her house I can play with. Says she'll make me lotsa dresses."

"Omega, you just got here. Your new home. You're going to help me plant flowers — make a garden. Plant Mama's rosebush. All kinds of things."

Her fingers were now stuck in her mouth, a sure sign that she was on the verge of tears. "I'll have to sleep in a room by myself. Aunt Lizzie says I can sleep on a little bed by their bed."

Liza turned on Uncle Joe. "I think we'd better have a little talk. I can see the talking you've already done to Omega." Her eyes swept over the presents stacked on the bare pine floor. "It was nice of you to bring all these. But Tom and I can get along without them."

Uncle Joe looked at the young woman before him. She might not look much like his sister, Nora, but she had her spunk. She was the spitting image of Grandmother Eleanor, whose portrait hung in the dining room at Oak Grove. He could see his plans falling apart. It would take a little more wheeling and dealing than he thought. He knew one thing. He wouldn't stand a chance of a dead dog in the sunshine if he lost his temper. It would be like throwing fat in the fire. "Better go easy," he said to himself.

"Looka here, Liza! No use to git your tail feathers ruffled. Me and Lizzie want to be friendly-like. Reason we brought you presents. You and Omega are our kin, my dead sister's children. Come on out to the buggy. I got a little unfinished business I wanta talk over with you." His voice was mild with no hint of threat or anger.

"Any business with Liza is my business now," Tom spoke up. "You talking to my wife. Omega's ourn. She's gonna be my daughter." Tom's manly words were what Liza needed. She knew she faced a crisis.

"Course, Tom," Aunt Lizzie soothed. "We didn't mean no harm. Course you got Liza's interest at heart. Don't blame you. I wouldn't have it any other way. But jist listen to what Joe's got to say. Then we'll go. No hard feelings."

Tom took Liza by the hand and followed Joe to the road. Omega sat on the steps with Aunt Lizzie. At nine she was still a baby, but she knew that what was being said would determine her future. Now she wasn't sure what she wanted.

Liza had been Mama since Mama came back in a box. She loved her big sister with all her heart. Still Liza had Tom now. They couldn't sleep together anymore. Aunt Lizzie had dolls and dresses — a whole drawer full she'd have. Different one for each day in the week, and Uncle Joe had watermelons. But Liza told the best stories. She could read herself now. Count to a hundred. Make her letters. She bet Aunt Lizzie had books, too. All kinds of fairy tales. Omega turned Cinderella over to test her cry and waited.

Joe Brown stood facing the young couple, one foot on the buggy board. He searched their faces, calculating their responses. The proposition he was about to make had been thought out – only as a last resort. Clearing his throat, he began.

"Tom, you probly didn't know me and Liza's mama had diffrences. Even so, she was my sister, closest kin. I didn't want her to get messed up with somebody like George Marion. Liza, I don't want to say nothin' against your Papa. You know what he is. What he'll always be. That's water under the bridge now. Tom, you got a fine wife — smart like her Mama — will be a real helpmate. I woulda give anything if Nora woulda give her to us when she was an infant. That's water under the bridge, too. But Liza, you done good spite all you been through. You got a good man who loves you. He'll take care of you. Nora would be proud of you both. Me and Lizzie gittin up in years. It's good to know we got kin on this side of the river we can depend on. I'm willing to help you get started. Reason partly we'd like to take Omega. Course, you know we been hankering after a youngun, an heir. I put my foot down when Lizzie wanted to adopt one we didn't know. Omega, she's my flesh and blood. We'd be mighty proud to send her to school. I can buy her all the books she could read. Never cared much about books myself. You and your Mama and now little Omega care about that stuff. Anyway, she'd never want for nothing. It would't be like you wouldn't see her. Plantersville ain't that far away."

Liza made a move to speak. Joe stopped her. "Now, wait, Liza, 'fore you say anything. I don't want you to git me wrong. I ain't trying to buy Omega exactly. Jist trying to make things better for all concerned."

"Just what are you trying to do, Uncle Joe? Split what little family I got left. I promised Mama to see after Omega. Tom agreed before I married him. I fought Papa for her — threatened him." Now her voice broke. "You don't know what I've been through. You didn't care enough to come see about us when Papa brought that woman in my Mama's house. This is too much. But let's call it what it is. Exactly what are you offering for my little sister?"

Tom put his arm around Liza's shoulders. "Liza, you don't have to do nothing you don't want to do. Nobody gonna force you. Let's let Uncle Joe here have his say and let him go on his way."

Uncle Joe cleared his throat again. "Liza, you know me and Nora was the only younguns in the family. The rest died at birth or before. Our Mama died in childbirth. Papa left me the land. I didn't trust one Brown acre or thin dime in George Marion's hands. It woulda been gone in corn liquor in a year. Haven't felt quite right about Nora gittin nothing. I'm ready now to square accounts with you." Joe Brown was now ready to gamble. "Irregardless of Omega, I got money here." He reached inside of the buggy and drew out a leather-skin pouch. Here's Nora's share in the Brown holdings. Thousand dollars in cash."

Liza covered her face with her hands. "My God," she

thought, "how Mama could have used this." Yet Uncle Joe was right. How much would have been sunk in Little Pee Dee frolics she didn't know. Was it possible that Uncle Joe was now trying to ease his conscience? She didn't think so. An old dog doesn't abandon old tricks. She recognized the gamble. Smart old codger. He had her now. Just where he wanted her. If she said no, she would be showing how selfish she was to deprive Omega of the shining future—even the full Brown land holdings. Omega loved books and stories even as she and Mama. She could have the chance neither she nor Mama had had. She remembered that afternoon years ago, Omega an infant of three months in the cradle — Mama shelling her beloved butterbeans – she herself shouting, "I hate you, Mama; I even hate Omega." Mama had refused to let her go stay with this same man, determined to have his way, even if it took years to accomplish it. And Omega? What if one day she turned on her and said, "I hate you, Liza. You should have let me go with Uncle Joe." Yes, nobody could underestimate Mama's brother. He had bided his time, had lured her with thirty pieces of silver, and capitalized on her own conscience, her innate sense of right. He had counted on her not taking the money unless she gave him Omega. Smart Uncle Joe! Yet she had to be honest with herself. How did she know him so well? There was a chunk of her in this little man. No wonder she could read his thoughts.

Tom was speechless. He had never seen so much money in his life. What could he and Liza do with it? Make this house a mansion. Put a down payment on a farm. But it wasn't for him to say. This was truly Liza's business. But he knew her well enough to know she would accept the money only if she gave them Omega. He had sensed that honesty and that practical judgment from the first. What could he say?

"Liza, honey, what you want is what I want. You do what's best for you."

"You win, Uncle Joe. You knew you would. You should have been a lawyer. You are more fitted for that than a gentleman farmer. But I have a condition, too. My part of the bargain. If Omega's unhappy, she comes back to me. If you won't give her back, I'll take her." Her dark eyes flashed steel bolts. "I'll find a way just the way I did to get her from Papa. And I got to see her — often. I'll want to know how she's doing. Not from a letter but from Omega's mouth."

"It's a bargain, Liza. I give you my word. My word is my bond."

Liza turned to her little sister and clasped her in her arms. As she smoothed her blond head, she said steadily, "It's all right, Honey. You can go with Aunt Lizzie and Uncle Joe. They're going to bring you back the moment you want to come. Liza loves you. You'll always be my little sister. My first little girl!"

Liza and Tom stood watching the buggy turn the bend in the road. The last thing they saw was Omega's little head hanging out of the side, one hand waving and the other undoubtedly clutching Cinderella. "Maybe she's at last going to the ball," Liza whispered. With that she turned to her young husband's arms and sobbed bitterly.

CHAPTER FOURTEEN

TRANSITION

IN THAT FIRST YEAR OF THEIR MARRIAGE Brown Hill cautiously regarded the newcomer, not precisely as an alien from another planet but certainly not of the same species as other brides who settled into their new homes showing proper deference to their husbands and most assuredly to their in-laws—especially mamas. They viewed her with a mixture of awe, envy, curiosity, amazement, and even respect. To look Minnie Brown in the eye without a flicker of fear was just short of a miracle, maybe not of the magnitude of the one at Cana but certainly a marvel. They watched her little make shift leanto turn into a trim little farmhouse with glass windows and curtains and a yard sprouting flowers overnight. They were downright shocked the way she socialized with niggers and Indians. Yet she was a mighty pretty woman and a smart one. The women would like to know her secret—no sign of a youngun on the way after a whole year. Tom Brown was lucky even if his missus was peculiar. One thing for sure—she wasn't cut out of the same piece of cloth as the rest of the wives.

What they didn't know was that Liza herself had undergone change, so subtle that not even she could account for it. The acid tongue of the Neck was blander; seldom did her voice rise above normal pitch. In short, the furious rage had abated, allowing her to look at people with almost a cool, philosophical detachment. She spotted the insecurity in her mother-in-law and speculated on the cause. Had she been Papa Gideon's second choice? Had her Mama been his first?

Her eye examined the difference in the people here— hardworking farmers who supplemented their meager incomes dipping turpentine, working sawmills, hiring out on larger farms—counting each fifty cents made, hoarding each dollar to purchase another tract of land. These were people, though poor, who dreamed of better days, whose wealth like that of their English forebears was counted in acres of land, not dollars in the bank. It was a different breed from the people in the Neck; yet the two shared the same intolerances, prejudices, and readiness to brand newcomers like Liza as "peculiar and uppity" if they deviated from their way of thinking and doing, but Liza held her tongue, to save it for bigger issues. To her, the black Aunts and Uncles, titles given to them because they were "good niggers," were objects of pity and far more lovable than many of their white counterparts. So when Aunt Della helped her in the yard or garden, she rewarded her not just with old clothes or scraps of meat to take home, but money. Like her mother-in-law she, too, had a title among others she supposed—"nigger lover." Liza didn't mind, preferring to be called a lover rather than a shrew. Tom gently admonished her that folks were talking about the way she spoiled niggers, making them reluctant to work for white folks for the usual handouts. Only then would Liza bristle, "Tom, they are human beings just like us. Color of the skin is the only difference." He would respond, "Folks say you done read too many books. Like them abolitionists up north that caused the Great War." She would counter, "You think I read too many books, Tom? You think I mean to cause trouble?" His arms would close around her and he would whisper, "I don't care how many books you read or gonna read. I love you, Liza. Just always love me. Promise?" Her lips under his gave him the answer he needed.

Perhaps it was her young husband's unswerving devotion that had tempered her. Such stability she had never known until he had brought her into this little house, which as she had predicted earlier, had undergone dramatic changes. Now on their first wedding anniversary, it was a place most frequently photographed. Uncle Joe's money had brought them a Brownie camera through whose lens, though in black and white, moss roses bordered pine logs outlining the sandy walkway to the road screened with crape myrtles. A wooden trellis supported a Paul Scarlet rose, too small to put forth many blossoms but whose rapid growth promised a spring array in future years. Red geraniums trailed from earthenware pots down the banister of the porch, which had a swing and two rockers. Wooden shutters had been replaced with glass windowpanes from which hung frilly curtains. Liza's first purchase had been a treadle sewing machine that had done double time, particularly on long winter nights as it stitched decorations and dresses. They had not been extravagant. They had saved a good portion. A little money had gone a long way. They both loved the comfortable dwelling so magically altered. Tom, on his knees beside their bed each night, thanked God for his home, his beautiful wife, his new farm fertile in cotton, corn, and fodder.

Liza, from the bed watched her husband's nightly devotions, but somehow she could not bring herself to share them with him. Prayer was too personal, the most private of conversations—which sometime took place in her little vegetable garden behind the house as she staked Mama's running butterbeans on gum saplings, or in her kitchen as she kneaded floury dough for biscuits. Certainly it was not her kind of prayer that she heard in Brown Hill Baptist, where a dozen or so worshippers vied with each other for the loudest, longest petitions. She would never forget that first Sunday when her mother-in-law, tight-lipped and restrained except when she loosed her venomous tongue, had screamed, "Glory! Glory!" and had waved her arms wildly in the air and set out down the church aisle shouting her praises to God. It was as if the tight springs of her being had been loosed, her emotions vented in her fervent cries rocking the church among "Amens." Liza, wide eyed, accustomed to the matter-of-fact hell and doom of the Hardshells, stared at her mother-in-law. Here at last was a woman free, her bonds loosened by God himself, who even allowed a woman to assert herself in his house, if not in her private home. Liza had looked at Gideon, her father-in-law, his head bent over the Bible in his hands. Tom, at her side was audibly joining in praises. Liza couldn't help wondering to whom God listened more attentively—the inaudible contemplation of and meditation on the beauty of an almost perfect dahlia or this release of raw emotions unhampered—unrestrained in ecstatic outpourings of word and gesture. It was one of those questions to which she found no answer but from which came the recognition of a truth—that people were what they were—could, for example look at a field of corn with different eyes—one seeing the yield per acre, another the yellow goodness enclosed from a bearded ear on a green stalk rising from black earth. Perhaps God looked on earth's creatures with different eyes, too. The Bible said He noted the fall of a sparrow; surely if He looked down tenderly on a diminutive bird, He must find equal spots in His divine heart for the Minnies and Lizas of the world and for Birdie, the first real friend she had made at Brown Hill.

On Gideon's farm at Port Hill, where he planted fields of corn and cotton, another young married couple resided, their little shack just steps away from the springs that fed into the Great Pee Dee. Zack and Birdie, his young wife, sharecropped for Gideon. They provided the labor and shared the profits, most often so little that had not their industry provided them with food grown on the farm, many days they would have felt sharp pangs of hunger. Liza had met them in the fall when she, like the other women of Brown Hill, went to the fields armed with croker sacks to pluck the bolls of cotton from dry brown hulls. On that first day she and Birdie were paired, sharing one row. Immediately Liza felt a strong affinity with her. It may have been the fact that Birdie was dark complexioned like Liza. Long straight plaits, swarthy skin, high cheek bones, eyes that seemed to look at you and say "I don't care who you are; I am interested in what you are." However, "who you are" had isolated her from Brown Hill. Birdie was half Indian, descendent of the Cherokees from the up country. The couple had abandoned the mountainous clime of North Carolina to seek their fortune in the flat tidewater, where crops were more productive and the growing seasons longer than those of the hills. Fortune had not come rapidly; still they worked together, not socializing with Brown Hill except in the fields, but even there existed a sharp demarcation, an invisible barrier divided them. Liza on that first day crossed the line. "I'm Liza, Tom Brown's wife," she had greeted, proffering her handshake.

Warmth and surprise collided in her deep brown eyes. "I'm Birdie. I belong to Zack, yonder." She pointed a tapered finger to a short bearded man in overalls adjusting the cotton scale. Her voice was soft, pleasing—different from the low country drawl. "Glad to meetcha."

As the two bent over their work, Liza, curious, couldn't help questioning. "Birdie, you don't sound like you come from these parts."

"No, Ma'am." She pronounced it in one syllable. "From North Carolina. Ever hear of Cashiers? I was born a few miles out in a place called Horse Shoe. I'm part Cherokee. Mama and grandparents is full blood," she continued. The added information posted a kind of stop sign, warning Liza not to pursue pleasantries further.

"Why, Birdie, you're the first Indian I've ever met. I've read a lot about them—Native Americans, you are. You got here before we did. I even know about the Trail of Tears."

"I heard about it. I can't read myself. Would love to be able to. I growed up hard. My Papa left us when we was little."

"Then I'll teach you, Birdie. I came up hard myself. Mama taught me. But as the saying goes, I took to books like a duck takes to water."

"Liza," Minnie called. "Keep to your work. Field ain't no place for talk, 'specially with half-breeds."

Liza straightened and faced her mother-in-law picking in the next row. She said levelly, "I'd rather talk with half-breeds than with those with no breeding." Minnie did not quite understand the statement, but she got the sass in Liza's voice. Birdie, on the other hand, sensed that she now had a champion.

It was the beginning of the first friendship for both of them at Brown Hill, one that would grow as the years passed and would endure. Liza felt such comfort in the gentleness of Birdie's nature. On late afternoons when Liza waited for Tom to finish "laying by" the crops for planting, she loved watching wild turkeys amble to Birdie's steps, waiting for her hand to dole out cracked corn. Often Runt, her pet squirrel, raised from birth, his mother having fallen to the hunter's gun, curled around her shoulder. This was truly a child of nature, Liza thought—one who found companionship with God's lesser creatures rather than his noblest of creations. Brown Hill tittered. "Tom Brown's woman was something else. Rather have Indians and niggers as friends than upstanding white folks."

There was one who did not criticize: Gideon, whom Liza now addressed as Papa Gideon, her special name for him. Sunday afternoons would find him at his desk writing in his ledger paper diary. Once she asked, "Papa Gideon, what are you writing?"

"Oh, things. Trifles. Not worth much. Might be something I seen. Something I felt—new idea—corner of a thought. Not worth much, Liza," he repeated.

"Would you let me read sometime?" She wondered if Mama's name was somewhere on those pages.

"Maybe. Tell you what." His eyes smiled over the tops

of his gold-rimmed spectacles dropped down over his nose. "It'll be yours someday. I won't be here to see you laugh at a poor man's spelling."

"Papa Gideon, you know I wouldn't laugh."

"I know you wouldn't, Liza. Your Mama wouldn't either." There was an added softness to his voice.

Liza didn't ask him again. They shared other things that didn't need to be read or for that matter spoken. They both loved Tom; they both like Birdie, loved nature. They both sought the solitude of thought where they might relive the past or seek guidance for the present. Tom was her emotional mate, but Papa Gideon belonged to her soul.

Birdie, Tom, Papa Gideon, a trinity. Yet there was room for one more. Uncle John MacDonald. He and Aunt Mary lived diagonally across the road. Uncle John had heard talk of Tom's brainy wife and her high-faluting ways. He was curious to meet this intellectual who had landed in Brown Hill. To his surprise and delight he found her a bright child with an inquiring mind. To Liza's surprise she almost effortlessly made a new friend. He had shown her his "liberry," as Tom called it, on that first afternoon. She couldn't even count the books that lined the shelves. His fingers would run over names and he would talk about them as if they were old friends—names Liza had never heard before. Plato, Sophocles, Kant, Voltaire. Frequently, he would read to her favorite snatches. Holding a dog-eared volume of John Donne, he commented dryly with a mischievous twinkle in his eyes, "One sermon from John Donne would shut the mouths of every preacher on this side of the Great Pee Dee—if they listened, that is. "Listen to this Liza, 'No man is an island...Any man's death diminishes me for I am involved in mankind.'"

Liza, fascinated, would gaze at this ancient pedagogue.

Upon leaving, she always carried a book—most often a novel or sometimes a volume of poetry. Dickens and Thackeray became her bedfellows, while Keats and Housman rang in her ears whether she worked in field or home. "Beauty is truth; truth, beauty." "Brooks too broad for leaping, the light foot lad is laid." That year was the happiest that Liza had ever known. She didn't really mind so much the discordant notes of Brown Hill; it had become her home. She could take a little of the bad when so much good had fallen in her lap.

The one thing that marred her happiness was the absence of Omega. How she missed those childish questions, those imperious demands, those outbursts of affection, those blue eyes enchanted with witches, goblins, elves in fairyland. There was no doubt, however, that Liza had made the right decision. Omega now occupied the throne in Uncle Joe and Aunt Lizzie's kingdom. In her little hand she held the scepter. One wave brought her devoted subjects to her feet. Omega had become their daughter on whom they lavished all the love stored for years while they waited for a child that never came. This devotion by this elderly couple was returned four-fold. Not once when the buggy made a trip to Brown Hill did Omega register any desire to remain with her sister. She had to go home to feed the new puppy or to see if the rabbit had had babies, or Aunt Lizzie was going to take her to Georgetown to buy school clothes. At Christmas they had come bringing presents, and Omega was sporting a winter coat — maroon velvet trimmed in tiny blue flowers down the front with a fur collar that buttoned close to her throat. She had picked it herself. Uncle Joe and Aunt Lizzie, grateful to Liza for giving them this little bundle of delight with angel wings, were generous in gifts and heaped on praises. Liza had overheard Uncle Joe say to Papa Gideon: "God Amighty, Gideon. That niece of mine is one smart youngun. Your boy ain't so bad neither. Them two gonna have something; be something." Joe Brown had made an investment—a wise one. The return was far more than he had anticipated. He was pleased with himself.

The second year of their marriage was about to begin. As Liza faced Tom across the cake where a lone candle burned, she said, "Make a wish, Tom. Don't tell me what it is. I'll make one, too. Next year we'll see which one will come true. Mine, yours, or both." They clasped their right hands and then both blew out the candle.

CHAPTER FIFTEEN

CELEBRATIONS

ANOTHER YEAR HAD SLIPPED AWAY. A second anniversary. Two candles, two new wishes. Again they clasped hands, their breaths mingling to snuff the candles. Liza said, "What was your wish? Did it come true?"

"Not yet. It will. I hoped there'd be three of us. Maybe a little girl. Spitting image of you. A boy would be alright. God knows best. I take what he sends."

"You really believe that, Tom? With all the troubles in the world God decides whether we have a boy or a girl or none at all?"

"Course, I do. What was your wish?"

"I wished not to have a baby."

"Liza, what's the matter with you? It ain't natural for women not to want babies. Reason to get married. My poor Ma's heart broke when no more came after Jess."

"Tom, don't you understand? My poor Ma's heart broke cause she had one every year or so. She was worried to death about how she was going to feed another mouth. You know why she named her last one Omega? She wished she would be her last." She was about to add "Thank God" but caught herself. "Haven't we had two good years, just you and me? Working together?"

There was a troubled look on his face. He started to speak and stopped himself. "Come on, tell," Liza coaxed. "What's worrying you?"

"Liza, I been wanting to talk serious to you. 'Fore I say anything, you know I love you. Ma's been after me for a long time." Liza's eyebrows arched. Tom added hastily, "I know you and Ma don't see eye to eye. But Ma, she has our interest at heart."

"I bet she has." There was no mistaking Liza's sarcasm.

For the first time Tom's voice rose; his cheeks flushed. "Liza, she's my Ma. She brought me into this world. Wanted me—wanted younguns. You got to respect her." His last words drew fire. She could almost hear George Marion yelling, "You got to respect Jane."

"What about her respect for me? She has never, not once, addressed one civil remark to me. From that Sunday when she cut me to this very day when I asked her and Papa Gideon to have supper and celebrate with us, you know how she answered my invitation? 'Working folks ain't got time for sich doings. 'Pears like some folks got nothing to do 'cept cook cakes in the middle of the week.'"

"Let's leave Ma out of it. We ain't gittin nowhere jawing over her. Ma's got a sharp tongue. She's had it hard. Bad things happened to her."

Liza's laugh was mirthless. "She's had it no harder then me. Don't give me that excuse for bad manners. But let's, as you say, leave her out of it. Just what is it, Tom, you need to talk about?"

"Alright, Liza. May as well git it out. I can't hold it no longer. Folks been talking. They say you keep company with the wrong kind. That half-breed Birdie —and those niggers. You been seen eating at the same table with a nigger. I don't see no harm in it myself; folks in Brown Hill ain't use to such doings. Don't think that way. I want folks to like my wife, to be friendly-like with them. They say you got airs—toting all them books from Uncle John. Time for you to be a mama. They think maybe some nigger work voodoo on you so you can't git in the family way." Liza now shook with laughter. Tom grabbed her by the shoulder. He was angry. "Don't laugh at me, Liza," he threatened.

Liza looked at him straight in the eye. "Don't try to make me feel little. Don't blame our inability to have a baby on an innocent old black woman who has been a better friend to me than any white on Brown Hill. It's a pity Brown Hill can't read. They might learn what prejudice and narrow-mindedness mean. It's a pity these good Christians don't know how Jesus felt about such attitudes."

"That's another thing, Liza. They say you ain't no Christian. We had four revivals since you in the family. You ain't made no move to the mercy seat, confess your sins, git baptized, jine the church. They say you ain't fitten to teach

Sunday School. You tell the younguns things contrary to word of God. Like it took longer for God to make the world than seven days." Tom stopped for breath. His grievances had tumbled out; he waited for her wrath.

Liza got up slowly from the table and moved to the kitchen stove. A pot of fresh vegetable soup bubbled; before she slept it would go into jars for winter days. She lifted the ladle and stirred it, wiped her hands on a kitchen towel, and began clearing the table.

"Ain't you gonna say something, Liza? Come on. Throw something at me. Kick me. Say something."

"Tom, there is nothing for me to say. What I could say will make you madder. You picked the wrong wife."

"Liza, we got to live here. I just want peace. I don't want people talking 'bout you behind your back. I love you, Liza."

She swung around to face him. "You love me enough to defend me to your precious Ma? To tell your good Christian church that Liza Brown confesses her sins only to God, not to the curious ears of Brown Hill? I thought Shiloh Hardshells bad; I'd welcome a seat in their pews to the ones I have to sit in every Sunday. You tell them Liza shouts; only it's so quiet only God hears it. Tell them that, Tom. I dare you." Her black eyes blazed. "Then I'll believe you love me."

Tom pushed his chair back from the table and saw Gideon standing in the doorway. Low country doors are left open on summer evenings.

Gideon walked over to Liza, her back to the door, and patted her on the shoulder. "Happy Anniversary. Got any cake left?"

She turned a tear-stained face to him. "Course, Papa Gideon. I saved a piece just for you. I'm afraid this anniversary is not too happy though. Tom's finding out he made a mistake in picking a wife."

She drew the knife down through the chocolate cake and lifted a thick slice to a plate. She handed it to Gideon and motioned him to sit down. "Would you like a glass of milk to wash it down"?

"No, thank you, Liza. I want you both to set down here and talk about the trouble. I heard some of it. It's best to let it out. It will fester like a sore."

"Pa, I was jist trying to make Liza see we got to git along with people we live near. That's all."

"Depends on what it takes to git along. Never knowed myself how to please everybody. I don't think I want to."

"Oh, Papa Gideon, Tom's unhappy with me. I know people don't like me. I can't help it. I got to be myself. If I can't be me, then I won't know who I am."

"Tom, I'm going to do some straight talking to you now. I'm your father. I know a thing or two. You got to learn when to listen and when to shut your ears up. It's like hoeing corn. You pull up the weeds and let the plants alone. Only way to get a harvest. You got to weed out what people say to cause trouble between you and Liza. Your marriage won't grow. Listen to me, son. You promised God to love her, protect her, stand by her until death parts you. Do it." He took another mouthful of chocolate cake. "There ain't nothing on God's green earth should keep you from standing by your wife, not your Pa, Ma, nobody."

Now he turned to Liza. "You got to find it in your heart to forget what these people say. They don't know no better. They ain't been further than Port Hill. Bide your time. Someday they'll come around. Do what you know is right. Forgive. Somebody better'n us done it. He did it from the cross." He made an invisible design with his fork on the empty plate and added softly, "Your Mama done a lot of forgiving. You can do it, too."

Liza's eyes filled with tears. She reached over and clasped Gideon's hands. She couldn't find words. This man was so different from anyone she had ever known. He was not learned in books like Uncle John but wise—like the Greek philosophers about whom she had been reading. And there was tenderness, compassion, and suffering in those gray eyes. Maybe that's how you got to be the way he was. You had to hurt first.

"When's your birthday, Liza?" Gideon asked.

"October fifteenth."

"Listen Liza, I'm gonna barbecue a pig and we gonna celebrate. You'll be twenty-one, won't you? Bible says to love your enemies. We gonna invite them to the party. I'm gonna invite your friends, too. Zack and Birdie's good folks. Aunt Della, too. Anybody you say. Write to your Uncle Joe. It's time for you to see Omega. Things gonna look up, Liza."

"Pa, what's Ma gonna say?" Tom could not believe what Gideon was proposing.

"She's gonna help us. She'll make the rice—bake a caramel cake. Liza here can make a batch of tater salad. Ask the folks coming to bring a dish. Don't worry about your Ma, Tom. She still thinking she done lost a son. We gonna make her see she gained a daughter."

"I don't know, Pa," Tom added doubtfully.

"Listen, Tom," Gideon's voice was stern. "I done told you where your duty lies—with your wife. Just like mine does."

The last dish had been dried and put away. Six jars of soup stood upside down on a cloth on the kitchen table for cooling. Tomorrow they would join rows of other jars in the smoke house — a shelf for vegetables, one for fruit, one for pickles, one for meat. Liza closed the back door and walked out on the porch. Tom sat in the swing, smoking his pipe. He didn't smoke often—only when as he said he had to study out something. The stars seemed unusually bright. The moon, invisible from the porch, had risen over the long leaf pines which curtained the cotton fields behind their house and looked down on Liza's flowerbeds—on Mama's roses, now a floral canopy on the trellis. It seemed a night for romance, the second anniversary of their love. Yet neither of them moved to each other as they had in the inn in Georgetown. Tom was still smarting over Gideon's reprimand. His father had taken Liza's side. He even supported her. Giving her a party and inviting all kinds of people. A vague sense of doubt pulled at him. Liza had managed to come between him and his parents and the people with whom he had grown up. Other men had wives who fitted in. In his heart he knew Liza would always stand apart from Brown Hill, would stand apart even from him. A pang of jealousy had struck him when he saw the closeness between Gideon and her. In his arms at night they were one. In daylight they moved apart. Their heads didn't seem to get together. But he could see how it was with Liza and Gideon. He was ashamed of himself—jealous of his own father.

Liza spoke first. "Tom, I'm sorry I've made you unhappy. I want to be a good wife." Liza sat down in the swing beside him. She continued, "I got obligations to you. Just like Papa Gideon said you got to me. I'll try harder to be like what you want. I don't know how to get on the good side with your Mama. But I promise to try. You've been so good to me. You took me out of the Neck. You gave me a home. Things I never had before. I thank you, Tom. I love you, Tom," she finished.

Tom reached for her hand, his fingers moved around the gold wedding band. Somewhere from the dark woods came the sound of a whippoorwill. A breeze lifted her loosened hair which brushed his cheek. His voice was soft. "Liza, I love you more than anything in the world. I want to make you happy. I don't know exactly how." His voice broke. "Maybe you the one who picked the wrong husband. I'm jist a country boy. Country ways all I ever knowed. I can't read all them books. I don't even want to. I can't stand for folks to talk about you. I can't see why we all can't be peaceful-like. Nothing you do bothers me. I guess Pa is right. I got to learn how to shut up my ears." He leaned over and kissed her lips. She took him by the hand and said softly, "Let's go to bed."

Long after her husband slept beside her, his head nestled on her breast, Liza stared into the darkness. A distant roll of thunder drew her to the open window, which she closed against the coming rain. On impulse she dropped to her knees beside the bed, her words directed to God's own ears. Then she settled in beside her husband, closed her eyes, and slept.

CHAPTER SIXTEEN

REUNION

LIZA WAS IN THE KITCHEN IRONING, one half of the table padded with quilts serving as her ironing board. Even though it was June, burning coals coated with fine white ash glowed in the hearth. Whenever the iron cooled down, Liza lifted its metal cover and added more coals, careful to check for any stray tag of soot which might soil Tom's Sunday shirt and then require another washing. Replacing the lid, she would test the heat by licking her index finger and touching it quickly to the iron. A sharp sizzle told her the iron was ready.

Frequently, she rubbed the bottom of the iron with beeswax, giving it the slick finish that sent it gliding over surfaces. Liza loved to iron. Her favorite domestic activity gave her the time to plan, to dream, to remember, to create. Her hands transformed balls of starched clothes, rolled tight in towels to preserve their dampness, into snow-white smoothness. Already shirts, blouses, dresses, scarfs, tablecloths, little monuments to her skill, decked the kitchen chairs. Outside, the slow June rain drizzled down the windowpanes through which she could see Mama's butterbeans rife with blue blossoms. The soft hiss of the iron against wetness, an occasional crackle of a burning log, the gentle patter of a raindrop—these were what Liza called "homely silences." They made her feel safe and special, their sounds audible only to her acute ear. Here was the place to iron out not only the week's wash but also the wrinkles of her life. Since their anniversary when Gideon had taken Tom to task, there had been a difference barely perceptible, but Liza had caught fleeting glimpses in a hasty negative response to her suggestion or the quick defense of his Ma when even her name was mentioned. She had overheard some of the men in the field joshing him about no children. "Not man enough for that pretty woman of yourn," she had heard one tease. Mama used to call that kind of remark "farm boy humor." Like Mama, Liza found it distasteful. She knew Tom, however, took such talk seriously, though he recognized its harmless intent. So as Liza ran the iron over leftover batiste from a blouse she had made, she actually wished for a baby. Maybe this time next year, I'll be ironing a frilly cap for little Nora, Liza thought. There had never been any doubt that her first daughter would bear Mama's name.

There was a sharp knock at the front door. She glanced at the hands of the clock on the shelf by the stove. It wouldn't be Tom. He and Papa Gideon were working in the blacksmith shop, taking advantage of a rainy day to build another coffin. Brown Hill and surrounding communities buried their dead in Gideon's pine boxes. Her mind flitted to Little Ida and the day Liza learned the word *sepulcher*. Shaking off the painful memory and smoothing her hair, she dropped her apron on a nearby chair and prepared to answer the door.

"Papa!" She threw her arms around his neck and kissed his cheek. Taking him by the hands, she drew him inside the living room. Her voice was full of welcome. "Oh, I'm so glad to see you, Papa. I can't believe it. I was just thinking about Mama and Little Ida. Do sit down. Here, let me take that wet coat. I have a fire going in the kitchen. It will dry in no time. Oh, Papa, you just don't know what this means. Have you actually come to see me? It's been two whole years, Papa. Have you had dinner? Let me fix you a plate."

George Marion stood in the middle of the room taking in the settee, chairs—mantel with a cuckoo clock over the gleaming white washed hearth, lacy curtains caught back in a saucy bow.

"Well, Liza, I seed you done right well for yourself. Fancy house and furnishings. Shore didn't know Gideon Brown made this kinda money making coffins and farming. Ain't nobody on my side of the river got nothing like this."

Papa's words struck terror. He had not come to see her. What she had mistaken for fatherly concern was no more than a visit for covetous inventory of her situation. He was right. Papa Gideon didn't have that kind of money. But Papa would not have been able to figure it all out by himself. Jane reared her ugly head. She could see her now, drawing Mama's wedding ring from her dress and throwing it at Liza's feet. Nevertheless, Liza was determined to remain calm. She would find out soon enough the object of Papa's visit. However, her voice had lost its former elation.

"How is Jane, Papa? And the new baby?"

"Jane's fat and sassy. ' Specting agin next month. Josh, he over a year old now. Younguns slip outta that woman like greased lightning." He ended with a chuckle.

There was a certain coarseness in Papa that had not been there with Mama. Shiftless and uncultivated as he was, no slack, shady talk had marred the charm of the penniless lovable nature boy. The blue eyes appeared hardened without their former sparkle.

"And Joey?" Liza questioned.

"That youngun is a growed up man now. Thinks he knows more than his Papa. Been in trouble with the law twice. Gonna go to the chain gang if he don't watch out. He runs around with that gang of Mishoe boys that'd steal pennies off dead man's eyes. I ain't seed him now in two or three months."

"Oh, Papa, that's awful. I'm almost afraid to ask about Mattie."

"That gal! She the talk of the Neck. Done left her husband. Running after anything with britches on and money in his pockets. Reckon two of my younguns done gone to the dogs. They ain't lucky as you and Mega. By the way, Liza, where's Mega?"

She knew by the way he asked it that he already was privy to Omega's whereabouts. Liza measured her words. "Omega lives with Uncle Joe and Aunt Lizzie. Remember they tried to get you and Mama to let them have me. They couldn't have children themselves. They're sending her to school. Nobody could love her more. They can give her so much more than I can. She's not too far away. I see her often. She's so happy with them," she finished.

"Well, now, Liza, I give up that youngun to you, not Joe Brown. He never give me the time of day. Dirt under his feet, I wuz. It don't seem quite right he done got one of my youn-guns when Jane needs all the help she kin git." A sly smile crept across his face. "Thing is, I don't rightly know why you give her up."

"I've already told you, Papa. With them she can have every advantage. She's bright. They'll educate her. Of course, I didn't want to let her go. I tried to be unselfish. Looking out for her future."

"Jane says she bet Joe paid a pretty penny for her." His eyes swept around her comfortable little home. "Any money change hands, Liza? 'Pears to me I oughta have a little dip into the pot, being as I'm her own Pappy. Course, me and Jane could use Mega. She be mighty good help now that she's done growed up."

"Is this blackmail, Papa?" Her voice was taut with anger.

"Me and you a lot alike, Liza. 'Pears to me we done been through this before," he said evenly.

"You are absolutely right, Papa. I threatened you to save Omega from that bitch's clutches. My God! What has she done to you? Taken the last drop of decency out of you. I don't recognize the man my Mama married nor the papa who bought us Easter clothes and who stood up in Shiloh among the whisperings and went through a ceremony to please a woman he loved." Her high voice made a quick turn and teetered off into a sob. She covered her face in her hands and dropped her head in her lap.

Liza did not see the pained expression that crossed his face. He reached down and picked up the loose leather shoe laces of his boot, drew them tightly together before tying them in a bow. Liza lifted her head and spoke. "Okay, Pa! I still hold the winning card. I'd do anything short of murder to keep Omega away from that wife of yours. Are you still making moonshine, Papa?"

"Feds done found it and tore it up. I need money awful bad. I reckon I'd do anything to git a little cash."

"Well, you get that smart wife to help you build another one. She's been smart enough to pull the wool over your eyes. It may be Clara's real Papa could help out." Liza had not meant to let that slip. Fear and anger had conquered reason and robbed her of any sense of propriety.

"What you mean by that, Liza? You better 'splain what you jist said." His voice was threatening. He crossed the room and took her by the shoulders, shaking her like a rag doll. "George Marion may be pore as church mice, but he ain't gonna let nobody, not even his own youngun, accuse his wife of being a whore."

"Papa, I didn't mean to say it. I got so mad." Liza knew that such an excuse wouldn't do. She had opened a can of worms, and they were crawling all over her once immaculate little world. Like Pandora, she had made a fatal mistake. But had she? If she destroyed Jane in Papa's eyes, then Jane would no longer be a threat. It was a risk to take. But Omega was worth it.

"All right, Papa. Remember I wouldn't have told you except I lost my head. You remember you met Jane at the Paul's barn raising. I remember, because it was Mama's birthday and you weren't at home. You came in at daylight—a little too talkative—the way you get when you have had one too many. You talked about a redheaded gal named Jane Port. Little Clara was born six and a half months later. I'm sorry, Papa. Two wrongs don't make a right. I did wrong to tell you."

A queer expression came over his face. Something was happening to George Marion. He looked smaller than he had been earlier. Her words had reduced him to a husk, a scarecrow, rattling in the wind. He had lost all desire to intimidate and power to carry out threats. But he had lost something even more valuable, the only smidgen of self-esteem—pride in his manhood and the faith in his women. He did not know the word cuckold, but he could hear the laughter behind his back in the Neck. George Marion had been played the fool.

He took his hat and coat and started for the door. Not one word had he uttered. Liza was terrified. He had two rivers to cross and somewhere in the swamp he would find a jug to help him either to forget or to restore temporarily a sense of pride, however false.

"Papa," she clutched at him. "Spend the night. Let's talk. Don't leave like this." He thrust her aside and strode out of the house, which one-hour before, had sat in peaceful stillness. The echoes of words bounced from wall to wall, finally settling in Liza's ears, which would ring with them for months.

A week later, word drifted across the black waters of the Little Pee Dee, to the Big Pee Dee and on the shores bordering Brown Hill. Eventually it found its way into the little cabin scented with spring flowers and yeast rolls rising. George Marion, drunk, had beaten his wife and unborn child unmercifully. The next morning, following their deaths, in cold sobriety, George Marion had hanged himself to a cypress on the edge of Parker Landing. Liza received the news wordlessly, without a visible tear. Not even Tom could see the depth of her pain. Only Gideon sensed the meaning of her unnatural silence, though not even he could imagine the slash across her soul.

CHAPTER SEVENTEEN

THE PIPER PAID

LIZA'S CHEEKS LOST THEIR COLOR; her dark eyes deepened and settled back in their sockets. Going about her daily chores, she would frequently forget what her mission was as she found herself in the house, garden, or yard. There were times when Tom, returning from the field at mid-day, would find the stove cold, his dinner uncooked, his wife out in the garden furiously attacking the weeds. At night there was neither joy nor passion in their bed, only submission. He might have been making love to a stranger. Afterward, he would press her tenderly to him and whisper, "Liza, what's the matter? You miss your Papa so much? Don't fret. It's not your fault, honey." Then Liza would turn from him to the wall. Her eyes, dry as her body, stared into the darkness. Hours later, Tom would pass his hands tenderly over her face, seeking her closed lids, instead, feeling her lashes still ajar, brushing his fingertips.

As days passed, she became thinner, less likely to respond to words. People around her might have been on another planet. She lived with the ghosts of the past. At first they came to her at night in the darkness of her bedroom—— Mama in her white dress bending over Little Ida's grave which yawned and gave up the beet-red body of her little sister that then faded into a casket upon which flickered a single candle. Worst of all was the slow unwreathing of the darkness and Parker Landing and Papa, his feet dangling over dark water. Then came the scream of a newborn baby. She did not know it was her own cry until Tom's arms closed around her. "What is it, Liza? Talk to me." The words stuck in her throat—too horrible to voice. To hear them might make permanent the dream, which came almost nightly. So she fought sleep to ward off the terror. Then came voices in daylight that followed her as she made a bed or washed dishes. One day while drawing water from the well, she thought she saw her face dissolve into Papa's face. The filled bucket tilted in her hands and the water soaked her clothes. Aunt Della was at her side, taking the bucket from her hands. "Youse done got yoself all wet. Miz Liza, youse needs to res.' Youse done be in a family way, I spec. Youse go dry off. I do de washing. I gon make you some sassafras tea. Make youse feel better while youse breeding."

After that, heavy poles crisscrossed the curb of the well until Tom removed them to draw fresh water morning and evening. Aunt Della did all the laundry. Liza walked aimless-ly about the house and yard. Ironically, as she closed her doors to Brown Hill, it opened its doors to her. No talk now of uppi-ty or keeping company with niggers and half-breeds. On Sundays Liza's empty pew brought no criticism. Instead, they asked anxiously about her. At last there was something they could share with Liza. Each had felt the emptiness of a departed loved one. A few had known the added horror when violence accompanied the death stroke. So her name was on their lips in evening prayers. Liza, through no effort of her own, had, however temporarily, invaded the hearts of Brown Hill.

One day Minnie appeared in her daughter-in-law's kitchen, carrying a bowl of chicken soup. Liza was standing over a dishpan of sudsy water scouring a pan already shiny. "Liza," Minnie's voice was kind, "I brung you some soup. You been looking porely lately. Tom's fretting about you." Liza continued her activity, not acknowledging the words. "I'm mighty sorry about your Pa. The Lord moves in strange ways his wonders to perform."

Liza's hands paused. She said woodenly, "It wasn't God; it was Liza." Her hands resumed their vigorous cleaning.

Minnie moved closer to her daughter-in-law and faced her over the dishpan. "Looka here, Liza. Ain't nothing hap-pens that God's hands ain't in it. I don't care how a body might think; we ain't moving a finger 'less He says so. Course, we move sometime 'thout asting Him first. Don't matter. He'd a stopped you if He'd a thought best. Mighta needed to learn you something."

Liza placed the pot on the counter, dipped her hands in the dishpan and dried them on her apron. She turned her dark eyes to face her. "Oh, Mama Minnie." It was the first time that Liza had used such a familial term of address. It was enough.

Minnie opened her arms and clasped her. "Liza, git it out. Tell me, Tom, Gideon—best of all God. It's gonna bust you wide open 'less you git rid of it."

For the first time since she had heard of Papa's death, sobs racked her body. Minnie gently steered her to a rocker by the hearth and eased her into it. Pulling a chair close, Minnie sat holding Liza's hands. The sharp edge of her tongue had disappeared. "Liza, I done wrong many a time. Spoke 'fore I ast God. You ain't no diffrunt from anybody else. You ain't got nothing to be afraid of. Whatever you done, God done forgot it."

"But I don't forget. I can't forgive myself. I am bad. Pure bad."

"Bad people ain't sorry. Bad people don't cry. You done suffered enough. Jist look up. God's smiling down. You don't have to tell me nothing. You ain't done nothing but what anybody'd do to protect they loved ones."

Liza looked down at her mother-in-law. How was it possible that this woman knew so much? Her next remark startled her even more.

"Omega's a mighty happy little girl, but she fretting about her big sister. Gideon done wrote them. We 'specting them tomorrow night. Do you good to see your kinfolks. You gonna feel better. You gonna be all right." Minnie reached for the chicken soup and began spooning it into Liza's mouth. Liza sipped it, and Minnie continued feeding her as if she were a baby.

At that moment Birdie appeared in the doorway. In her arms she carried a small puppy, silky red hair and bright brown eyes and ears sticking up like antennae. When she saw Minnie, she drew back. "Come in, Birdie. I jist got Liza to eat a bowl of my chicken soup. Whatcha got there?"

"I brung Liza a little baby puppy, Miss Minnie, to keep her company. It ain't but five weeks old. It ain't hardly weaned from its mammy."

Minnie motioned her forward. Birdie advanced uncertainly and placed the puppy in Liza's lap. Brown eyes looked up at Liza and a little red tongue licked her hand. Then it rolled over on its back, four little feet kicking the air.

"Oh, Birdie! I never had a dog before. All we had was hounds Papa kept for hunting." Suddenly Liza realized she had uttered that name casually and normally.

"She's a little girl-dog. Old folks say to name a dog after you bring good luck."

Liza turned the pup right side up and lifting her by her front paws looked into her eyes. "I need lotsa luck." Without hesitation she said, "Your name is Betsy. Betsy, you bring Liza luck?" Betsy wagged her tail vigorously before curling up in Liza's lap for an afternoon nap.

Birdie and Minnie looked at each other knowingly. Minnie spoke. "We gonna leave you now. 'Member what I said." The two walked out the front door together. They went their separate ways, their mission accomplished, their mutual satisfaction unspoken.

In the kitchen Liza leaned her head back against the rocker, closed her eyes, and slept. A movement in her lap and a yip stirred her. Brown eyes examined her. "Are you hungry, Betsy?" A miniature thunder from a small tummy answered her. She spied the remainder of the chicken soup on the kitchen table. With Betsy in one arm, she poured rice and bits of chicken in a saucer. A little red tongue met her finger moist with broth. In minutes Betsy had lapped the saucer clean and was gazing adoringly on her new slave. Liza cuddled her to her cheek and rocked slowly.

Time too rocked the summer months away. Some days to Liza the rocker creaked seldom; others it was steadier—speedier. Tom now looked at his young wife with hope. Gradually her eyes regained a bit of their luster, her step, sprightlier—the vacant stare less frequent. September and cotton picking moved into Brown Hill. This year, however, Liza did not return to the fields.

One afternoon she sat on the front porch knitting, her eyes drifting over her yard. Nimble fingers having memorized the stitches, she was free to peruse the first signs of fall, the silvery needles never missing a stitch. Steamy summer days had disappeared; now a pleasant dry wind ruffled the dogwood beginning to lose its green. Asters and marigolds, standing upright in circular beds, were now brilliant in purple and gold array. "They don't even know about frost," Liza mused. A playful tug at her skirt and a sharp nip at her ankles drew her attention to Betsy, three months old in puppyhood. "And you don't either, Bet. Never heard of Jack Frost, have you?" She dropped her sewing and scooped up the now big ball of red fur, shaking her gently and reproving her mildly. "Bad, bad, little girl. You've forgotten you just a little dog. You think you own Liza." She tweaked her ear and continued, "Lucky little Betsy! No worries. No yesterdays. No tomorrows either." Betsy turned her head sagely from side to side. "Why couldn't I have been born a puppy," Liza laughed softly, "and had a fool like me for a mama?"

Betsy wriggled out of her hands and commenced nibbling on the ball of blue yarn. Liza tugged it out of tiny teeth and pushed it into the safety of her apron pocket. "You musn't chew on little George's blanket." Somehow she knew the life beginning to stir inside her was a boy. With all her heart she wished him to be blue-eyed and blond, not dark like her. It would be a good omen—a sign of atonement for that which each day she was more successful in pushing into a corner. And Tom was so happy, so solicitous. The evening when she told him the news had become a bright light illuminating the dark recesses of thought.

The two had been in the garden picking Mama's butterbeans, which had miraculously produced a second crop, the first ones having dried into brown hulls—dead as the way Liza had felt. Liza's fingers automatically found the plump green jackets heavy with seed. Tom, not so astute, often plucked those still slender with immature fruit. "No, Tom," she admonished, "Let them grow to fullness. See? Like these." She held out a handful of fat beans. "You know these go back two or three generations. In late spring they are reborn. It's a kind of miracle. Like the miracle here." One hand patted her stomach.

Tom dropped the basket of beans, scattering them in the furrow of the row. "What's that you say, Liza?" He took her by the shoulders. "You mean? —-"

"Don't look so alarmed. It's been happening to folks year after year." She smiled. "Like beans. Only this one ought to be earlier. April, I'm thinking. Around Easter." Her thoughts swung around, took a nosedive into other Easters—wedding, proposal, death. Tom's strong arms swung her back to the present, lifting her from the ground, his head buried in her hair.

"Liza, Liza," he whispered. "It's the answer to prayer." She had never heard a man cry before. Somebody had said that it was awful to hear men cry. She didn't think so at all. It was like muted music, each tear dropping a note.

"Let's name him George, after Papa. If you don't like George, Marion."

"We'll name him anything you say." Betsy let out a yip. She had been forgotten among beans, babies, papas, names. Tom added playfully as he gently dislodged her from his pant's leg, "Anything 'cept Betsy."

Now she let the pup down easily to the floor and ordered, "Go find Betsy's doll." As her hands resumed their knitting, Betsy ran to a corner of the porch, appearing momentarily with one of Tom's knitted socks in her mouth, ready for a game of tug-of-war.

The gate attached to a chicken wire fence Tom had erected to keep the new resident in the yard opened, and Gideon came up the walk. Without having to look up, Liza knew who it was by the gentle click and the shuffling saunter of his step.

"Papa Gideon." There was warmth mingled with gladness in her greeting. "Do come sit down. I've been wanting us to have a nice long talk." Gideon reached down to pat Betsy's head and then settled himself down on the top step in full view of Liza, whose needles still busied themselves in the blue wool yarn.

"Looks like me and Minnie gonna have a baby. To hear her talk, it's not gonna be yours at all. Don't let her spoil it like you done this little mongrel." Betsy was now waving her sock doll in front of him.

"You know, Papa Gideon, I think in some ways it's better just to have dog babies to pet. You can spoil 'em and not worry about the consequences. I'm scared. I never really wanted to be a mother. Now that I know I'm going to be—-I don't know whether I'll be the right kind. I'm afraid he won't understand me. Like me with Mama. I didn't know how good she was until it was too late. Papa Gideon, what's wrong with us humans? Why are we so blind? Why do we have to hurt each other—to drive each other into——" She was about to say hell and then changed her mind. "To drive us into damnation," she finished.

"Liza, you so young to ask such deep questions. Ain't no real answers to them. But I think it's kind of important to keep asking them. Makes us stay in touch with what humans is. Weak vessels. Strong vessels. We break and then find ourselves soldered back. Some say it's time do the soldering—some say God—some say ourselves. I don't know; kinda think it's all of 'em." He chuckled. "Maybe sometime it's a little four-legged critter." He tugged the sock that Betsy was holding onto tenaciously.

Liza smiled in spite of herself. She dropped her needles and leaned forward. "Papa Gideon, I think I killed my father, his wife and unborn child." Her words fell like lead on the still afternoon. Gideon did not speak. He waited for her to continue. "Papa threatened to take Omega away. I promised Mama to look out for her. Jane put him up to it. Bad as she was, she didn't deserve what happened to her. I was mad. I told him the truth about the first baby, Clara. It wasn't Papa's. I took away the little self-esteem he had. You know the rest. I saved Omega, but I've lost part of me. I don't know if I'll get it back." She finished and waited.

When he spoke, there was neither surprise nor condemnation. "Liza, we all kill in one way or another. Lotsa times we don't even know it. Maybe that's a blessing. It's a curse when we do know. Can't tell you that you'll ever get over it entirely. Jist remember you ain't God. He'd a done it different. I'm not excusing you, Liza. What you done was wrong. But you didn't drink the whiskey that drove George Marion out of his good senses. What you done, I can tell you this, Nora woulda done. She woulda lied, fought, and maybe even killed to protect her child. You got a lotta Nora in you. Nora didn't break promises. You don't neither."

They were both quiet for a long time. Even Betsy decided to snooze, her little black nose on Gideon's leg. A wagonload of cotton drawn up in burlap sheets trotted down the road. An old hen that had strayed from the hen yard scratched contentedly around Liza's flower bed, not threatened by the usual "Shoo." A flock of robins fluttered by, wending their southward way. A yellow butterfly topped a purple aster and flitted to a clump of four o'clocks, ready to open their pink blossoms. Liza noted the movement around her and felt some of the heaviness in her breast move also. Gideon had been her priest and confessor. He had not absolved her of guilt, but his words had seemed to ferry her across troubled waters to the shore where she shared a comforting kinship with those who had also erred.

"Papa Gideon, you know just what to say. Uncle John gave me some plays to read—written thousands of years ago. By Greeks. They're all about suffering. They say the only way to learn is to suffer. It didn't take a Greek to tell you that. You must have done a lot of hurting, too." She was not questioning but making a statement. His response confirmed it.

"Yes, Liza. I done my share. I done my share of killing, too." His gray eyes met hers. "I best be gittin' along. Upsets Minnie to be late for meals." He rose slowly, pushing Betsy aside. "Minnie done her share of hurting, too. No woman wants to play second fiddle. No man neither." With that he walked down the steps to the gate and turned homeward.

CHAPTER EIGHTEEN

THE CIRCLE WIDENS

LIZA'S BIRTHDAY CAME. There was no party. "Papa Gideon," she said, "Let's save the celebration for your grandson. There will be other birthdays. Besides, right now I don't feel much like a party."

"Alright by me, Liza." Gideon returned. "'Pears to me reason for the get-together kinda straightened out itself." There was a twinkle in his eye.

It was true. She was not entirely integrated into Brown Hill. Many still looked at her askance, but for a time the mutterings had ceased. Often, as she sat on the porch sewing scraps or knitting, neighbors would pause at her gate to exchange harmless chatter about late frost, how the collards and turnips would still be bitter until a freeze sweetened them—where the best wild straw was. Cousin Nellie boasted that she could tie the straw broom so tight that it never came loose until it was "wore out." Quick to admit her ignorance of the art of broommaking, Liza enthusiastically accepted Cousin Nellie's kind offer of a lesson. Cousin Daisy shared her fruitcake recipe and brought her a bucket of black walnuts that "give a cake a good flavor. Course fruitcake ain't fruitcake without watermelon rind preserves," and since Liza's "jarring up" during the summer had been curtailed during her "mourning spell," cucumber pickles, beets, beans, and watermelon preserves found their way to a shelf in Liza's smokehouse. In church Liza joined in with her neighbors as they sang, "Blest be the tie that binds," and she was grateful.

Minnie, however, was another story. After the day of the chicken soup, there had come an easiness, though not a closeness. Minnie's tongue was less tart, but the fence she had built around her still bore the "no trespassing" sign. Only when she was "in the spirit," in church did the bars collapse as her feet found their way up and down the aisles, her eyes closed, her tongue shouting praises, her whole body rocking to an invisible band of music. At her home, Tom, alone, could cross that threshold at will. Not even Gideon enjoyed such privileges. Jess, the second son, stood in about the same proximity from his Mama's gate as Liza. Each was content to maintain a comfortable distance.

The two years in Brown Hill had not produced a defined relationship between Liza and her brother-in-law. Theirs was an affable surface of pleasantries. Liza knew he liked her, and she liked his playful teasing manner. Sometime he would jest to Tom, "Bud, lock your doors when you go to Port Hill. I jist might steal that pretty woman of yourn." Oddly enough, Jess had no girlfriends. While other young swains escorted their lasses to church, Jess, when he attended church at all, sat with the fellows on the backseat, a position not acceptable in Minnie's eyes. Unlike Tom, Jess had not made a profession of faith and like Liza, remained a sinner. On one of those Sundays when Liza, too, "had forsaken the congregation of the righteous," and remained at home, Jess dropped by. Betsy had been with her for three months and was already claiming her lady dogship. Jess found Liza in the breezeway between the house and kitchen tossing a rubber ball, Tom's gift to Liza's toy.

"Well, Liz," he had elected to shorten her name from the first day, "you a sinner like me today. Ma's gonna git after you proper. It's downright sinful staying home from church to play with a dog. Ain't you shamed of yourself?"

"What about you, Jess?" she returned tartly. "The pot can't call the kettle black," she laughed. Picking up Betsy, she beckoned him toward the kitchen. "Come on and have a cup of coffee with me. I might be able to find a piece of pound cake to go with it."

Settled across the table from Liza, Jess blew into his cup before sipping. "Hottest damn coffee I ever seed. If I wasn't in company, I'd jist pour it in my saucer and slurp it the way I do at home."

"You go right ahead. Table manners are for company. You're not company." An awkward silence ensued. This was the first time she had been with Jess without Tom or others present. Past the repartee of greeting, they both waited for the other to speak. Liza searched for an opening.

"Well, now that we have a little time to ourselves, tell me about yourself. I have been in Brown Hill over two years. I still don't know much about Tom's brother. It's time to get acquainted, don't you think?" Jess's eyes dropped in studied reflection of his cup. She had meant to put him at ease. Instead, her words had induced certain diffidence, even embarrassment. She added lightly, "I'm not trying to get you to tell me any deep dark secrets, Jess. Save those for the wife you'll be bringing home someday."

"Don't think there'll be any wife," he said slowly, now taking a swallow of coffee. "Tom beat me to the best one out there," returning quickly to his usual banter.

Her tone was serious. "Come, now, Jess. None of that. You know when I was a child, I swore I'd never marry. I had had enough of babies. But time changes things." She made a semi-circle with her cup in the saucer. "Look at me now. Married, pregnant—the whole bit. I don't blame men to stay single. It's different with a woman. Without an education, she has little choice. Don't misunderstand me. I love Tom. But if I could have gone to school—always loved books—always wanted to be a teacher. Someday a woman will have choice. Someday you men even going to let us vote," she quipped.

"You smarter than anything in Brown Hill, Liz, 'less it's Uncle John. I always wondered why he came back here. Me. I wanta get away. Tired of wagging tongues, revivals, hard work that gits a fellow nowheres. No wonder some fellows take to the bottle. We ain't free neither, Liz."

"Yes, you are. No woman depends on you. If you want to leave, you can. There's a big world out there waiting for you. Brown Hill has no strings on you."

Jess looked her fully in the face. "I wish I could git up the nerve. Shake off Low Country mud. Find higher ground.

Find folks think like me. Feel like me." He dropped his eyes once more.

Betsy, who had just learned to bark, exercised her lungs as Tom opened the front door. Coming into the kitchen, he bent and kissed his wife. "Well, you two sinners missed a good sermon. All about David and Jonathan. We had a new preacher for a trial sermon. He talked about friendship. You woulda liked it, Liza. Tamer than the usual fare. Less hell fire and damnation." He pulled up a chair and hit his brother playfully on the back. "Bud, what's doing with you? Ain't found you a girlfriend yet?"

"Stop it, Tom," Liza interposed. "Why in the world would Jess want to saddle himself with a wife? He has better sense than his brother. He can come and go as he pleases."

"You right about that, Liza," he jested. "Old married men like me lost all the fun in life." He smiled at her across the table and picked up her left hand. "Yep! This little old ring here hems a man in. Keeps the horse in the stable as the old saying goes."

"Speaking of horses, I best be checking on Old Blue. Had the colic last night. Me and Pa had to drench him and give him a dose of salts." Jess rose from the table. With a flourish he bowed to Liza. "Thank you, ma'am, for the coffee and for the advice," he added, as he disappeared through the back kitchen door.

"What kinda advice you give him, honey?" There was concern in Tom's question.

"Oh, nothing important." Liza had no intention of sharing their conversation.

"I worry about my brother. He don't seem to have much direction. I wish he'd settle down. Have a home like me. Ain't no man luckier than me. God's been good to me."

Liza rose from the table and busied herself at the stove. She said levelly, "Tom, some men are not meant to marry. My Papa was one of them. Papa was not cut out to be penned in. Jess may be like that. My advice to you is don't try to tie him down."

The subject was closed. Tom never indicated that he had given her words a second thought. Liza, however, never forgot that morning coffee or that look on Jess's face as he confided his wish to "shake off Low Country mud." How vividly would that conversation return years later.

As fall slipped around to winter, Liza slipped back into the routine of Brown Hill—the comfortable circle of a rural village. At last she could sleep without nightmares. "Far from the Madding Crowd," Liza thought, as she finished her first Hardy novel. Life around her was uneventful, but inside of her something exciting was happening. The quickening turned to butterfly stirrings and then became vigorous kicks as her twenty-two inch waistline disappeared over a bulbous middle. April seemed such a long way off, so the morning she looked out on her flowers coated with a thin frost, she did not grieve. Spring promised not only their return but also the advent of little George, now lying close to her heart.

Christmas also held promise. She would see Omega. Now in a private school for young ladies in Georgetown, Omega spent only weekends with her aunt and uncle, who were reluctant to relinquish one precious moment with their little idol. Liza had not seen her since summer and could hardly remember much, the heavy cloud having so enveloped her, that even Omega was indistinct. In just a week all of them would be coming. Omega would stay with her; Uncle Joe and Aunt Lizzie, with Uncle John. Liza threw herself into decorations. The whole house smelled of cedar and pine, which, along with holly and berries, hung from each corner of the living room. Garlands of looped greenery interspersed with mistletoe and stars cut from stiffly starched organdy met the corner arrangements. Near the chimney a graceful longleaf pine lifted its branches to the ceiling. An angel, a doll robed in white organdy but stuffed with straw, spread her white starched wings over green needles laden with floury snow. Over the chimney hung five stockings—Liza's, Tom's, Omega's, Betsy's and that of one who would remain invisible until April.

Mixed with the freshness of greenery was the pungency of wine-soaked fruitcake. Even Minnie approved. Wine had two purposes—for the stomach and for fruitcake. For these reasons each fall Minnie dutifully gathered grapes from the arbor behind her house, fermented their juices, and preserved them. On the day before Christmas, the oven added the smell of roasting ham and cinnamon potato pudding, while hot apple cider gurgled contentedly in the cast iron kettle. Liza, buxom in her white apron, closed the door of the oven. Betsy, aroused from her afternoon nap on the pillow by the hearth, let out a volley of barks. A queer sound came from the yard. It was neither fowl nor beast. It was like the untutored notes of a horn in the hands of a tone-deaf prankster. Rushing to the door, Betsy at her heels, she beheld to her amazement a buggy without a horse. In the driver's seat sat Uncle Joe; beside him perched Aunt Lizzie. Already on the ground was Omega waving, her yellow curls bouncing under a red silk bonnet. Liza clasped her sister to her. At that moment George Marion's ghost receded, replaced by a blond sprite beaming with life from cloudless blue eyes.

"Oh, Omega! You are so beautiful!"

"Oh, Liza! You are so fat!" Their peals of laughter rang

through the crisp December air. Betsy, clamoring to be included, danced on two legs, tugging at Omega's coat. "You've grown so, Betsy. Just like Liza." Omega knelt to greet her properly.

The two in the Model T watched. They had imagined a grand entrance to Brown Hill; yet they didn't mind that the scene before them had taken a backseat to their horseless equipage. Now Liza turned to them. "For crying out loud. What kept you from driving that contraption into the ditch, Uncle Joe?"

"Liza, I can drive it, too. Just as good as Uncle Joe. Only thing is I can't crank it. Uncle Joe has to do that. But I'll learn."

Liza looked down at Omega. "I just bet you will. Just bet you will," she said proudly.

Brown Hill suddenly came alive. They streamed from every direction to examine this strange phenomenon. Even Uncle John wrested himself from a dusty tome to listen to Uncle Joe expound the mysteries of the mechanism, this harbinger of the New Age. "This piece of steel gonna bring changes. Folks gonna ride on the ground thirty miles an hour. Omega here gonna ride in the air. Couple of fellows up in North Carolina done invented a airplane. We ain't seen nothing yet. Gotta lotta learning to do."

"Humph," growled Uncle John. "Folks haven't learned what the past could teach 'em, much less the future."

Jess, who had joined the crowd asked, "Mr. Joe, how much a thing like this cost?"

"A pretty penny, boy. Pretty penny. I swapped in a brand new buggy. It set me back four hundred smackers. Worth every dime of it. Ain't no holes in shrouds as I've heared of," he added humorously. "Tell you what. Me and Lizzie and

Omega be around a few days. We come for Christmas. Anybody wanta go for a spin, we'll try her out," he finished good-naturedly.

A chorus of thank-you's followed his offer as the crowd, having examined every inch of the little black vehicle sitting on oversized wheels, dispersed. Jess lingered, lifting up the side covers to the engine, passing his hands over the warm metal. "Mr. Joe, reckon they hire lotsa people to build these, don't they?"

"Reckon so. Factories all up North though. They ship 'em down here by train. You ain't planning to leave the farm for the big city, is you?"

"I don't know. Kinda thinking 'bout it," Jess returned softly.

Old Blue pulling a wagon of firewood drew up. Tom jumped to the ground to greet the Model T first, forgetting completely his hostly duties. In due time, the appropriate warm welcome made, Tom ushered their company inside to show off their Yuletide splendor. Liza was rewarded with approving ah's and delighted cries. She could not remember when she had been so happy as she gathered her family into the kitchen to sip hot cider and munch on a slab of black fruitcake. Even Betsy was privileged to a morsel of its nutty goodness.

The stockings on the chimney were empty, the Christmas dinner had been eaten, Aunt Lizzie had decided to nod off by the chimney in an easy chair, and the men had gone for a ride in the new Model T. Omega and Liza curled up in bed under Aunt Lizzie's wedding present, the Star of Bethlehem quilt. At last they had time for a sisterly talk. Omega opened the conversation.

"Liza, what happened to Papa?"

The question shot in the air like a firecracker ready to explode. Liza propped herself up on one elbow and looked at Omega. "Don't you know, little one?"

"I know he's dead. Jane, too. I want to know how. Why? Uncle Joe says it's best not to ask too many questions. He still treats me like a baby. I'll soon be thirteen. He was my Papa, too, you know. I want to know," she repeated.

Liza picked up a blond curl and twirled it around her finger. "He killed himself, Omega. He hanged himself at Parker Landing."

"Why?"

"He was sorry that Jane was dead. He had beaten her up. He wouldn't have done it, but he had too much to drink."

"Why was he mad at Jane?"

If she answered this question, she knew what the others would be and where they would lead. Should she lie or tell the truth? How desperately she needed the wisdom of Papa Gideon now. She searched for a middle ground. "Omega, grown people do terrible things to each other. Most of the time they don't really mean to. They're awfully sorry later. Papa was like that. He was good to us most of the time. In his way, I know he loved us. He loved Jane, too. But Papa had problems. He didn't have money like Uncle Joe. He felt bad about it. That's why he took to drinking. Whiskey made him forget awhile. We all want to run away from the bad things we do. Papa was like that. He couldn't live with himself knowing what he had done to Jane. But he had a good side, Omega. We got to remember that side. Remember that last Christmas before Jane came? We were all together. We had such fun even without Mama, partly because Papa was there—loving us— taking care of us."

"I'm glad Jane is dead. I'm glad Papa beat her. She beat

me, Liza. She beat me when you weren't around. Dared me to tell. Said she'd give me a worse beating. I hate her. I'll hate her to my dying day. She made me call her Mama."

Liza was grateful for the sudden turn from the direction the conversation had been going, but she cringed at the venom of Omega's words, at the hate glittering from her child eyes. "Omega, I should tell you not talk like that, but I know how you feel. Jane did bad things to both of us. She was the evil witch in the fairy tales we read together. But, Mega, she was a real person. I bet somebody beat her when she was little. She was simply copycatting."

"Liza, I wouldn't copycat on anybody. I can't even spank my little dog, Spot, when he messes up in the house."

Liza gave her a hug. "Omega, you are so dear! I love you as much as this little baby growing inside of me. You know what I'm going to name it if it's a boy?"

"Uh huh. You gonna name him after Papa."

"How in the world did you know, Omega?"

"'Cause you want Papa back. Like I do." She twisted the little locket that she had received in her Christmas stocking. "Liza, you ever hear of reincarnation? I read about it in my history book. It's what Indians believe."

"Yes, I read about it, too. I keep telling Betsy I want to come back a little dog to somebody like me—or you. Wouldn't that be a good life?"

Omega giggled. "Not unless little dogs got fed candy, ice cream, and cake, and—-"

"Watermelons," Liza finished for her. They both laughed. " Somebody else loves you, too, Omega. Uncle Joe and Aunt Lizzie think you hung the moon."

"I know. But you're my fairy godmother." She turned her blue eyes to meet her sister's dark ones. "You saved me from Jane, didn't you, Liza?"

"I saved you from Jane. I'm glad I did." The front door opened to Tom's step. A thud told her he had put another log on the fire. The warmth that she felt, however, was not coming from the chimney.

CHAPTER NINETEEN

POST-PARTUM

THREE DAYS AFTER CHRISTMAS the company had disappeared around the bend, chug, chugging down the road rutted in black mud from a warm December rain. Uncle Joe had bade his farewell to Brown Hill with intermittent beeps of his horn. Liza and Tom stood in the yard waving good-bye. Turning to her husband, she confided, "Such a wonderful Christmas; but I'm just as glad it's over. It was too perfect. Scares me. You don't think something bad is on the way? Uncle Joe and Aunt Lizzie are like real parents. And my dear little Omega! Oh,

Tom, I did the right thing to let her go with them. I'm sure of it now. No matter what the cost. It's what Mama would have wanted.

Hand in hand they walked back to the house, Tom reaching around her waist to give her extra support up the steps. "Honey, I didn't know your Mama. I sure woulda done the same with Omega. And your Papa, too," he added. "He had faults—like all of us, but he'd a wanted the best for Omega." A chill inched up her spine. Only Papa Gideon knew the truth of Papa's last visit. Only Papa Gideon and God. In spite of the uncommonly warm day, she shivered.

"Cold, Liza?" There was concern in his question.

"No, Tom. I'm suddenly very tired. I think I'll go rest for a while. There's plenty cooked for supper. Little George must be tired, too. Haven't had a kick out of the little fellow all day. And, Tom, will you check on Betsy? I left her in the backyard. A bowl of dinner scraps is for her on the kitchen stove."

Stretched out in their bed Liza pulled the quilt to her chin and closed her eyes. Her hands caressed her stomach. Little George must be taking a nap, she thought. He had been such a strong little fellow. He must be taking time out for rest. Uncle Joe and Aunt Lizzie had invited her to come to them to have the baby. She could have a doctor, not a midwife. It would be right, they said, to have her first one in the bed where her Mama was born. How she wanted to see Mama's home. Go to Mama's church. But little George would be coming corn planting time. Tom deserved to be near when his son was born. And Mama Minnie and Papa Gideon. They shouldn't miss out on the big event. Tom had been so sweet—willing for her to go near her time. She had sensed his disappointment. She told them she'd just have to think about it. But no! She wouldn't do that to Tom. Little George would just have to take his chances with Mrs. Marsh, who had delivered practically every baby in Brown Hill, including Tom and Jess.

She closed her eyes, but sleep wouldn't come. Tom's words echoed. "And your Papa, too. He'd a wanted the best for Omega." What would Tom say if he knew? How did she stand with God on the issue? If she had to pay for driving Papa to do what he did, what would be the cost? For weeks now she had been able to push these thoughts aside; now they came crowding in on her. She turned quickly on her side to shake off such horror. At that moment she felt something warm seeping down her legs. "Tom," she screamed. He was at her bedside. "Something terrible is happening. Run get Mama Minnie."

That night a perfectly formed little boy, though not fully developed, was placed in one of Papa Gideon's coffins and carried to the country cemetery, the destiny of many others like him before the days when science and technology might have saved him. To Liza, however, Little George's still-birth was the price Papa demanded. "Are we even now, Papa?" she whispered.

Tom's hands soothed her forehead, damp with perspiration. "What's that you say, honey? Just close your eyes and try to sleep. I'll be right here."

Liza dreamed of Mama. She was with Addie and Sally in the wood near their house, bending over picking violets. Liza could not see her face but she recognized the white organdy dress. When she straightened, Liza saw a stain running like a red stripe down the front of the dress. In her arms she carried a blond blue-eyed infant. Then her face dissolved into one with dark hair and black eyes. A scream tore from Liza's throat. Despite the loving arms that enclosed her, she was powerless to stop the cries that wrenched her body.

Even in Brown Hill New Year's Eve was a time of celebration. They crowded into church to sing songs and say prayers, to give thanks for the dying year and for a prosperous one being born. Firecrackers and Roman candles would decorate the sky. From husband, to wife, to child would the words be repeated, "Happy New Year." Somebody would tug the cowbell in front of the church and ring out the glad tidings. Then they would go to their several beds—some would pour a glass of grape wine declaring, "good for the stomach after all the Christmas vittles." Tomorrow is a new day, a new year. With God's help there'd be good seasons – plenty of rain and bumper crops. There might be enough to buy another piece of land. Good to leave your children a home after you've gone to the great Up Yonder. One o'clock would find most of Brown Hill sleeping, the thoughts of the day neatly tucked away in feather beds and quilts.

In one house neither the serenity of the hour nor the celebration of the New Year had crossed its threshold. Tom looked down at his wife and wondered what this second lapse into a world he neither shared nor understood would bring. Course Liza had had it uncommonly hard. Losing her papa in that way and now the baby. But women had been having to stand sich since the world begun. It was the curse put on the woman in the Garden of Eden. A body jist had to ask God for help, brace up, and go on. Ma had lost baby after baby. You jist couldn't let life wear you down. He had tried to console Liza with these thoughts. She had turned away and said nothing. She didn't scream anymore after that first night, but he didn't know which was worse—this awful silence or her cries.

"Liza, you feel alright? Can I git you some warm milk? Ma says it helps you sleep." Liza tossed her head "NO." He blew out the kerosene lamp and lay down beside her. There was no response to his touch. He knew her eyes were staring into the darkness. He did not know that the darkness of the room could not compare with the darkness inside of her.

In due course, they all came. Mama Minnie was there almost daily. In the beginning she took charge of the house — cleaned, washed, ironed, cooked. Liza half aware of her presence lay on her bed. Minnie spoke little. There seemed a bond that needed no words. Now Minnie concentrated on nourishment for Liza's thinning body. From experience she had learned the futility of trying to save her soul. God would have to do that. In the meantime, she coaxed her to eat thick potato soup, ham simmered hours in corn meal, biscuits sopping with butter and sorghum syrup. Some days Liza was more responsive—would finish her plate, would thank her mother-in-law. Others, she sat vacantly staring on the bare trees and the ice collected in Betsy's outdoor water bowl. In the evening Gideon would turn to his wife and question, "Any change, Minnie?" "Not much. Takes time. Only a woman knows what 'tis to lose a youngun. Takes time."

Gideon with words tried to break through the wall of silence. "Liza, ain't any use blaming yourself. These things happen. Happened to Minnie more times than I can count. Life got to go on." Liza said nothing. One day he said, "Liza, it ain't fair to Tom. He's a good boy. Loves you. Ain't just your life. Somebody else to consider. Your Papa's gone. Little baby's gone. Tom's alive. It ain't right to close your door to him."

Liza heard the logic of his words and even caught his gentle reprimand. Still she could not lift herself from the morass—hope and desire mired in the swamp of guilt and grief.

Even Jess found his way to the door and teased her that thin women always appealed to him more than fat ones. When she failed to spar with his humor, he became serious. "You and me a lotta like. We feel things different. We ain't like most people walking around. Reason we kinda stay in touch. You don't know what you coming to Brown Hill mean to me. I shore hate to lose you. Me and Tom both," he added.

Liza took his hand. "Don't worry, Jess. I'll be all right." She gave him one of her rare smiles. "Only the good die young. I got a long way to go."

"Me, too," he said thoughtfully.

At last Birdie came. Expecting a baby herself, she had stayed away on purpose. Seeing her might make Liza worse. Her warm heart could not stand the distance between her and this friend. She came bringing greens from her garden, sorted and washed, ready for the pot, along with a new straw broom tied as sturdily as Cousin Nellie's. Betsy, not understanding the neglect of the past weeks, greeted Birdie with all the vigor that her barks could muster. "Where your Ma, Betsy? Tell her I here," Birdie commanded trying to settle four dancing feet.

"I'm in here, Birdie." The voice came from the bedroom. Birdie found Liza at a tiny chest that Papa Gideon had made for her birthday. Each drawer was open and empty. On the top were neat piles—one blue—knitted wool blanket, cap, booties, sweater; one white—flannel edged in blue embroidery. "I'm glad you came. I was just packing all of these up for you. Hope it's a boy. Regardless they will keep it warm."

"Don't give 'em to me. Others come. Save 'em."

"I never wanted to be a Mama anyway. No more. No more!"

Birdie said softly, "Liza, even little mama animals lose babies. Seen 'em. Not half grown. Nature got funny ways.

Maybe nature decided. Maybe it won't ready to be itself. Maybe you done decided what itself would be. Couldn't be nothing but itself. Nobody else. No two leaves alike. Much less babies."

"What do you mean, Birdie?"

"I mean nothing take the place of something else. You think this little thing inside me gonna take the place of a Papa I ain't never had? Gonna have its own place. Its place be special. All nature special."

"Oh, Birdie! Don't. I can't take much more."

"You special, too, Liza. Nobody like you."

"I'm not special to anybody. Not Tom. Not even to Betsy. She looks for Tom to feed her. I'm lost. I'm caught somewhere between the Little Pee Dee and the Big Pee Dee. One water's dark, not deep. I can't even stand in shallow water. The other—big—very deep. I can't swim, Birdie." She buried her face in the unused blue blanket and sobbed. "I'm so alone."

"You need your Mama. She dead. I know. Go back to where she was. Put yourself on her ground. Look at things she looked at. Walk where she walked. She speak to you from there."

"Birdie, it's Papa. He won't speak to me."

"He done spoke, Liza. The reason little George in the graveyard. You can't play hopscotch. Walk straight up to what's between you and your Papa. He leave you then. Leave you for good."

It was late March. The leaves on the trees had the gold hue just before they turned green. Liza thought on what Birdie had said for days. Over supper she turned to Tom. "Tom, I would like to spend Easter with Omega. I've never seen Mama's old home. I've never been to her childhood church. Maybe the change would help. I won't go if you don't want me to."

"Go, Liza. May be the answer to prayer. You still looking peaked. Been three months. You oughta be feeling better. Tell you what. Write Uncle Joe. I'll take you in the buggy half way. You get ready to come home, write me. Course I'll miss you. I jist want you back to your old self." Unashamed tears glistened in his blue eyes.

Liza cupped his face in her hands and kissed him on the lips. "Thank you, Tom," she whispered.

CHAPTER TWENTY

OAK GROVE

THE MODEL T BUMPED COMFORTABLY ALONG, Uncle Joe yelling out above the noise. Liza clutched her hat with both hands fearing, an April wind would send it into the swamp. "How much farther, Uncle Joe?"

"We here, Liza. Yonder's Oak Grove. That's what your mama and grandmama called it. They liked fancy names. Me, it's jist home." Gnarled oaks wearing gray moss stood guard on either side and met overhead to form a canopy of light and shade. Through the trees emerald fields of rye grass stretched out, broken only by occasional shrubs. The car, slowed to a lazy horse's gait, belched two or three times and stopped. "Danged thing. Knows it's home, I reckon. Gimme a little time to git her started."

"Uncle Joe, I'd like to walk the rest of the way. You mind? Seems kinda right." What she did not say was that she wanted to feel the same earth under her feet, to follow in the footsteps of other Brown women. She remembered Birdie's words: "Put your feet on her ground; walk where she walked."

Liza left Uncle Joe making jerking revolutions with a crank. The engine made a momentary effort to catch and then died again. As she ambled down the lane, she heard Uncle Joe proclaim, "Dad blast it. You out of gas?"

Unlike the dead car, Liza felt a strange rejuvenation. Her head swirled with pictures of the past — carriages taking young brides, carriages propelling young and old to their final resting places. Her eye caught a small enclosure marked by a wrought iron fence. Lifting her skirt, she jumped the narrow ditch and headed toward the site. One marble tomb, taller than the others, was shaped like a pine. It stood like a sentinel around the others. On the left was a smaller monument. On either side small pointed marble slabs bore only dates. **JOSEPH EBENEZER BROWN**. 1800 – 1878. Woodman of the World. **NORA ELIZABETH JOHNSON**. 1802- 1845. *Wife and Mother*. "Mama, you should be here with them," she whispered.

She retraced her footsteps to the road. Uncle Joe had evidently persuaded the Model T to move. A short stroll farther and she could see it parked near the stables. Rounding a curve, Liza glimpsed the house framed in magnolia and pecan trees. It was a modest structure in comparison to other plantation houses along the river. Still it was a two-story white wood frame with a wide verandah supported by ionic columns. The yard, boxed in with sculptured low hedges, which also out-lined the walk, ended at the front entrance with a trellis where a Paul Scarlet rose would bud in mid-May profusion. To the left a wisteria trailed its lilac blossoms heavy with fragrance. To the right a giant Cape Jessamine, loaded with buds, awaited a June opening.

Aunt Lizzie stood on the porch waving. Liza had never seen Oak Grove before, yet sensed the joy of coming home after having been absent so long. Like the oak trees which spread aged roots in all directions, Liza mused that she, too, would find her roots and entrench herself so firmly. Now she ran into Aunt Lizzie's waiting arms. "Where is Omega?"

"She's still in school. We have a new schoolmaster. Also our Vicar. He comes from England. Me and Joe been missing Omega off at the boarding school. Mr. Westbrook's full of learning. Graduated from Oxford. He started a school in the Parish House. Younguns like him. Omega's crazy 'bout him."

"Why, Aunt Lizzie, I didn't think you and Uncle Joe were much for church going. 'Do my praying at home,' I've heard Uncle Joe say."

"You're right there, Liza. We got Omega now. It don't seem right not to bring up a youngun in the church. That's what her mama done. Shiloh wont her church, but it was church jist the same."

Uncle Joe was now in the yard lugging two suitcases. "You beat me here," he said , panting. "I'm plum give out from trying to crank that old tin lizzy. 'Bout ready to buy me anoth-er buggy. That mare of mine is tired of standing round doing nothing. Ain't used to easy life. Dog if I ain't beginning to side with that old wisecrack John MacDonald at Brown Hill. Better content with what we know. Ain't good sticking our noses out to ever new fangled thing come along."

"Oh, hush up, Joe. You wouldn't take a pile of gold guineas for that piece of metal. He tinkers with it all day, Liza," she confided. "He's kinda like a baby with a sugar tit. Gracious goodness! Here we stand jawing. Bring in the bags, Joe. Liza must be give out."

They guided Liza into the hallway, from which a circular stair wound its way to the second floor. On the left was the dining room, centered with a banquet walnut table over which a chandelier hung. Against the wall stood a handsome hand-carved sideboard. Above hung the portrait of a dark-haired woman, her face haloed by a transparent white bonnet ornamented with a cluster of anonymous flowers. Around her shoulders draped a shawl matching the bonnet. It was the eyes that caught Liza. They were hers — the same black eyes that stared into hers. "Who is she?" Liza asked breathlessly.

"Your great grandmother, Eleanora. Papa said she was French – from Hugenots in Charleston. He said she had the second sight. See ghosts. Tell fortunes."

"Another Nora," Liza said. "Looks like all the girls are either Elizabeth or Nora. I bet those eyes could see anything. Sometimes eyes see too much."

Across the hall in the parlor were a pedal organ, a red velvet sofa, gold and cream colored French chairs upholstered in faded brocade, a lamp whose chimney was topped by a hand-painted glass shade—old—beautiful in mellowed age. It was not the furniture that held her. Over the marble mantle was Mama. She must have been sixteen or seventeen at the time. Ordered blond curls, an unlined high forehead, smooth rosy cheeks—no hint of worry marring the youthful brightness of blue eyes or the smile that played about her mouth. "She looks so much like Omega, don't she?" Uncle Joe commented.

"Where are all the Brown men?" Liza inquired.

"There's only great grandpa. I bet Grandma made him set for a painting. Rest of 'em like me. Don't see no need to spend hard earned money to paint ugly faces. Picture cameras can do that. Grandpa's facing Grandma in the dining room. He's over the highboy."

"Liza, Liza!" Omega dropped her book satchel and ran to her sister. "I just couldn't wait. I've been telling Mr. Westbrook 'bout you. How many books you read. How pretty you are. You know what he said? 'Omega you're about to exhaust superlatives.' He's got the funniest way of saying things. He can't say *a*'s like us. You'll see. I can't wait for you to meet him. Liza, I think I'm in love for the first time."

They all laughed. Uncle Joe scolded mockingly. "Shame on you. You forgit he's your preacher. What did he say in his sermon last Sunday? 'God's vicar on earth.' Ain't decent to run after holy men."

"Omega, take Liza up to your room. I put you in with Omega, Liza. Course, if you want, you can have the spare."

"Oh, no, Aunt Lizzie. I want to be with this bad little sister of mine. I have to straighten her out. Talking about falling in love at thirteen." Liza mussed her blond curls.

"Juliet was only thirteen. 'Romeo, oh Romeo, wherefore art thou, Romeo?'" Omega bent to an imaginary garden and called theatrically. Linking her arm through Liza's, she drew her into the hall and up the stairs, prattling about everything from Mr. Westbrook's beautiful voice to inquiries about the absent Betsy.

"I had to leave her with Tom. He'd be so lonely without both of us. These last few weeks she's been more his dog than mine."

At the top of the stairs, Omega stopped. Her little voice was full of anxiety. "Oh, Liza, you feel better? I'm so sorry about the baby. I didn't know what to write. You understand?"

"I understand," she assured her. "I didn't know either."

They ate in the small alcove off the kitchen. Aunt Lizzie explained, "Didn't bother about the big table. Saved that for company when we ask Mr. Westbrook. Been waiting for you to get here. You can talk proper like to him about books and things. Me and Joe old fogies. Omega's been dying to ask him. I thought maybe we could send word by Omega for Saturday night. That's if you feel like it. We could wait awhile longer."

"Oh, no, Aunt Lizzie. I'm better already. Besides I can't wait to meet this God wrapped up in schoolmaster and preacher clothes. I hope he's not a wolf in sheep's clothing. I bet I won't get a chance to talk much. Omega will take care of that," she smiled mischievously.

The grandfather clock downstairs chimed twelve, then one, then two. Liza looked up through the crocheted canopy overhanging the four-poster. From the high ceilinged window curtained in lace and slightly cracked for fresh night air, moonlight played hide and seek, dancing shadows over the white counterpane neatly folded at the foot of the bed. Omega, curled like a little bunny in her white flannel nightgown tied with pink ribbons, breathed evenly. Images swirled in Liza's head like the flitting moonbeams. Here Mama had slept, perhaps dreamed of a blond Viking and love like meteors trailing fire. There had been no shooting stars with Tom, but there had been a river that offered escape and the tenderness of a good man who gave her his love and his protection from the swelling quicksands of the Neck. "Mama, we both compromised,"

Liza said softly. "You traded security for stars, and I traded stars for security."

And Papa! Liza had known little of Mama and less of Papa. Mixed images loomed around her: lovable, unlovable, unloved — Papa with a string of fish, Papa staggering up the front steps, Papa emerging from the swamp announcing Mama's death, Papa leaning against the tree the morning at Parker Landing. Liza clasped the pillow, burying her head in the soft down. "Oh, Papa! We both used the river to escape. It didn't work, did it? For me or for you."

Now on the brink of womanhood, Omega's head was already swimming with notions about love. What was it with women? Were men likewise slaves to dreams? Was the feminine psyche so love-starved that she created her own reality? Or had the years of subjugation to a society whose laws were so ordained driven her to seek power with the only weapon she had, with and without conjugal bed? How would it be with Omega? Would she alone, among the Brown women Liza knew, find that idyllic union? Liza smiled. "Omega, you and I both have read too many fairy tales. Living happily ever after is simply the ending made up by some dreamer. Like you or me." Sometime she would like to open such speculations to Papa Gideon or even frosty old Uncle John. However, she really needed a woman's point of view. Mama might have answered many questions, but Liza seriously doubted Mama would have opened up even to a daughter. Living in seclusion so long made anyone's attempt to break barriers an intrusion. No wonder communication was such a rarity. The world seemed to be divided into two groups: those unwilling to let down the bars and those with no bars to let down. Most talk was just clatter, Liza decided.

There had been a few breakthroughs where Liza had

been permitted glimpses of inner worlds. Birdie, Papa Gideon, and even Jess. What would it be like to have a permanent pass to share deepest joys and deepest fears? Perhaps that relationship existed only with God, but his presence came for the most part unsolicited — sometimes in the shape of a budding tree or the sound of the trill of an anonymous bird.

Her thoughts wandered and picked up death. Did it open up mouths or was there total silence, more silent than earth? Where was Papa, Mama, and the little boy who would have been named George? Maybe Omega's Oxford vicar had tapped into some of these mysteries. She had never met a scholar. She was sure she would not know how to talk to him either. What did she have to offer anyone now but a broken spirit? She had read books, but mostly what she knew about life had come from living — a mass of opposites — cruel and kind – and agony; about the ecstasy she had had no experience. It was just as well. She was content with the comfort of Tom's arms and a little surprised that she missed him. He would be sleeping soundly at this hour, to be ready for the long day in the fields. Tomorrow she would write him. Easier to put in a letter the things she felt. Tom would not understand her doubts. So good! So trusting! So blessed! He didn't need a river to escape. He's not like me. Not like Jess either.

The clock chimed three. Omega stirred in her sleep. Regressing to babyhood, she stuck her fingers into her mouth and dreamed on. Liza touched her cheek lovingly and then slept herself. Mama stepped out of the portrait over the mantle and came up the spiral staircase. This time she carried a bouquet of Paul Scarlet roses that she handed to Papa as he stepped into his boat and disappeared around the bend of the river. Liza smiled and then sank into dreamless slumber.

An April day dawned cloudless and mild. Liza was up

early enough to see Omega skip down the path for the two-mile walk to Master Westbrook. Time on her hands, she strolled through the wood. What a glorious palette it was — wild yellow forsythia, white dogwood, redbud and honeysuckle mixed with the gray of dead trees and various hues of green of the live ones! She took off her shoes and walked on the green moss, careful to avoid the violet or the daisies and even the lowly dandelion. Bruised, she did not want to bruise.

In the afternoon she wandered over to another visit of the cemetery. How strange that the great grandmother and grandfather of the dining room were not here. Only the son and his wife. What had happened that they were not at Oak Grove? Their portraits but not their graves. She must ask Uncle Joe.

A flock of purple martins flew overhead. From the window that morning she had seen the gourds strung in double rows from poles, the homes of summer guests. Uncle Joe had expounded on martin lore. He said he cleaned the gourds each winter before their spring arrival and left bits of woodchips and straw nearby, material for nest building. "Why, Uncle Joe," Liza had exclaimed, it's not like you to encourage laziness even in birds." "Woods full of hawks, Liza. Little fellows come a long way — fur as South America, some say. Least I can do is hep 'em along." Here was another side to Uncle Joe. She must tell Birdie. Uncle Joe might even enjoy her brood of wild turkeys. Come to think about it, he was not the hunter nor the fisherman like Papa, the swamp fox. Marion was just the right name for Papa. But Uncle Joe belonged to the land — to these waving fields of grass, and corn and watermelons, she thought humorously. Watermelons. One of his charms for Omega.

"Liza, Liza!" It was Omega. "Guess what. He's coming Saturday night. Mr. Westbrook. He talks so proper. 'Most kind of you — will look forward with pleasure to Saturday evening.'" Omega mimicked his accent. "Let's get Aunt Lizzie to use the cloth that belonged to Great Grandmother and you make flowers for the table. Remember like you made at your house. And Liza, do you think you could get Aunt Lizzie and Uncle Joe not to say *ain't*, just for Mr. Westbrook. And Liza, did you bring the red dress you made last summer? You looked so pretty in it."

"Wait a minute. Calm down. If Mr. Westbrook is as wonderful as you say, *ain't* won't matter a bit. Course we'll make the table pretty. I didn't bring the red dress, but I'll manage so you won't be ashamed of me."

"Liza, you 'spose he's got a girlfriend back in England? You know what I think? I think some cold-hearted damsel broke his heart. That's why he left. Why he decided to be a preacher. Not like Catholics, you know, not like monks and nuns. He's not that religious. I'm just dying to know."

"You have read too many books. Your little head's crammed full of broken-hearted knights and ladies and English schoolmasters."

The flurry of activities directed by Miss Omega herself ended in a table set with a gleaming damask cloth over which French Haviland, edged in gold and splashed in apple blossoms, welcomed this honored guest. A fetching piece of dogwood and forsythia draped a royal Sevres vase. Fresh candles in the chandelier flickered on the face of Great Grandmother Eleanora, whom Liza imagined smiled down on her family treasures. Aunt Lizzie and Uncle Joe donned their church clothes and looked admiringly on the festive preparations. Omega was radiant in blue chiffon, with a wide sash, her blond curls tumbling around her rosy cheeks. Liza wore a black skirt with a scarlet cummerbund, the color repeated in a velvet band at her throat just above her high-necked white blouse. In a drawer she had found an old mother-of-pearl comb which now glistened in the black upsweep of her hair.

From the kitchen came the mingled aromas of fried chicken, yeast rolls, English peas with new potatoes and spring onions, the work of Aunt Dinah, who lived nearby and who helped out at Oak Grove when company was coming.

In readiness the family in the front parlor awaited their guest. From the window Omega spied him as he rounded the bend. "Look, Liza! There he is."

The figure approaching wearing a dark suit and clerical collar moved in unhurried gait, his hands clasped behind him, neither eager nor averse to complete his journey. He appeared more interested in perusing the blue wisteria or measuring the height of the magnolias. Before he could mount the front steps, Omega was already at the front door. Instead of the animation Liza expected, she opened the door and said primly, "Do come in, Mr. Westbrook. We have been eagerly awaiting your arrival." Liza could scarcely restrain laughter. She could imagine Miss Hostess endlessly rehearsing that elevated introduction in front of her mirror upstairs.

Liza stared into gray-green eyes set in a high forehead with slightly wavy blond haircut in monk fashion. A strong square jaw with just a hint of a dimple did not seem to go with the slightly sensuous mouth. This tall angular man should have been handsome. Taking each feature separately, he was. Maybe it was the nose, a little too long for the lean face. Liza could not quite decide, but when he spoke, she forgot the face. His voice was deep, scaled to a pleasing pitch. "How very kind of you to invite me." Then in a humorous turn from the stodginess of his greeting, he added, with a merry glint in his eyes, "I hope that Omega's pressuring an invitation for an old schoolmaster did not inconvenience you too much." His words were directed at Uncle Joe and Aunt Lizzie, but his eyes were on Liza.

Now Omega, aware of her duties as hostess, said, "Mr. Westbrook, this is my sister, Elizabeth."

Liza raised her eyebrows and smiled. "The name is really Liza. Everybody calls me that except on rare occasions." Liza extended her hand. He took it in his long tapered one, so different from Tom's big work fingers.

"I'm Charles Westbrook, Liza. I'm quite at home with just Charles. But Mr. Westbrook to you, Omega, at school and in church." For once Omega's words stopped. She couldn't quite understand whether he was giving her permission to "Charles" him tonight. Uncle Joe extending his hand, cordially asked, "Well, Reverend, ain't you hungry? The vittles hot and waiting. Aunt Dinah's ready to put it on the table."

Embarrassment flushed Omega's cheeks. Uncle Joe couldn't remember anything. Sensing Omega's consternation, Uncle Joe rephrased, "Is you bout ready to eat?"

Charles took Omega by the hand and said gallantly, "Lead me to your table, my hostess."

The meal served, Omega could not eat for staring at the funny way their English guest moved his food forward with his knife to his fork as he cut a piece of chicken. Liza punched her, and Omega picked up her fork and knife, trying desperately to imitate Mr. Westbrook's table manners.

Uncle Joe, a drumstick in his hand, waved it. "Reverend, down here in the South we eat our chicken with our fingers. You welcome to join me. Gnawing the bones is the best part."

"Thank you, Mr. Brown. Most of the kings and queens of England followed the same etiquette. So if you don't mind,

I'll be delighted to join you." He took up his chicken breast and raised it gingerly to his mouth. At that point Omega decided it proper to follow suit.

Across the table Charles and Liza exchanged knowing smiles. Now she asked impishly, "Speaking of chicken, Mr. Westbrook, which came first, the hen or the egg?"

"Neither, Liza" was his prompt reply. "I believe it was the rooster."

"Oh, Mr. Westbrook, how unlearned you must be in barnyard procreation. I was not asking about the fertilized egg. Only the egg we ordinarily eat for breakfast."

"Touche! That being the case, I would say the hen. Certainly her gender is more important than a mere egg."

Uncle Joe thought it time to butt in. "Don't forget, Reverend, that Adam come first. Eve, if I remember the good book rightly, came out of Adam."

Liza perked up. "Uncle Joe, maybe you men concocted that story. It gives you another weapon to hold over our heads. Keeps us in our place like our colored neighbors. One day we're going to show you. I wager within ten years we women will be marching to the polls with you men."

Aunt Lizzie spoke now. "I wouldn't know who to vote for anyway unless Joe told me."

"Mrs. Brown, many English women share your sentiments. It sounds as if your niece belongs to the New Generation. Feminists, I believe is the term."

Liza challenged him. "And you, Mr. Westbrook, how do you feel about these women upstarts? I believe your church like the Baptists has barred us from Holy Orders. It's not that I would ever want to don the collar. Platitudes are not my specialty." Liza blushed. "I'm sorry. I have been rude."

"Not rude. Honest." He leaned toward her and said

pointedly, "It is refreshing to meet a beautiful woman who thinks and who is brave enough to express herself."

Liza dropped her eyes and concentrated on her food. Aunt Lizzie, aware of the awkward silence, picked up the platter of fried chicken and passed it to her guest. "Thank you," he said. "Liza, Omega tells me you are a voracious reader. I'm addicted as well. Tell me. What brought you to love books? A great teacher?"

"Mr. Westbrook, don't let Omega mislead you. I have never been in a classroom. My father was barely literate. My mother loved books. She taught me to read, or maybe I taught myself. My library as a child was a shelf at Mr. Haskell's general store. He let us check them out. To be completely honest, I can't explain what happens between words on the page and what happens in the head." She stopped to examine her words. Why was she talking this way to a stranger? "Anyway," she added, "books are good company."

"Liza you ought to hear Mr. Westbrook read poetry. It's like he wrote it, not somebody dead for a hundred years."

"Omega, you are my greatest admirer. I do love to read. I know the magic to which you alluded, Liza. I find poetry in my books. The Bible. The Prayer Book. Come to church tomorrow and I'll do my best to convince you that the sound of the well-phrased word even softens the platitude."

"Well, Reverend, reckon we can't hardly do nothing else. But Liza here has not been well lately. It's up to her," Uncle Joe finished.

"I would love to come, Mr. Westbrook. I have never been in my mother's church. My church experience has been limited to Hardshell or shouting Baptists. Don't misunderstand me. Good people. I just guess I'm not temperamentally a Baptist. In fact, I don't really think I'm very religious.

Speaking of poetry, do you know the American poetess, Emily Dickinson?"

"Not well. Perhaps you would be so kind as to introduce me."

"She was an upstart, too. She was a feminist by modern standards. In one of her poems she says she spends her Sundays staying at home while others go to church. She goes on to say she has birds for choristers. That God, a noted clergyman, appears in her orchard, and doesn't preach very long sermons."

"I'm not much on sermons myself. I think I'll lift one of Dean Donne's tomorrow. He writes far better than I."

Liza laughed. "I heard an old codger say the same thing. Uncle John. He is Brown Hill's claim to scholarship."

Uncle Joe chimed. "John MacDonald's one of the queerest old ducks I ever knowed. You'd like him. One of your kind, Reverend." Suddenly realizing the import of his words, "Sorry, Rev, reckon I put my foot in my mouth that time."

They all laughed good-naturedly. The dinner ended, Westbrook rounded the table to assist Liza's exit. As he drew her chair out, his fingers touched her shoulders lightly and lingered before she turned to lead him into the parlor.

The conversation after awhile waned. Aunt Lizzie and Uncle Joe, their duty done, excused themselves to complete last-minute chores. Even Omega, having seen her idol at such close range, slipped out to feed Spot. Mr. Westbrook stood up to go. Looking up to the portrait over the mantel, he asked, "Your mother, Liza?"

"Yes."

"Striking. But I think the daughter surpasses the Mother."

"Did Oxford teach you the art of flattery, Mr. Westbrook?" Liza asked artfully.

"If Oxford taught me anything, Miss Liza, and I don't think it taught me much, it was to accept a compliment graciously," he scolded mildly.

"Touché, Mr. Westbrook." She followed him to the door. "I shall see you in church tomorrow." She held out her hand. "Thank you for coming. I apologize for my bad manners. I shall work to try to mend them."

He lifted her hand to his lips. "Don't try too hard. Oxford men take an arcane delight in impertinent young women." He dropped her hand and disappeared down the steps.

As Liza undressed, Omega, already in bed, hugged her knees and questioned her. "Liza, you like Mr. Westbrook?"

"Of course. He seems very nice."

"Not what I mean, Liza. Do you really like him special like? Like say could you fall in love with him, or somebody like him?"

"Omega, I'm a married woman. The only man you like special is your husband."

"That's not what the books say. Anyhow, I could tell he liked you, special like."

"Omega Brown, that's the biggest nonsense I've heard in a long time."

"Then why did he kiss your hand?"

"Well, he was being polite. Gallant. You know. Like what the books say."

"Uh huh!" Omega responded as she slipped under the covers and prepared for sleep.

CHAPTER TWENTY ONE

PRINCE FREDERICK

NEITHER AUNT LIZZIE NOR OMEGA chose to go to church the next day. Aunt Lizzie felt she was coming down with a spell of hayfever; Omega elected to stay with her and finish the book Mr. Westbrook had let her borrow. So it was Liza and Uncle Joe who set off to church in the Model T. Liza would have preferred the walk, but Uncle Joe insisted they ride since Liza "had been under the weather so long." As they bumped along the dirt road at a snail's pace, Liza turned to her Uncle and asked, "Uncle Joe, do you believe in God?"

"Great God, Liza! What a question? Course I believe in God."

"Do you love God?"

"Well, I reckon so. The Reverend says you got to love God to go to heaven."

"What is heaven, Uncle Joe?"

"Heaven is where you ain't got nobody to keep asking danged foolish questions." He accelerated the motor and lurched forward; the engine sputtered his annoyance at Liza's foolishness. God in heaven, Uncle Joe thought, deliver me from a thinking woman.

A steeple with belfry topped with a cross lifted itself above a small stucco structure set behind a lych gate with a wrought iron fence to which half a dozen horses and buggies were hitched. Uncle Joe's Model T was the only car. No wonder, Liza thought, he wanted to drive it. On either side of the church a few imposing monuments stood sentinel. The churchyard held a modest congregation of parishioners to whom Uncle Joe began introducing Liza. "Folks, this is my niece, Liza Brown, sister to Omega. She come from Brown Hill. You probably heard of Gideon Brown — makes coffins — well, Liza married his son, Tom." Among the "Glad to meetchas," Charles Westbrook in black cassock descended the steps of the church. His eyes sought Liza, and when they found her, a smile spread over his face. Liza smiled back and took the proffered hand when her turn came to be greeted.

"I'm glad you're spending this Sunday coming to church," he whispered, paraphrasing Dickinson.

"I'm glad, too," she responded. He made a quick survey of her blue muslin dress, his eyes traveling from the neckline edged in lace to her softly rounded bosom over a pointed waistline. Liza felt the approval in those gray-green eyes and

in spite of herself blushed with pleasure. He nodded to someone overhead, and from the steeple came the Westminster
chimes, a gift from a wealthy parishioner now under one of the
imposing marbles.

Liza and Uncle Joe followed the crowd into the tiny
church, whose sanctuary could seat no more than thirty-five or
forty souls. The clear glass gothic windows on either side provided the only light. Liza noted with interest that each parishioner bowed before entering the pew and then knelt for quiet
prayer. Uncle Joe, behind her, pushed her gently toward a pew
with a plaque bearing the name of Joseph Ebenezer Brown. As
her uncle pulled the prayer cushion forward, Liza knelt beside
him and looked at the cross on the altar, flanked by two
unlighted candles. At that moment Mr. Westbrook re-entered
from the side of the altar, bowed to the cross, lighted the left
candle, bowed again, lit the right candles and bowed again
before leaving. Looking around her, she saw some praying,
some sitting, but none speaking. How very odd, she thought.
Now came Mr. Westbrook, wearing a purple robe with a hole
cut in the center for his head. Bowing once more to the cross,
he turned to his congregation and said in that beautiful melodious voice, "The Lord be with thee."

"And with thy spirit," the congregation responded.
Uncle Joe now handed her a small leather bound book. *The
Book of Common Prayer.* Vaguely she remembered one like it
bearing Mama's name. Mr. Westbrook was on the right side of
the altar, reading from Corinthians; now from the left reading
from Matthew. Now the entire church was saying the Nicene
Creed— belief in "all things visible and invisible." She would
have to think about that. "Resurrection of the dead and the life
everlasting." These words were no strangers, except now they
were being said in unison above which she could hear Mr.

Westbrook's voice. Imagine! A sermon not more than five or six minutes. About love and forgiveness. She remembered a line from Longfellow, "Lend to the rhyme of the poet the beauty of thy voice." Now came the words, "We acknowledge and bewail our manifold sins and wickedness — heartily sorry — miserable offender." A tear slipped down her cheek. She followed Uncle Joe to the altar rail and knelt beside him. Mr. Westbrook did not offer her the cup. Instead he made the sign of the cross over her head and whispered a prayer. She tried to imagine Mama on her knees here — Mama who didn't get married here — Mama and Papa far away — Tom in church at Brown Hill. Dazed she returned to her seat. She was glad when it was over. She needed to think — to find out if the God of Shiloh and Brown Hill also lived in this quiet place — if this God could take away the despair that seemed to be crowding her.

She was making her way to the Model T when she felt a light touch on her shoulder. "Did you hear poetry, Miss Liza?"

"Oh, yes, Mr. Westbrook. You almost persuade me to be a Christian," she said lightly.

"Can't we talk sometime soon? I mean, I would like to explain about the church and its history. Much older than your Baptists," he laughed.

Uncle Joe, half listening to the proposal, said, "Sure, Reverend. High time Liza got to know about her kin people's church. Can't tell her much myself." He punched the priest playfully. "Come at least twice a year — Christmas and Easter. Yes, sir, Rev, come on up anytime and give her a lesson."

Charles Westbrook eyed Liza. Should he take the plunge? How would she react? Before he could stop to decide, he heard himself say, "The church is the best place to instruct.

In this old church English and American history meet. You know, Mr. Brown, if Liza would like a short lesson, I could offer her a biscuit and a cup of tea. Afterward, I would walk her back. Liza's cheek flushed. "It's such a beautiful day," he continued. "An afternoon stroll would be pleasant."

Before Liza could say anything, Uncle Joe spoke up. "Sure thing, Reverend. Only don't forget Liza here is a mighty pretty girl. She's married, you know," he quipped.

"I certainly will remember." As Joe turned toward the Model T, he added, "How could I forget."

Inside the church, Mr. Westbrook launched into the typical tour of the docent. The two candles – Jesus the man, Jesus the divine; the sign of the cross; the reason for genuflection. His tone was formal and impersonal. Then in a more intimate voice he ended with, "Now if you were in Westminster Abbey or even St. Michael's in Charleston, you would have stained glass windows, a pipe organ, a choir. Old Henry the Eighth, unfortunately, stripped the church of its statuary. Do you have any questions?

Liza had remained silent for a long time. Finally she asked, "Mr. Westbrook, how do you know whether you're worshipping God or the beauty of the service?"

"Liza," his voice was soft and reverent, "if God is truth, eternal, but invisible, we need something concrete to make him visible. The beauty of the service makes him visible. Poetry, remember? The bread and the wine are tangible, providing the table of communion with Him."

"Then why was I deprived?"

"I would not have deprived you, Liza. But the church has law. As a priest I am ordered to follow that law. You have never been baptized, have you? Nor have you been confirmed?"

"I can't imagine the loving God of which you spoke caring about such trivialities. Don't be shocked. I know I'm an upstart. Anyway, I'm confused, Mr. Westbrook. Sometime I think what you preachers say is just talk. Frankly, I wonder if there really is a God. If there is, why does he allow such pain." Her dark eyes filled with tears. "Anyway I haven't found him in the churches I have attended. I don't know whether I can find him here. I am more likely to find what I think comes closer to what we speak of as God at odd moments when I don't really need him. When I do need him, he doesn't show up. Out on other business, I suppose."

"Do you think that just because I am a priest that God is always real to me? He isn't. I can anticipate your next question. Then why are you living a lie? And my answer is I don't know. I don't seem to have any other choice. If man could be completely self-reliant, perhaps God is not necessary. I am not that kind of man. I need him if he exists. I need him if he doesn't exist. I have no choice except to seek him. Books break the loneliness; sometimes, rarely, people." His eyes searched hers. "They never erase it."

"I know, Mr. Westbrook."

"Liza, would you call me Charles?"

"I think I should go now." She moved toward the door.

"Have I offended you, Liza?" His eyes were troubled. "I hoped you would share a bit of lunch." He pointed to the parish house that doubled as rectory and school.

"Oh, no! But thank you just the same. As you said, it's a lovely day. I will like the stroll. Alone," she added.

"Will I see you again, Liza?"

Liza looked at him questioningly. "Do you think it's wise, Charles?" Before he could answer, she closed the door softly and turned her steps homeward.

Late afternoon found Liza on the front porch in a rocker. So much in her life had ended and begun on a porch. On
a porch she had first spoken to Tom; she had made earth-shaking decisions; she had heard words of wisdom. Now she sat
looking out on the neat-boxed yard, the oak-lined drive, not
straight but curved so that she couldn't see the end. Like the
river at Parker Landing. Like the bend in her life. On her lap
was paper to write Tom. Should she go back to Brown Hill
now? Yet she had been here less than a week. Nothing had
happened; everything had happened. "Will I see you again,
Liza?" Something very frightening was taking place. She felt
on the edge of an abyss into which she was afraid to jump but
to which she was magnetically drawn. If she stayed in Oak
Grove, another meeting was inevitable. She should go back
now, to her little home in Brown Hill, to the good man who
loved her. She picked up her pen and wrote:

> *Dear Tom,*
>
>   *I am enjoying being with Omega and seeing Oak Grove.*
> *Uncle Joe and Aunt Lizzie are pampering me. I do feel better most*
> *of the time. Today I went to church with Uncle Joe and walked*
> *home alone. The spring weather is fine and the flowers are so pret-*
> *ty. Take care of yourself and Betsy. Will write often.*
>
>   *Your loving wife,*
>   *Liza*

CHAPTER TWENTY TWO

SECRETS

AT FIRST IN THE DAYS AHEAD, Oak Grove yielded few secrets. Somebody besides Mama had loved books, or maybe books were a necessary ornament to a plantation house like velvet draperies to a window. In the front bureau in the hall behind gothic glass paneled doors were shelved volumes where pages had never been parted — handsome leather bound sets — *Great Events of the World* in twenty volumes — the complete works of Shakespeare, an unabridged dictionary, a history of the world, a set of Dickens, and collected poems.

She could almost tell before opening the books which ones Mama had read. Some of them even bore her name. Here Mama had tasted romance vicariously.

Below the glass doors a writing desk let down, behind which were a number of tiny drawers and cubby holes containing odd assortments of foreign stamps, staff pens, buttons, empty drawstring pouches. In the larger drawers beneath the desk were photographs of old men and women who looked out with stern uncompromising candor. There were a little boy baby in a frilly dress and little girls, some wide eyed, some subdued — all unnamed. What secrets did they carry with them to some country graveyard? Why was the little burial plot at Oak Grove confined to one generation? Where were the rest of them? Her blood and theirs were perhaps the same. As she examined one picture after the other, her finger touched the stiffness of heavy paper. Turning it over, the face of a little girl rendered in watercolor stared at her. Black wavy hair framed limpid brown eyes – intelligent, inquiring eyes set in skin the color of honey. There was a hint of flat nose over wide lips whose smile got lost in sadness. Uncle Joe's hands now took the picture from her hand. "Who is she?" Liza questioned.

At first he said nothing. He simply gazed as she had done on the beautiful, alert little face. He cleared his throat. She could hardly hear his words. "Must be Lucinda. Ain't never seen her. Heared about her once or twice. Kinda family skeleton. You know, Liza, nigger in the woodpile."

"But Uncle Joe, who was her Papa? He must have loved her. Somebody did this watercolor. I don't know much about art, but this looks good to me."

"Don't know all the ins and outs of the story. Papa wouldn't talk about it. I got most of it from other people. Seems like after Papa was born, Grandmother Eleanora got kinda unhappy. She had lost a lot of younguns before Papa. Then she fell into a spell of sadness. Kinda like you been, Liza.. Anyhow, she went down to Charleston to visit her folks. Well, she stayed. She met a fellow. He was French like her. They fell in love. She wrote Grandpapa asking for a divorce. Grandpapa took the boat to Charleston. Was gonna kill the fellow. Grandma must have got wind of it. She left the baby, my Papa, with her people. The two of 'em went to Canada. Grandpapa brought my papa home."

"Oh, Uncle Joe, how sad for both of them. But how did this Lucinda come into the picture?"

"Well, that's another story. Elberta lived on the place. She was high yaller nigger. Named for the peach, I reckon. Grandpapa got her to come in to look after the baby. Lucinda here was born when Papa was five or six. Elberta lived here at Oak Grove. Plantersville had nothing to do with him after that. When my Papa was eighteen, the two of them left the country. Grandpapa left Oak Grove to Papa. I don't know where they went; don't know where they died."

"So that explains why they aren't in the family plot. But Uncle Joe, what about Lucinda? Did she go with them?"

"Nope. She stayed here. Papa was good to her. Sent her to school. She went to Voorhees, school for niggers in Denmark. Become a schoolteacher. She married some nigger from the North. I reckon she's dead now. I heared her son come back, one of them nigger professors at a college in Columbia for awhile."

"And you never saw her. Did Mama?"

"I done told you. Just heared about her. Lucinda done growed up and grown when me and Nora come along. I don't rightly know where your Mama knowed the whole story or not. We kinda kept it hush hush. Folks that knowed about it are dead now. I reckon there's a skeleton in every closet." He handed the picture back to her. "Liza, the Reverend wants to take the school younguns to Georgetown and spend the night at the Gladstone. He wants to show them around historical places. Wants to know if you'll go with him to see after the gals while he tends to the boys. Omega's been lotsa times with me and Lizzie. Course she'll go with the school."

Liza's heart quickened. What should she say? Charles had planned that trip for her. He was gambling on her accepting. God in heaven! Great grandmother Eleanora, Mama, and now Liza. History was repeating. Her head was saying no. But what harm could it be? There would be children. "You are thinking crazy, Liza," she told herself. "Think about Tom. Brown Hill."

"When is he planning the trip, Uncle Joe?"

"After church Sunday. The tide goes out 'bout two o'clock. You catch the boat at Chapel Creek. It's just an afternoon ride to Georgetown."

"Tell Mr. Westbrook I'd love to go."

Liza sat at the desk, holding Lucinda in her hand. "So you are my great aunt? My great grandpapa's daughter by Elberta. So the English Browns have colored kin. What would Shiloh and Brown Hill say?" She laughed in spite of herself.

Liza's hand pulled out another drawer.She unfolded yellowed linens, fringed napkins with heavily embroidered flowers – daffodil for one; roses for another; wisteria for another. There were dainty little luncheon napkins with the initial E.M.B. Reaching for the next drawer, she slipped out another carefully concealed drawer beneath. "Ah," she said. She had read about secret drawers. This was like a fairy tale. It was a very thin drawer, not more than an inch in depth. Inside was an envelope, still sealed. **To my husband, Joe.** The ink was brownish with age. Did she have the right to intrude? Her fingers decided for her. Liza's hands trembled.

August 4, 1798

Dear Joe,

When you put me on the boat in Georgetown, it will be the last time we see each other. I can't come back to Oak Grove. There are too many memories buried here. At last you have a son. Little Joseph. He promises to be blond like the Browns, not like the Miotts with tainted blood. I wanted to be a good wife. I'm sorry it didn't work out. Elberta will see after you and Joseph. Try to be happy now.

I am yours faithfully,
Eleanora

So Joseph Ebenezer Brown had never even read it. What did she mean by "tainted blood?" Why did she tuck the letter away in such a secluded place? Was it meant for her husband or did her "second sight" foresee kinder eyes reading it now? "Oh, Grandmother," she whispered. "Did you know about Elberta all along? Did you ever hear about Lucinda? Did all the babies you lost have a darker skin?" Goose pimples covered Liza's arms. And Grandfather. Did his knowledge of his wife's ancestry explain his generosity to his daughter, Lucinda? What she would give to unlock the doors to these secrets. She was tempted to write her name and the date on the envelope with a message. "Liza Brown, great granddaughter of Eleanora Miott Brown read this letter June 2, 1915. She is proud of her heritage." Instead, she folded the letter, replaced it in the envelope, and closed the secret drawer.

In the dining room Liza's eyes sought her great grandmother's gaze in her portrait. "Our eyes are identical," Liza whispered. She wondered if the artist had tampered with the skin color. There was such a faint blush on her smooth white cheeks.

CHAPTER TWENTY THREE

THE RIVER WIDENS

LESS THAN A MILE from Prince Frederick Church was Chapel Creek Landing, a small outlet to the Great Pee Dee, the navigable route to Georgetown. Here boats came twice a week from town, loaded with, salt, sugar, and other staples. Farmers and small tradesmen met the boats, which depended upon the tide for added speed. Having unloaded their cargo, they took on passengers and produce, such as crates of chickens and boxes of eggs headed for the tables in hotels and inns. Each Sunday a small passenger boat with a capacity of fifteen or twenty made one run, picking up travelers. Some sought respite from Low Country quietness; others had pressing business in town early Monday morning. Of course, the schedule varied with the tide. Now Liza stood with Uncle Joe and Omega, waiting for Mr. Westbrook and his entourage of little tourists, already fifteen minutes late according to Uncle Joe, who every few seconds checked his gold pocket watch secured by the fob chain which dangled over a portly middle. The two-level craft, its back wheel gently chugging, also waited, the other passengers having boarded and now standing watch at the rails on the upper deck. "Reckon the Reverend got wound up and preached too long," Uncle Joe commented dryly. Liza had elected not to attend church. Instead, she had washed her hair and taken pains to fluff the slightly curling bangs around her face before crowning her head with heavy ropes of hair now obscured by a wide sunbonnet. Aunt Lizzie had packed a basket of ham biscuits, teacakes, and dried apples just in case that hotel had closed up on Sunday. As Liza watched the river, its waters grayish green, not so dark as the Little Pee Dee, she wondered where it would take her this time. Would it lead her into forbidden channels? "Oh, no! Not me," she whispered. Contrary to her words, her heart gave a curious lurch.

Rounding the curve, the schoolmaster with his little charges, his blond hair slightly ruffled in the brisk wind, strode toward them. There were three little boys—Timothy, Paul, and Andrew, who were scarcely out of their third grade primers— and three girls—Mary Louise, Elizabeth Anne, and Charlotte, in bright spring dresses with matching hats—all soon to be on their way to hear from Master Westbrook how a little part of England still claimed a part of Georgetown, though no longer a subject of the crown. Each hand carried a small satchel—each face wide-eyed and animated, happy to miss school a couple of days for whatever reason.

"'Bout time you gittin here," Uncle Joe complained. "We been waiting right near an hour."

"So sorry. I had a few unscheduled stops along the way." His eyes smiled and sought Liza. "I missed you at church. You had a better sermon in your backyard, I suspect." His words were playful.

"Oh, no, Mr. Westbrook. Liza had to wash her hair. It takes a long time to dry. She wanted it pretty for the trip." Liza felt the color mount her cheeks.

"Omega, you talk too much," Liza remonstrated mildly.

"Let's get on a move." The words came from the pilot. "Sundown not too long from now," he added, motioning his passengers aboard.

With a quick goodbye to Uncle Joe, Liza joined Charles to herd their crew up the steep stairway—some to their seats, some to watch the receding Chapel Creek as the waterwheel gained momentum and headed down the river. Liza and Charles also stood at the rail. Liza waved her hand ceremonially to the shore and turned shyly to her companion. "We meet again."

"We knew we would, didn't we?" Charles replied. The boat slipped out into the Great Pee Dee. Liza looked straight ahead, not daring to meet his eyes. She hoped he could not hear her heart pounding.

Their destination lay twelve miles east. Liza watched the water darken to a grayish black as the river widened. On the swamp side were the familiar trees—sweet gum, tupelo, and maple—leafed in shades of spring green. Among them water oaks dressed in slick greenish brown bark towered supreme to eighty feet above their lowly brethren. Cypress knees dotted the edges and received the waves rippling in the wake of the boat. On the marsh side lay what had once been vast outlays of rice and indigo fields, where Tideland planters amassed huge fortunes, counting themselves among the richest people of the world. Now brown marsh grass rose over the ruined empires, from which occasionally a marsh hen rose, trusting her eggs to the watery sod. Liza turned to Charles and commented, "No wonder rice was on every table in the Low Country. The mother-in-law tested a bride's culinary art in rice. Soggy rice forecasts a poor cook and bad marriage. The bride who produces a bowl of rice, thoroughly done but with each grain standing apart, met instant approval. Mama could cook rice that way," she added. "Mama's ability to cook rice didn't add fortune to her life. Ruined like rice fields," she finished.

"Tell me about your Mama."

"I didn't really know her until after she was gone. I mean, I lived with her, but I didn't know her. She died so young. It's so strange. People we love most are sometimes strangers. Odd that death opens the door to the realization." Liza brushed the corner of her eye.

"Love and understanding don't always unite," Charles said thoughtfully. "When it does, something very rare and very wonderful happens, I imagine. Browning talks about it. I wonder if he, too, dreamed of it. Was the idyllic marriage that has been handed down a reality? His wife, Elizabeth, also died young. Their lovestory makes good reading anyway. Still one wonders about the reality."

"Look!" Liza pointed overhead. "Isn't that a bald eagle?" Its dark wings outspread and its hooked white beak steering skyward, the massive bird soared across the water and headed toward the swamp. "I've seen only one or two eagles' nests and very few eagles. Another rarity, like rice fields and indigo and love," she added cryptically.

"Don't be bitter, Liza. Life is not over. For either of us," he added softly.

"No, Charles. You are right. You have a future to make it what you want. We women don't have that kind of leeway. Mine is pretty set in a little Low Country village with a husband, a good man who loves me, who hopes God will bless us with many children. It could be worse. It's certainly better than what Mama had," she finished.

"We men aren't free either. If I had the freedom of which you speak, I would take what I want, what I think would make life complete. The only trouble is, happiness doesn't feed on somebody else's misery." Their eyes met for a split second. Liza turned abruptly toward the mid-channel of the river.

"Odd that I have heard almost the same words from someone else. Jess, my brother-in-law, a kind of lost soul. He's like me in many ways," she murmured. Now her voice brightened. "Goodness gracious! Let's talk about pleasanter things."

"Of course. Whatever you want. Name the subject. Enlighten me on some of your Southern folklore," Charles suggested.

Omega edged her way between the two. "Omega, Mr. Westbrook was just asking me to tell him about southern folk tales. Help me out," Liza begged.

Glad to be included and eager to show off her knowledge, Omega launched forth. "They say, Mr. Westbrook, that haunts, hags, conjure men, and plat-eyes are loose in the woods and swamps around here. The only way to keep them out of your house is to have a blue trim. Blue comes from the indigo flower that they used to make dye out of. So because blue is the color of heaven, the home of God, evil things don't like it and won't come near a house with blue on it," she finished proudly.

"My! My! Omega. That makes sense to me. You know the Hebrew high priests as well as Greek and Egyptian gods wore blue. And Arabs wrapped their children's necks with blue beads to keep off the Evil Eye. But pray tell what are plat-eyes? My education is sorely lacking about them," he laughed.

"Well, everybody knows about plat-eyes," Omega said archly. "It's a god-awful thing that creeps around in the darkest hours of the morning before the sun comes up. Once upon a time they were human beings, but somehow they never had a proper burial. No preacher or priest prayed over the body before it was put in the ground. So they have to wander around, floating around graveyards and swamps. They have huge fiery eyes that get bigger as they get closer and closer. They can be in the form of a dog, cat, horse, raccoon, or even a sand crab. If one gets close, it'll burn anybody up — shrivel up like a dry weed. Best thing to do when you come across a plat-eye is close your eyes quick and run away as fast as you can. It's not easy to run with eyes shut at night in the woods and swamp," she confided.

Liza and Charles laughed heartily. Liza, putting her arms around Omega, asked, "Don't tell me you have seen a plat-eye?"

"I've seen things a lot scarier than a plat-eye, Liza. You have, too."

"So right, little one. Looks like we can't get away from such things. Look!" She pointed to the sawmill on the horizon and the row of stores edging the Sampit River. "Remember you and Tom and I spent our wedding night at Mrs. Brinkley's inn." The moment the words were out, she regretted them. Turning to Charles, she said, "I'm so looking forward to really seeing the old town. With you," she added softly.

Three short whistles heralded the steamboat, which anchored on the Sampit River's brackish water running behind Front Street, the principal artery and shopping center of Georgetown. The buildings on the riverside included the town clock, housed in a two-story brick structure which had accommodated, since 1842, the jail, police department, and the Chamber of Commerce. Next door was the *Georgetown Times*, printing since 1797 obituaries, earthquakes, hurricanes, feuds, politics, and industry. From these pages the traveler could glean Low Country life spanning almost a century and a half. As the town clock struck the hour of six, the tourists from Plantersville crossed over Front Street to where the Gladstone awaited their guests. At that moment the electric streetlights flooded the little metropolis and the cobblestone street, where both automobile and buggy parked side-by-side or clattered and clopped along to the night's destination. "It's just like Uncle Joe predicted," Liza commented; "the twentieth century will bring big changes. I bet in ten years there won't be a horse and buggy anywhere in sight or a kerosene lamp. Makes you wonder what the *Georgetown Times* will be printing fifty or a hundred years from now."

"Well, Tennyson had the same ideas. In one of his poems he says he 'dipped into the future far as human eyes could see. Saw the heavens filled with commerce.' He saw the heavens filled with deadly weapons, too," Charles added.

As Liza's eyes swept the street, she tripped on a stray brick. Charles steadied her with his arms until they were at the Gladstone door. A black man in a white tunic over dark pants greeted them. "Come right in. We be 'specting you." He took both Charles's and Liza's valises. "I puts de missus and mister in de bride room wid de ribber in sight."

"Oh, no." Charles said quickly. "Mrs. Brown will share a room with one of the girls. I'll be with the boys. Mrs. Brown was gracious enough to come with me to chaperone the young ladies."

"Youse not married then. I be making nother mistake. Reckon cause me and Lily Mae so happy I wants everybody hitched," he chuckled. "I'm Sam. I'm gonna git you all settled in. Last call for supper seben. We's bettah git a move on."

Inside, the squat bald-headed hotel registrar looked down on the group from his black-rimmed spectacles, which had slid down to a beaked nose. His smile sported regular white teeth with reddish gums that clacked as he greeted his guests. "Welcome to Gladstone." Liza looked around the spacious lobby, divided at intervals by columns with sofas and chairs arranged in intimate groupings on a rich red carpet decorated with pink roses and green leaves. Certainly the little inn where she and Tom had stayed bore little resemblance to this. To the left she could see the dining room. On the tables draped in white linen, a candle flickered. Worried she turned to Charles, who had just signed the book and now carried a handful of keys. "We can't afford this. I mean, I can't."

"Look, Liza, not to worry. You are my guest and a necessity when I have young ladies in my charge."

"Just the same I don't think it's quite right—-"

"Stop it, Andrew," Charles commanded. The redheaded boy had slid down the stairway and was ready to lead his chums on a similar expedition. "Let's get them settled, shall we?" He motioned the group forward while addressing Liza.

Three rooms had been engaged upstairs. Charles steered his three little boys, not quite subdued even after a stern reprimand, into their room. In the second room Mary Louise, Elizabeth Anne and Charlotte explored their premises, bouncing on beds and pulling out empty drawers. The door closed upon their squeals and chatter. Liza and Omega entered the third room with considerably less animation. Hanging her hat on the convenient tree, she plopped down on the bed and closed her eyes. "I shouldn't have come," she told herself. "How foolish!"

Omega, who had already opened the door to the balcony, called out, "Come, Liza! We can see the river. Oh, Liza, wasn't Mr. Westbrook nice to bring us? He's so wonderful. It's much more fun to come this way than with Uncle Joe. Liza, do you think Mr. Westbrook's handsome?" Now she was back in the room. "What's the matter? You tired?"

"No, no, Omega," she said extending her hand to beckon her sister near. "I'm worried about who's paying for this."

"No need. Each one of us gave Mr. Westbrook money. I wasn't going to tell you. I wanted it to be a surprise." She opened up her little satchel and handed Liza twenty dollars. "Uncle Joe wants you to buy something pretty. He wants you to have a good time."

"Omega. How can I repay them and you"?

"Liza, you've been sick. You better now?"

"I'm better, little sweetheart. And I'm going to have a wonderful time." With that she rose and walked over to the lavatory and splashed her face with water. Her deep socket black eyes stared at her from the mirror. Fluffing out an extra curl here and there, she opened her bag and pulled out a mother-of-pearl comb, which gleamed like a miniature halo in her dark hair. There was a knock at the door.

"Are we ready?" Charles called.

Smoothing her blue muslin dress, Liza opened the door. "We are ready." Charles bowed gallantly and offered her his arm.

"May I escort you, my lady, to dinner?"

"Thank you, my lord," Liza returned graciously.

Sam met them at the door of the dining room. "Dis way." He seated the boys and girls at a long table. To a side table for two he steered Liza and Charles. Holding out her chair, Sam remarked, "You sho pretty lady."

"Isn't she?" Charles offered agreement. Liza looked over at Omega, who she knew would have preferred being with them. She wondered who had made the seating arrangements. Charles's smile answered her question.

"The excursion was rather wonderful, don't you think? I learned so much about haunts, and plat-eyes, and blue-trimmed houses. I don't think our English tales can hold a candle to yours."

"I'm afraid I talked too much. I would like to hear about England. I've read books, poetry, seen pictures. Will be as close as I'll get to Britain. Course, I was born in Britton's Neck," she laughed. "I fear the muddy banks of the Little Pee Dee have no resemblance to merry old England."

"Oh, I don't know. Actually I was born near water, too. A great deal of water in fact. The Lake Country, Wordsworth Land. In the vicarage in Grasmere. St. Oswald. My father was the village priest; but Mummy really ran the church. She was a strong little lady with a mind of her own. Like you, Liza." His hand toyed with the knife, making a pattern on the white starched cloth. "Both my parents now lie in the little churchyard at St. Oswald between the village and the lake. In it are buried Wordsworth, his wife, and sister Dorothy. Also Coleridge's son. Grasmere is the color of your dress. We have mountains, too. Only they are not so high as America's. The highest one is less than four thousand feet. We call them pikes. They are most beautiful when they are snow-covered."

"Your soup, Missus. She-crab soup. Fresh each day."
The waiter bowed as he left the table. Liza glanced over where
the little school crew were spooning in theirs hungrily. She
couldn't help noticing how Omega lifted the spoon daintily to
her mouth and sipped from the side. My little sister is class,
she thought.

Turning her attention to her own, she remarked, "This
is delicious! I've never had this. Seafood inland is freshwater
fish from the river and streams. Papa was a great fisherman.
He would bring in strings of bream, shad, bowfin, catfish.
That is, if he remembered after several swigs of moonshine.
Don't let me get started about the Neck. Why did you leave
such a beautiful place to come to a godforsaken mosquito
infested swamp? You would have done better in Tidewater
Virginia or even in Charleston."

"I came on a dare really. After too many swigs of your
Papa's moonshine. That's another story. Maybe my coming
was not just an accident. Any place where Liza Brown is, is not
godforsaken."

Liza met his eyes. "Please. Such talk is nonsense. A
few weeks from now you will look back on our meeting as—as
a little reprieve from daily routine. Casual and pleasant."

"You are the one talking nonsense. Meeting you has
been anything but casual since I saw you first standing under
your mother's portrait. You know I planned this excursion for
us. We are too forthright to banter."

"What are you saying? Don't you know who I am? I
am as unreachable to you as the little country maid in
Wordsworth's Lucy poems would be to the Prince of Wales."

"I prefer to think we are the twin Longdale Peaks of the
Lake District. Wordsworth says that when the storm rides
high—let's see just how he says it— 'Methinks that I have

heard them echo back the thunder's greeting.'" The words rolled off his tongue organ-toned. "Side by side we could ride out any storm."

Liza said nothing and now concentrated on the main course, shrimp in a rich sauce, watercress, and English peas. Finally she said, "Have you forgotten you are a priest? Someone who weighs words carefully, someone who does not deliberately hurt, someone aware of consequences." Her voice dropped to a whisper.

"I understand my duty as a priest," he said solemnly. "I am also a man. Remember the two candles on the altar? I make no claim to divinity. I'm human. I want something besides books and liturgy to break the isolation. Liza, I don't speak irresponsibly. I'm not sure that I was ever fitted for Holy Orders. I can always teach. I think we both know what loneliness is."

"I'm alone, too," Liza admitted. "I suppose I am the second candle as well, but I am also a wife. Tom can't talk like you. Tom has never read a book other than the Bible. But he loves me as much as he is capable of loving. He would give his right arm for me. It's bad enough to hurt those who hurt you. I know what that is. I helped send Papa to suicide. I know what hell is." She kept her eyes lowered. "It's nothing like the hell that comes when you know you have deliberately hurt someone who loves you. Don't ask me to do that," she finished, her voice wavering.

Moments passed before he answered. "I have the tragedy that whenever I have felt deeply, my feelings have not been returned. Unrequited love I believe we call it. Now I have met someone who feels the way I do. I'm sure of it, Liza. You don't have to tell me. Twin peaks. Close but not one. That's hell, too."

Liza was glad that at that moment some little hand sent a water glass crashing to the floor. Charles hurried over to the table to sort things out and settle a giggling mob.

Liza finished her plate. When Charles returned to the table, she rose. "I have a headache. I don't care for dessert. Would you excuse me, Charles?"

"What have I done." It was not a question. "I got carried away. I don't want to hurt you. I don't want to spoil the trip for either of us. I promise to control my tongue."

Liza looked him fully in the face. Even in the candlelight he could see the deep creases in her forehead. "You and I both know there's no going back. The words have been said." With that she turned and disappeared into the lobby.

Later she stood at the window and watched Charles stroll down Front Street. Omega was at his side in animated monologue. Minutes passed. The clock struck nine. She looked down at the heavy gold wedding band, which had not been removed since Tom placed it on her finger at Parker Landing. Turning it gently, she was surprised at how easily she could slip it off. At that moment a dozen feet clattered up the stairs. Liza opened the door. "Did you have a nice walk?" Her question was directed to no one in particular.

"Yes, we did, Miss Liza." His words were clipped, polite, and impersonal. "I'll just take these young lads along. We'll see you ladies tomorrow. Breakfast is at eight." With that he proceeded down the hall, three little boys following him.

The town clock struck twelve. Liza, wide-awake, listened to Omega's quiet breathing. She wondered if Charles had also heard the clock. Despite the warm flannel blanket, she shivered. Sleep came slowly, but she dreamed of being held close with no guilt at all that the arms were not her husband's.

Charles was already at the table when she and two girls came into the dining room. It was half past eight, but Mary Louise had fussed with her ribbons forever, and Charlotte, the sleepy head, had to be removed bodily from her bed. Omega and Elizabeth Anne, early risers, had insisted upon going down earlier. Already finished with their breakfast, they now occupied themselves at the window, watching Front Street come alive. Sam had taken the three little boys out back to see the pond of gold fish. The three took their assigned places, Charlotte and Mary Louise now at an empty table.

Liza sat down opposite Charles, who had a copy of the last week's *Georgetown Times* in his hands. "Good morning, Liza," he said without lifting his eyes. Liza reached for the carafe to pour a cup of coffee. Instead came a tan stream of tea. "I'm sorry. Did you want coffee?"

"I'd like to try it the English way." She reached for the cream and dropped a lump of sugar in her cup. She stirred the cup slowly and raised it to her lips. "Did you sleep well?" she asked politely. "I didn't sleep much," she confided. "I don't seem to be able to make anyone happy, not even myself."

"Some philosophers say to seek happiness is the lowest aim. Today I'm an Epicurean. I shall eat, drink, and be merry. So what do you want for breakfast?" he finished glibly.

"I'm not very hungry really." A black waitress placed a plate of ham, eggs, and grits in front of her. "It looks like the egg comes first this morning." It was her attempt to be humorous. Charles did not respond but continued reading. Once more Liza broke the silence. "After this trip, I promise I won't trouble you again." Her hand shook and sloshed the tea in her saucer. She lifted her dark eyes to his.

His hand touched her free one. "I didn't sleep either. At least we have today." He looked down at the heavy gold wedding band. "I had no right," he whispered. "Forgive me. Then perhaps I can forgive myself."

"Forgive me, Charles," she said simply and busied herself with her food. "I shouldn't have come."

He did not answer. He folded his paper and walked toward the table where Charlotte and Mary Louise were finishing their breakfasts. Liza heard him say, "Girls, guess what a little genie whispered in my ear. 'God's in his heaven. All's right with the world.' "

Mid-morning they were assembled in front of Prince George. Enclosed by a brick wall matching its façade, its rounded bell tower ended in a simple cross. As they entered the church, the organist struck the beginning notes of Tallis, strange but curiously appealing to Liza's ear. She stole quietly into a nearby pew to give the music her full attention. She tried to follow the progression of notes, to determine what turns and directions they would take, to discover if they could speak to her. With half closed eyes she listened. She remembered Abe Lawrimore's fiddle, the hymns sung at Brown Hill and Shiloh, without accompaniment, raised by untrained voices, some following the key while others ran off erratically. She could hear Charles's reverent melodious voice unlocking the mysteries of the old church, born out of the Church of England, ravaged during the revolution, after which its name changed to Protestant Episcopal. Now the music changed, its trumpet notes swelling as the organist wandered into Purcell and Elgar and then Handel, names she had read in books but could not have identified. The music climbed, descended, and then soared to the beams of the old church. Liza thought her heart would burst. Never before had she heard such glory. Charles touched her on the shoulder. "May I stay here for awhile?" she whispered.

"Of course. Meet us at the Town Clock noonish. You'll hear the chimes."

Now she was alone with the music, which climbed gradually to a crashing climax and then trailed down to the tender strains of the finale. The quiet harmony still echoing, her mind ambled into the dark carvings of the altar rail and the triptych centered with a cross and flanked by a seven-branch candleholder. Above the cross the stained glass window featured the Christ, his hands outstretched. On each side stood two figures—angels or saints. Now the sun touching the windows transformed them into an exotic mass of reds, creams, purples, and greens. Over the Christ head, caught in his halo, a white dove hovered, ready to soar heavenward. She remembered Charles's words—since he is invisible we need something visible. Here he was, beckoning, but not smiling. Perhaps he knew that those who gazed at him did not smile either but sought the love and understanding that he had promised. Liza pulled the prayer cushion forward, crossed herself as she had seen Charles do, and prayed silently. She did not know how long she had been there, but the music had ceased. She rose slowly from the pew, and as she left the church, she turned to the altar and genuflected. Making her way slowly to Front Street, she heard the twelve bells of noon. They were already at the clock, seated on the benches nearby. Omega, seeing her, jumped up, taking the hand of a boy in blue overalls. Then she recognized Joey. "Oh, Liza! I found him at the sawmill. He works there. Didn't know him at first."

Liza opened her arms and drew him close. He smelled of sweat, sawdust, and turpentine. He was Papa, younger, with unkempt hair and unshaven face but the same blue eyes. A jagged scar marred his smooth high forehead. "Oh, Joey. I didn't know where you were. I tried to find you after Papa. Where did you get that scar?" Liza touched it with her fingertip.

"Some nigger axed me. Up in the county jail. Nearly bled to death. I'm alright now. Got me a job at the mill. I'm making out. Nough to eat and sleep on. Little extra on the side for Saturday night," he grinned shyly.

"Joey, do you hear anything about Mattie?"

"Nope. Reckon she gittin along. Mega here begged the boss man to let me off a hour. He didn't believe me and her brother and sister. Mega ain't fergit how to talk. Boss let me go." He smiled. Three of his front teeth were missing.

"Joey, we need to talk. I want to know about you."

"Ain't nothing to tell. Ain't done good as you and Mega. Won't never smart nohow. More like my Papa. Jist hope I don't end up at Parker like him." Liza thought she saw his eyes moisten. He added quickly, "Got to git back to work now. Don't need to git fired."

"Joey, when can I see you again?"

"Don't know, Liza. Maybe one of these days." He broke away suddenly and hurried down the street in the direction of the river.

Charles moved toward them. He said, "It's time to eat. Our boat leaves at one-thirty. I thought it best we not stay another day. The weather looks threatening with rain likely tomorrow. We've had a good morning, haven't we?" he addressed the group.

"Yes, sir." There was no exuberance in their voices.

"Don't worry," he said cheerfully. "No school tomorrow."

Liza was so busy with her own thoughts that she scarcely heard a word at lunch or even sensed the disappointment at the sudden change of plans. On board the boat once more, she sought a quiet seat.

The sun was warm but an icy fear clutched her. The image of a row of bricks that she had stood upright around her Mama's grave loomed. Once she had touched the first one, they fell domino fashion after the other. Mama had touched that first brick when she fell for George Marion and had unwittingly set off their lives — Papa's, Little Ida's, Mattie's, Omega's, Joey's, her own, even Jane's and her unborn child's. Charles's hand touched her shoulder. "Liza, my dear, tell me your thoughts."

"I was thinking that," her voice broke, "we are doomed to choose. Doomed to accept the responsibility of choice."

"You are an existentialist and don't even know what it means. It's a complicated and rather terrifying view of life. Existence precedes essence, they all say. Dostoyevsky didn't come right out with the assertion like the present day philosophers. But it's there. You must read *The Brothers Karamazov*."

"What does it mean? 'Existence precedes essence'," Liza questioned.

"It means that to think we have an essential self is just an illusion. Ourselves is just what we have become. We begin with nothing. We have the freedom to act, to make choices, but unfortunately, we have to live with them."

"Where does God fit in? This morning at Prince George, I thought for a moment there was something—invisible but very real. I don't know now. My poor little brother."

"Some existentialists deny God's existence. I believe there is a God, but we can never know his purpose. To know God we must take 'the leap of faith' as Kierkegaard put it. I believe in the goodness of what Christ taught. If our choices were based on his teachings, we would have an ordered universe, a more nearly peaceful self. But Liza, he was God; we are human."

Liza reached out and clasped his hand. "I have never heard anyone say the things you say. It's almost as if you are saying my thoughts, although they are more ordered. You put them in a way that makes sense." She raised her dark eyes to his. "If I live to be a hundred, I shall never forget. Something quite wonderful has come into my life, even for a short time. I might never have known that it existed. Thank you," she said simply.

Charles dropped her hand as Omega stood before them. Liza reached out to her. "Omega, I am so sad about Joey." She touched her blond curls. "You are going to be the Brown to make us proud, to make Mama proud. You are going to make the right choices. You just have to, for you and for me."

Charles drifted off to the others and the two sisters sat, neither speaking for a long time. Finally Omega said, "Liza, if you hadn't married Tom, you could have married Mr. Westbrook."

Liza didn't answer. Instead she tweaked her nose playfully. "You are so dear. I wonder if you inherited the second sight from Great Grandmother Eleanora."

The boat drew into Chapel Creek at five. Together they took the public road to Prince Frederick, a short walk by Clyde Williams's General Merchandise, the only place in Plantersville with a telephone. Andrew and Elizabeth Anne found their fathers there. A mere two-mile walk in opposite directions from Prince Frederick would bring the remaining travelers home. Liza took charge of the ones she would drop off on the way to Uncle Joe's. About to take leave, Liza turned to Charles and extended her hand. "Thank you for everything. You know I would like communion before I go back to Brown Hill. I don't suppose that's possible," she added. "I haven't even been baptized. I should have let myself be dunked at Parker Landing," she commented humorously. "Bad choice. Yes?" she quipped philosophically, as she turned homeward.

Back at Oak Grove a letter awaited her from Tom. Aunt Lizzie handed it to her as she came up the steps of the porch.

> *Dear Liza,*
> *I got a surprise for you. Your sister Mattie done come over from Britton's Neck to see you. Been awful smart cleaning up and cooking for me and Betsy. Told her it won't fitten for her to spend the night over here. Been going to Ma and Pa's at bedtime. Mattie goes to church. Got in the spirit last Sunday. She can outshout Ma. I don't think Ma like it too much. Take your time coming home. Want you to git your health back worse than anything.*
>
> > *Love,*
> > *Tom*

Liza read the letter written ten days ago a second time. So Mattie had moved in on her. She had probably heard somehow that she was with Uncle Joe. She dropped down into the rocker and stared at the old oaks which guarded the entrance to Oak Grove. Neither human nor tree had ever protected her. One battle after another. Never an ally. Always alone. This time maybe she wouldn't fight. Let the future take its course. To choose not to act. But that's choice, too, she thought.

"What Tom got to say for hisself?" Aunt Lizzie asked.

"Mattie is visiting him. Cooking, cleaning. Spending

the nights at Papa Gideon's."

"Well, Liza, ain't that nice. Ain't got to worry about him. Stay long as you want." How innocent Aunt Lizzie is, she thought mistakenly.

"You don't know my sister, Mattie. She's been a flirt as long as I can remember. I wouldn't trust her with any man, not even Tom. I can't throw her out either. She's my sister." Liza's voice broke. "I saw Joey today. He works at the mill. He's been in jail. Got beat up. Aunt Lizzie, Mama said I could manage. She left me to see after all of us. I don't know what to do—where to turn." Her eyes dropped to the letter and focused on its awkward scrawl.

Uncle Joe had come up the steps. "Let me see that letter." She handed it to him. He read it, folded it, and handed it back. "Now, you listen to me. You go back now you gonna fight with Tom and Mattie. Tom's a good boy. He kin take care of hisself. When he sees what she's after, let him do the throwing out. It won't take him long to catch on. Sides, way I heard it, she don't stay with any man long."

"But suppose something happens between them? Tom's conscience would kill him."

"Looka here, Liza. That's Tom's choice. You can't stop him. Best you can do is be there when he falls flat on his face. If he does, help him up. Lizzie knows what I mean," he commented meaningfully.

"What about me? Who's going to help me? What about my feelings?"

"You'll manage. You that kinda woman. You got more strength in them hundred pounds than anybody. You stood up to your Papa. By damn stood up to me." What he said next startled her out of would-be tears.

"I'm danged proud of you, Liza. I'm proud of Omega,

too. But specially you. You got the grit to you. You a credit to the Brown name." Uncle Joe took her hand and pulled her up. Come on and git some supper. You look give out. Hand feels mighty hot. Ain't coming down with something, is you?"

That night Liza really wanted to be alone. She had no appetite for small talk even with Omega, who must have sensed Liza's mood. "Liza, I want to read — finish *Jane Eyre*. I don't have to go to school tomorrow. The light might keep you awake. I'll sleep in the other room. All right?"

"You're not mad at me?"

"Course not. I just want to read. You didn't sleep much last night either. You got to get well so you can go back to your husband." She picked up her book and walked across the hall, closing the door gently behind her.

Somebody had told her that half the Southern women had hooked themselves on opium during the War Between the States. Now she craved anything that would blot out her thoughts and bring a dreamless slumber. Nothing in her life was right. Now she could understand why Papa killed himself. Just make a list, Liza, she told herself. Omega has a crush on Charles—jealous of her sister—disappointed the trip cut short—saw him holding her hand. Behind that closed door Omega wasn't reading. She was wrestling with how much she owed her sister and the guilt of wanting her out of the way. And Joey and Mattie. She hadn't really tried to provide for them. That guilt lay heavy with her. Now Mattie was striking back—threatening her home, the secure life she had with Tom. Uncle Joe was probably right. She would let Tom learn for himself as she would have to learn for herself if she kept on seeing Charles. If she postponed leaving what would happen? Every fiber of her woman's being wanted Charles Westbrook. Just imagining being locked in his arms, feeling his intimate caresses and listening to his voice made her whole body ache. There was no future with Charles—a clandestine affair that would end in guilt and despair. The truth was that she and Mattie were not so different. Jess's words came back to her. "Shake off Low Country mud." If only she could escape. She had nowhere to go. No training, no means of support. God, where are you? She had left him in a stained glass window in Prince George. His outstretched hands had not touched her; yet his blazoned image flashed under her burning eyelids. A drowsy warmth suffused her. Toward morning she woke with a dry mouth and aching throat. She felt her cheeks. They were hot to the touch. "Water," she mumbled. She made her way to the pitcher of water on the washstand. The room danced around her. Earthquake, she thought. Then she fell, her head striking the footboard of the heavy walnut bed.

Omega rushed across the hall. "Liza!" she screamed. She ran to the top of the stair. "Uncle Joe. Come quick. It's Liza."

Uncle Joe lifted her to the bed. "Smelling salts," he ordered. "Burning up with fever. Git some aspirin. Wet cloths. I'll go down to Clyde's store. Call Dr. Massey. She bad off sick."

A little later as the Model T, stretched to its top speed, passed Prince Frederick, he saw the Reverend, clippers in hand, trimming a wisteria determined to climb a dogwood. Uncle Joe did not pause, not even to lift a hand. I wonder what he's up to, Charles thought. Old bloke. Salt of the earth. I like him.

The wisteria, for a time disciplined to climb its own trellis, Charles turned to re-enter the rectory and begin his daily office. Now the Model T was returning, slowing down. "Reverend, Liza burning up with fever. Fainted—dead to the world on the floor. Been to call Dr. Massey. Be here soon as he kin git some youngun born. Reckon you could jist mention her name to the Almighty. I ain't much hand at praying. Preachers better at it, I reckon."

"Let me come with you. I know a bit about high fever. I have some medicine I brought from home in the event I became ill."

"Sure. 'Preciate it. Wanta git back soon as I kin."

As the two men entered the room, Omega and Aunt Lizzie had just finished changing Liza's gown. Omega, weeping silently, was taking the pins out of her sister's hair and was whispering, "Liza, you feel better?"

"Fever's down," Aunt Lizzie whispered. "I spec she got flu, pneumonia, typhoid, or malaria." She had run the gamut of diagnoses. Charles walked over to the bed and picked up her hand, testing the pulse in her wrist. Liza opened her eyes and managed a smile. Then she closed them and slipped off again into sleep, where she dreamed that the outstretched hands in the stained glass window had touched her hands.

In the days that followed, Oak Grove scarcely slept as they kept vigil around her bed. Pneumonia. Lobar. Mustard plasters were changed hourly to break the congestion. Liza's sides turned beet red like Little Ida's. At intervals Aunt Lizzie tried spooning a concoction of raw eggs laced with whiskey through Liza's parched lips. They decided not to get Tom. He would bring Mattie. Liza didn't need to be upset. On the fifth morning as Liza was about to go through her crisis as the doctor had predicted, Charles Westbrook took Uncle Joe aside. "I need to baptize her. Give her holy unction. She expressed the wish to be baptized so that she could take communion."

"Sure, Reverend. Whatever you say."

With Omega, Aunt Lizzie, and Uncle Joe standing

around the bed, Charles Westbrook sprinkled holy water on her dark hair, its long tresses lying limp on her white pillow. "I baptize you in the name of the Father, the Son, and the Holy Ghost," he intoned as he made the sign of the cross on her forehead. Liza slept on, unaware that her priest's voice dwindled down to a mere whisper and got lost on the word *Ghost*. From a small vial he dipped his finger in holy oil and then touched her brow and breast. "Her temperature's dropped. She'll need to be kept warm. The next few hours are crucial." He turned to go down the stairs. Omega ran after him.

"Mr. Westbrook, is Liza dying?"

"I don't think so. I think she will be all right." His gray green eyes glistened with tears.

"You love her, too, Mr. Westbrook?"

"I love her, too, Omega." He put his arm around her and they descended the stair together.

The next morning Liza opened her eyes and saw Aunt Lizzie asleep in the rocking chair. Her gray bun at the back of her neck had loosened, hairpins scattered on her bosom. "Aunt Lizzie, what time is it? Why aren't you in bed? What day is it?"

Aunt Lizzie was on her feet. "Liza, you gonna be all right. Doctor said so. It's Sunday. You been awful sick. Double pneumonia. We were worried out of our minds, Joe, Omega, the Reverend. We all been right here. You been sleeping. Out of your head most of the time. Liza, the Reverend baptized you yestiddy. I couldn't help crying. He even cried, I think. You don't remember nothing? He left you something." She pointed to a red leather pocket size book on the bedside table. *The Book of Common Prayer*.

"It's all so vague. Like a dream. I felt like I was in a hot oven. I thought Shiloh's hell had finally got me. Then I got cold. Dante's *Inferno*.   Ninth circle.   Solid ice."

"You hungry? Got some chicken broth ready to warm up."

"Sounds so good, Aunt Lizzie." She cradled her aunt's hand against her cheek. "Where's Omega?"

"Sleeping. She set up first part and I took over at two. We ain't left you a minute. We all took turns with Joe. When we weren't here, the Reverend was. I declare he was jist as upset like you was his kin. He's a real man of God, that Mr. Westbrook."

Liza couldn't help smiling. Dear Aunt Lizzie. So naïve. So good. She tumbled her thoughts around to find which one was the last lucid one. Opium. She had wished for sleep. To forget. Her wish had been granted—by chance, God, or the congregation of little germs. No time to worry about that now. "I'm going to get up, Aunt Lizzie."

"Oh, no, you ain't. Doctor said not to put your feet on the floor for five days."

Liza lay back and felt so good. She could never remember having been surrounded by such love, such care. Oak Grove had taken its daughter into its arms after all, protected her like those oak trees in the driveway. She liked something else too—gray-green eyes and a beautiful voice who had worried about her, had wept for her, had performed the official duty of the church not just as a priest but as a man who cared about her. She would indulge herself with the thought just awhile longer before she let it go. She didn't ask for Tom. She suspected he didn't know. She would think about that, too, later, she decided. Now the heated broth tasted good, warming her body as her heart was already warm. Silently she prayed, "Dear God, wherever you are and whoever you are, thank you for this moment. I shall carry it with me always. Sipping the last spoonful, she said, "Thank you. I think I'll sleep awhile. I love you, Aunt Lizzie. I love everybody." She turned her head on the pillow and dropped off to a peaceful nap.

The next few days were some of the happiest Liza could remember. She lay back, basking in the sunlight of their solicitude. Omega insisted upon staying out of school to help nurse her sister. They curled up in bed like old times and read together. Often their conversation veered to intimacies where little sister questioned big sister about the mysteries of womanhood and marriage. Such talk invariably ended with — "Omega, you get yourself ready for out there. It's not all fairy tales. You can have that knight in armor, maybe. But if he doesn't work out, if his shield tarnishes, if you are trained in a vocation, there are good things still in store for you. You can have pride in yourself, your work, your independence. Honey, you have that opportunity; don't let some romantic illusion rob you, Omega." Her voice was deadly serious. "It happened to Mama. You must know her life was a tragedy."

"And you, Liza?" Omega questioned. "Was it like that with you? Like what Mama did?"

"Not exactly. Tom Brown is nothing like Papa. He's good, honest, hardworking. He took us both out of the Neck."

"But did you love him? Like maybe Mama loved Papa?"

"Mega, there are different kinds of love—special love for special people. Like my love for you is different from my love for others."

"Did you love Tom?" Omega persisted. "Like you love Mr. Westbrook?" she asked cautiously. Her blue eyes focused on the book in her hand.

"I love Tom. I am not permitted to love Mr. Westbrook in the way you mean. You know that." The subject was closed.

Liza knew she had not answered the question to Omega's satisfaction. She didn't dare tell her the truth.

Another Sunday came, a drizzly Easter Sunday, and Omega and Uncle Joe dutifully took off to Prince Frederick. Liza, feeling much stronger, despite Aunt Lizzie's dire admonitions, had commenced walking around her bedroom, venturing into the clawfoot tub at the end of the hall, laving the salty sweat of feverish days. Standing in front of the full-length mirror, she surveyed her slight figure, which seemed out of proportion to her heavy hair. "Why not?" she said to herself. On impulse she grabbed the scissors on the dresser and snipped a coil. She liked what she saw. Strand after strand followed until her heavy locks were reduced to a crop of slightly wavy tresses even with her ears. A few more snips made wisps around her face that fell surprisingly natural into a side part. She gathered up the long ropes of hair and pondered their loss. The day she met Tom she had been sunning this very mane. She could imagine what Brown Hill would say. "Liza Brown, have you gone stark raving mad crazy?" Aunt Lizzie stood wide-eyed in the doorway, a glass of buttermilk in her hand. "What have you done to your hair?"

"Cut it. Like it? Who said women have to be burdened with all this weight? Uncle Joe cuts his hair. Why shouldn't I?"

"It ain't fitten. Everybody be laughing at you. Sometimes I think you Browns ain't had the sense God promised a billy goat."

"That's why you love us. Right?" She pivoted in front of her aunt. "You can't say it's not becoming. Besides, think how much cooler, how much easier it will be to wash." She laughed impishly, "Want me to barber you?"

"Liza Brown, you done beat all. One foot out of your

grave and you come up scrapping. You ain't never happy with how things is. I can't rightly think where you heading."

"Aunt Lizzie, I try to go on. To survive. It's the only way I know to get out of the rut—shake off Low Country mud."

"You gonna shake yourself out of a husband and home if you don't git back to Brown Hill. I heared what Joe said. Stay here. Let Tom be. Depend on him coming back. If a woman don't look out for her interests, the door gonna be slammed shut in her face. Perticularly if she ain't got nothing to depend on—learning, land, money."

"I know. A few more days and I'll be leaving. You have been so good to me. Mama couldn't have been better. I will do what I must. This time I have no other choice." She spoke without emotion. "Brown Hill, not Plantersville, not England, is where I will live. Where I will die. If cutting my hair gives me a little freedom, don't scold me."

Aunt Lizzie put the glass of buttermilk down on the washstand. "Liza, I ain't had no younguns. I wanted you since you was born. Your Ma wouldn't let us have you, but I love you. I ain't educated, but I ain't dumb. Ain't no future in Charles Westbrook. He would have to give up the church. The church won't allow him to marry a divorced woman. He would blame you some day. Tom Brown is your best chance."

"I know that, Aunt Lizzie." She reached out for her hand. "Thank you so much for caring. Thank you so much."

There was a loud knock at the door downstairs. "Wonder who that could be," Aunt Lizzie said. "I ain't expecting nobody 'till after church."

Liza slipped into a fresh cotton gown and had just lifted the glass of buttermilk to her lips when the door opened. Tom stood there, his light brown hair tousled, falling over his blue eyes, now startled to see Liza, shorn of her long hair. She was thinner than when he had seen her, her eyes even larger, darker, and somehow forbidding.

"Liza, Aunt Lizzie told me you been near death. Nobody told me. What happened to your hair? Did the sickness cause it?"

For a moment Liza thought she was going to fall. Steadying herself from one piece of furniture to another, she made her way to the bed and sat down. "I just cut it, Tom. It felt too heavy to manage. I have been ill. I'm all right now. Just a few more days to get my strength back and I'll be coming back to Brown Hill."

"Oh, Liza!" He dropped down into the rocker and studied the hooked rug, his hands interlocked. "I reckon you might not want to be coming back. Reckon I done messed things up. I reckon it ain't fitten to ask you back."

Liza waited. Finally she broke the silence. "I reckon you took my sister to our bed."

"How did you know, Liza?" His voice was between a sob and a question.

"I got your letter. I know Mattie. What are your plans, Tom?"

"I ain't got none. I talked to Pa. He told me to come tell you. Told me to let you decide."

"What did you do with Mattie?"

"I give her what we had in the bank 'cept what Uncle Joe give us. Every dime I made last year on the farm, floating logs, dipping turpentine. She didn't give me no sass. Just took the money. Left. It happened like this, Liza."

"Stop! I don't want the details."

"Liza, it won't in our bed. It wasn't like it was with us. Devil got into me. I been praying hard about it. God done turned a deaf ear. I can't sleep. That's when I told Pa. He said make it right with you first. Then make it right with God. I'll do what you say. Only don't keep me up in the air. Jist got to know one way or the other."

Liza reached out and took his hand. Her voice was kind. "Tom, stop beating yourself. You're not God, you know. You're just human, like the rest of us." Where had she heard these words before? "I'm not saying it doesn't hurt. Life hurts. We both need time. Maybe it's like cutting my hair. Maybe we have to cut out the past and start again," she said quietly.

Tom turned to her hopefully, his arms outstretched. "No, Tom," she said, gently pushing him off. "Not now. I have my own stone to roll up the hill." Like Sisyphus, she thought. "It keeps tumbling back down again. Maybe one day we can meet at the top of the hill."

His face was puzzled. "I don't rightly know what you mean, Liza. Only thing I know is I love you. I loved you when I first saw you drying your hair. I love you now without your hair. I'm willing to wait for you at Brown Hill. Ain't much of a hill there, but I'm more than glad to meet you there. Anytime you say."

Liza smiled sadly. Somebody else would have known the myth. At least she knew that such sharing was possible. Browning's words came to her. "A man's reach should exceed his grasp else what's a heaven for." She changed the subject abruptly. "Betsy. How is my little Betsy?"

"She misses you. Birdie does. Pa, Jess, even Ma. Me most of all. I best be going. I got a ride with Abe Lawrimore. He's moved over on this side of the river. Got him a car. I got to meet him back at the landing by one o'clock. He started toward the door. "Oh, I forgot. Uncle John sent you this." He handed her a slim leather book. "I'll sleep better tonight. Be counting the days 'till you come back." She heard his footsteps descend the stairs and looked at the title of the book. Dante's *Purgatorio*. She had read the *Inferno* before leaving Brown Hill. She rather suspected she wouldn't attempt the third volume. Paradise was just another fairy tale.

Liza picked up the Prayer Book that Charles had left her without an inscription. His visits had stopped abruptly since her recovery. She was grateful. The silk white ribbon marker lay on the General Confession. She had struck through words "provoking most justly thy wrath and indignation against us." The God she sought was not an angry God.

The days ahead gradually restored Liza's energy. Once downstairs she began taking long walks around the tilled fields of grain and corn, its green fronds thrusting themselves upward through the dark warm earth frequently bathed in April showers. What were the lines she had seen in the little magazine *Poetry* to which Uncle John subscribed? Written by a young woman not much older than Liza. "When I am dead and over me bright April, shakes out her rain drenched hair; though you should lean above me broken-hearted, I shall not care." She couldn't remember the poet's name but recalled Uncle John's wry remark. "Good metaphor but a little soppy." But the word picture had stayed with her, though she had to admit the sentiment cloyed. Now she looked down the furrowed rows of corn and wondered what she would be doing when its stalks tasseled. Unlike the poet she didn't wish for death, although life back at Brown Hill held little allure. She was in limbo—like the ones in Dante's Inferno—somewhere in between— neither living nor dying—neither caring nor not caring. The image of Tom rose. Seared for the first time in his life by guilt, he had made a piteous plea for forgiveness. His simple nature would find peace once she returned to his bed, absolved by her and

God. It was not so with her or with Charles either, she imagined. The forgiveness they sought would have to come from within. Anyway it wouldn't hurt to try communion. As a priest he was empowered to say those words after the confession. She quoted them aloud. "Have mercy upon you; pardon and deliver you from all sins." Besides, the words coming from his beautiful voice might even tempt her to believe in forgiveness. She wondered if it would be possible to have a private communion, an experience with Charles and God. The trouble was would she be able to focus on the priest, not Charles, the man with whomever, however briefly, she had shared something rare, though undefined.

That evening she wrote him a letter.

> *Dear Charles,*
>
> *When I return to Brown Hill, I can tell my mother-in-law that I have been properly baptized, omitting, of course, the method. At least I won't have to join the other converts at Mill Pond after a revival. Yes, I shall become a member of the Baptist Church and be the dutiful wife of a deacon; that is, if they will accept me without a public airing of my sins, among which would be confessing that the deepest feelings of my life are for a man not my husband.*
>
> *Would it be possible now to receive absolution and communion? I prefer it to be private; however, the decision is yours.*
>
> *Gratefully,*
> *Liza*

Next morning she gave Omega the letter. "Please give this to Mr. Westbrook. It is a request for communion before I leave," she said truthfully.

That afternoon Omega handed her a letter. "From Mr. Westbrook," Omega said without comment.

Dear Liza,

> *Although I receive good health reports from Omega, I have wanted to see you but dared not. I cannot express the depth of my anguish and the joy your letter brought. It would be spiritually beneficial for your first communion to be with another priest. In the absence of one available, let me schedule tentatively Saturday afternoon at two. If I hear nothing more, I shall expect you then.*
>
> > *Sincerely,*
> >
> > *Charles*

Liza folded the letter and tucked it in the envelope and put it in her hand satchel for safekeeping. At supper she turned to Uncle Joe. "It's time for me to go home. Tom needs me. These weeks I won't ever forget. You have all been so good to me. I wonder if you could drive me back to Brown Hill Sunday. I—-"

"But Liza," Omega interrupted, "what about communion?"

"Mr. Westbrook will give it to me Saturday. The church is the proper place now that I am well," she finished.

"Be glad to take you. I need to git an early start. That old tin lizzie apt to have another flat tire. I'm gonna miss you, Liza. You welcome to come back any time."

"Thank you so much. Mama would be pleased at how you looked after me." A sudden gush of tears sent her from the table. Omega followed Liza, who stood in the parlor in front of Nora Brown's portrait. Omega put her arms around her sister's waist and together they wept.

CHAPTER TWENTY FOUR

COMMUNION

THE MINUTES, DAYS, HOURS, before Saturday stretched out, Liza's moods swinging from anticipation to fear, from elation to despair. With all her heart she wanted the experience to be one that reached into the recesses of her anguish, where by some miracle or magic The Divine Presence would obliterate the spectral image of George Marion on Parker Landing and soften the harsh light of the world ahead at Brown Hill with Tom. To hope for such spiritual sustenance meant relinquishing the all too potent desire for Charles Westbrook, who, she knew, however transitory, offered her nourishment of mind and heart. Suppose in a weak moment the search for God got lost in gray-green eyes and a soft voice, where they both would witness earthquaking tremors, laying waste both of their lives. Suppose, even if she could avoid that devastation, that God's outstretched hands did not come close enough for her to grasp them. Then she would have to return to Brown Hill, her back still burdened and her heart left with a priest who was unable to provide either lasting love or lead her to the peace that she craved. Such thoughts interposed themselves between food and sleep. At moments she was tempted to cancel Saturday altogether. Better to entertain in the years ahead what might have happened than to know that nothing had— that she had left Prince Frederick as she had come, alone, guilt-ridden, lost.

Friday morning after she had said her good-byes to Oak Grove—the little cemetery where her grandparents slept, the old oak trees guarding the trellis now abloom with Paul Scarlet roses, and the verdant fields over which purple martens homed their way to their brown globular abodes—she found herself in the kitchen with Aunt Lizzie, busy at her wooden tray, kneading the day's bread. A light dusting of flour lay on her creased cheek where her hand perhaps had carelessly brushed away a straying wisp of iron gray hair escaping the tight bun on her neck. There was warmth in her voice and eyes as she motioned Liza to a nearby chair. She slapped her hands together, to get rid of the excess flour and spread a towel over the mass of inert dough in the tray.

"Set down, chile. I been waiting to talk to you. Sunday not far away. I can't hardly stand to see you go." Wiping her hands on a towel, she filled two coffee cups from the blue pot speckled in white on the stove.

"Sugar?"

"No, thank you. I have been having mine black recently. I'm getting a taste for it. I suppose you can get used to anything after awhile. Even life. There's not much cream and
sugar in my cup these days." She laughed as she sipped.

"That's what I wanta talk about. I'n worried to death
about you, Liza. I heared what Tom said. I heared what you
said. I was right at the door. Listened cause I care about you.
You done the right thing." She added a half trickle of cream.
"I know it was hard. I been there myself. Us women ain't got
much choice. Jist the same you done it like a lady. I wont no
lady. I said words. Cuss words. Screamed. It didn't do no
good. I felt shamed after. Let myself go." She reached out and
took Liza's hand and rubbed the gold wedding band. "I want
you to know if I'd had my say, things woulda been different for
your Mama. I told Joe pot couldn't call the kettle black. That's
men fer you. I jist want you to know that you ain't all to blame
for what happened to your Papa. Joe coulda done it different.
He coulda looked out for his sister and her husband, who
mighta mounted to something if he'd had a chance. I look at
Omega. She something else. Gonna be somebody. She oughta thank her lucky stars she got a sister like you."

Liza clasped her aunt's hand. "You are so dear. I'm so
glad you have Omega. She's headstrong. Talk to her the way
you're talking to me. She has a bright head on her shoulders.
Don't let her get carried away. You know what I mean."

Aunt Lizzie laughed. "Already carried away. Know
what she told me yestiddy when she was out picking English
peas? She said after she finished college, she was gonna marry
Mr. Westbrook. Said girls married men twice their age in
England—happens all the time in the books she read."

Liza did not answer. She drained her coffee down to

the brown dregs. In them she could see blond Omega in Charles Westbrook's arms, her tongue no stranger to the books and ideas they would share. She winced at the sharp pang of jealousy. However, she said calmly, "Omega is fanciful. It's not likely a school girl crush will end in matrimony."

"Liza, I know it's hard for you. Too bad the Reverend didn't come along before Tom. Ain't no guarantee in this world things work out to our liking. Maybe that's what heaven's about."

"I'm all mixed up about heaven and hell and God. It seems to me some of us have seen enough hell on earth. I just don't know about the great hereafter."

"Me neither, Liza. I jist do the best I kin. I'm willing to tell St. Peter I done it. I can't think we'll be turned out."

"Oh, Aunt Lizzie!" Her dark eyes welled with tears. Their hands entwined, they sat for a long while, neither speaking. There was no need for words.

On Saturday, Liza ate little. By noon she was ready to set out on her two-mile trek to Prince Frederick. She wore a plain black skirt and high-necked white blouse with a cluster of Paul Scarlet roses caught in her buttonhole. Omega watched her as she combed through her short black bob falling into curls over her dark eyes.

"Liza, may I go with you?"

"No." Liza's reply was quick and sharp. In a softer tone she said, "Omega, I really want to be alone. I have lots of thinking to do. You understand, honey. There are times when we just have to be by ourselves. Right?"

"Uh-huh." She picked up *Pride and Prejudice* and pretended to be engrossed.

Liza descended the stairs slowly and made her way out the door and down the lane. Uncle Joe, turning the corner sputtered to a stop and yelled out, "Want me to give you lift?"

"No, thanks. I want to walk." She hurried on down to the road and turned her face to her destination. As she walked along, she tried to divert her thoughts. Five thousand and two hundred and eighty feet in a mile. Roughly fifteen thousand to walk. A step is a foot. Fifteen thousand steps. One, two, three, four, five; one, two, three, four, five. The numbers became a rhythm of questions. Pentameter—five stressed syllables to a line. What is this about? One, two, three, four, five. How will this help me? One, two, three, four, five. Why do I do this? One, two, three, four, five. The answers, not syncopated, asked other questions. Counting didn't work. Meter belonged to the poet who had worked out even lines. She might as well submit to doubt and fear.

Charles was standing by the lych gate, his blond head crowning his black cassock figure, his eyes intent on the direction from which she would come. Why does he not come to meet me, she wondered. Is he afraid like me? Her heartbeat quickened even as her pace slowed. "This is it," she whispered.

His first words startled her. "Liza, do you know what this is?" He handed her a string of beads around a crucifix.

Liza's fingers perused them. There were one large bead, three small beads, large beads, many small beads. "No." Then she added. "Yes, I read about it. The rosary."

"It belonged to my grandfather, an old high churchman who revered every tradition of the church. But the use of beads in religion is older than Christianity. The word "bead" comes from the Saxon "bid" which means *to pray*. It became a method of prayer long before the Reformation. Protestants object to the Hail Marys. They are simply an affirmation of the faith in the incarnation, my old grandfather would retort to an objector."

As her fingers counted the beads, a curious calmness enveloped her. Her heart was now steady as she asked, "Are there specific prayers for each bead?"

"Oh, yes. I must confess sometime I make up my own. Interesting devotion. Just the rhythm sometimes takes me out of myself. The Rosary seems to appeal to both the scholarly and the simple."

"I suppose I am in the last category." She smiled as she handed them back to him. "It seems to me the less you know, the fewer questions."

"Liza, the questions are important. Those who accept blindly may be happier, but on the other hand, their faith has never been tested. Who knows what grade they will get before God?"

"Oh, Charles! How you put things." She raised her eyes to his.

He smiled as he said, "Liza, if you want me to hear your confession, you must address me as Father. My old grandfather would insist upon it always, in or out of confession." The lightness in his tone made them both chuckle.

"Yes, Father," she responded, as he led her into the church.

Two candles flickered on the white draped altar. On each side of the candles sat a small brass vase from which trailed fronds of blue wisteria interspersed with white dogwood. He whispered, "I arranged the blue wisteria to keep out the plat-eyes. You are safe here. Nothing evil can come in."

What was there about him? Not only his voice—the words, not even carefully thought out, but coming with such spontaneity and with such rightness and curiously double in meaning. Yes, she wanted to tell him everything. Even to admit that she loved him, and if it were a sin, she was not a bit sorry.

He seated her in a front pew and handed her a small book. "Liza, this is the order of Confession. I am going to sit behind you. We both need to keep our thoughts in order. I must admit that your eyes divert me." His admission was gentle, tender. "When you are ready, begin. Take as long as you need. If you decide against confession, it's all right."

Over and over she read the Preamble. Over and over she crossed herself. Over and over she prayed silently "The Lord's Prayer." Finally she said aloud, "Father, give me thy blessing."

"The Lord be with thy heart and lips...Confess in the name of the Father and the Son and the Holy Ghost."

Now she began the ritual: "I confess unto God Almighty, the Father, Son, and Holy Ghost, before the whole company of heaven, to you, Father, that I have sinned exceedingly in thought, word and deed...."

She was now ready to enumerate.

"Father, my problem is that for some of my sins, I am not truly sorry. If I had the same choices, I would perhaps repeat them. The Prayer Book says we are forgiven if we are truly penitent. What about us who are not?" She paused.

"Go on." His voice came from the back of the church. She marveled at his understanding. How his nearness might so easily disconcert her.

"At my mother's wake, I drove the women sitting up out of our house, because they were calling my mama sinful, because I was conceived out of wedlock. I slapped them—called them bitches. I suppose this is a sin; I lost control , but I'm not sorry."

It was good that he was not near, unsuccessful that he was in suppressing a giggle.

"My father hanged himself from a tree in Britton's Neck. I told him that he was not the father of my stepmother's first child. He got drunk; beat her and their unborn child to death. Sober, he ended it for himself. I am so sorry that I caused it. But I did it to save Omega from going back to the Neck to a cruel stepmother. I didn't mean it to end the way it did. I made the choice, and as the existentialists say, we have to live with it. I have. It's been hell. I don't think I would repeat it. I honestly don't know. Every time I look at my happy, bright little sister, I take heart. Does God understand my dilemma?" She paused.

"Go on."

"And I married Tom. I felt affection for him. I respected his honesty, his love. But the truth is he was my meal ticket out of the Neck. I have tried to be a good wife; but I can't seem to fit into the mold of what he expects, what Brown Hill expects. You see, Father, if I be somebody else, then I am losing me. I'm sorry I can't be the wife he should have had. But I can't give up me. Then I would be lost forever. Jesus was a man. Does he understand women like me?"

"Go on."

"I suppose my greatest sin is I don't know really how to love God. When you love somebody and feel that love returned, you feel close. I get glimpses of what I think God's love is. The day I was in Prince George Church, the music I had never heard." Her voice broke with emotion. "It was like I was part of it, floating up on those notes, up, up, up. And then the hands of Jesus, outstretched in stained glass window, even in his hour of death—caring about others—caring maybe about me."

Charles drew a handkerchief out of his cassock and wiped his eyes.

"And, Father, recently I have truly felt love, but it's not the love for either my husband or for God. Although I think sometime it is close to God, because, because," she was searching for her words and remembering, "it's like twin peaks who have waited eternities to be united into one big mountain and then it happens. I am not sorry, Father. The only sorrow is that I must stay on my own little peak and hope that someday—maybe what we call the Great Hereafter—there will be a mountain. I have other sins," she finished saying simply. "These are the ones most oppressive." She waited, her hand clasped tightly in her lap for his answer.

At last the Vicar of Christ spoke. His words, laden with emotion, came softly. "The God of the cross was human. Every single sin you have described, he experienced as a man. In anger he drove the moneychangers from the temple, as you drove those women from your home. He sacrificed himself that others might live and experienced the agony of choice on the cross as you have over the choice of your father and life of Omega. Liza, he didn't fit into any mold either. He ate with the Gentile dogs; he healed on the Sabbath. He forbade the stoning of an adulterous woman. Yes, he understood women. The Bible does not tell us that he loved a woman as a man. I cannot imagine that he didn't. But he knew his destiny. As you know yours. The choice was not easy for him to make either. Remember the words in the garden, 'Father, if it be thy will, let this cup pass.' And on the cross, Liza, he doubted for a moment the love of his Father. 'My God, my God, why hast thou forsaken me'? Liza, God has and will forgive you. My penance is that you must forgive yourself. But in spite of all that, there will be, like St. John of the Cross said, 'a dark night of the soul' for you."

Now his voice intoned the absolution: "May the

Almighty Lord grant thee absolution and remission of all thy sins, space for amendment of life and the Grace and Comfort of his Holy Spirit."

He now moved to the front of the church, picked up the folded chasuble, the robe of Christ, and began the Eucharist. Liza's hands trembled as she crossed them to receive the bread, and a tear may have slipped into the silver chalice as she sipped the wine. As she rose to return to her seat, there was lightness in her step that matched the lightness in her breast. She sat and watched him as he snuffed the candles. At the gate he met her, now shorn of his priestly vestments, not even wearing a clerical collar. "I want you to have this." He held out his grandfather's rosary. Before she could answer, he wrapped his arms around her, his hands caressing her short hair. "I like your hair. It's like the new Liza." Then he kissed her on the lips. His gray-green eyes met her dark ones. "I love another man's wife," he murmured hoarsely. She returned his kiss, knowing it was their last. They broke away at the same time; he, into the church; she, down the road that would take her back to Brown Hill and her husband, Tom.

CHAPTER TWENTY FIVE

BROWN HILL
REVISITED

ALONG WITH RICE, fresh greens from the garden are Southern fare from the humblest pine board in the kitchen to the beveled walnut banquet table in the dining room. They are in season year round—mustard in early spring and fall—collards planted in summer provide hardy heads throughout winter along with their neighbor turnips. A black iron dinner pot simmers a ham bone awaiting leafy masses which wilt rapidly, making room for additional loadings from dishpan or sink, doubled Saturdays for leftovers on Sunday. The preparation is long and tedious, from plucking tender stems from the dark earth to "picking" in the kitchen, the first process where each leaf is carefully scrutinized before washing. To Liza the preparation was not a chore but an hour when her thoughts could wander independent of her hands and eyes. Her little kitchen, unlike most others in Brown Hill, sported a sink with a red water pump attached, making the trip to the well obsolete except for flowers and laundry. The convenience had been Tom's gift to her upon her return to Brown Hill, now three years past. How proud he was, like a little boy, as he led her into the kitchen! She had been touched by his thoughtfulness, though the image of gray-green eyes floated between them. The disappointment at her lack of enthusiasm so transparent on his honest face elicited a whispered thank-you and a forced smile. Only later did she note the empty rack that had supported his rifle, a Winchester inherited from his grandfather who fell at Gettysburg. Tom had sold it to Abe Lawrimore. It was such tenders of affection that made surrender to his caresses easier even as she tried vainly to imagine other arms enclosing her, arms no longer extending the cup at Prince Frederick. At first it was a great comfort to know that an ocean separated them and that somewhere in the Lake Country he was gazing on the Twin Peaks and remembering. As the news of the Great War wafted its way even into the swamps and savannas of the Low Country, she saw him in uniform holding a canteen of water to the lips of a thirsty soldier in a trench in France. Oddly enough, she never saw him dead. He was as permanent as the rosary she had hidden between the table linens brought back from Oak Grove. On sleepless nights, listening to Tom's regular snores, she would draw it forth from the lavender scented folds of a napkin monogrammed EB, her fingers exploring the delicate contours of the silver crucifix and advancing bead by bead in silent meditation. To be truthful, too often the memory of Charles' hands upon it as he had said on that last day, "I want you to have this," stopped whatever prayers she might have addressed to God.

Yet she and Tom now had little Josh, who had come to them in that first year. If she had taken the story of "manna from heaven," literally, she would have called the lovable red-haired elf with Papa's blue eyes a gift from on high. For him she had crossed two rivers to descend once more into the Neck, her own inferno, though she was adamant that they should not land at Parker. Tom, eager to please, was willing to take him. Now Joshua Marion, her half brother, was their son, bearing the name Brown and calling Tom Papa. Even now he was perhaps trotting behind Tom in the cornfield, his childish six-year-old treble begging to let him plow. One day Tom had laughingly told him he'd have to eat more biscuits before he was ready for men's work. His sturdy little feet hustled into the kitchen, demanding, "Biscuits, Liza. Then Papa will let me plow."

She heard the front door open, and Josh stood before her. "Look what Papa Gideon made for me." He held a little wooden wagon replete with tongue and moveable wheels. The little finger of his left hand was missing, evidence of the abuse and neglect of the first three years of his life. She would never forget the day she had seen him first, a scrawny little boy in a torn dress, his little face begrimed with dirt, his unshorn red hair as long as a girl's. Abe Lawrimore had told them that Jane's people had taken him in and that while little Clara had found a good home with the Pauls, Josh was with people who had neither money nor values. It was Tom who had whispered that night, "Liza, let's go git him. He's your blood kin. Ain't nothing but right. We lost little George. Seems fitten for us to have your papa's youngun." Now he held out the little wagon, his sparkling blue eyes under his red mop so much like Papa, his untroubled face glowing with his new toy. She wondered how much he remembered. Only recently had the cries in the middle of the night ceased. "Liza, can I have a teacake?"

"May I," Liza corrected. "Yes, you may, Josh." Already he was opening the tin doors of the safe perforated in stars for air to circulate.

"Aw, Liza, why come I can't talk like Papa? When I'm growed up, I'm gonna say ain't, ain't, ain't, ain't a hundred times a day and Mr. McDonald won't be round to slap my hand with his old ruler." He giggled mischievously. "Can I help you, Liza?" His choice of *can* was deliberate, waiting for correction he was sure would come. Liza lifted into the pot a mound of greens glistening with water, tamping them down with a wooden spoon, another piece of Papa Gideon's craftsmanship. She drew him close; she spoke without levity.

"Josh, you may say ain't as many times as you want to, just so long as you know you have the choice of another word. I want my little brother to be able to talk like Papa Tom or Mr. McDonald." She picked up the little wagon and admired its art. "Josh, one day you might decide that you would like to build lots of little toys. You are so handy like Papa Gideon with a whittling knife. You might make enough to sell—make you rich—have a fine car like Uncle Joe's. So you need to be able to talk both ways. You know you learn very fast. You already know your multiplication tables. We need to read more, but you're a whiz with numbers. Better than I am. You're just like your real Papa—smart as a whip."

"Liza, how come Papa Tom's not my real papa?" Liza had been dreading this question. She turned to the wooden icebox, another gift from Tom, and poured out a glass of milk from a fruit jar. Josh perched on the stool, the milk in one hand and the teacake in the other. Liza chose her words carefully.

"Josh, your papa was my papa, too. You see, you're my little brother. The only difference is that we didn't have the same mama. Omega's your sister, too. But you're also Tom's and my little boy now."

"What happened to my real papa and mama?"

"There was a bad accident. They both died. Someday, when you are older, we'll talk about it more. All right?"

"When I get big enough to plow?"

"When you get big enough to plow."

"Liza, what does it mean war? Is it like what Mr. McDonald says? Growed up men shooting each other dead? What they want to do that for? I can't see why Jake shoots little birds. They too little to eat."

Liza smiled. George Marion may have given him his blue eyes but not a trigger finger. The boiling pot demanded another feeding and stirring. "Josh, I don't understand war either. Men make war. Maybe women do too, but not as much. Maybe there will one day be enough men like you to stop war. Wouldn't that be nice?"

"Papa Gideon said we in war. He said Papa Tom and Uncle Jess might have to go way across the ocean to fight the Germans. Who would make them go? They might get killed." He was whirling the little wheels on his cart, but his little voice was troubled.

Jess stood in the doorway. He crossed over to the stove where Liza was now settling the iron lid securely over the footed dinner pot of greens. There was sprightliness in his step that matched the animation in his voice. "Look at this, Liza." He handed her the *Georgetown Times*, almost a week old. She read

aloud the bold black headlines: WAR RESOLUTION
PASSED BY BOTH HOUSE AND SENATE. UNITED
STATES NOW AT WAR WITH THE GERMAN EMPIRE.
RESERVE FORCES TO BE CALLED. Liza scanned the article
quickly. She looked up to see Jess tickling Josh's ribs and bat-
tling with two little fists pummeling his sunburned face. The
laughter of man and child joined the peaceful gurgle of steam
issuing from the stove. Liza could not help noting the irony.
War and laughter had stolen side by side into her little kitchen.
Life had such wry humor.

"I've been expecting it. I have mixed feelings. England
needs our help," she added softly, "but I'm a pacifist at heart.
Only fifty in the House agree with me," she finished, quoting
the dissenting vote figure from the paper.

"They calling for volunteers. I done been by the post
office. Filled out my application. Reckon I qualify. I got good
teeth, good hearing, good eyesight. Ain't overweight. Tall
enough. They don't say nothing about brains. You reckon
they'll have me?"

"Oh, Jess! Do you really want to do this?" Now she
remembered that Sunday morning years ago. "Shake off Low
Country mud," he had said. How could this gentle country
boy who couldn't care less about hunting the swamps of the
Great Pee Dee, who even at thirty had not killed his first deer
and got his face smeared in the animal's blood — how could he
with such joy enlist to shoot men? Perplexity registered on her
creased brow.

"I know it sounds crazy. Reckon plenty of jobs without
shooting guns. I'm a pretty good cook. Reckon I could help
out in the hospitals. They ain't gonna put me behind no gun
when they see how bad I is. I never hit a bull's eye 'cept by
accident." He grinned and poked Josh's ribs again. "Give me

a chance to see the world. I ain't been nowhere. I wanta see someun diffrunt—meet diffrunt people. Find me a buddy we kin do things together. I ain't scared. Brown Hill scares me more than them Germans."

A smart yip and a scratching at the door took Josh to let in Betsy. In her mouth she held a letter. Uncle John had challenged his pupils, saying a dog could learn faster than some of his blockheads and forthwith proved his assertion by teaching Betsy to fetch. She was now the official postman. Josh eased the letter from her mouth. "Good dog! Smarter than me. Better be glad you just a dog. You don't have to go to school—do sums—speak proper—write funny letters all joined together. You don't have to go to war neither. Like Uncle Jess." Betsy, unaware of her superiority, wagged her tail and waited for the treat she knew was coming. Josh reached for a sliver of ham left from breakfast and reserved for her Highness in the scrap dish.

Liza was already deep into Omega's letter. "Omega's excited about the war, too, Jess. Talks about a Miss Daisy Nolan, a teacher from Georgetown enrolling in the Naval Reserve as Yeoman. Omega would like to do the same thing. Uncle Joe said over his dead body. Omega's going to college come fall. My little sister is something else. She's going to make waves wherever she is. I bet she'll be marching with Suffragettes in Columbia next year." Now she read silently. Omega's words: "I wonder what has happened to Mr. Westbrook. Funny he doesn't answer my letters I send to his home. I say my prayers for him every night."

"You and Omega two peas in a pod," Jess commented. " I ain't never seen sich women. You got minds of your own. I won't never fergit the first Sunday in church when you come in with all your hair cut off around your ears. I went specially to hear what Brown Hill would say. Ma even fergit to shout. Some of your nerve done rubbed off on me." He reached over and tousled Josh's red hair. "Your Uncle Jess gonna be a soldier man. Gonna bring you back a surprise from all the way across the ocean."

"Just don't get killed." Josh's voice trembled. "Not like Papa Gideon's papa. Not like my for real Papa," he added soberly.

Liza turned suddenly and wrapped her arms around Jess's neck and drew his cheek to hers. "Jess," she whispered, "I know somebody like you. You may not be two peas in a pod, but both of you are kind and sweet—no thoughts of killing. I don't know how much good my prayers will do. I can't pray as loud as Mama Minnie. You'll have them anyway. Both of you," she whispered inaudibly. She kissed his cheek, picked up the wooden bread tray and began measuring out the flour for the day's biscuits.

June yielded a bountiful crop. April and May had been generous with frequent slow rains that fell gently into the warm soil, bathing the roots of black bottom acres of grain, cotton, and vegetable. Little Josh had his own little farm parceled off a big field. Papa Gideon had fashioned a minia-ture plow that Tom adjusted to the traces of antique Old Blue, slow and rheumatoid, but still faithful. The little Eden, though irregularly sown by Josh's hand, had produced a conglomerate of popcorn, peanuts, and watermelons. After plowing time,

Josh had enclosed his little kingdom with leftover sweet gum poles used to stake the running butter beans in Liza's kitchen garden. In the emerald twilight of a late afternoon, Liza and Josh sat on the front porch with a pan of beans, zipping down with thumbnails to release the multicolored legumes. Ever so often Josh's productivity slacked as he stopped to count each separate bean. Liza had promised him a nickel for each hundred he shelled. She doubted seriously that pay-off would bankrupt her purse what with the counting and the eternal chatter as they waited for Tom to return. He had been gone three days now. He had boarded the train in Lambert for Columbia, where he would have his medical examination at Camp Jackson. Almost anytime they expected to hear the chug of Abe Lawrimore's ford bringing Tom back from the depot.

Jess was in training in Oklahoma but had made it home one weekend from Jackson. Brown Hill had gathered around its hero, the only one to volunteer from this part of the county. For the first time Jess Brown enjoyed the admiration and adulation of his hamlet and walked with a swagger that even he did not know he possessed. His Ma, who had been highly disapproving of his enlistment, seemed to feel a certain superiority as she confided to neighbors that the Lord would provide for her son in the service of his country. In the simple breast of his brother, Tom, however, no flames of patriotism burned, and the stern voice of duty remained silent. It was the summons from the draft board that transported him from his burgeoning fields of green to imagined horrors of life and death in the muddy trenches of a foreign field. On that last night before he left for Columbia, Tom had turned to Liza, his voice cracking. "If I got to go, I got to go. Don't see no reason in it. I don't even know what they're fighting about. Grandpa knew what the other war was about. This one ain't none of my business. I don't see why this country made it our business. I don't mind dying so much. The Lord will take care of that. I'd jist like for it to be at home, with you standing by close." Liza had drawn his head to her breast and caressed his hair. She searched for reassuring words. "Tom, you have faith. Try not to be afraid."

"Here they come." Josh's pan clattered to the floor, his beans scattering like pebbles. Liza knew by his gait the bad news. Josh did, too. He ran to Tom and clasped him around the knees. Tom swung him up high and mounted the steps. Liza rose and waited. Placing Josh on the floor, he took her in his arms. His voice was making a desperate effort to be steady. "Liza, you got a husband healthy as a horse. That's what comes from such good rations," he quipped.

"When?" she asked.

"Next Friday. I tried to get deferred for farm. It mighta worked if we'd had more younguns." Too late he knew his words had stung. He added hastily, "It ain't your fault no more'n mine. Maybe God is punishing me." So that red devil guilt still ate him. Mattie's name had not been mentioned since Liza's return. The penance that Charles had exacted of her —-"forgive yourself"—-Tom, too, had not been able to handle. A rush of tenderness overwhelmed her. She cradled his face in her hands. "Tom," she spoke with authority, "God's not like that. He's not holding a whip. He loves you. I love you, too, Tom." It was the first time she had said those words. She kissed him slowly, deeply and felt the warm response of his body. Little Josh, who had been rescuing his pan of beans, broke the moment.

"Look, Papa. I shelled fifty beans. Liza got to give me two and half cents. How she going to cut a penny?"

"Well, bud, I don't hardly know. Maybe she'll let you have a half on credit. Anyhow, you the man of the house now. Papa's got to go see about them mean old Germans. You gotta run things and look after Liza 'till I git back."

"Yes, sir." There was no joy in his little face. Tom reached into his pocket and drew out a sack of marbles, jostling around in their yellow mesh enclosure. " I reckon we better get in a couple of games 'fore Friday. I used to be able to shoot pretty straight. Reckon that's what Uncle Sam 'spects me to do, eh?"

CHAPTER TWENTY SIX

THE DARK COLORS
OF COURAGE

IN THE TWILIGHT of the late next June, Liza sat, like her mother before her, with one foot rocking the cradle, but reading by lamplight the closing acts of Shakespeare's *Julius Caesar*. Little Nora had come in April, an almost effortless birth. When Liza heard her lusty cry, she wondered if it were a protest against having to leave her snug little world to be thrust into one often loveless and despairing. Was this little mite of pink flesh wailing for her father dug somewhere in the trenches of a country where he neither spoke its tongue nor

understood its struggle? Gentle Tom's empire extended no farther than his plow, his wife, and his home. Each letter ached
with nostalgia and underlined the fear that he might never
come home. He had written, "Liza, I ain't no hero. I don't
wanta kill nobody. Not even Germans. I jist wanta live—I
wanta see that little baby. Reckon God'll bring me home to see
it? Reckon he still wants to punish me and let me get killed?"
Liza had replied hastily, "No, Tom. God's not like that. He
didn't promise an easy life. He didn't have one either. The
cross, remember? Try to think about His love, my love, Josh's
and our little baby's, even Betsy's. I can't tell you why you have
to be where you are. I do know it hasn't anything to do with
a wrathful God." As she wrote, she had the oddest feeling that
Charles was dictating her words. What kind of letter would
the priest be writing and to whom? Had he found someone
who could share his thoughts, who was free to love the whole
of him? Useless and painful, she told herself, to dwell on such.
So she turned her attention to what was close by, Josh, and
now Nora, and even Betsy, her charges far from the threat of
guns and dying men.

Jess had written often. As he had predicted, he had
been assigned to a medical unit where he saw "plenty of them
poor fellows, some dying, some dead, some living with sawed
off legs. Worse than them is the shell-shocked. You ain't never
seen sich torment, Liza. Me and my buddy, Samson, believe it
or not a nigger from New York, course I don't call him nigger—almost white as me—good heart—make you laugh even
when you wanta cry. He calls me Dixie Brother—says his
mammy and mine probly related way back. Wonder what Ma
would say 'bout that? We gonna git leave pretty soon. Me and
Samson gonna have a look around Paris. War makes funny
things happen. I never thought my best friend would be a nig-

ger. Learnt a good deal. One thing color ain't got nothing to do with how you feel about a person. You knowed that before I did." Liza smiled. So old Jess had turned philosophical. She wondered if after the war, he would bring his buddy to Brown Hill. That would cause more of a stir than her cut hair or her choice of a half-breed for best friend.

Now that Tom was gone, she had seen more of Birdie, a mother of two little boys, wild little Indians, Liza had told her—free spirits like their Mama, one with a pet pig, Archie, and the other with Quack-a-wack, a duck who lived in the nearby pond growing heftier by the day with cracked corn fed by tireless little hands. "Want them to love everything, Liza. Not jist people. Great Spirit of my people love the wind, trees, moon, stars, sun, rain, and all the little live things creeping around. Best way to git along with yourself. Can't hate yourself when you love everything around you."

One day Liza played the devil's advocate and asked, "What about Minnie Brown? She calls you a half-breed, an infidel. 'Never darkens the door of the church,' she says. Your boys should love her?"

Her answer was quick, spontaneous. "Miss Minnie, she all right. She jist ain't learned that some churches ain't got no walls. She one of us. Jist a little behind, that's all." Liza had burst out laughing. Birdie was cool wind fanning musty dogma. How she wished she could share her with Charles. He would find the same delight in her natural goodness and wisdom expressed with such candor.

"Zack kinda feels left out," Birdie confessed one day. "Both Tom and Jess gone. Zach got turned down cause he not tall enough. I told him this country don't know yet you don't measure a man by inches. A midget kin be braver than a six footer. Inches inside what counts." President Wilson might benefit from Birdie's counsel, Liza thought. Poor man! What with the army in France and suffragettes picketing the White House and attempting to burn him in effigy, he could use a down-to-earth advisor like Birdie. She might even provoke a laugh.

But war was no laughing matter. Recently she had discussed the subject with Uncle John. Wit and wisdom sprinkled his crusty comments. "Nothing new, Liza. The haves and have-nots at it again. It's all about power. When gimmes turn takers, that's war. Read *Julius Caesar*. That old fellow from Stratford said it all. Power never satisfies. The world would be better off to follow a cranky old fool like me. I covet no man's land nor his wife. My best friends are right here on these shelves. They don't care a whit for power and glory." His bright eyes twinkled in his wizened face. "Odd thing is, they are power." Birdie and Uncle John, equal pedagogues, one with nature as her specialty, the other with the minds before him. Liza felt blessed.

"There is a tide in the affairs of men," she read from the play. This little girl lying so peacefully beside her had made waves already. Liza had not been able to imagine the surge of emotion when she first held her. From her and Tom had come a new being, who would grow, learn, laugh, think, hurt. She felt so close to that other Nora, who had slaved, begged, compromised for her little ones. She had tried to shield them as best she could, giving them the armor of literacy as she painstakingly taught them by firelight. Even so, she had not been able to protect them. Poor Mattie! From one man to another—searching, never finding. Joey. Who knew where he was. A convict at sixteen. At least she and Omega had fared better. Liza had managed as Mama had predicted; only Mama had not anticipated the cost. It may be that little Ida was the lucky one. Liza shook off that dismal thought as a tiny fist curled her finger. "Nora," she whispered. "I'll manage."

She had written Tom the good news.

Dear Tom,

We have a little baby daughter whom I have named Marian Eleanor Brown. We'll call her the middle name, Nora, short for my mama. The first name is for Papa, with the different spelling for a girl. She is a beauty. She looks like you when you were a baby, Mama Minnie says. She has your blue eyes. I can't tell the color of the hair yet; she's quite bald. I hope that doesn't last. We don't need a bald-headed daughter. Your parents think she is an angel and a little afraid she might sprout wings and fly away. I wish she could for just a moment—to let you see her. I cannot believe how much this little girl means to me. Remember our first quarrel when I wished not to have a baby? If we have done nothing else worthwhile, little Nora is our gift to each other. She smiles in her sleep. I think she is dreaming of her father. I want her to call you that—a different name for a different time.

Your wife,
Liza

Nora's head turned slightly, her little lips moving as though she were feeding. Such perfect little hands raised with palms up. It was good that she had not inherited Tom's fat fingers. Since her arrival, the image of Charles had become less distinct. She and Tom had finally joined each other—on the hill she had mentioned to Tom on that Sunday morning of that terrible confessional. The magnet was a blue-eyed baby. She would write Tom again. She wondered if he had sensed the division that this little girl had now closed. It was something she must share with him. It would give him hope and make him less fearful. She hoped that there would be a letter from Tom tomorrow, full of Nora. News of her must have reached him weeks ago. Tomorrow she would write again. Her eyes felt heavy. I'm glad Josh is with Birdie tonight, she thought. It's a good time to snooze. The cradle stood idle and her book slid softly to the floor.

Betsy's yip startled her. Automatically her foot resumed its motion. Nora lay in her bed—awake—alert—silent. "Liza." It was Papa Gideon's voice. Goodness! What time is it! The door so often left open had been closed for the night.

"Yes, Papa Gideon." She slid the wood bar. Both Papa Gideon and Mama Minnie stood before her. One look told her the news. "Is it Jess or Tom?" Papa Gideon held out a yellow slip of paper. Somewhere between dreamland and reality the paper came alive. "Liza, we done read it. Came by telegraph to Georgetown. They sent it down tonight. I thought it was for me." Papa Gideon finished.

Liza moved toward the lamplight. "The War Department regrets to inform you that Private Thomas Arthur Brown died in action at Belleau Woods, June 11. We offer sincere condolences." Liza looked into Nora's blue eyes, surveying the ones around her. The silence hung thick, cold, immutable on a summer night. A strange impulse propelled Liza to the chest of drawers where she drew out the rosary from the linen cloths. Summoning both of them, she knelt at Nora's cradle. The lamplight gleamed upon the crucifix. Liza handed the left strand of beads to Papa Gideon; the right hand to Mama Minnie. Crossing herself, she whispered, "In the name of the Father, the Son, and the Holy Ghost." She began the Lord's Prayer. Now a trinity of chants surrounded the cradle. Liza led them through the Twenty-Third Psalm. As they continued kneeling, Liza slipped her arm around Mama

Minnie's neck and brought her face to hers, where their tears mingled, sealing the treaty ratified by death.

Papa Gideon spoke. "Liza, I kinda knowed it. Felt it in my bones when I seen him last." He blew his nose. "Wish I could put him in one of my coffins. Reckon it can't be. It's hard not to know where his resting place is. Anyhow, he ain't got to be afraid no more. He's home for good. Me and Minnie here gonna see after you and this little girl of his'n. You all we got left of Tom. We come to spend the night. Course if you want to be alone, it's all right. Sometime it's better to be by yourself when you got a lot of hard thinking to do. You say."

"I want you to stay. But let's try to remember Tom alive." She held the crucifix up. "We all think He is alive, don't we?" She finished. Now it was the time for sobs which shook the room. Only little Nora, wide-eyed in her little bed, remained silent.

Long after the communion around the kitchen table had ended and each of them had responded to Papa Gideon's words, "We bettah git some rest. Tomorrow people be coming in," the three lay in their beds staring dry-eyed in the darkness. Each heard the clock on the mantel strike the hour; each saw a face with blue eyes and thick brown hair swathed in airy wraiths spun by private looms. The mother saw a little boy toddling toward her outstretched hands, taking his first steps; the father, a bruised finger when the small hammer missed the nail; the wife, a boat on the Little Pee Dee and a voice, "Why, Liza, it ain't fitten to take a lady on the river." Each asked the ageless questions that had no answers; yet they had to be asked—over and over—as necessary as a tongue seeking the sore place and knowing it would hurt. "Why?" For Minnie Brown whose sturdy faith had withstood every gale—loss of so many stillborn babies—awareness that another woman, though long dead, lay between her and Gideon— tonight her faith was less than a slender broom straw, battered, limp and useless. Never before had she asked such questions; never before would she have dared. Blasphemy. A streak of lightning would strike her dead. Tonight she wasn't afraid of the bolt. In fact, she just as soon it came as not. So she, too, asked. "Why?" Where were you, God? I thought it was you who got me my baby. It won't you at all, was it? Just some of my crazy thinking. You don't give something and take it back. Decent people don't do that. Specially not God. Maybe God was dead. Like Tom. Liza had held in her hands a dead Jesus on the cross. A shudder crept up her toes through her body. She couldn't stop shaking. What was she to do tomorrow and the next day with a dead son and a dead God on her hands? Gideon's arms stole around her and drew her close. "Minnie, my dear. I know. I know." His calloused carpenter hands stroked her back gently. Finally she said, "No, Gideon. You don't know. Something turble happen to me. I done lost Tom. I done lost God. I ain't gonna darken no church door agin. I'm gonna jine up with that half-breed Birdie. She got more sense than me."

"You got me, Minnie. His words were soft, gentle, soothing. No chastisement. No disputing. He went on: "I can't go it by myself. You can't neither. We in it together."

Slowly her body relaxed into the warm tenderness of his embrace that enclosed her and her alone. "Gideon, my husband," was all she said.

In the room across the hall, Liza touched Nora's cheek. She had brought her from her bassinet to share her bed—to help her sort out her thoughts—to explore the ground on which she stood and find some firm corner stable enough for emotional conflicts and practical affairs. Mama's voice spoke from the darkness. "You'll manage." The farms now would be hers—both insured and paid for now that Tom was gone. Half of Uncle Joe's money still lay in the bank and had been drawing interest. No doubt there would be compensation for Tom's death. Still there were Josh and Nora, her sole responsibilities—to see them schooled—boy and girl, Nora as much as Josh. This little girl would have a different life. Liza had managed for Omega. She could do no less for her child. And herself. Uncle John had said he would help her to study. If she could pass the tests, she could get a teacher's license. The farms she would put under the direction of Zack and Birdie. Tobacco was the rising crop—brought more money than corn and cotton. The war had increased the demand for cigarettes. If she got in on the ground floor, she might double the farm income. Of course, she could go back to Oak Grove. Now that Omega was off at school, Uncle Joe and Aunt Lizzie would be glad to have her. No. That would not be fair to Papa Gideon and Mama Minnie. She wouldn't feel right to leave them. There had been something strange in Mama Minnie's eyes tonight. Not one time had she mentioned God. Her lips had been oddly silent when the three had knelt around Nora's cradle, but the two of them had made their peace now. Liza listened to the even soft breath of Nora and knew that Minnie Brown had felt more keenly than wife or father, a blow that had sent her reeling, threatening her special place which she had believed she shared with the Almighty. Tonight kinship had been born between them, springing not from cherished beliefs but from acceptance of a world unknowable, incomprehensible. Neither would verbalize the reason for the change, Liza thought; each would, however, find it was good. Her life now belonged to Brown Hill. Tom's death had rooted her in its soil and had given his mother a daughter at last. Looking down at Nora cuddled on her breast, she, too, shivered. The darkness swirled with images. Little Ida's diminutive frame in her Easter dress—Mama planting forget-me-nots around the mound of dark earth—Mama Minnie denied that humble privilege to mark her son's grave with a cedar or arborvitae—green the year round. No greater sorrow for a woman, Liza thought. Last week she had been looking at Uncle John's latest purchase, a collection of photographs of Michaelangelo's works. *La Pieta* had arrested her. A mother with a dead son in her arms, a body too large and too heavy to carry, had looked down on her child in mute resignation. The artist must have had something of a womanly instinct to create such heart-rending magnificence in marble. Liza's fingers had touched the soft folds of her headdress as she contemplated the despair of losing Nora. Here she was safe in the curve of her arm. She would never know Tom, whom she would call Father, a fitting formal address, since the two had never met.

Liza wandered back to the day she had met Tom. Death had been their introduction. He had been so careful to spare her the news of Mama and had loved her from that day, he had told her. She had been grateful and had come close to returning his affection, but she realized those were the times when she reached for him, not as a wife or lover, but as a mother. She relived that Sunday morning at Oak Grove and his open confession and those nights riddled with the horror of leaving her and going to war—these were moments when her husband was her little boy for whom she wanted to be the anodyne for his guilt and fears. It was the best she could give then. Maybe she and Papa Gideon had more in common than either would acknowledge—the shadow of someone else between husband and wife. Nora had brought her closer to Tom, but then Tom was away in France dug into a trench. Now he lay somewhere in an unmarked grave, consigned to anonymity except for those in Brown Hill who had known his sweet, unselfish nature. Now she would never know with his gift of Nora to her, whether or not she could have returned the depth of the love he had for her. As death had provided introduction, it had also brought closure. At least she could teach his daughter to love him—not to mold him as a dying hero for his country but as a human being ennobled by a simple, loving heart. The words from *Julius Caesar* came to her now: "The elements so mixed in him that nature might stand up and say to all the world 'This was a man.'"

"Listen, Nora," Liza said softly, "I am proud Tom is your father. We couldn't have picked a better man."

CHAPTER TWENTY SEVEN

WIDOWHOOD

"FOR EVERYTHING THERE IS A SEASON, and a time for ever purpose under heaven: A time to be born, and a time to die; a time to plant, a time to pluck up what is planted." Liza read these words from Ecclesiastes and contemplated their meaning. Was there a predetermined pattern of life which man could neither understand nor change? Everything happens at a fixed time says the bold biblical philosopher. Lately she had turned to the Bible and discovered to her surprise such kinship with the teacher or preacher of this ancient text. Since

Tom's death she had done soul-searching to find what she believed and how to adjust that belief to her life. She found herself in accord with this Old Testament sage. God is the inscrutable originator of the world, but his ways remain inscrutable to his creation. She questioned whether he was the determiner of man's fate and explored once more the question of choice. How strange that Shiloh's Calvinism seemed a bit more reasonable. Ecclesiastes pointed out clearly that character and accomplishments do not change destiny. She now saw the real danger in banking on a God who supplied every need and gave protection from every adversity. Look what that kind of thinking had done to Mama Minnie. Not once had she entered the church since her son's death; not once had she given an explanation. Papa Gideon had remained silent on the subject. Liza suspected, however, that Mama Minnie's faith had been buried in a grave in France. No one questioned her. No one dared. One afternoon in late November she had said to Liza, "Reckon you thought I was half-cracked them days showing myself in meeting. I ain't got nothing to shout about now." "You have another son," Liza replied. " The Armistice was signed on November eleventh. Jess should be home by Christmas."

"Humph," she retorted. The unspoken words might have been, "Why couldn't it have been Jess, not Tom, my first-born." Liza felt a certain gratitude to fate or whatever, that she would have the one child. At least there would be no favoritism. How terrible for Jess to return to learn of his brother's death and to see on his mother's face the resentment that it was he, not her beloved Tom, who had been spared. Liza almost wished he wouldn't come home—that he would shake off Low Country mud for good and find companionship with his buddy, Samson, too far away to be hurt by comparisons Brown

Hill would silently make between the good dead son and the live one who "never was much account." Impossible though she knew it was to make the homecoming the welcome Jess deserved, she still tried to lay stepping-stones to make the path easier.

"Mama Minnie, I loved Tom. He was my husband, the father of my child. He was a good man. He didn't deserve to die. But Jess doesn't deserve to feel like you wish it had been the other way around. He's your son, too. I've learned to love Jess. He has the same sweetness as his brother. The only thing is—he just hasn't found himself. War makes people grow up. Give him a chance at least. He can't be Tom. Let him be Jess. Tom would like that."

Papa Gideon, standing in the doorway of the kitchen, had heard her speech. He walked over to the stove to his wife, stirring a pot of grits with one of his long-handled wooden spoons. He reached an arm around her waist; the other hand closed upon her hand on the spoon and together they stirred the bubbling white mass. It was a tender gesture, the first overt sign of affection Liza had ever witnessed between them. She was touched. It was so simple and yet so intimate that she almost felt an intruder. Papa Gideon spoke. "Mama, reckon you oughta add a bit more water to these here grits? They look kinda thick to me. Me and Jess like 'em thin, remember? Put red-eye gravy on 'em and eat 'em like soup, specially if a egg sunny side up on top. Be sure to save that last year's ham for Jess. Ones this year ain't had time to cure." Now he turned to Liza. "How about staying for supper? We got plenty. Me and Minnie kinda like company. Specially you. I can go fetch Josh and little Nora."

"Not tonight, Papa Gideon. I'm trying hard to get ready for the test for my teacher's license. I can't see why I have to know algebra and geometry to teach little ones, but Uncle John says they are on the test. I bet he's pulling my leg. He keeps on like a parrot. 'Knowledge is power.'"

"John ain't got the sense God promised a brass monkey." It was Mama Minnie sounding almost like her old self. "He ain't never seen much 'cept the writin' in those dusty old books. He ain't hurt much. Ain't got no younguns. He oughta be ashamed of hisself tolling you off to learn younguns when you got younguns at home. It ain't fitten."

Her last words brought back Parker Landing and a young man in a boat taking his love around the bend of the river. There was a catch in her throat as Liza answered, "Mama Minnie, I need to earn money. More than that, I need to get out—feel useful. I have the best nanny in the world for Nora. Josh will be in school. I wouldn't leave her if you couldn't keep her. I don't know what I'd do without you."

A smile played around the corners of Mama Minnie's mouth. "That little gal ain't no trouble. Jist like her daddy. Not fussy like Jess wuz. Hongry all the time. Don't fret, Gideon. I done saved up the ham. I reckon Jess gonna be glad to git home rations. I reckon the army don't feed 'em chicken pilau."

Liza reached for her coat. "Liza," Papa Gideon said, "send Josh around after supper. Me and him got a little business going on in the shop. We wanta be done by Christmas. Josh is startin to smile agin. It's been real hard on the boy. Real hard."

"Yes, Papa Gideon," Liza said softly as she opened the door letting in the brisk nip of an early winter—as chilling as the cold curling around Minnie Brown's heart.

Liza watched an evening star wink at the moon, now veiling herself modestly with floating wisps of diaphanous clouds. The light in the window and the welcome yip of Betsy drew her back from any such poetic reflection of a moonlit night.

Liza stood on the kitchen stool and fastened the five-pointed star to the top of the cedar tree. Nora had pulled herself up to a chair and was engaged in rattling her latest toy from Papa Gideon, a tiny gourd painted blue and containing dry corn. Josh was busy hanging the last of the stuffed figures crafted by Liza's hands—the magi in velvet—angels in chiffon—donkeys and sheep in paisley and gingham. Red hearts edged in white lace ran diagonally from the star, crossed in the center and ended on the last branch. Each bore an embroidered name: **Tom, Josh, Nora, Liza, Omega, Aunt Lizzie, Uncle Joe, Mama Minnie, Papa Gideon, Betsy.** Attached to Jess's heart was a green bar with WELCOME HOME. Climbing down from her perch, Liza surveyed their handiwork. "Liza, this is the most beautifulest tree we ever had." She was glad to hear the animation in Josh's voice. "I wish Papa Tom could see it," he said wistfully. Liza drew his red head close. "Maybe he does, Josh. Who knows? There's something magic about Christmas."

"Well, I wish the good fairy would bring him back. I druther have him than the dime the tooth fairy left in place of my tooth." He lifted his freckled face to display the gap in his front teeth. "Liza, you believe in magic?"

Just then Nora wobbled three steps toward them. Liza caught her up in her arms. "Of course, I believe in magic. Nora's walking! First step, Josh. Absolutely unheard of in an eight month old!" Liza cuddled the baby head under her chin and twirled a little tendril of a blond curl. "Nora's a big girl now. She's strong like her father; smart like her brother, Josh." The excitement of Nora's first steps had diverted attention from the door, which had opened ever so softly. Jess, still in army uniform, stood before them. "And brave like her Uncle Jess," Liza gasped.

"Uncle Jess," Josh screamed. "Magic, Liza! Magic! Just like you said. Maybe Papa Tom will come next."

Jess swung the little boy high in the air. "Good Lord, Josh. You growed up like a weed. High as a bean pole." He set Josh down and moved toward Liza, who placed Nora in his arms. "Nora, this is Uncle Jess. Give him a kiss." Her baby mouth brushed his cheek.

"Uncle Jess, you didn't bring Papa Tom, did you?"

Jess staggered slightly and eased himself in a nearby chair. His blue eyes, set back deep in their sockets, glistened with tears. "Sorry it won't me, Josh. I woulda give anything for it to be diffrunt." His voice broke. Nora pulled at the medal on his uniform.

"Why, Jess. Medal of Honor. Look, Josh," Liza said. Jess unpinned the silver bar and handed it to Josh. "Yours, fella. I done told you I'd bring you a surprise."

"Jiminy Crickets. I bet I'm just about the only boy in the whole world got one of these. What did you do, Uncle Jess?"

"Nothing much. Jist rescued a couple fellas. No big deal. Anybody'd do it."

Josh walked over to the tree and detached the red heart and handed it to Jess. Nora's hands closed around the ornament. Immediately it was in her mouth. "Nora, no. It goes back on the tree," Liza admonished. "Welcome Home, Jess." She encased his hand in her own. "You must be hungry."

"No, Liza. Ma made me a pot of grits with ham and gravy and eggs. It beats army chow to pieces. I never thought Brown Hill could look so good. I never thought a bunch of stuff. Reckon I bettah git on back. I'm gonna lend a hand to Pa in the shop. I had to come see you and the younguns." His eyes filled again. "Awful hard, Liza. Awful hard."

Long after the door had closed behind Jess, Josh examined the medal. "Liza, why come Papa Tom didn't get one of these? Wasn't he brave, too?"

"Of course, he was. Every bit as brave. Only nobody saw him. Lots of people do wonderful things and don't get medals you can see. Their medals are invisible. You know like knights can be. Like magic, Josh."

The kitchen table was too small for Liza's family now. So was the kitchen for that matter. Papa Gideon had foreseen the problem. Christmas Eve Jess and Josh had brought in a beautiful oak table with drop leaves and placed it in the living room. Now Liza knew the business Josh and Papa Gideon had going in the shop for months. Besides, there were a high chair for Nora and a little rocker.

Now they sat around the table for Christmas dinner. They were all there: Uncle Joe and Aunt Lizzie and Omega, home from college and looking her regal self in red velvet. Of course, there were the Brown Hill Browns. Papa Gideon sat at the head of the table; Mama Minnie sat at the other end. Each of the ladies had contributed to the feast. Ham, turkey, yams, dressing, turnip greens—southern fare for Low Country palates. Uncle Joe had been given the honor of returning thanks. "The Lord be with you." "And with thy spirit," Aunt

Lizzie, Liza and Omega responded. "Give us grateful hearts, our Father, for all thy mercies, and make us mindful of the needs of others; through Jesus Christ our Lord. Amen." Omega signed herself with the cross. Around her throat lay a slender gold cross, centered with a ruby. Mama Minnie, noting the gesture, dropped her eyes to her plate. Now, Josh spoke. "Liza, can I—may I say a grace, too? The one Papa Tom used to say when he was in a hurry?" Liza nodded. "Thank the Lord, what we got, Christ sake, Amen." Silence hung heavy across the table. Mama Minnie excused herself to go to the kitchen for biscuits. Nora in her high chair held her baby spoon in midair, making no effort to beat it across the tray. Papa Gideon cleared his throat and picked up the knife to carve the turkey. It was Jess who broke the silence.

"Mega, I seen them chaplains cross themselves over and over. I kinda like it. There was this one fella, English, I got to talk to a lot. He said he had been to America—preached in a church down your way. I fergit his name right now." Jess was now helping himself to the turnip greens. Each now was beginning to serve himself with the dish nearest his plate. Papa Gideon had commenced carving the turkey.

"You don't say, Jess," Uncle Joe said, looking up from his already filled plate. "Name Charles Westbrook ring a bell? He preached at Prince Frederick a year. Liza met him." Uncle Joe now took a biscuit from the pan that Mama Minnie was passing. Omega's and Liza's eyes locked.

"Mighta been. I can't say for sho. We called him Father. He didn't mention what church. He was dressed like them Catholics but can't believe he was one. Nice fella. I liked to hear him talk. Course it was diffrunt. I ain't never heared a man talk like that. Kinda low. Music like."

"What happened to him, Jess?" It was Omega. She had

made no effort to serve herself the potatoes in front of her.

"Don't rightly know. Fellas move in and out so fast. One day I jist knowed he wont around. Probly got sent to another front. Nice fella, though. He mighta made me jine up with the church if he'd hung around longer." Jess laughed. "Hope nothing happened to him. Can't never tell," he finished soberly.

Liza felt suddenly faint. She could feel the blood rushing to her head. Omega eyed her sister and then countered, "Too much of a coincidence for him to be the same. It would be like something in these domestic novels some women read. Anyhow, he would have mentioned me. I was his star pupil, wasn't I Liza?"

Liza sipped water from her glass. Nora banged her spoon on her tray. Aunt Lizzie spoke, "Feed that youngun, Liza. She's hongry."

Dinner over, Uncle Joe reached under the tree and drew out a bottle hidden under Christmas wrappings. "Brought along a little port. It helps settle these vittles. I'd like for you all to jine me in a little Christmas cheer. Not you Josh. Not yit. We need to celebrate the end of the war. Things gonna git back to normal now. Boys done come home."

"Some ain't come, Joe. Some won't never come." It was Mama Minnie. "I think I'd like a taste. Been sampling fruit cake wine. It seems like it been kinda good for my stomach." All eyes had turned to the speaker. Jess could not suppress a gasp. Even Papa Gideon looked at his wife in astonishment.

"Be a good time to try them wine glasses I brung you," Aunt Lizzie suggested. "Belonged to your great grandmother, Eleanora."

Liza rose to fetch the glasses on the top shelf of the corner cabinet. They made the softest tinkle as she placed them by Uncle Joe, who poured a finger or so for the ladies and a healthier serving for the men. He raised his glass and looked directly at Minnie Brown. "Here's to the ones here and the one who ain't." Liza touched her glass to Omega's. They smiled, each knowing that not one but two were missing from the table.

Around four Omega roused Uncle Joe from his afternoon nap. "Don't you remember? We have to go."

"Doggone it, Mega. Done forgot. Gitcha Aunt and we'll be on our way."

"Why, Omega," Liza said. "we haven't had a proper visit. I've been so busy with the preparations. I had hoped so much we could have a nice chat."

"Omega's been invited to a Christmas shindig at the Guignards. Mixing with muckety muck these days. Pretty soon she gonna grow out of Oak Grove. That's what a little larning and going to college does to a gal. Gets 'em 'bove their raisings." Uncle Joe's eyes twinkled as he patted Omega on the shoulder. Both pride and adoration gleamed in his eyes. "Yep, she done right well for herself. That Reverend started her off aiming high. You ain't done so bad yourself, Liza Brown," he added. "Got your license to teach school. You smart enough not to have to go to college. I reckon Mega's the dumb one, eh?" He tweaked her ear playfully.

"A teacher's license and a college degree are two different things, Uncle Joe. I just wish we could spend more time together. May be next summer Omega and I could plan a holiday together. Nora will be old enough for me to leave her then. I'd love to go to Charleston. I know you've been, Omega. You could give me a guided tour."

"I'm not sure about that. A group of my classmates are planning a trip abroad. England. I'd particularly love to go to the Lake Country. The Romantic Poets are my favorites. I just have to talk Uncle Joe to finance me." She put her arm around his waist and batted her blue eyes.

"I don't know about that yet. Tom foolishness trotting across the ocean." There was not the slightest hint in his banter that would indicate Omega wouldn't go.

Liza looked at her sister, poised, cool, and already confident of her charms and how to use them. What had happened to the little girl who, one Christmas years ago, had called her fairy godmother? Now she stood, slipping into her riding coat, beautiful and detached. Liza moved to embrace her. "I love you, Omega. I always will." For just a moment Omega returned her hug. Then she brushed her sister's cheek lightly and mumbled, "Love you, too, Liza."

With Nora in her arms and Josh at her side, she watched the car disappear around the bend of the road and realized that her life had taken another turn. As she mounted the steps with her little ones, she felt very tired. "Merry Christmas, Liza," Josh said. His little hand sought hers. "Don't worry. I'm the man of the house. Papa Tom said so." Her dark eyes smiled into his blue ones. "Course you are, Josh. We'll manage."

The door closed behind them. Somewhere, Liza thought, there is laughter and song. Somewhere there is the music of the spheres. The words came back to her from *The Merchant of Venice*. "Such harmony is in immortal souls; but whilst this muddy vesture of decay, doth grossly close it in, we cannot hear it."

CHAPTER TWENTY EIGHT

THE WOMAN
OF PROPERTY

PLEASANT GROVE SCHOOL, three miles from Brown Hill, squatted within a grove of long leaf pines, a two-room wooden building with a porch running across the front. After Labor Day, when the corn was safely in the barn and the last leaf of tobacco had been cured and sold, the door would swing open to welcome boys and girls in grades one through six. Come October, learning would cease for a month, when even the smallest hand plucked bolls of cotton and dropped them into burlap sacks. When school reopened in November, the dullest pupil would be happy to exchange backbreaking chores for the hard two-seater desks. On a day in mid-September, at the sound of the handbell, older and younger students marched in parallel lines to their respective classrooms. They had come to learn reading, writing, and arithmetic—enough schooling to write a letter, figure how many board feet of lumber to build on an extra room for a growing family, read the Bible, and order from Sears Roebuck catalog. Liza scanned her little ones on a Monday morning and tried to spot the faces of the ones who would want more than the three R's and to whom she could unveil landscapes painted in words and prepare them for even larger canvases. It was her first assignment and carried a stipend of thirty-five dollars each full month, and although the extra income was certainly needed, Liza's excitement was not measured in dollars and cents. On a good day she would walk to school; others she would take the buggy and Old Blue. As the children scrambled to their desks amid a chorus of "Good morning, Miss Liza," her heart raced with thoughts of implementing the plans on which she had been working all summer. She wondered about her colleague, Miss Gertha, who had been teaching the upper grades for years. Did she feel the same animation and anticipate the challenge? Like Liza, Miss Gertha's credentials rested on a General Education Certificate; unlike Liza's, she had been standing in the same position many Septembers. This morning, armed with her yardstick which doubled to draw a straight line on the blackboard and to crack a knuckle of an inattentive or recalcitrant student, she also surveyed her students who shuffled past the living legend of the old maid school marm who had never altered her hairdo or the gray high-necked dresses in her twenty-year tenure at Pleasant Grove.

Liza closed the door softly and mounted the raised

platform upon which her desk rested. Behind her stretched the blackboard, over which the alphabet in upper and lower case letters was boldly outlined in black on paper yellowed with age. To her left was the row of windows which provided both ventilation and diversion. On this warm end of a summer day, they were raised to permit whatever breeze stirred the humid air. Even now some little eyes were following busy chickadees and English sparrows as they flitted on and off the bird feeder that Papa Gideon had made for Liza's first class. Miss Gertha had taken a dim view of such tomfoolery. "Hard enough to keep these little people, (her pet title, resented by her pupils) on their lessons as is," she had snapped, and although Liza had said nothing, she felt there was equal disapproval of the sandbox in the back of the room and cut-outs pasted on window panes. Nevertheless, Liza had smiled amiably and countered with "Maybe you're right." At that point she wanted neither to make an enemy nor to abandon her plans. The best way was to placate Miss Gertha as best she could and go her own way.

"Boys and girls, we have two weeks before cotton picking to learn wonderful things. How many of you want to go on a trip with me?"

Fifteen pairs of hands waved the air and that many "Me's."

Liza twirled the globe on her desk. "Do you know what this is?"

"No, Miss Liza."

"It's the earth. We live right here." Her index finger pointed to the spot. "Now we can go anywhere. All over the world." Here she gave the globe another spin—"to strange lands. You know what is going to carry us?"

"No, Miss Liza."

"This." She held a book up. "Books will take us to the North Pole, where it is frozen in ice all year round, or to the equator, where it's scorching hot all year round." Each time she pointed out the locale. "Guess what? The trip won't cost a penny or a nickel. It's free. Only thing you have to do is to learn to read. Right now I'm going to take you to Africa, where a little black boy, whose name is Epaminondus, is sent on an errand to his grandmother's." Liza turned and wrote EPAMINONDUS on the board, pronounced it, and beckoned her students to repeat. Fifteen variations of her pronunciation filled the room. She launched into the story of the little lad who completely confused his grandmother's instructions and came home with melted butter running down his face and a wet puppy that he had cooled in the water instead of the pat of butter. The story ended in gales of laughter, which elicited a sharp thump on the wall from Miss Gertha, whose classroom was as silent as a midnight graveyard. Liza raised her fingers to her lips to calm her charges and set them out on the trip among a sea of letters and words. At the end of two weeks, Liza's fame had spread far beyond her pupils' homes and followed them into the cotton fields, where they repeated her stories and sang their ABC's. Even Josh, still in school at Brown Hill with Uncle John, begged to accompany Liza to be in her class. Uncle John, pleased himself as her mentor, commented dryly, "Well, Liza, guess it's another case where Plato outsmarted his teacher, Socrates." Miss Gertha continued to complain about the noise next door but grudgingly confessed "Liza had a way with children."

The first school year slipped by, and the business of classwork, farm, and family left little time for brooding. At night before fatigue gave way to sleep, the darkness sometimes yielded images of Parker Landing and Papa, Tom and Belleau

Woods, and Omega in England near Lake Grasmere. Only rarely did she indulge in memory of a low voice quoting poetry. Then she would hear the soft rustle of little Nora turning in her cradle, sucking contentedly on her thumb. "At least I have her," she would whisper.

Under the direction of Zack and Birdie, the farms, now free of debt, prospered, especially the tobacco that had grown in such demand during the war. Liza's tobacco barn for curing large quantities was among the first built. Talk of the pretty widow, with her bobbed black hair and flashing dark eyes, a teacher as well as a woman of property, spread beyond Brown Hill and even as far as Oak Grove. Uncle Joe began to tease her that he knew half a dozen fellas dying to come a courting. He also added that he had warned them they had little chance with his niece unless they had a book in one hand and a hefty bank account in the other. One day Aunt Lizzie had asked shyly, "Liza, you ever think of the Reverend?" to which she had replied, quoting Marlowe, "That was in another country and besides the wench is dead." "Nothing dead about you, Liza," her aunt had replied. "Too young not to git married." Then she added laughingly, "Better git to the Reverend before Omega. That youngun still got crazy notions."

And Omega did get her trip to England but never mentioned that she had found Charles, nor did Liza question her. The old bond between sisters had loosened, and Liza grieved for those days when their laughter and tears had mingled. Another chapter in my life closing, Liza thought. Yet there was never a day when she would not have gladly reopened it. Her losses, however, had not been without compensation. Tom's death had brought financial stability as well as closeness to his parents, especially Mama Minnie, who now attended church irregularly but never again "in the spirit" of former days.

Life's little ironies. The heathen daughter-in-law now taught adult Sunday School, where she led Brown Hill graybeards through the journeys of Paul to strange places, even to the Greek Acropolis and the Island of Lesbos. Like her primary classes they sat rapt as she toured the city which worshipped the goddess Artemis with a thousand breasts or re-enacted dramatically Paul's epiphany on the road to Damascus. Uncle John had laughed himself hoarse when he heard about her depiction of the prostitution on the outskirts of Corinth. "Great guns," he had shouted. "What's the world coming to when dyed-in-the-wool Baptists relish the stories of Sodom and Gomorrah more than the blissful heaven paved with gold over which thousands of angels flit, welcoming the faithful into the pearly gates." Between the church, the school, her home, Liza moved, not happy, not unhappy. Her feet stood steady on the level ground, and unlike Jess she was content to sink her toes for the moment in Low Country mud.

The spring when Nora was three, Liza contracted to add two bedrooms and a dining room to her house. She and Uncle John drew up the plans, but it was Papa Gideon who worked out the specifications. That was the spring death once again stalked Brown Hill.

It was an April Saturday. School had closed for the term. Every free hand was now needed for planting—dropping corn seed, scattering manure from the stable, setting out tobacco, carrying water to keep plants alive if God had not seen fit to send rain. And he had not chosen to drop even a sprinkle during March. Now in mid-April the plow "laying-by" or "busting out middles" turned the black earth into clouds of gray dust. Oldsters shook their head and believed the Almighty had pronounced anathema on Brown Hill. "Somebody done sinned," they said. "God don't like ugly."

Liza listened and said nothing. She smiled to herself and remembered old Oedipus, with whom the gods had become angry. Drawing the analogy with Uncle John, Liza playfully quipped, "Know anybody around who has killed his father and married his mother?" Still she went with them to church to pray for rain and was amused that not one of them censured heathen Birdie, who, they had heard, had commenced sunrise rain dances at Port Hill. Uncle John with his typical wry wit commented, "God moves in mysterious ways His wonder to perform." Farmers, however, did not discuss the subject with such levity. Every withered stalk of corn and every bean that didn't sprout meant a lean larder as well as repetition of hard labor. Liza on this Saturday morning stood with Nora in her front yard, each with watering cans giving the beds of verbena and thrift a drink. Behind them Papa Gideon and a couple of skilled carpenters were hammering the last strip of tin roof over the additions of her house. Even Josh was in the act. Liza loved the syncopated rhythm of the rain on tin—the pelting downpours and the slow drizzle that lulled her to sleep. Looking up at the cloudless blue sky, she, too, lamented the drought, not only for her neighbors but for herself as well and admitted once again that after eleven years in Brown Hill she found herself indissolubly linked with its natives.

"Mother," Nora asked, "you bake Nora a birthday cake? With candles? Three of them?" She held up three fingers. "Chocolate?" Tipping her miniature water can, she doused the flounced hem of her green gingham dress.

"Chocolate and candles, Nora." Liza righted the watering can. As she stooped to wring water from Nora's dripping dress, the sound of a shot pierced the still air and echoed among the trees. The hammers on the roof stopped simultaneously. Papa Gideon descended the ladder first, taking two rungs at a time. Behind him came his helpers. Only Josh remained, his little hammer in midair and his gaze directed toward Papa Gideon's barn adjacent to the shop. "My God, Liza. It's Jess. I knowed it was coming." Papa broke into a run, the two men at his heels. Now Josh had scrambled down the ladder. Liza caught his hand. "No, Josh. Stay here. You mus- n't go." Josh wrenched his hand free, ignoring her command. Liza jerked him back. "Josh Brown, you stay here. Don't you move one inch from this yard," she threatened. She had never spoken to him that way before. He burst into sobs, equally fearful of the terror in her voice and the shot that had halted their hammers. Liza marshalled the two of them up the steps and into the house. In the kitchen the three of them waited. Now Nora's sobs joined Josh's. Liza handed Nora a sucker from the candy jar and gathered Josh in her arms. "Oh, Josh! Josh! I'm so afraid. I need you with me. Remember Papa Tom said you were the man in the house."

"What did Papa Gideon mean, Liza? Is there some- thing wrong with Uncle Jess? He didn't come to help this morning. You reckon he got drunk again?"

"I don't know, Josh." Again she whispered. "I don't know." What she couldn't understand was why lovable tender Jess, never climatized to the soil, had been planted in an alien field, and destined to wither like the crops of Brown Hill. The two and a half years Jess had been back she knew had not been easy. There had been only snatches of conversation between them. She had been so busy ordering her own life. When Jess had come around, she was occupied with schoolwork or at the sewing machine, or helping Josh with his lessons. Still she knew that Jess was unhappy. He had confided once that Samson, his colored buddy, was one of the men he had res- cued. One had lived, but Samson had died in his arms. He had returned home to a family grieving for the good son, and although the prodigal son had been welcomed, the fatted calf had not been killed and the feast never spread. Mama Minnie had tried, but her altered life proclaimed fully her loss of the favored one more than any words. Rumors had it that Jess was drinking more and running around with shiftless white trash, one man in particular. Once Liza had suggested to Jess, "Why don't you go get a job in town? You'd make a good mechanic. You are not a farmer, Jess." He had answered, "I ain't much a nothing, Liza. No credit to myself nor to my folks. My parents ashamed of me, Ma specially. I wish it coulda been me stead of Tom." So he remained in limbo—unhappy where he was and afraid to move out.

Birdie stood in the doorway. She had eased herself in as siilently as her ancestors had flitted through virgin pine. Working in Liza's fields with her husband, Zack, she, too had heard the shot. Now she stood in Liza's kitchen, dark earth still clinging to her hands, the green fuzz of pine pollen caught in her braided hair.

"Where?" Liza questioned.

"In the barn. You needed up there. I come to stay with the younguns."

"Whatcha mean, Birdie?" Josh cried out.

"Your Uncle Jess dead. Shot himself."

"How come?" It was Josh again.

Birdie moved behind Josh, wrapped her arms around his neck, and dropped her dark head on his red one. "Don't know, Josh. He never felt at home here. Been wanting to git away a long time. He jist rushed up his going a bit. He's happy now."

Liza was already at the door. As her feet raised the dust on the road, she heard Jess's voice. "Shake off Low Country mud." Well, he had done it at last. At the door of the house, she stopped and prayed fervently. "God, let me find the right words." Never before had she pleaded. Charles's words came back to her. "Whether there is a God or not, I have no choice except to seek him." This morning she needed God desperately for herself and those two old people who had now lost both sons. She found them in the room where Jess and Tom had been born. Mama Minnie was sitting on the bed, her husband at her side, his arms holding her close. Liza dropped to the floor and clasped their knees. Mama Minnie spoke. Her voice was dry, unemotional, measured, and fell on the silence like clods of earth. "I called him pervert." Liza groped for words but found none. She grieved for Jess, for Papa Gideon, but for Mama Minnie the slash cut deeper. Again the three mourned together, this time more terrible than the other.

That night it rained. It started just at sunset as kind neighbors placed Jess in a coffin his father had built. Liza, sitting with Josh and Nora at the supper table, heard the first plop on the tin roof. It had come as unexpectedly as the morning shot, and now it fell steadily, gently, without even a rumble of thunder. It continued throughout the night—as unremitting as the tears that fell in Brown Hill. It marked the end of the dry season and the beginning of a bountiful harvest. Liza remembered having read that gods die in April, that their deaths replenish the earth, that spring is the evidence of their rebirth. Easter was next Sunday. Teasdale's poem came back to her. It was almost as though she could hear Jess saying it.

> When over me bright April
> Shakes out her rain-drenched hair;
> And though you lean above me broken-hearted
> I shall not care.

This time the sentiment did not cloy.

A slow drizzle continued, laying the dust and sinking deep into the earth. "God's mercy," Brown Hill said even as the soft drops fell upon Jess's coffin. Her face showered with tears, Liza clutched the hands of Josh and Mama Minnie and prayed that this heavenly dew would cease and that Brown Hill was in for a dry spell. Not so. Years after, there would be talk of the bounties of the land. Every seed sprouted, the corn grew taller, tobacco cured golden, and the cotton bolls were massive. The Gods were appeased. Temperate days and nights replaced scorching summer suns as the yield of crops multiplied under seasonable rain. And so there was rejoicing among such plenty with barbecues on the Fourth and frequent "dinners on the ground" after church on Sunday. It was, indeed, a time to celebrate, and although sympathy for a grieving neighbor existed, "God's will had been done."

In one house there was no joy. The two moved like ghosts from room to room and stared silently at each other over plates of food scarcely touched. The saw and hammer lay idle in the shop and the beans left unpicked, dried up on the stalks. Watching them was so painful that Liza would often leave abruptly to vent her grief. Not even Nora, prattling her baby nonsense, could rouse them from their stupor, but Liza was grateful that her little daughter, untouched by and unaware of loss, still laughed merrily as she chased butterflies or frolicked with Betsy in her playhouse built in happier days by Papa Gideon in the backyard.

Josh was another story. Her heart ached as she saw him each morning pin the Medal of Honor to his overalls, and she wept silently as she watched him coming from Papa Gideon's, his little feet viciously kicking whatever lay in his path. "How can you explain, Uncle John," Liza asked, "to a twelve year old untimely death—especially its violence?" For once the old philosopher had no answer and shook his head wordlessly. And so the season of plenty for some was a barren one for others.

September and the end of summer once more found children on their way to village schools proudly carrying Baby Ray primers and Elson Basic Readers. Pleasant Grove had added another room to accommodate the seventh grade and another teacher, Megan McGillam, fresh out of normal school, who was named principal. Megan, a native of Charleston, and barely twenty, boarded with Liza. With her auburn hair pulled smartly into a tight bun, she might have been a younger edition of Miss Gertha, but her green eyes sometimes glinted with mischief, and Liza suspected there might be a warm heart beating under her high-necked starched blouse accented with a gold cross dangling from a filigreed chain. Brown Hill had heard of Roman Catholics but had never seen one. They doubted that a heathen should be teaching their children, but Liza assured them that Rome was, indeed, Christian and worshipped the same God as the Baptists. With the extra income, Liza bought a car to transport the two of them to school along with Josh, now in the seventh grade. The runabout would also provide Friday passage for Megan to catch the local train in Lambert for weekend visits to Charleston.. Buying the car had another purpose. Liza hoped Josh's learning to drive would give him new interests and assert him once more as "the man of the house."

School that fall offered not only the usual challenge but also temporary respite from the gloom of past months. Mama Minnie, Nora's nanny during school, showed the first sign of life when Liza suggested that perhaps a three-year-old was too much of a handful for her. "That youngun ain't no trouble. Her granny knows jist how to manage her. These old hands done had practice with two rowdy boys." At that her eyes moistened and Liza quickly said, "Oh, Mama Minnie, she loves you as much as she loves me. I wouldn't for the world change her nanny if you feel up to it." So the matter was settled, and for the third year Liza readied herself to teach bright little faces and some not so bright that the world extended far beyond Brown Hill and that the mountains, which Liza had not yet seen, had once, millions of years ago, lain under sea-water like the ocean at Pawley's Island.

Miss Gertha was prepared to dislike the new principal, younger and better qualified on paper. So when Gilbert Williams, the seventh grade bully, brought a green snake into the classroom to present to his new science teacher, Miss Gertha could not hide her smug satisfaction when Miss McGillam's shrieks elicited howls from the boys and screams from the girls. Even Josh enjoyed the fun. Liza, realizing that her colleague's tenure in the classroom would be ending almost as soon as it had begun unless things were brought under control, gingerly picked up the snake and draped it around Gilbert's neck. The young prankster let out blood-curdling yells that surpassed those of his teacher and made him the laughing stock of his peers. "Gilbert," Liza said softly, "bring your pets to me next time." Turning to the applauding class, Liza raised her right eyebrow famous for restoring order. "I believe Miss McGillam is ready to continue. I'm sure Miss McGillam will be glad to discuss with your parents any other problems." With that she closed the door behind her. The act made her the unofficial head of Pleasant Grove and won her the adoration and respect of Megan McGillam. Even Papa Gideon laughed when he heard the story, and Liza Brown inched up another notch in approval among the residents along the Great Pee Dee River.

During cotton-picking break in October, Liza accompanied Uncle Joe and Aunt Lizzie to Columbia to see Omega crowned "the most womanly and the most likely to succeed" at the girls' school where Omega was now a senior. The title, a secret until the event, was evidently no surprise to the poised young woman who knelt before the college president to receive the school's highest honor. There was no mistaking why she had been chosen. Besides being a top student, Omega was breathtakingly beautiful. Masses of golden curls framed flawless skin set with large blue eyes that could smile graciously or dismiss contemptuously, while the angle of her determined chin signaled beware to those who would attempt to cross her. No vestige of the frightened little girl from the Neck remained. Proud of her though she was, Liza mourned the lost sweetness of her baby sister replaced by a remote statuesque stranger. Even so, as Liza stood by Omega in front of the mirror as they dressed for dinner, she tried to recapture something of those former years. "I have missed you, Omega. Remember the times when we curled up in bed and read to each other? I want so much for my Nora to get to know you. Actually, she looks so much like you. She's smart like you, too. She's already talking in sentences."

"I'm afraid I'm not the maternal type. Motherhood fits you. When Nora is older, I'm sure I can relate to her more. Babies have no part in my plans now and maybe ever. They tie you down and age you quickly." Omega looked at her sister's reflection in the mirror. Liza's lithe figure and dark beauty, as striking as her sister's, belied Omega's dire pronouncement. In fact, something about the warmth of Liza's eyes and softness around her mouth may have been more arresting than the cool demeanor of her sister. "Of course," Omega hastily added, "motherhood becomes you. To each his own," she added lightly.

Liza felt the door close sharply between them, leaving a whiff of cold air. Did Omega remember and perhaps resent the sacrifices she had made for her and was afraid that payment would be demanded? Could it be that she still smarted over the affection that had developed between her and Charles? Leaving the questions hanging, Liza forced a smile and repeated, "To each his own," and added silently "So be it."

The four dined in a restaurant of the Wade Hampton Hotel. Uncle Joe in his new serge suit and black bow tie was jubilant. A couple of toddies earlier in his room had loosened his tongue and warmed his heart. Flushed with pride and corn liquor, he was ready to broadcast to strangers at neighboring tables, boasting unabashedly of Omega's accomplishments. "My niece here, she's got brains and beauty. Genuine southern belle. Straight out of the Low Country of this great state. First to secede from the Union. One day this young gal gonna be Mistress of Oak Grove. Yes siree. She won't want for nothing. It will be a mighty lucky man to win her hand. Course it's up to her to carry on the line. We Browns go back to seventeen hundreds. Old English stock. Oak Grove was a land grant from King George himself. I had a great, great, great uncle in Parliament. 'Spec Mega got some of his brains."

Omega, embarrassed that her assets were being so blatantly advertised, tugged at Uncle Joe's white cuff, hoping to draw his attention away from the amused listeners at a nearby table who had been speaking with a decided New York twang. Liza, however, was enjoying herself immensely. Deviltry in her flashing eyes, she was about to interject that half of Mega had not sprung from English peerage but from a father of peasant stock whose ancestral home, if you wished to use a euphemism, lay deep in the woods around the Little Pee Dee, where his liquor stills had provided a meager existence until the Feds broke it up. Before she could enlighten the Yankee tourists about the "other side," a tall young colored waiter who had been pouring water from a silver pitcher addressed Uncle Joe. "Sir," he questioned politely in a voice with not a trace of southern dialect, "did you say Oak Grove? Could that possibly be a plantation near Georgetown, outside of Plantersville?" The question was neither hostile nor derisive. The speaker with skin just a shade darker than the guests in the dining room bore little resemblance to Low Country servants. Liza's eyes widened, and before Uncle Joe could respond, she answered. "Of course, young man. How in the world could you happen to know Oak Grove?"

"My grandmother, Lucinda Brown, was born there. Joseph Brown was her father and benefactor. She graduated from Voorhees. She became a teacher. All of us have followed her footsteps. My family's all in education."

Taking a small pad from his white coat, he continued, "I can recommend the prime rib. The trout meniere is also very popular." A stunned silence had fallen on the group. Each of them had seen the watercolor of the little girl whose intelligent brown eyes had stared from a honey-like face framed with wavy black hair. Now she had become very real to them. She was no longer a portrait tucked under old photographs in an eighteenth century breakfront at Oak Grove. The young man who stood before them with pencil ready to take their order was her grandson. Liza tried to make a mental calculation of exactly where this tall, alert stranger stood in the pool of Brown genes. Lucinda was grandfather's half-sister. That would make her Uncle Joe's aunt and her great aunt. Did Mama know about her Aunt Lucinda? Life's little ironies, thought Liza wryly. Now a distant cousin, well spoken, poised, his dark blood mixed with Anglo-Saxon, no longer in servitude to his blond ancestry, looked curiously upon them with perhaps secret amusement. Liza turned her attention to the others at the table. Uncle Joe, caught off guard by this sudden pronouncement, studied his menu carefully while Aunt Lizzie stared openly into the waiter's face. Liza smiled to see that Omega had lost some of her hauteur and like Uncle Joe concentrated on her order as though the choice were a weighty decision with earth-shaking consequences. Liza, to the amazement and consternation of her party, extended her hand. "I'm Liza Brown," she offered. "You are a distant relative. This is my sister, Omega, a college senior, and my Aunt Lizzie and Uncle Joe. And your name, young man?"

"Samuel Butler the third." He bowed lightly, acknowledging her greeting without taking the proffered hand. It was a gracious gesture, carefully considered, not choosing the more familiar but electing instead the formality that put him in complete command of a situation that might bring embarrassment. Uncle Joe, not quite recovered, ordered for all of them. "We'll all have the prime rib."

"Very good, sire," returned Samuel, bowing once again as he strode confidently toward the kitchen.

Uncle Joe, his voice lowered to protect them from curious ears, whispered. "Great guns, Liza. You want to show the world we kin to niggers. If you got no respect for me, think about your sister here."

Liza smiled archly. "I have the same respect for you that your grandfather had for his offspring whose mother was a Negro servant. He evidently respected his child enough to finance her education. I suspect that both Omega and I would have had a great deal in common with Aunt Lucinda." Liza stressed the name. "All three of us are educated southern women. The fact that one had a darker skin makes no difference. Liza picked up Omega's left hand on which she wore her class college ring. "Latin, isn't it, Omega? *Non Quem Sed Quid.* Not who but what," she finished judiciously.

"God Almighty, Liza! You talk just like those abolitionists that caused the war. I reckon you got respect, too, for that SOB Sherman that burned half of the South. You got a pile of kinfolks killed at Chickamauga. You got no respect for them, I reckon."

"Uncle Joe," Liza spoke softly but with conviction. "I do not believe in human slavery nor do I believe in war. What I do believe in and what I most admire is anyone who judges a person not by ancestry, money, or race, but by his courage to fight intolerance and bigotry. The men at Chickamauga, both sides, Rebels and Yankees, have my respect and my pity. They, like my Tom, were drawn into a war they didn't make and didn't even understand. Yes, I admire and respect Lucinda. She has passed down to her children her love of learning. With all my soul I hope I can do the same for my Nora."

"Danged if I know where you git such idears. Omega, here, she got more larning than you. You ain't heard her Aunt Lucinda-ing to a nigger. Some of that way-out talk sounds like that English preacher, Charles Westbrook. I'm sho glad it didn't rub off on Omega. I got nothing against niggers so long as they stay in their place."

"And does that place include a white man's bed?" Liza's eyes flashed as her words hit the target.

At that moment Samuel approached their table rolling a teacart laden with food. As he ceremoniously served each one, Liza turned her attention from her irate uncle to Omega. Expecting at least token agreement, Liza was taken aback at the hostile glitter in her sister's blue eyes. What had she said that had sparked such anger? Then she remembered Uncle

Joe's words. Yes, what she had uttered, indeed, might have come from the lips of Charles Westbrook. Omega had recognized the twin spirits and felt shut out. Resentment burned her smooth fair cheeks as she saw the futility of competing with her older sister, who could still outsmart her. As their eyes locked, Omega knew instinctively that Liza had read her and hastened to brush off the discussion with an imperious "Disagreement is so tiresome. Remember this is my party."

"Is there anything else, sir?" Samuel had caught Omega's words as he waited dutifully for further instructions. Uncle Joe nodded no, but Liza motioned him to her side. "May I have coffee now?" she whispered. Then she added, "Is your grandmother still living?" "Yes, in New York." Without another word he retreated toward the coffee bar. When he returned with her coffee, there was a scrap of white paper under her cup. Liza slipped it into her purse and picked up her fork.

Uncle Joe uncharacteristically left a handsome tip, far exceeding the usual ten percent. Liza, who never missed anything, smiled at Uncle Joe, who smiled back sheepishly. Samuel was nowhere in sight as they left the dining room. Liza thought idly that perhaps he, like Falstaff, considered discretion the better part of valor.

Back in the room that the two sisters shared, Liza turned to Omega. "I'm sorry about the argument. But Mega, there are some things I just can't keep silent about. Do you know what I mean, honey?"

"I suppose so. Goodnight, Liza." Omega switched off her bedside lamp and pulled the covers up. Liza's eyes welled with tears. Opening her purse, she drew out the paper on which was printed in neat black letters: Mrs. Samuel Butler, 130 West 63rd Street, New York, New York. The bedside drawer yielded hotel stationery. Not in the least sleepy, Liza began, "Dear Aunt Lucinda."

Christmas of '21 was the first year that the Browns of Plantersville did not celebrate with Liza. Omega was in a whirlwind of activities with college friends and parties thrown in plantation houses along the inland waterway. Although they were more elegant and larger than Oak Grove, the doors were, nevertheless, thrown open to welcome the charming, beautiful Omega. Liza felt emptiness in the Yuletide but decided separation from her sister was better than the aloof demeanor and sometimes icy shoulder that Omega thrust upon her. Still there was Nora, almost four, who every night had a different request for Santa Claus. Josh, a teenager who handled the car better than Liza, had a much shorter list. Liza noted the absence of shells and bullets; since Jess's death, Josh had not once taken his rifle or gun from the shelf in the hallway. After all, a shot had ended the lives of the two men he had loved most. So sadness lurked in the corners garlanded with bright Christmas holly and shiny silver tinsel and dimmed the star on the top of the tree, but Nora's laughter sprinkled the gloom with cheer as she clattered around the room pulling her new doll in a red wagon. At the Christmas dinner, Liza bowed her dark head over her plate and waited for Josh, now the man of the house, to offer thanks. She was startled and profoundly moved by his words. "We thank you, Lord, for letting us be together. We miss the ones who used to be here. I reckon that's about it, Lord. Amen."

Mama Minnie stifled a sob, but Liza facing her brother smiled as she said, "Oh, Josh! That was beautiful."

On New Year's Eve, Liza stood in front of her mirror. Though the red coals glimmering in the fireplace warmed the room, a shiver shook her body enveloped in her fleecy nightgown. It had been over four years since she had felt a man's touch. Her hands pushed back the dark curls clustering her forehead. She stared into her eyes, two smoldering coals in her white face. "Who are you?" she questioned. A log broke and collapsed into the burning embers. She heard a long, slow sob. It came from the figure in the mirror. The face disappeared as Liza eased herself into the softness of her feather mattress and dreamed of twin peaks reflected in a blue lake.

School reopened on a cold January day. Josh, trusted now to meet the train in Lambert, had fetched Megan McGillam back to her boarding house. Liza welcomed her return. In the months since school had opened in the fall, a warm friendship had grown between the two school marms. Liza, ten years Megan's senior, had gradually become the young woman's mentor and confidante. Megan, grateful for Liza's diplomacy and expertise at school, where Megan was titular head, looked upon the older woman with respect and genuine affection. On long winter nights they had exchanged stories of childhood, so oddly different even though the two had discovered that they shared the same kind of loneliness and the same love of books which had made both of their lives less isolated. A grandmother who spent a great portion of the day praying novenas and reciting the Holy Rosary had reared Megan, whose parents had been killed in a freak train derailment. There had been little warmth in the stern old lady's crumbling Victorian house only a short walk from the Battery. School with the nuns had added little diversion, except for Sister Louise, whose heart opened up to a little girl starved for affection and glutted with endless saints, prayers, and masses. It was Sister Louise who gave her courage to break away. Much against grandmother's wishes, after her normal school teacher training, she had landed in a rural low country school, scared, inexperienced, and alone until some saint had chosen to answer one of her many prayers and send her to Liza. Strong family ties and guilt propelled her back to Charleston weekends and holidays. As little entertainment as Brown Hill offered, sharing Liza's hearth was cozier than the rattling radiators in grandmother's rambling house. So it was with genuine affection that the two embraced as Nora tugged Megan's skirts to get her to acknowledge Pretty Girl, her new doll.

"Megan, your hair!" Liza exclaimed. The tight bun had disappeared. A brown wavy bob now made her green eyes more prominent, while lip rouge had turned her cheeks to a rosy glow. "You did it. You look beautiful."

"It's all your fault, Liza. Grandmother says you have corrupted me. She's quite sure now that I'll end up Protestant and go straight to hell."

"Me go, too?" Nora begged. The word *go* always sent her into a frenzy of expectation regardless of the destination.

The two broke into peals of laughter, which rang out among the Christmas decorations still there until Epiphany. Nora, deciding that a trip was not in the offing, climbed up on the sofa and was ready to perform for the returning Megan. With Liza's occasional promptings, Nora, sometimes on key, chortled out the Twelve Days of Christmas. Even Josh joined in the applause.

"Megan's got a boyfriend. Megan's got a boyfriend," Josh sang out.

Color suffused her cheeks. Danny O'Malley, whom she had met at church, had accompanied her on the train to Lambert, where he continued his journey to North Carolina and to his bookkeeping job at a cotton mill. Josh had seen him escort Megan from the train and thought he had seen him kiss her goodbye. Megan stoutly denied the intimacy but was full of Danny during supper. At bedtime, just before Liza turned down the wick in the last lamp, she stole into Megan's bedroom. "I'm so happy for you, Megan," she whispered. With that she slipped back into her own room and settled herself down under the quilt bearing the wedding ring design. Mama's heavy gold band still occupied the third finger of her left hand. On impulse, she drew it off and transferred it to her right hand. Staring into the darkness alive with memories, Liza indulged herself in daydreams. She clasped her Rosary, which she had not shared, not even with Megan, since the night of Tom's death, and fingered each bead on which his touch still lingered. Chastising herself for unholy thoughts, she whispered her favorite Psalm: "He that dwelleth in the secret place of the most high shall find shelter under the Almighty." Before she finished it, she sank into uninhibited dreams, unaware that her body moved in rhythm with another's.

Spring burst upon Brown Hill unexpectedly. One morning frost glistened on plowed furrows waiting planting. The next, purple iris, crocus, and buttercups pushed their way out of the dark earth around the white picket fence enclosing Liza's yard. Plucking a handful for her desk perhaps to inspire some little hand to pen the magic of rebirth, Liza remarked to Megan, "You know it's such a beautiful time. I can't help feeling a little uneasy though. It's brought such sad events into my life." Her high forehead wrinkled in memory as she resurrected the closure of past springs—Mama's, Tom's, and Jess's death. Megan, young and now desperately in love for the first time, playfully jabbed a daffodil behind Liza's ear. "Stop it, Liza. This spring is different. I read the cards for you this morning. Excitement and change are on the way."

"Speak for yourself, Megan," Liza rejoined, paraphrasing Longfellow. Liza smiled wistfully and unlatched the gate to board the honking car with Josh at the wheel. His impatience at their loitering no doubt had foundation in a certain little Cindy Lou, whose big brown eyes had been following him. Liza had seen them recently share their lunches and thought it was time to have a serious discussion about the birds and the bees. Liza waved a kiss to Nora on the porch with her grandmother and settled herself in the rumble seat as the runabout lurched forward to Pleasant Grove. She noted with some alarm that no one was stirring at Uncle John's but supposed the old pedagogue had proclaimed a holiday from school, an event that had occurred more frequently during the past months. When Liza had questioned him about the mandatory hundred and forty days required by state law, Uncle John had shrugged his shoulders and wryly commented, "Let those educated fools in Columbia try larning the blockheads. They reach a saturation point, Liza. Most of my scholars look no farther than a mule's behind. A two-horse farm is the height of their ambition. I haven't spotted a Cicero or a Socrates yet. I reckon you're young enough to still keep looking. Good luck!" Although she knew the futility of argument, she had said, "Uncle John, you spotted me." A smile had spread across the old man's face. His arm encircled her shoulder and lingered unexpectedly. She had never seen him make an overt gesture of endearment to anyone, not even his wife, Aunt Mary. Liza was touched. Neither of them spoke. Words were unnecessary.

That afternoon as the trio rounded the bend in the road where Brown Hill lay stretched out, the crowd around Uncle John's house told her the spring once more had brought closure. Josh stopped short of their own front yard. Papa Gideon in his Sunday suit separated from the crowd and broke the news. "Mary found him this morning. He died in his sleep.

Reckon you better call off school for a couple of days."

On Sunday afternoon Liza stood surrounded by Brown
Hill by the open grave awaiting the plain unadorned pine box
Papa Gideon had fashioned according to the specifications left
with Aunt Mary.   There had been no church service. His
instructions were that Liza Brown should read the third chapter of Ecclesiastes, verses one through eight and finish with the
last verse of "Thanatopsis". Without a quaver in her voice, Liza
intoned:

> For everything there is a season,
> And a time for every matter under heaven:
> A time to be born, and a time to die;
> A time to plant, and a time to pluck up what is planted;
> A time to kill, and a time to heal;
> A time to break down, and a time to build up;
> A time to weep, and a time to laugh;
> A time to mourn, and a time to dance;
> A time to cast away stones, and a time to gather stones
> together;
> A time to embrace, and a time to refrain from embracing;
> A time to seek, and a time to lose;
> A time to keep, and a time to cast away;
> A time to rend, and a time to sew;
> A time to keep silence, and a time to speak;
> A time to love, and a time to hate;
> A time for war, and a time for peace.

Liza now turned to Bryant's poem. She wished with all
her heart for a laurel leaf. In its absence she substituted purple
crocuses and narcissi. "Royalty," she murmured as she dropped
them on the casket. Then the words:

So live that when thy summons come to join
That innumerable caravan which moves
To that mysterious realm, where each shall take
His chamber in the silent halls of death;
Thou go not like a quarry slave at night
Scourged to his dungeon, but sustained and soothed
By an unfaltering trust, approach thy grave
Like one who wraps the drapery of his couch
About him and lies down to pleasant dreams.

Liza, her eyes brimming with tears, moved away. A small hand clutched hers. She looked down into the face of a little boy in overalls, who whispered to her, "Mister John, he learned me good." Liza scooped the child up in her arms and whispered back, "He learned me good, too."

That night Aunt Mary left with her people for the Up Country. There was no rancor in farewell to Liza. "John loved you more than anybody. He left you everything. I belong to the hills. I have missed them all these years." With that she climbed into the car beside her brother. Not once did she look back.

CHAPTER TWENTY NINE

VOICES
FROM THE PAST

SCHOOL CLOSED IN LATE APRIL. Every hand was needed in the fields. Liza, now the owner of a two-story house filled with furniture and books, decided that it would become her new home. Her own house, although more spacious now with its added rooms, could not accommodate Uncle John's books, which she valued as much as the treasury notes. In his spidery script Uncle John had written a note on the packet, "A little learning is a dangerous thing; see that Josh and Nora drink deep of the Pierian Spring." Two thousand dollars and the two acres of land upon which the house was sitting were now hers. John, with no ties to the landed aristocracy, had invested in books, not farms. First editions of Dickens and Thackerary and Taine's history of England Liza knew were treasure troves that one-day would belong to Nora. So the month of May marked the transition to the house across the road. Aunt Mary, a meticulous housekeeper, had left each room scrupulously clean except for the library into which her dust mop had not been permitted to enter. Elsewhere, the heart of pine floors glowed in mellow richness, the silver service sparkled, and the French china shelved in a heavy mahogany corner cupboard, although unused for years, bore no trace of dust. Liza, that first night as she lay in the canopied four poster, imagined herself in Mama's bed. She had closed the door to her first home in Brown Hill and entered the heavy oak portal of her new one. She wondered if she were opening a new chapter in her life, one written in a sturdy hand, as sturdy as the seasoned lumber and the man who had once called its walls his domain. In time, Mama's Paul Scarlet rose would climb a trellis in the yard. Already the red pump that Tom had installed at the expense of selling his grandfather's gun had found its way to the back porch. Yes, a portion of the first chapters in Brown Hill would be included in the pages yet to be written.

For the time being, Liza had also inherited the Post Office. Proximity to the little building and teacher literacy made her an appropriate replacement. Letters to Brown Hill were few and a dozen subscriptions to the *Georgetown Times* and *Progressive Farmer* made sorting the mail an easy task occupying not more than fifteen minutes of her time. Occasionally, there came catalogs from Sears Roebuck, from which one could order everything from clothes to plow shares. Outdated issues found their way to the outdoor privy. Liza's interest in the dresses lay in the design which her nimble fingers could copy. Hasting's seed catalog, however, was her favorite. From there she ordered the bulbs and tubers that became spring's array of tulips and daffodils.

One day she received an invitation to Omega's graduation to which she responded with a letter of regret in not attending and containing a money order "to use to buy something special when you go abroad this summer." Has the Omega chapter closed as well? she asked herself. Too busy to dwell upon the reversal of their relationship, Liza thrust herself into the management of farms and home, reserving quality time for Nora and Josh. Midnight hours would sometimes find her in Uncle John's library, where she renewed acquaintances with old friends and made new ones. She discovered with delight *Tom Jones* and relished his rollicking escapades almost as much as the women's chicanery and subterfuge in *Lysistrata*. Now that women could vote, she duly registered every housewife at the post office, much to the disgust of their spouses, who thought "ladies," like " niggers, "should stay in their place.

The pleasant days of spring drifted into the sultry ones of summer. A letter from Megan announced her approaching marriage to Danny O'Mally with a note insisting that Liza be her matron of honor. The wedding bells were set for October, coinciding with the school break. Liza wrote back immediately, promising to be on hand to fasten the wedding veil. It would be her first trip to Charleston. Josh would accompany her to be one of the ushers. In the meantime, the Department of Education decided to close Brown Hill School and consolidate Pleasant Grove, adding two teachers, one to replace Megan and the other to accommodate the overflow from Brown Hill. Josh, now an eighth grader, would board in

Lambert and attend the high school. Liza, looking back over the past months, shook her dark head beginning to thread in premature gray and mentally cataloged the changes. Perhaps Megan's reading the cards was more truth than fancy. One day, as she stood in the little post office distributing the mail in the cubby holes and contemplating the months ahead, she discovered a letter and a small package addressed to Mrs. Liza Brown, one postmarked New York; the other the United Kingdom. Collapsing in the swivel chair, she examined the letter first. Her name was neatly printed in black ink. The parcel must be from Omega, she thought. Perhaps it was a gesture, a bid for renewal of their old relationship. The letter piqued her curiosity more. Her index finger made a careful slit to draw out the missive.

> *Dear Cousin Liza,*
>
> *My mother, Lucinda, received your letter which she treasured until the day she died, Christmas the 25th. She shared it with me. I, too, was deeply moved and like mother searched diligently for a way to answer it. I apologize for both of us for our negligence. Neither of us had ever dreamed that one day we would be acknowledged by that side of the family. You must be a very rare person. My son, who is a student at Allen University, has never ceased talking about you. He says that he sees his grandmother's spirit in you and is proud to claim kinship. It was his choice to go south. He believes that to understand himself is to understand his roots. Several weekends he has visited Plantersville and has seen his grandmother's birthplace. Obviously he has not called on the Browns at Oak Grove.*
>
> *You may be interested to know that your great grandfather and his common law wife Alberta lie side by side in a country churchyard just outside Utica, New York. Mother visited their*

grave so long as her health permitted. She never forgot her father's generosity and was grateful that she could care for them in their last days.

I have been retired from teaching for a number of years. Samuel is my only son, although I have three daughters all in education. Should you ever come to New York, my children and I would be privileged to meet you. Had mother lived and had she been able to travel, there is no doubt in my mind that the two of you would have met.

Again forgive our negligence. You must understand how overwhelmed we were to have heard from you.

Gratefully and cordially,
Cousin Samuel

Liza smiled to herself. Would she dare to ask young Samuel to Brown Hill? She would have to think about that. From the past loomed the cold night and the hooded horsemen. She shivered remembering the potato bank where she and her siblings had crouched, waiting terrified lest the returning stampede make a final stop at "the nigger lover's house." And the morning afterward. She could see the solemn, silent procession bearing the still figure on a makeshift litter. She thought of Josh and Nora and felt deep shame. Coward that she was, she could not risk putting them in danger. Maybe they will be braver; maybe the young Samuels one day could knock unafraid at Oak Grove's front door and be welcomed. At least, she thought, I can write. That resolve did little to ease her conscience.

"I'll deal with that later," she said audibly as she turned to a pleasanter prospect. It was a neat package. Perhaps some store or friend had mailed it for Omega. Certainly the handwriting was not familiar. On top of a black velvet box there was a letter.

Dear Mrs. Brown,

 Fr. Charles Westbrook passed away Easter. He had been in failing health since the war, sustaining a wound that left him with a painful limp as well as a severe diabetic condition. Nevertheless, he served our little parish, St. Oswald's, faithfully and delivered his last sermon Easter morning. It was so beautiful; he read an imaginary last sermon by Sir Thomas a Becket. After a quiet lunch at the rectory, I found him late afternoon in his favorite chair where he had a nice view of the Twin Peaks. He seemed to have fallen asleep, smiling about some pleasant memory.

 Just last week I finished clearing the rectory getting ready for our new vicar. In a drawer in Fr. Westbrook's desk I found this letter that I had completely overlooked previously. Written just a few weeks before Easter, he must have sensed death was imminent. Quite coincidentally your sister, Omega, while passing through Grasmere, stopped. She was kind enough to verify your address. I did not take the liberty of reading his letter to you, but a card inside of the box bore the message FOR LIZA. I am so happy that I can carry out his wish.

     Your humble servant,
     Hannah Craig

Wiping her blinded eyes on the corner of her apron, Liza read aloud:

My Dear Liza,

 Almost ten years ago I watched you pass through the lych gate retracing your steps down a narrow road leading to the life we would be unable to share.

I know the decision was best for both of us; still the ache has lingered. At such odd moments I see your cropped dark hair, your flashing eyes. I do not even attempt to stifle a chuckle when I hear your voice call the mourners at your mother's wake "bitches," and I'm delighted that you had not the least remorse. Of course, my dear, I was quite smitten by your beauty, but more than that I admired and loved your candor in expressing convictions, making you a woman quite out of time. I read that American women now have the franchise; your English sisters follow suit. Much to the amazement of my brethren, I champion their cause, and I foresee the Church of England extending Holy Orders to your sex before this century ends.

I loved your forthrightness, but even more I remember moments we were one in thought. How rare to find someone with whom silence is the speaker filling the vast and lonely spaces. I have no qualms expressing these feelings. I know in my heart they are yours.

What joy to find such immutability, not just in art as Keats so beautifully stressed, but also in another person! You were that person for me. You gave me so much in such a short period. I like to think that I gave you God, not in the burning bush but in the loveliness of his entire creation and in his infinite love. It seems, therefore, "fitten," as I remember you southerners saying, that you should have my mother's ring, which I began wearing on my right hand soon after my return to England. It symbolizes the priest's vow of celibacy. The cross with which I had it etched is for God. The diamond is for you.

God Bless!

Charles

Fr. Westbrook +

Liza opened the box. The ring, snug in its velvet niche, glowed in its twenty-two carat gold richness. On the cross-beam winked a small diamond. Mama's gold band still encircled the finger of her right hand, where she had placed it one of those dreamless nights when she had indulged in dreams. Now without hesitation she slipped his ring on the third finger of her left hand, a perfect fit. She whispered, "With this ring I thee wed." Through her tears she spotted a cardinal on the windowsill. He had come to partake of the last breadcrumb of his morning feed. Catching her eye, he paused for just the briefest moment before flapping his wings and becoming a scarlet streak skyward.

CHAPTER THIRTY

AUTUMN LEAVES

FALL IN THE LOW COUNTRY does not have the colorful palette which limns the trees climbing the hills, where an invisible brush strokes the green forest of mountain pine and fir topped by a clear blue sky with the gold of maple and the scarlet of sweet gum and dogwood. Liza had seen paintings of such splendor. On days like this one in October, Liza felt as flat as the land that surrounded her. The water oaks sloughed dull brown leaves that needed weekly rakings. The air had lost the steamy summer heat, but still her damp dark hair clung in ringlets to her forehead as she piled the fallen leaves into pyramids. Not a wind stirred to scatter them. Tomorrow, Saturday, would be time enough. Leaning the rake against the tree, she turned toward the porch, where Nora was busy making her own mountains in crayon on yellow lined tablet paper. Josh would be coming home from school soon full of news of his high school and eager to visit the cookie jar and lift the lids of the pots simmering on the stove. Zack had offered to fetch him from Lambert. Liza dropped down on the front steps, draping her gray gingham skirt over her drawn up knees over which she laced her fingers. Across the way was the house that Tom had built, now occupied by Zack and Birdie. Birdie missed the swamp of the Big Pee Dee, but most of all she missed her wild friends. "Don't feel quite right, Liza. Mornings I watch my wild turkeys creep out of the woods. I had two little fawns uster play around the around the edge of the yard. Course I go back to feed 'em. Ain't the same though. They good company. Bettern most people. Course Zack needs to be closer to the farms here. Your house bettern ourn. Still —." Liza caught her hand.

"I know, Birdie. Lately I've had the strangest feelings. I thought once I left the Neck, I'd never want to go back. Now and then I get a hankering for that black water, feel the sand under my toes, in the shallow water, watch it creep up the cypress knees as the tide comes in. I have a sister somewhere in the Neck. A brother, too. Funny though how you can't wait to get away, but then something pulls you back. You hate it and love it. There's a big word for that, Birdie. Ambivalence."

Birdie bent down to pluck a clump of crab grass from the tender shoots of a fall mustard bed. She held up the roots clinging to the dark earth for Liza's inspection. "Reckon I know what you mean. I thought I'd never want to see red clay again. You don't find black dirt in them mountains. I'd kinda like to see sourwood growing out of stone—turned bright red by now. Makes the sweetest honey. Kinda like life. It's hard making a living in them hills, but you ain't never tasted such water gushing over rocks or felt such a breeze even in July. Even the bees know the diffrunce. That how come the honey so sweet."

Liza reached an arm around Birdie's waist and drew her close. "Oh, Birdie. One day you are going to show me those mountains. One day maybe, I'll see the Langdale Pikes. The twin peaks." The tiny diamond sparkled on the finger of her left hand. "At last I have found a measure of peace."

Birdie picked up her hand."He made you find yourself. He opened up your ears and eyes. That's what your mama done give you. She had him waiting for you at her home. Ain't nobody gonna steal him from you. You can hear him in the song the wind make; you can see him move on still water. Like the Great Spirit. He everywhere."

"Oh, my dear, Birdie! How did you know?"

Birdie smiled and then pointed her index finger toward her heart before pressing her high cheekbone on Liza's. Just as Charles said, Liza thought, silence speaks louder than words.

Liza's eyes moved now to her laced fingers and studied the ring. "Mother," Nora prattled, "look what Nora made." Cross-sticks of red, green, yellow, purple swam in front of her. Liza pulled her child close.

"That's good, Nora. What is it? You have to give it a name." Nora turned her blond head from side to side in deep thought as she contemplated a name. One chubby finger traced the configuration of the cross and diamond on the ring.

"What it mean, Mother?"

"Love, Nora," Liza whispered.

"That's what my picture's name," she returned solemnly. Little arms stole around Liza's neck. Joy and sorrow met in Liza's tears.

Nora heard the chug of the car first as it rumbled toward Brown Hill. "Josh," she shouted. Minutes later, the Model T slowed and gasped to a stop. Josh, behind the wheel with Zack at his side, waved a greeting with Nora already scrambling up the running board to give her brother a hug. Liza watched from the porch as Josh approached. One arm carried Nora, licking the red lollipop he had brought her, and the other carried a suitcase. This visit would be extended. Next week Liza and Josh would leave for Charleston for Megan's wedding. Liza smiled as she surveyed the tall boy in knickers, his red hair mingling with his sister's blond curls. Liza rose and clasped both of them.

"Good to have you home, Josh. How is school?"

"Got a "A" on that story you helped me with. Gosh, Liza, you know more than them teachers."

"Those teachers, Josh," Liza corrected gently.

"'Aw shucks. Those teachers. I can't get away from school even at home," he complained teasingly.

"Those teachers," Nora repeated. "See? I speak correct."

Josh and Liza laughed. "Correctly, Nora," Josh said as he tugged at one of her blond curls.

The candelabra flickered shadows on the damask white tablecloth. They had eaten in the dining room to celebrate. Now that the last piece of fried chicken had disappeared and all but one of Liza's biscuits remained, Josh and Nora waited for Liza, who minutes before had disappeared into the kitchen. Now she stood in the doorway, holding a chocolate cake on which candles burned. "Happy birthday to you; happy birth-

day to you; happy birthday, dear Josh; happy birthday to you."
Liza sang in a clear soprano, accompanied by Nora's warbling
on and off key. As was the custom, Josh's gusty breath quaffed
the fourteen candles encircling the cake.

"But, Liza," Josh commented, "my birthday's next
week."

"I know. We'll be in Charleston. We couldn't let Nora
miss the celebration, could we?"

"Guess not," he grinned. "I reckon since she can't go,
she should have the first piece."

Given such distinction, Nora did not voice her usual
question as to why she should not be permitted to accompany
them. Since Josh and Liza would be occupied in the wedding,
there would be no one to see after Nora, who each time insisted
she was big enough to sit by herself. Cake taking precedence
over a trip, Nora concentrated on her slice, her tongue alter-
nating between fork and fingers as she licked the chocolate
goodness.

Light flickered on Liza's left hand as she, too, partook
of her culinary pièce de résistance. Josh, noting the sparkle of
the ring, asked, "Liza, the ring is new. Where did you get it?"

"It belonged to the mother of someone I used to know.
Someone very dear." There was a catch in her voice. Josh
looked at her curiously. "He's gone now." She hesitated a
moment before she said quietly, " Dead."

"Did Papa Tom know him?"

"No, they never met. Want another piece of cake? It
is your birthday."

Like Nora, Josh, too, forgot momentarily to inquire further at the prospect of another slice. Years later he would
remember the ring and ponder who its sender was. Now he
only thought it odd. He had never before seen a cross cen-

tered with a diamond and was not sure he liked it. Actually he preferred the gold wedding band that she now wore on her right hand. He couldn't really explain why except it reminded him of Papa Tom. He was glad Liza married him instead of somebody else who had a mother with such a funny looking ring, he thought. He wouldn't be about to give a girl a ring like that. A diamond solitaire would be more his style.

CHAPTER THIRTY ONE

CHARLESTON

LIZA LEANED AGAINST THE RAIL and stared at the straight gray line of the Atlantic Ocean where it met the sky. Behind her lay the battery and the antebellum homes built by dukes, barons, and earls, a young country's new nobility which had found wealth in the dark lush soil of the Tidewater. That morning she and Josh had purchased a walking tour map and had tramped winding cobblestone streets. They had peered down alleys and over walls into hidden gardens guarded by iron-scrolled gates. Their tired feet finally rested in a pew of

St. Phillip's, where Liza had knelt, crossed herself and lifted her eyes to the gold cross on the altar, behind which the stained glass window featured the Good Shepherd, robed in scarlet and leading a herd of white sheep. She was glad that no one was playing the organ. As it was, it was hard to contain herself. She was glad also that Josh had chosen to amble around the sanctuary gazing at the splendor that held little resemblance to Brown Hill church. Closing her eyes, she tried unsuccessfully to recapture a voice from that past. She could not even summon up his face, although she could isolate certain features that did not meld into a whole—the gray-green eyes, the strong jawline with a hint of a dimple—the nose a bit too long—the hair caught in sunlight as he stood at the lych gate. "Gone," she said silently. Looking down at the ring, she whispered, "Not quite." Josh had interrupted her reverie with questions and was soon impatient to move on. They had found their way to the museum, founded in 1773, the oldest museum in the States, a vast collection of natural history specimens, most of which were connected to the city in some way. The bones and the account of the first man and woman who were hanged for murder intrigued Josh. Together they now stood looking out over Charleston Harbor. Charles had set sail from here. Mama had made her first and final trip here. Undoubtedly great grandmother Eleanora had fled with her Huguenot lover, escaping Oak Grove and the husband she had no longer loved. Strange that she could recall so vividly her portrait when she could not assemble Charles' face. Across the street several colored vendors were hawking their wares in soft guttural Gullah, most of which Liza could not understand. There had been that subtle hint in great grandmother's letter that she, too, like Lucinda, sprang from dark blood. Liza smiled as she realized that she was one of the few Browns of

dark complexion among the blond blue eyes of Saxon ancestry. It was no wonder that the image of Eleanora was fixed in
her mind. After all, she looked at herself each day. And what
irony that great grandfather and his colored mistress Alberta
had followed Eleanora's example and said goodbye to the
South, which still preserved strict color lines. She smiled and
thought if she could have shared with Charles her African
ancestry, he, too, would have been amused. No wonder she
felt such affinity with color. Birdie, her closest friend from
another color line was more like a sister than blond Omega.
She wondered now how Omega had taken the news of
Charles's death. A schoolgirl crush grown into an obsession
had shut out a sister who was a rival. Liza felt somewhat
responsible, having filled Omega's head with knights in shining armor to brighten the gloom of the Neck. Charles per-
sonified gallantry to little Omega. Perhaps it was good that
Omega had not seen him, a man more than twice her age,
dying slowly. In this way she preserved the dream. Liza did
not envy her that. When a woman is confident of a man's love,
Liza thought, she does not mind other women's admiration. It
makes her even prouder to be the chosen one. A light breeze
blew wisps of dark hair into her eyes. Brushing them aside, she
turned to see a tall gray-haired man in morning clothes eyeing
her. She flushed under his bold stare and was about to move
away when he said, "Pardon me, madam. You looked so much
like someone I used to know. I can see now I was mistaken.
Please forgive me. My grandfather's sister had your eyes and
your coloring." He bowed his portly figure and turned toward
the park, his cane clicking on the cobblestones. Liza, her
mouth agape, could say nothing. She stared at the retreating
back of the spokesman and stifled an urge to stop him to ask
for more details. Once more he looked backward, caught her .

eye and then, as though embarrassed, increased his forward pace and lost himself amid a gaggle of schoolgirls in blue uniforms taking a history lesson from a wimpled nun.

"Liza," Josh giggled, " was that man trying to pick you up? What a stupid excuse! Saying you looked like kinfolks."

Liza squeezed his hand affectionately. "Maybe not, Josh. I had relatives who used to live here. It would be a coincidence, I admit, but then," she murmured philosophically, "life is full of them, Josh. A chance meeting can change your life. Exciting but scary, don't you think?"

Josh, his young eyes focused on a ship just appearing on the horizon, proffered no serious speculations. Liza smiled as she read the dreams in his blue eyes, not unlike her own at fourteen she supposed. "We must be getting back. Megan is expecting us."

In spite of herself Liza wept throughout the wedding — St. Michael in candlelight, the pipe organ blessing the kneeling couple in quiet strains of Ave Maria, the hushed reverence of the onlookers, many of whom had also stood in front of the same altar, making solemn vows—some broken, some unbroken — the light in Megan's eyes as she lifted her face to her young husband and Josh, smart in his rented suit, standing proud as the chief usher who had escorted Megan's grandmother to her place of honor. Liza's dark eyes glistened with happy tears. When she closed them, however, she was back at Shiloh with Mama and Papa ringed with their children robed in homemade finery in rainbow colors, and she saw clearly the proud tilt of Mama's head despite the titter that followed, " I pronounce you man and wife." These were the tears that fell unrestrained on the bride's bouquet of white roses nestled in baby's breath. As the organ trumpeted out the triumphal recession of the bride and groom, many eyes followed the regal matron of honor gowned in rose chiffon which clung softly to her lithe figure and which matched the color of the deep rose pinned in dark curls, and they wondered who this woman was with the remarkable flashing eyes. For the second time that day Auguste Baptiste stared at the stranger, and because he, too, had a philosophical bent, said to himself, "La vie est etrange."

CHAPTER THIRTY TWO

DEPRESSION YEARS

NORA WAS TEN and Josh was in his sophomore year at college majoring in engineering when the roaring twenties ceased to roar and Wall Street collapsed, banks closed – millionaires one day became paupers the next – America and the world staggered under the weight of the shock of financial ruin which drove former tycoons to suicide and lengthened bread lines in cities. In the Low Country of South Carolina few were hungry or cold. They filled their larders with pork from the sties, grits from the fields, and fruit from the trees, while their homes were warmed in winter with oak logs cut from the woods. Still little money jingled in their pockets. A popular song played on their phonographs summarized their financial status: "Four cent tobacco and forty cent meat; how in the world can a poor man eat." Uncle Joe, the wise old business-man that he was, had escaped the disaster without great loss, having trusted the stability of postal savings, treasury bonds, and fruit jars buried in Oak Grove's back yard. Liza heeded his advice and did not feel the pinch of that of her neighbors even though prices of cotton and tobacco had plummeted. Sometime her teacher's salary was in the form of vouchers. Many of the farmers, unable to pay their fertilizer bills, piled their belongings in a train car and moved up country seeking jobs elsewhere. The ones hardest hit were the sharecroppers, whose profits were divided with their landlords in return for their manpower. Those lacking the industry to grow their own food, preferring bologna sausage sold in country stores to the cured hams they might have had in smokehouses, often found their way to Liza's door, where she shared from her bounty. "Encouraging laziness—shiftless nogoods," her neighbors would say, but Liza remembered the lean years in the Neck and the scathing tongues of Shiloh and gave to colored and white alike. She had the respect and admiration of her fellow landowners, but the less fortunate of the citizenry idolized her. "The Lawd gonna sho bless you, Miz Liza," she would hear over and over again. Then Liza might add, "Next year this time you can have your own garden, have your own meat with this old sow I'm giving you." Some heeded her counsel, while others remained the downtrodden, beaten not only by bad times but also by the accident of birth and resignation to the kind of life in which parent and grandparents had existed. She remembered conversations with Charles and wondered if he would agree that though man was doomed to choose, was it really choice when programmed by genes, sex, environment. In these ruminations her mind turned toward Mattie and Joey. How could she account for the difference in hers and Omega's worlds? Her land now extended from Brown Hill to the shores of the Big Pee Dee. In a few years Papa Gideon's timbered acres and cleared land would be hers. Recently she had been unanimously elected President of the School Board, an office never before held by a woman. Some even suggested that she run for the state legislature and pull the country out of the economic hole. Liza smiled and thought that even a little dot on the map like Brown Hill could change. In the meantime, she relaxed, feeling security for herself and her little ones. Josh would, undoubtedly build roads, marry well, and have only a vague recollection of the ragged child she and Tom had brought home from the Neck. Nora was already spinning out her future that Liza suspected would take her away from Brown Hill. Omega had done well for herself. The wife of Philip Guignard, she was mistress of Live Oaks and hostess at the parties promoting Guignard Lumber Company, old enough to weather the current slump. One day Oak Grove would be added to her fortune. Her statuesque beautiful sister, the ice maiden that never melted, would reign in cool detachment over her empire. There had not been the slightest thaw in the years since she had graduated from college that might reveal a little girl crying for her mama and naming her big sister fairy godmother who had rescued her from the wicked witch. Maybe the difference was that she and Omega had used their heads while Mattie had used her body, the only asset she had to combat the poverty of her life. Poor Joey—too much like Papa. Somehow she had to find them. It wasn't right that she had so much – so much and yet something was missing –

something lost – something so fragile, so elusive that it was rare, even in dreams, that she could catch hold of it. One night she stood in front of Aunt Mary's beveled gold leaf mirror and examined the tiny lines beginning to crease her forehead. There was a swatch of white in the dark hair around her temple. She wondered if the figure staring back at her was really Liza Brown or just some persona created by Liza Marion, who had died long ago in the dark waters of the Little Pee Dee.

Another face joined her in the mirror. The blond head caught her just below the shoulder. "Mirror, mirror on the wall, who's the fairest of them all?" Nora chanted impishly.

"One who's fair and blue of eyes; One whose beauty none denies," Liza rhymed in answer.

"Oh, Mother, I wish God had made me a brunette."

"Nora, the wicked witches are all dark. The good fairies are blond like you."

"My good fairy's not blond. Mr. Ralston says the prettiest woman in Georgetown County has curly black hair. He says he'd like to drive her to the teachers' meeting next month. He says something special is going to happen there. It's a big secret. I promised not to tell." Nora pressed two fingers to her lips to show that she could be trusted with a confidence.

Liza arranged the silver brush and comb in the center of the dresser. With her feather duster she whisked away a dusting of powder and readjusted Tom's framed picture on the left. "Since when did you get to be such friends with Mr. Ralston?"

"Oh, he visited our room today. He picked me to recite *Little Boy Blue*. He put a gold star on my reader."

"And when did this little conversation about driving the prettiest woman take place?"

"When Miss Mildred sent me to his car to fetch the

extra spellers. Since the Cribbs moved here, we ran out."

"Nora, if what he told you was a secret, why are you telling me?"

"But, Mother, don't you see? He said I could tell you. But nobody else." Nora smiled wisely. She not only knew that she had been used but was thoroughly enjoying being a key player in the strategy.

"Nora, a wise old writer once said, "Two can keep a secret if one of them is dead." The two giggled together.

"You going to the meeting with Mr. Ralston?"

"He hasn't asked me."

"I bet a nickel he will."

Theodore Ralston was the newly elected superintendent of education of the county. In the months past, Liza was quite aware that he had observed her class more frequently than he had her colleagues' and had also noted that his interest in her was not completely academic. A graduate of Harvard, Mr. Ralston, soft spoken and mild mannered, clipped his words and sounded his final consonants as though the new accent had been recently acquired. Liza smiled to herself as she mentally compared the language of George Marion of the Neck and that of his daughter and speculated that Mr. Ralston and she shared similar backgrounds. Neither speech nor his impeccable dress had changed his marital status and at fifty, he still remained eligible. There had been jovial teasing by the other teachers. One of them wondered if he wooed with or without the accent. Liza had secretly wondered if his ineptness with the ladies had deep roots in his psychological make-up. These thoughts turned toward Jess, the lonely outcast and anomaly of Brown Hill. In her, Jess had found a friend but not one close enough to keep him from "shaking off the dust of Brown Hill" in that last violent act. It was not that she thought she could have been his savior; she was fatalistic enough to believe that only the peculiar mixture in the psyche made one able or unable to survive the "flaw" inherent in everyone's nature. Still she felt sharp guilt about Jess and determined to make a real effort to put Theodore Ralston at ease, who for the most part had confined his conversation to choice of textbooks or the pros and cons of Dewey's radical ideas on education. Now as she and Nora stood before the mirror, she wished with all her soul that this little girl had such elements so mixed that she, too, like her mother, "would manage" as the older Nora once predicted. At the same time she resolved to draw the Harvard pedagogue out and proffer her friendship. Tweaking her daughter's nose playfully, she retorted, "I bet he will, too." They laughed like schoolgirls contemplating future conquests.

Two weeks later, Liza sat in the Gladstone Hotel in Georgetown across the table from Ted Ralston. During the trip to the meeting, their relationship had moved to a first-name basis with the conversation actually turning from academic to such trivialities as Low Country weather and table fare. Ted had commented that the brilliance of mountain fall had escaped the flat lands, and the two of them laughingly admitted that while most of the vittles were very palatable, neither of them had developed a taste for chitterlings. Now as she looked at the plaque bearing the words *Elizabeth M. Brown, Teacher of the Year of Georgetown County*, she turned a quivering smile on her host as her dark eyes misted a second time that evening. "You know, Ted, I've always been Liza. I doubt that I have a birth certificate. Britton Neck, where I was born, didn't always register its children except in the family Bible on pages between the Old and New Testament. This Elizabeth is a stranger or maybe the other part of a split personality with whom Liza is unacquainted—like two people in one body. Life is so strange," she murmured. "Maybe a different person emerges as one meets different people—many personalities revolving around a center." Her right hand made a circle with the stem of her water goblet. "Goodness! What might you think of these solemn meanderings? I suppose this glass of champagne you brought to celebrate has loosened my tongue. I promise to shut up." She lifted her eyes to his and smiled. "After all, I should know something about this Liza and Elizabeth. We've been living together thirty odd years. I'd rather like to hear about you, Ted." She flashed a warm encouraging smile across the table.

Ted Ralston rearranged the silver at the side of his plate. Without lifting his eyes to meet her open glance, he returned softly as though he were measuring each word that had already been tested before utterance. "I understand, Liza. At the moment I'm not quite sure which part of Ted is coming out. The truth of the matter is I'm quite shy." Now his steady gray eyes met hers momentarily. They were nice eyes, Liza decided. He was not a bad looking man at all, even though his brown hair line had receded to a widow's peak. Still there was no evidence of a pot belly like most men at fifty, and his gray pin-striped suit with a tie coordinated to match was evidence of his careful taste. The gold Phi Beta Kappa pin on the lapel of his coat testified to his scholarship. He raised his wine glass and said, "Here's to Liza, whom I would really like to call Elizabeth, because I would also like to think that a special side of Liza is emerging for me," he finished, stammering slightly.

"Why, Ted, what a nice thing to say. I'll drink to that." She touched her glass lightly to his. Then she continued mischievously, "Oh, how children's and teachers' tongues will wag in their matchmaking. Brown Hill especially cannot conceive of friendship between the opposite sexes." These words were meant to set the record straight. She was rewarded with his bantering rejoinder in a deep southern slur.

"Why, Miss Liza! How you do talk. You done dashed a man's hopes." The accent though exaggerated, seemed more natural than the clipped words of the classroom, and their shared laughter moved them to another plane of easiness. Liza felt confident that this was the beginning of a friendship but was content for now to relax in light chatter about the events of the recent teachers' meeting, safe ground forming a foundation for the future.

As they sipped their after dinner coffee, the conversation turned suddenly to a more serious note. It began with Ted's question, "Elizabeth, would you tell me about the ring on your left hand?" The request was made in such a way to indicate there would be no offense if she chose not to answer. Liza looked down at the small diamond that caught the candlelight as she turned her hand. She had never really discussed Charles with anyone before. How odd that she felt a kindred spirit in this man, with whom she had spent only a few hours.

"A number of years ago I had dinner in this same hotel with the man who gave me this ring. We loved each other," she whispered softly. "But I was married to Nora's father. He was a priest in the Anglican Catholic Church. He's dead now. This was his Episcopal ring. It symbolized his vow of celibacy. The diamond he added later—especially for me. It sounds like a Victorian novel, doesn't it? Except it's true. A part of Liza died with Charles," she finished quietly.

"I understand. I lost someone, too." He gave no further details. Neither he nor Liza thought them necessary. It was enough that their grief was mutual.

Brown Hill in the months ahead noted the frequency of the superintendent's roadster parked in front of Liza's house.

Of course, they speculated on romance. They felt that the brave smart widow had found a match in the educated schoolman who talked so funny. Of course, Liza would not marry a dirt farmer. Not one of them ever thought or for that matter cared that she had never been to college. To them she was as smart as a whip but had never let "larning go to her head." There was one thing about Liza Brown. She treated everybody alike. Niggers loved her as much as whites, and while some didn't quite understand her camaraderie with the lesser citizens, they grudgingly admitted that "she was no respecter of persons" and supposed that just as she had told them in Sunday School, Jesus wasn't either. Why had Mr. Ralston not popped the question? After awhile they decided that he had, but she had turned him down. Still grieving for her husband who died in the war they said. But it was strange that Mr. Ralston kept coming back, taking her and her daughter, Nora, on trips. What they did not know was that theirs, Ted and Liza's, was a warm friendship where on many evenings they shared their pasts and travelled the long road to their present situations. They both relaxed in the comfort of a brother-sister relationship, and Liza felt no jealousy when he squired ladies in Georgetown to social functions. Ted kept her abreast of contemporary writers. Into Uncle John's library had come new names: F. Scott Fitzgerald, Edith Wharton, and Theodore Dreiser. The two sometimes wrangled over the merits of writers and while Ted felt that the superficial characters that peopled Fitzgerald's novels would not render him a lasting place in literature, Liza saw the beauty of the sparkling images he created with such facility. Once in their conversation Liza had confided wistfully, "Ted, I would like so much to write. I don't have the easiness with words that you have. It would be like a catharsis. And yet there is a part of me still hanging—a loose line dangling over Little Pee Dee water."

Ted's response had been reassuring. "Oh, but you do, Elizabeth. Big words don't create great writing. Writing seriously is a full-time job. And you shouldn't keep that line dangling. You'll have to go back, you know. Walk where you once walked. I do that myself almost every year. I go back to Copper Hill, Tennessee. It's one of the most godforsaken places on earth. The sulphur fumes from the mines have killed every sprig of grass so that a milk cow would starve if her feed were not imported. But you know," his voice was reverent and fervent, "there is such ugly beauty in those masses of red clay coated with green slag. I left Copper Hill even as you left the Neck, but I think that, for both of us, escape is possible only if we go back." Liza found herself nodding in agreement and remembered almost the same kind of advice from Birdie years ago when she had urged her to go to Oak Grove. One day the Neck would claim her, but for now she pushed away the image of Parker Landing and a sister and brother still wandering somewhere in the heavy swampland that the sun seldom touched.

In the early spring of '32, Oak Grove also summoned her. Uncle Joe died. When he had not come in for supper, Aunt Lizzie had gone out to call him from his perennial chores of clearing out last year's gourds in preparation for the return of the martins. Two poles stood smartly dangling their triple rows of homes for the migrants tired from their flight across the sea. Each abode had undergone a thorough house cleaning, awaiting the bits of straw and lumber shavings scattered conveniently about so that they would not have to go far afield for nest furnishings. The third pole was leaning against the branches of an old oak tree. Nearby, lay Uncle Joe, the gourds destined for the last pole around him like scattered toys. His fall had smashed one of them, but his gold rimmed spectacles remained unbroken only inches away. "Looked like," said Aunt Lizzie to Liza, "Joe took 'em off to wipe trash outa his eyes. Had his handkerchief still in hand. Reckon he won't be needing them no more," she whimpered.

"Aunt Lizzie, we must see that the third pole goes up in its place, for the martins will soon be coming," Liza whispered. She smoothed back a wisp of gray hair and leaned over to kiss her aunt on the forehead.

"Done done it, Liza. Had Joby, Della's boy, finish it yestiddy. Joe wouldn't rest easy knowing there wasn't enough room for all coming. He counted over two hundred last year. Them crazy birds like his own younguns we never had. Course, we had one, Liza. Lost it. Joe said it was a boy. I never seen it myself." Her pale blue eyes looked intently into Liza's. "See me and Joe had to git married. I won't nothing 'cept a poor sharecropper's youngun, but Joe did right by me. Joe's gone, but he never had no right to treat your mama like he done. Reckon God punished him not letting us have other younguns. Course, Omega's been a blessing. She ain't the little girl we brung home with that Cinderella doll I give her that Sunday. I don't speak good English like her high-class friends. Me and Joe still love her. Ain't nothing gonna change that," she affirmed.

Liza pressed her aunt's wrinkled hand, splotched in brown and misshapen with arthritis. For the first time she felt a wave of hostility toward her sister. Looking up, she saw Omega standing in the doorway. Before Liza could say anything, Omega turned abruptly. Momentarily, Liza heard her rapid footsteps descending the stairs.

It was a simple prayer book funeral without a eulogy. As the pallbearers paused at the lych gate as was the custom,

Liza, holding on to Aunt Lizzie's hand, remembered. Omega and her young husband marched behind them. At the graveside in the family plot at Oak Grove came the solemn words: "Unto Almighty God we commend the soul of our brother departed and we commit his body to the ground; earth to earth, ashes to ashes, dust to dust." Liza made a mental calculation: Little Ida, Mama, Papa, Tom, Jess, Charles, and Uncle Joe. She thought about death—the mystery of it—the protocol that accompanied it. Uncle Joe looked so out of place in his satin lined box, spruced up in his best suit with his tie neatly knotted and his cheeks reddened with artificial color and his hands folded ceremoniously on his chest. Never in his life had she seen those hands idle. She could almost hear his pert remark. "Great guns, Liza. I don't look like myself." She smiled in spite of herself and drew a comic picture of Uncle Joe approaching a bearded St. Peter with "Jumping Jehosaphat, Pete! Let me in so I can shed these fancy duds."

Back in Oak Grove in the front parlor, Lawyer Jameson read Uncle Joe's will. There were only a few surprises. Aunt Lizzie was now in sole possession of Oak Grove. At her death it would pass into Omega's hands except for the portraits, which would be Liza's along with a hundred acres of timber "to my great niece, Nora, who is the namesake of my beloved sister." The biggest surprise came from Aunt Lizzie, who wanted to vacate the house and spend her remaining years with Liza.

The four of them—Liza, Nora, Omega, and Aunt Lizzie—shared the leftovers of the food sent in by neighbors for dinner. It was Philip's poker night with friends, Omega had explained. At supper the conversation was stilted, unnatural—part of the protocol, Liza mused. Even the usually effervescent Nora had little to say, although she asked Aunt Omega if the diamond solitaire she was wearing was real. Liza had not caught Omega's response. The exchange between the two sisters had been polite and formal, and Liza had made no move to break the icy barrier. At one point after supper, Liza found herself in front of great grandmother's portrait. She was going to ask Aunt Lizzie if she could claim her bequests of portraits now, when she heard footsteps behind her.

"You have always been fascinated by her, haven't you?" Omega's voice was matter-of-fact. "I suppose the reason is that you have her coloring. There is even something about the eyes that are yours. She's not a bit like the blond Browns. She must be Latin. French Huguenot, I believe. But like the Browns she must have had the curse of sterility. Brown progeny does not seem to follow typical southern reproduction.

"Except for Mama. Her lot was to have a baby every year. You don't remember five children cramped in that lean-to in the Neck, do you?"

"Of course, I remember. I haven't had brain damage. And I haven't forgotten the debt I owe the sister who was my avenging angel, rescuing me from the clutches of wicked Jane. I even know how I got my name. Mama didn't really want me. She hoped I would be the last. It's a pity she didn't call you Alpha so that you could have enjoyed some of the jokes that have followed me around. I dislike my name, but I think I dislike you even more. You are the reigning queen of the Brown clan. Everybody admires and loves Liza, the good Liza, the beautiful Liza, and the long-suffering Liza. Even that queer Ted Ralston never stops singing your praises. You attract them all. Men and faggots."

Liza's hand rose involuntarily to strike her sister, but she managed to stop it in mid-air. Her eyes blazed fire. "The last time I called a woman a bitch was at my mama's casket when they slandered her, because she was pregnant with me when she married our papa. I cannot change your perception of me, but I won't tolerate your denigrating my friends. I would put Ted Ralston's manhood up against any Southern swain's, including your husband's, in this or last year's cotillion. There is no comparison in the weight of his values or the contributions he is making. If a college education makes you ashamed of the people who loved you, then deliver me from a sheepskin. What in God's name makes you think you can flaunt superiority over people different from you or less learned. Look at grandmother Eleanora." Her finger pointed to the portrait. "She was destroyed by such prejudice. You know the reason she is dark? Somewhere in the past a young African scout mated with a French maiden. I am proud that I look like her. I am also proud to claim kinship with a colored educator in New York whose mother was fathered by this woman's husband. Despite your blond banners, Omega, a few drops of black blood run in your Anglo-Saxon veins. I just wonder what Charles Westbrook would say about your high-mindedness." The last sentence was the parting thrust. With it, her rage subsided. Liza dropped down in a chair and with her head between her hands sobbed. "God, Omega! What has happened to us?"

Liza heard Omega's footsteps climb the stairs slowly. Later when she and Nora lay in Mama's bed, she listened for some sound from Omega's room. She was tempted to try once more for reconciliation, but the possibility of defeat and the ensuing bitterness kept her silent. The next morning Omega had left. On the downstairs table in the hallway, Liza found an envelope bearing her name. Inside was a black and white photograph of a churchyard with mountains in the background. A cross inked in black marked one marble tomb. The note said, "I think you should have this. Maybe it will make you think me less of a bitch. Omega."

A month later, with Aunt Lizzie ensconced in a guest room and under the watchful eye of Birdie, Liza, Nora, and Ted set out on the long journey to the mountains and to see Josh graduated. It was a tedious trek over muddy roads with frequent flat tires. Liza watched with interest as the black soil of the Low Country turned to gray and then to red. The flat terrain gave way to hills and then as they neared Highlands, the destination for the night, Liza had her first glimpse of real mountains looming against a blue sky scudded with white wisps of clouds. As she looked at the purple peaks, lines from Millay's "Renascence" echoed. "And he whose soul is flat the sky will cave in on him by and by." Nora, asleep on her mother's shoulder, did not stir. Ted smiled and pulled over to the side of the road, where the hillside was sprinkled with Ragged Robins, dandelions, and Queen Anne's lace. "All that I saw from where I stood were three long mountains and a wood," Ted quoted, opening the poem Liza had just ended. Liza settled Nora's head on Ted's shoulder and eased herself from the seat and outside where a brisk wind whipped her hair. A few paces uphill brought a view of a lone cow grazing on sparse grass growing between jagged rocks. Just above, a waterfall gushed from a craggy cliff and trickled its way along a stream. That she was not close enough to see its thundering flow or hear its gurgle over rocks did not matter. She had followed its path with Wordsworth, where cataracts had haunted him like a passion. Now she closed her eyes and, like Lanier and his Chatahoochee in the hills of Habersham, followed the rippling water down its long descent to a river and eventually to the quiet flow of the Little Pee Dee reflecting phantoms on its liquid face. She felt such a oneness with hill and plain, with sea and sky. But there was such security in those hills that lifted leafy branches to a sky that even now was misting the top-most peak in a spring shower and would also clothe the naked limbs in winter with white. They would always be there, weathering nature's whims, and she decided that at last she had found where she truly belonged. Nora's hand broke her reverie. "Oh, Mother," she whispered. "It's prettier than the pictures. And the books say millions of years ago they were under the sea. It's scary. I mean what happens. Do you suppose one day Brown Hill will be a mountain?"

"Who knows, Nora. Maybe one day this little place called earth, now just a pin point in the sky, will explode into a million meteors."

"That would be like the end of time like Preacher Gibbons says. I wouldn't like that."

Liza hugged her daughter close. "Oh, yes you would. You'd be one of the brightest lights. I can see these golden curls streaking across the sky."

"You're so funny, Mother. But I don't want to be a meteor. I'd much rather be turned into a mountain. Then I could look down below and laugh at all the crazy people like Aunt Omega, who would really trade that big diamond she wears for your little one."

"Come now, Nora. That's nonsense."

"No, Mother. I saw her eyes think it when I asked her if hers was real. Remember what she said. 'Not really.' And all the time she was looking at your little one. Crazy. Right?" Nora questioned.

"Not really," Liza murmured.

There were two hundred young men graduating from Clemson in that year. Most of them received degrees in agriculture. South Carolinians referred to Clemson as a cow college. The graduates returned to the farm, where they implemented the modern methods learned in school or took jobs as agriculture teachers in high schools. A surprising third, however, had taken degrees in engineering. Josh was one of these. When the name *Joshua Cable Brown* was called, followed by the words *cum laude*, a trio on the front row stood clapping their hands. From another section of the auditorium Liza heard another applause. "Mother, it's Aunt Omega. She's come to see Josh get his diploma," Nora shouted. At this point she had climbed up on her seat and was waving a wild welcome. The people around smiled warmly at the sight of a golden-haired girl in red hat and jumper greeting a relative. Liza made no move to correct her. She and Ted smiled at each other, and the moment passed as the next graduate's name was called.

His arms around Nora on one side and Liza on the other, Josh in his gown faced Ted's camera. Looking on a few paces away was Omega. Josh broke the pose and rushed toward his half-sister. He scooped her up in his arms. "Mega, you made it. Now I know where all the whistles were coming from. You prettier than a movie star." Now it was Nora's turn to greet her aunt. For just a moment there was an awkward pause before Liza came forward to embrace Omega. "I'm so glad you came," Liza whispered. "It means so much to Josh. To me, too," she added quickly. Omega smiled and kissed Liza lightly on the cheek. No one could have guessed the scene a month before. Only when Ted took Omega's hand did a faint blush suffuse her cheeks. To onlookers an attractive loving family—cream of South Carolina croppings, surrounded the young graduate.

In the dining hall the President treated the graduates and their families. Josh had reserved a table for six, expecting Omega and her husband Philip. In his absence Josh had insisted on his roommate's joining them. Scott Farraday's family, who lived up in the West Virginia mountains, had not been able to attend. Right away Liza perceived the basis for Josh and Scott's closeness. Here was another, who like the others at the table, had had a beginning in a similar Neck. Omega, who also read the same picture, was unusually warm to Scott, who blushed often being the object of a beautiful woman's attention. Josh sensed his friend's embarrassment but eager to have some fun quipped, "Look, Scott, Mega's married. Stop making eyes at her. Low Country men still fight duels. I'd hate to be one of your seconds one early morning."

"Oh, no, Josh!" Omega countered. "Philip and I are getting a divorce. I have already moved to Oak Grove. Like Henry's Catherine I have failed to give the Guignards an heir. Phil has several other prospects," she said blandly. "No doubt Live Oaks will soon be filled with children's laughter." The sudden announcement of her change in situation ended with as little import in her voice as a casual change of address.

CHAPTER THIRTY THREE

THE RETURN
OF THE NATIVE

THE THIRTIES brought change to life in the Low Country and change to Liza. Josh, graduated, was working with the state highway department mapping out hard-surface roads that would eventually crisscross the state. Nora was in her last years at the newly consolidated school accommodating grades one through eleven. In the name of progress teacher training now demanded college credits, and Liza's provisional certificate required renewal with study that would take her away during the summer months from people for whom she felt responsible. So she dusted her last eraser and checked the last spelling paper in the four-room schoolhouse where she had been teaching fifteen years. She remembered with joy that first day when she had tried to introduce her pupils through books to the world outside of Brown Hill. She was gratified that with some she had succeeded in teaching them to love books and whether they followed behind a mule plowing a furrow or having babies year after year, there would always be escape in the magic of words. The traveling library from town now made monthly stops in Brown Hill. Liza was not the only customer to meet the little red bookmobile. Only a handful of her pupils, however, had moved on beyond elementary school and into high school. Aside from her own children, only one had graduated. Her pride and joy was Zack and Birdie's elder son. Forest, with an apt mind and agile body, had graduated and with Ted's help received a scholarship to the university. A promising athlete, his parents would have little financial responsibility. They were so proud and so grateful. Birdie confided to Liza, "The Great Spirit sent us from them hills to flat country and to Liza. My fir tree," that was her nickname for her tall son, "got all the height from me, but he strong like his daddy. He gonna grow, and grow, and grow 'till he hit the sky. Be something if a Cherokee git to be President," she laughed. As Liza rejoiced in the accomplishment of one red man, she looked across the road on winter mornings to see colored children wending their frosty way to school in the Negro church. She doubted the quality of the instruction and cringed at the unfairness where white schools consolidated and buses, however slow, now picked up white children each morning. She thought of Aunt Lucinda and her progeny, who unfortunately, had fled north when they were needed so badly here. Life held little fairness, Liza decided. Was it the Great Spirit, as Birdie had suggested, who directed certain favored ones into the life of "the privileged" or was it simply Lady Luck? And how did Omega fit into this chess game? With the attributes of a queen— beautiful, charming, and intelligent—what invisible hand had captured her and called checkmate, relegating her to lonely Oak Grove, where her solitude was interrupted only by weekend parties. Rumor had it that on occasion the old house rocked with the merriment of its guests fortified with Jack Daniels. She visited Brown Hill on rare occasions, one being the death of Aunt Lizzie.

One winter morning in January, Aunt Lizzie did not rise first to light the stove fueled by a carbide generator, which furnished the house with lights, a decided improvement over candles and kerosene lamps. Nora rising early to board the school bus, it was Aunt Lizzie's custom to have Liza's coffee ready along with a plate of grits, eggs, and country ham. No longer required to go to school, Liza had taken to sleeping late. Often she woke encased in rows of books which had led her the night before into the arms of Morpheus. The savory odor of brewed coffee usually wakened her along with the puttering steps of Aunt Lizzie, as she opened cupboards and closed doors. On this morning it was the mantel clock chiming nine that roused Liza. The silence downstairs and the absence of a redolent breakfast sent her scurrying to Aunt Lizzie's room, where she found Aunt Lizzie lying peacefully under a mound of quilts necessary on a winter's night. Liza touched her Aunt's forehead and realized that the inert little lady needed no more massive covers to warm her. The expression on her face was as though she were about to break into a smile. Liza had heard that frequently old people in the hour before death had visions of departed loved ones and wondered if Aunt Lizzie had sighted Uncle Joe. She and Omega had stood together in the family plot at Oak Grove, where Aunt Lizzie joined her husband and in-laws. As they turned toward the house, Omega had suddenly caught Liza's hand and whispered, "Thank you for making her happy." It was as close as she could come to expressing regret for the alienation from family. Only Nora, who looked enough like Omega to be her daughter, seemed unaware of estrangement. Liza smiled as she listened to the unforced chatter between her daughter and her sister. The premature lines in Mega's face and the gradual laxness in her attention to dress and hair saddened Liza, who found a measure of contentment that at least Nora could bridge the gap.

That night after Aunt Lizzie's funeral, Liza once again studied great grandmother's portrait, which now belonged to her. She had decided at Uncle Joe's death not to trust angering Omega more by claiming them then. Mentally she was hanging them in the parlor at Brown Hill when she heard Nora, who was in the front parlor with Omega, ask.

"Aunt Omega, how old were you when you fell in love for the first time?"

"You wanting to take a peek into my personal life, huh?"

"Well, at least it must be more interesting than my love life. I'm sixteen and haven't had even a prick from Cupid's arrow. Mother says she's glad. I don't know. My life is so boring. School and tests, and silly parties. Nothing happens. Just a kiss here and there. I just have to read about other people's romances. Like plain Jane and Mr. Rochester. Course, I can make up wonderful stories about me." She giggled. "I'm always beautiful, the put-upon heroine, but eventually my knight whisks me away. Not on a horse, though. In a brand new car with leather upholstery and a diamond big as the one you used to wear. You know, Aunt Omega, speaking of diamonds, Mother never has told me about the little one she wears in that funny ring. Shuts me up with 'Oh, Nora, somebody I knew years ago. Before you were born.' Do you know anything about it?" she asked inquisitively.

"Your mother has lots of secrets. Every woman does. One day you will have them, too. It's best to let your mother be. She's never talked about the ring to me. Unlike you, I wouldn't ask her. I let sleeping dogs lie, as the saying goes. It's best not to stir ashes in the fireplace unless you want to rebuild a fire."

Liza, not wanting to eavesdrop further, stole quietly from the dining room into the pantry Omega had converted into a small breakfast nook.

On the way back to Brown Hill, Nora had commented briefly, "Being an only child is not great fun. I wish I had a sister like you. I'd tell her just about everything. Course, I tell you just about everything. But it's different. You wouldn't talk the same way to your sister as you would to your mother."

Liza caught the hint. Nora was voicing her curiosity about the strained relationship her mother had with Omega. Liza slowed the Model T to a stop to let a stray hen scuttle her brood of biddies across the road. The engine died and the necessity of priming a restart of ignition saved Liza's response. Someday she would share Charles with Nora — some day when Nora had found the love her mother might have had.

That summer of '35 Ted Ralston on one of his visits came with two offers. Now that the post office had also closed and was incorporated in the town, Liza spent most of her daylight hours in her garden or library.

"You're going to seed. Liza, you need to be back at work. A night school is opening in the fall to teach people how to read and write. You know South Carolina leads the states in the highest percentage of illiteracy. You won't get paid much, but knowing you, money won't be your reward. But what's more exciting is the new project President Roosevelt has begun. He's authorizing the writing of a history for each state under the Work Projects Administration." Liza laughed heartily. "You don't understand. It's not the WPA of digging ditches. The staff will be teachers and writers, not employed. A Miss Montgomery from Columbia has asked me for recommendations. I took the liberty of sending in your name. You will be part of a team who will write the cultural history of South Carolina — identify the peculiar background of heritage, education, religion, customs. It's a chance for you to go back to the Neck. You'll see it now from a different perspective. I'm contributing an essay on Copper Hill for the Tennessee edition."

As warm as it was, Liza felt cold perspiration on her forehead. As the crow flies, she thought, only a few miles across two rivers separates me from the Neck. Yet she had never been back since she and Tom had brought her half-brother Josh, an orphan waif, to Brown Hill. She had heard that the house where she had lived with Mama and Papa and Little Ida, Omega, Joey, and Mattie had burned; but Parker Landing would not have changed, nor with it the dark waters of the past. "Oh, Ted, I'm not qualified. I'm not a writer. I'm not even a properly trained teacher. Ask somebody else who needs the money more. There are plenty of college graduates out of work. Ask Omega," she finished brightly. "She's qualified."

"Liza, you're just making up excuses. I submitted to Miss Montgomery one of the articles you wrote for the *Georgetown Times*. You have already been accepted. Of course, you don't have to cover that area. You could concentrate on this side of the river. But I think you should. You've always known you would go back. What better opportunity than to look with detachment through the eyes of a reporter at your childhood home? Writing about the past may bring reconciliation or even a kind of closure."

"Detachment! Ted, you don't know what you're saying. Every cypress knee, every moss-covered tree, every log that floats down the river will rewrite the past. Objective! Ha! You want me, like old Lear, 'to drown the stage with tears.'"

"I want you to render a valuable service to your state and in doing so, perhaps come to terms with what happened a long time ago. Give me your answer in a couple of weeks. I know you'll give it careful thought."

How right he was! The days following she thought of nothing else. Not even in dreams did she escape Mama at Little Ida's grave—Mama's voice "You'll manage" — Papa bringing home a string of catfish whistling *Turkey in the Straw*, his eyes bleary with too many swigs from the jug—Papa at Parker Landing, cut down from the same tree where he had many times tied his boat. She had resolved to say no to Ted's offer when strange news found its way across the Pee Dee. Papa Gideon had come to tell her that the last barn of tobacco had been cured, and it was time to rush up Zack, Birdie's husband, a bit to get the rest ready for market. The last barn had not even been taken off the sticks, much less graded and tied. He was afraid that prices that had opened that year at twenty cents per pound would drop even lower as the market wound down the season. As he started to leave the yard where Liza had paused in her weeding verbena and miniature marigolds, he said, "Liza, I heared a bit of news from Abe Lawrimore. He jist come back from the Neck visiting his sister. Seems like your sister, Mattie, done made a big change.

She's bought her a tent and goin' round holding revivals.
Doing the preachin' herself. Drives a brand new car. It 'pears
like religion turned her around and changed her luck. Abe says
people claimin' to gittin' saved, sanctified, and filled with the
Holy Ghost all in one night. Abe says the shoutin' and hol-
lerin' goin' on in the spirit would put Minnie in her shoutin'
days to shame. Course, I ain't got nothing against the way
people practice religion. Just 'cause it ain't my way ain't no reason for me to quarrel with it. Some people like me and you
like religion kinda quiet. Reckon I ain't never had the mind to
holler about it. It don't matter which road you take if all of 'em
leadin' to the pearly gates."

"Papa Gideon, did Abe see Mattie?"

"Yep! He went to one of her tent meetings. Said the
place was packed. She got fifty dollars in the collection plate
on the first go round."

"Oh, my!" Liza leaned the hoe against the fence and
dusted the dirt from her hands. "You know I haven't seen
Mattie in years. I've wondered about her. I have wanted to tell
her there are no hard feeling. You know. About her and Tom."

"I remember, Liza. I ain't forgot how broke up that boy
was afterward. Reckon a man can stand jist so much tempta-
tion. Ain't many men can say they eyes never gone out of his
wife's bed. Women, too." His eyes glanced fleetingly to Liza's
ring. "Bible warns us against it. Ain't nobody perfect, though.
Jist look at old David, one of God's pets. He got a man killed
to take his woman."

"Papa Gideon, Ted Ralston has asked me to do some
writing about the Neck to go into a kind of history book for
South Carolina. I think I'll take him up on it. I could leave you
in charge here. Birdie is better than I am at getting things
done. I think I need to see Mattie again—not to settle

accounts exactly, but to find out about her—how and why she's taken this path. She is my sister. I should have gotten in touch years ago."

"Might be a good thing, Liza, but just remember her way ain't your way," he iterated. "People got to be what they is."

"I know, Papa Gideon! How well do I know." Liza reached out and took his hand, the same stubby fingers like Tom's. She looked at the thumb that had been nicked by a saw—at the square nails where cuticle had never been pushed back. They were solid hands—as solid as the man who in his humble way had delivered a profound sermon on tolerance. "Papa Gideon, I don't know what I would have done without you through the years. Books have been minor teachers to you. You have been my greatest. It's a pity you don't put your wisdom down in a book for people like Nora, Josh, and Forest. You would be leaving them such treasure."

The old man squeezed her hand and dropped his head as though he were studying the foliage of the Paul Scarlet rose, now bereft of its perennial blooms. He drew out a handker-chief from his overalls pocket as he simulated a cough, but Liza did not miss the wetness in his blue eyes as he smiled into hers. Even his voice was dangerously close to breaking as he answered, "You been a blessing to me. To Minnie, too," he added. "I might let you take a gander at what I been writin down Sunday evenings. It ain't no good English. Jist thoughts I git in my head sometimes."

"Oh, Papa Gideon, some of the greatest books in the world aren't written in the King's English. Old Jim, the Negro slave in *Huckleberry Finn*, couldn't read or write a word, but what he said is better than most sermons on Sunday morning deliv-ered in the biggest churches."

With a car at her disposal, Liza decided to take the long road to Britton's Neck instead of the waterways. Her route took her through the little town of Lambert, renamed Hemingway for a prominent citizen. The small town of less than four hundred souls had served for years as a trading post. The Southern Railroad gave it added distinction and connected the little town to Charleston to the east and north to Hamlet, North Carolina, the junction of Low Country rails. One of Hemingway's citizens had distinguished himself by growing on a one-acre lot thousands of flowers such as gladiolas and dahlias as well as maintaining an orchard, vegetable garden, barnyard of fowl, pig, and cow. It had become a model for do-less farmers during the depression to encourage them to follow the example and become less dependent on "store-bought" groceries. Liza's home, though it had not received the public-ity, could have matched in industry the model acre. On to Ashboro, so named, because at one time or other everything had burned down except the artesian well. Just a few miles north, Liza turned her car east and traversed the red muddy water of the Great Pee Dee, where in recent years a fairly sub-stantial bridge had been built. She was now in the Neck, the narrow strip of land bounded on the west by the Great Pee Dee and on the east by the Little Pee Dee. The two rivers con-verged and flowed into the Waccamaw at Georgetown and on out to sea. Liza stopped at a filling station for refueling. In front of the store stood a bubble top gas tank, where one pumped the amber liquid to measure the gallons marked on its clear glass cylinder. The roof of the store extended into a shed which allowed farmers and field hands brief respite from the sun. As Liza emerged from the car, she met the open stares of two bearded natives, men perhaps in their sixties or older. Each held an RC Cola in one hand and a Moon Pie in the other. The unabashed curiosity in their eyes asked from what neck of the woods had come this woman, not only driving a car but also traveling alone. Few Low Country women learned to drive; the man's place was behind the wheel with his spouse at his side when they ventured a few miles from home to visit the doctor's office or a son or daughter married and living elsewhere. Convinced that this woman with bobbed hair and dress short enough to reveal shapely calves was not from these parts, the short pot-bellied customer ventured to satisfy his curiosity with a question. "You been travelling fur?"

"Not really. I come from Brown Hill in Georgetown County. Plan to spend a few days around here. I was born in Britton's Neck. My daddy was George Marion. I married Tom Brown. I haven't been back in a number of years." Liza knew them well enough that she might as well identify herself and avoid endless probing questions to ferret out her business. "I'm Liza Brown." She extended a friendly hand to each of them who awkwardly maneuvered moon pie and coke. The red-haired older one now spoke.

"Well, Lawd have mercy! Reckon me and you kinda kin. I'm Jed Port. My sister, Jane, married your pappy. Sho was bad what happened. Reckon it's better to stick with these kinda drinks." He held up his empty cola bottle. "Corn likker done drove many a man clean outa his head. After I got saved, I ain't never teched another drop."

Before Liza could respond, the store owner, who had suddenly appeared, was in the process of placing the gas hose into the car tank. "Reckon you wanta fill 'er up."

"Yes, thank you. Would you mind checking the oil and water. My left front tire looks as though it needs some air."

The first speaker took the last swallow from his drink and came forward to lift the hood and pull out the stick to measure the oil. "Bill," he said, addressing the attendant filling the tank, "this here's George Marion's youngun by his first wife. Member she died with cancer at Roper in Charleston? I went to the settin up." Liza felt the color mount her cheeks. She wondered if he remembered the scene when she had driven the mourners from the house. To her relief he rambled on in his reminiscences as he wiped the oil stick on a dirty rag. "My Lawd! Time do fly. Seems jist like yestiddy when we buried that woman at Shiloh. Here's her growed up good-looking daughter. I heared tell you been teaching school. And your sister, the youngest chile, married well—money. Can't recall her name. Kinda uncommon name seems to stick in my mind."

"Omega," Liza replied.

Drawing out the oil stick, he announced. "Bout one quart low, Miss Liza." The fact that he had put a handle to her name was acknowledgment that her situation now was far removed from what it had been twenty-five years ago.

Bill cut off the flow of gas as a few drops gurgled outward onto the ground. He placed the cap on the tank and turned toward Liza and held out a hand yellowed with nicotine. "I'm sho glad to meetcha. I'm Bill Mishoe. Usta run around with your brother, Joey. I ain't seen him in a coon's age. But that sister of yourn, Mattie Marion, she sho making a name for herself. Reckon the Lawd moves in mysterious ways his wonders to perform. Yes, siree. Heared her speaking in tongues jist last week."

Redheaded Jed now contributed to the servicing of the car by unscrewing the cap on the water tank and gauging the water with one squinted eye. "She's full right up to the brim. That old stripdown of mine runs hot ever' few miles. Always have to carry a jug of water around. Reckon these jobs ain't as likely to spew up steam even on warm days like this 'un. By the way, I seed Josh las year. I wouldn't a knowed him without that red hair. Most Ports got it. He come through here surveying a new road they gonna cut through the Neck. He stopped by and had dinner with us. Seemed right hongry for that mess of catfish Martha fried. Only kin I got ever gone to college. I'm proud to claim kin with him. He is sho a fine young man."

"Yes, I thank you. Josh is like my own son. My husband, Tom, and I adopted him, you know."

"That's what I heared tell," Jed replied.

Bill having replenished the oil from the drum under the shed, the three of them accompanied her into the store, where she paid for her gas and oil with a five-dollar bill. Bill handed her the change from a cigar box that served as a cash register.

"Can I buy you a dope?" Southerners often gave that name to soft drinks because of the cocaine that was originally an ingredient. The offer was made by the fat one who had attended mama's funeral but who had neglected to identify himself. Realizing his mistake, he said, "Done fergit my manners. I'm Jim Short. We lived 'bout a mile from Parker Landing. Reckon you could see the river from your house." With his pocketknife he cut a quid from his plug of Brown Mule chewing tobacco and stuck it in his jaw.

"Yes," Liza murmured. "And yes I would like a drink, thank you. An RC would be just right." He lifted the lid to the red metal box filled with ice and drew out a frosty bottle and opened it in the slot on the front of the box. The cap dropped into a metal can on the floor. Liza had seen decorative baskets made with sundry caps wired together. He placed a nickel on the counter. Handing a drink to Liza, he asked, "You planning to go to one a Mattie's meetins?"

"I suppose so, Jim. Certainly I want to see her. Since I'm going to be around for a few days, I wonder if I could locate an extra room to rent for a night or two. Nothing fancy. Just clean sheets and towels and a little breakfast. I will pay, of course."

Now Jed spoke up. "You sho won't pay. Me and Martha glad to have you if you can put up with the fare. The younguns all gone now. Married early. We got a company room we don't never use 'cept when the preacher comes. We Methodists belong to Pine Bluff. We have preaching onc't a month. No harm meant, but me and Martha ain't got much truck with the Holy Rollers. Being saved is enough for us. Don't zackly know what being sanctified and filled with the Holy Ghost means. 'Pears to me the Lawd could give it all in one dose, not drag it out to three. I reckon all the Baptists and Pennycostals think we going to hell since we jist been sprinkled. Course, I got it both ways. I was baptized at Parker Landing before I married Martha. She wouldn't rest easy until I got sprinkled by her preacher and jined her church."

"My father-in-law just said to me a few days ago, 'More than one way to the Pearly Gates.' Everybody must choose his own road."

"And that's the Gawd's truth," Jed replied. "If you wanta look at the room, we jist live a mile and a half up this road. I could ride with you and git you acquainted with Martha."

Liza smiled graciously and thought how different Jane's brother appeared to be. Then she thought about herself and Mega and Mattie and conceded that there was no law that made siblings carbon copies.

A half hour later, she was standing on the porch of Jed and Martha's' home. Looking out on the cleanly swept yards and the neatly trimmed rows of privet hedges leading to the front steps, Liza surmised that the inside of the house was as tidy as the outside. Martha Port, in a clean white apron tied

around an ample waist, welcomed Liza into the sparingly furnished company room, where stood an iron bedstead made up
with a chenille spread under which, Liza was fairly sure, a
feather mattress rested. On the marble-topped washstand,
over which hung a small mirror, sat a basin and pitcher, and on
the rack at the side hung a white towel and wash cloth. A lone
rocker by the bed completed the furniture. Indeed, the whole
house had that scrubbed look that showed Martha's scrupulous
cleaning. Liza looked at the couple standing in the doorway.
To turn down their hospitality would be to say that what they
had to offer was not good enough. Martha said, "It ain't much,
but it's clean."

Liza smiled and said, "I'd love to stay here. Is that fried
chicken I smell?"

"It sho is," Jed replied. "Martha here makes it crisp and
not greasy. Soaks it in buttermilk first."

Liza looked with wonderment at these two simple people. They both knew the fate of Jane Marion, and yet they
welcomed the daughter of the man who in a drunken rage had
killed her and her unborn child. There was a lesson here —
the kind that Papa Gideon taught. It was all about forgiveness
and not holding grudges, and although Liza had hated Jane
and blackmailed her, a well of sorrow brimmed close in Liza's
eyes for the woman who had not learned to cope with the
inner rage that had escaped only in cruelty.

Jed Port brought in her suitcase and filled the pitcher
with fresh water for her to bathe her face and hands before
dinner. In the kitchen they waited for their guest, proud that
one so far above them had chosen to stay with them.
Somehow Liza had to get down on paper what these people
were to share with posterity—simple goodness springing from
clean hearts. And yet they were part of the Neck, which for

years had haunted her and plagued her even in dreams. Now she found herself smiling and engaging in easy chatter with people, who two hours before, she would have been afraid to meet. At one point she asked, "Jed, what became of little Clara, Jane's first child?"

"She married one of the Mishoe boys, Bill's first cousin. They got a passel of younguns. Clara's got the Port red hair. She don't look much like the Marions though. Josh, now he got the Marion nose and eyes."

On dangerous ground, Liza steered the conversation in another direction. "Do you ever talk with Mattie? Does she have children? Did she divorce Buddy Wright?"

It was Martha who answered. "I don't know about no divorce, but Buddy died a few years back. He got his hand cut clean off at the sawmill. Bled to death. Anyways, Mattie took up with a travelling salesman who came through here selling Bibles. I heared she was living up in North Ca'lina. She ain't been back in these parts long. I ain't heared about no youn-guns. I reckon she coulda left 'em up the country. The two of you got a lot ta ketch up on. You gonna be plumb s'prised at how she's turned out. You gonna go hear 'er preach?"

"Yes." Liza surprised herself at the answer, but yes she would go. Now that she was here, she would see the whole of it. It was the only way to write about it — the only way to come to terms with it as Ted had said. If it meant going to a shouting camp meeting to hear her sister, purported to have been any man's woman if he could pay the price and now turned preacher, she would, indeed, go. Besides, she had to admit, her curiosity had been piqued. Would she find in Mattie a remnant of herself?

"If you want us to, we kin go with you," Jed offered. "I'm kinda curious myself about hearing a woman preacher.

Most folks don't believe in women preaching. They say none of Jesus's disciples was women."

Liza smiled wryly as she remembered the discussion of women priests with Charles. High Anglicans and country churchmen alike cordoned off their pulpits — holy ground not to be contaminated with females. But her sister had jumped the ropes. They had something in common after all. Liza thought of Mama and wondered if she would be pleased to see her three daughters, each in her own way having achieved a kind of liberation—each with a mind of her own—each escaping the life that had trapped Mama. Omega—educated, wealthy, divorced, childless—Mattie having defied convention, a veritable Moll Flanders, now a preacher woman invading masculine territory. And herself. She had done all right in a man's world. Poor Mama! What would have happened to her if there had not been a George Marion? Even so, Mama had held her head high, though the Neck had condemned her and her uppity ways and regarded her delayed church wedding with children as attendants a charade. Mama had bequeathed something of her spirit to her daughters. Even Little Ida had died reaching her midget arms high to obtain the forbidden. Suddenly Liza realized what she was doing. She was striking a dry rock of the past and was finding water, clear and cold like mountain waterfalls tumbling free, not dark and still like the river, where as a child she could not see beyond the bend. Nora Marion's girls had dared to round that bend, lifting the oars a boat that took them out of the narrow, gloomy channel to a wider expanse of sea and sky. Going against the tide had been a vigorous trek, Liza thought, but the exercise had toughened sinew and bone.

Martha's voice brought her back. "Eat the last piece of chicken, Miss Liza. We jist homefolks. Ain't makin you company." Martha passed a lone drumstick, left on an otherwise empty platter yellowed from the countless warm-ups in the oven. Liza, whose hunger pangs had ceased three pieces ago, took the offering, knowing that her hardy appetite would please them. Feeding a guest remained the primary way to entertain in the South.

"I'm not company. Please call me Liza. All of us are from the Neck. And as Jed said earlier, we are practically kin." Both of them smiled, pleased at the warm response. Liza looked down at her black checked skirt with green patent leather belt. A crisp white blouse with a bit of green ribbon attached to her collar with Aunt Lizzie's cameo completed the ensemble. Dress, speech, hair-do had drawn a fence between her and these people who acknowledged that barrier with "Miss." Liza was letting them know that she was willing to let down the bars. She was rewarded with warm smiles as Jed stammered, "Me and Martha done took you like homefolks, Liza," trying out her name without the formal greeting. "You sho done right by Josh. Done what my sister Jane couldna done. Me and Jane had a hard time growing up. It left her kinda mad at the world. Reckon you know about that."

Liza realized that Jed had opened the door for her to say more. But Liza decided to close it softly. "I'm grateful to Jane. Without her there wouldn't have been a Josh, and I wouldn't have had a brother who is really my son. Tom and I had a daughter. Nora was born while Tom was in France. He never saw her, but he regarded Josh as his son. Josh called him Papa Tom. Let me help you with the dishes, Martha," she offered, rising from the table and changing the subject tactfully.

"Oh, no, Miss — er Liza," she corrected herself awkwardly. "Be done in a jiffy. Why don't you lay down fer a spell and rest. There's a breeze on that side of the house. Jed will open the window. We got screens," she added proudly.

In the "company room" Liza could hear the soft exchange of their voices, pitched deliberately just below her ears and felt assured that she stood favorable with them. She drew back the spread under which the quilt's pattern was tediously assembled from small scraps that had once been dresses. The tiny uniform stitches in the quilting evoked scenes of women who sat around a frame supporting a new quilt inter-lined with cotton beaten thin and smooth from the fall crop. At the end of the day a new quilt could be added to the store of winter covers and another chapter in the lives of Neck housewives written from their exchange of neighborly gossip. Quilts, a quilting bee, and this soft feather mattress, the culmination of saving for years the down of fowl, wild and tame—these were the minute details of life without which the people would remain vague and unidentified. Indeed, as Martha knew, a breeze ruffled the starched white cottage curtains. Liza could bet they had been made from bleached sugar or flour sacks. The frugal housewife learned to utilize everything. On impulse Liza rose and took paper and pen from her suitcase. "A Day in the Neck," she wrote at the top of the page and began an epistolary account to an imagined urbanite in a bustling New York or a lumberjack in the frigid climes of Maine or Colorado.

That night she went alone to the tent meeting. She had turned down the Ports' offer to accompany her, making the excuse that she wanted, if possible, to visit with Mattie alone for an undetermined length of time. They seemed to understand and displayed no hurt feelings.

The tent had been pitched strategically at the crossroads that marked the route to the tobacco markets in town or to the boats now making daily voyages to Georgetown. Liza sat in her car and watched the people gather. They came by wagon, pickup truck, and car. Those living nearby walked. It was an odd assortment—young boys in overalls, old men with indiscriminate color and style of trousers hitched up by leather suspenders, a group of giggling girls—all dressed in long white dresses with chatter close enough that Liza surmised their purpose was not entirely to seek holiness. Nursing mothers, their breasts obscured by a diaper or handkerchief and old ladies tottering along with cane walking sticks or leaning on the arm of a more reliable relative. All made their way to the tent under which folding chairs awaited them. Liza wondered if Mattie had already arrived and was somewhere within the environs preparing her sermon. Afraid that the crowds would soon leave no empty seats, Liza emerged from the car and joined them. Jed had said that the meeting would start at sundown. Liza remembered that people gauged time not by the hour but by the heavens. She managed to stay on the fringe of the moving congregation and was a bit surprised to find a handful of Negroes bringing up the rear. Now she could hear the twang of a guitar being tuned to a piano note, neither of which appeared to be synchronized. The back benches in the tent were all filled with young people. A tall gangling fellow in white ducks and black bow tie with a wide blissful grin suddenly grabbed her arm with "Sister, we got plenty room at the front" and steered her to a space in the second row. By now the guitar and piano on the right side of a makeshift speaker's stand struck up a lively tune strongly resembling a hoedown in opry land. A clapping of hands joined the music and one brazen youth at the back yelled, "Let 'er go, brother." Directly in front of the pulpit was a bench stretching the width of the tent. It was unoccupied. Liza assumed this was the mourners' bench and felt uncomfortably close to it. A string of lighted lanterns dangled above the pulpit, unnecessary at the moment but sure to be of use before the end. Somebody started "We want Sister Mattie" and was momentarily joined by a chorus accompanied by shuffling feet and clapping hands. From the rear of the tent emerged a tall woman, not obese, but carrying her excess weight compactly distributed by a corset that pulled in the waist and raised her breasts to prominence. Her dress was white and long sleeved and flowed down to the tops of her white pumps. Her hair, a color somewhere between brown and gold, was finger waved back and ended in three neat balls at the nape of her neck. She wore no makeup, but her dark eyes flashed acknowledgement to the right and to the left and seemed to illumine the entire face. In the crook of her right arm she carried a black Bible and in the other a silver pitcher. "God in heaven," Liza whispered, "it's Mattie." At that precise moment Mattie's eyes met hers. A smile spread over Mattie's face. Liza would not have been surprised if she had stepped down from her raised platform to greet her. Instead, she placed the Bible on the stand and addressed the audience. "Brothers and sisters, tonight I'm gonna give you a drink of water." At this moment a hand proffered a glass and Mattie poured it half full from the silver pitcher. "This water came from a well. I poured it in the pitcher from a drinking gourd. Folks, this is the kind of water you drink everyday. But what I'm offering you tonight is a drink where you'll never be thirsty again. What's more, folks, this water has magic in it. Once you drink it, you'll never die." "Amen." "Praise the Lawd," burst from dozens of mouths. Mattie raised her hands to quiet them. "And where do I get this magic water?" This time she raised the Bible in the air. "It comes from the rock that Jesus left us. It'll be here 'till he comes back for us. And who knows? That might be anytime—even before the last prayer is sent up tonight in this tent."

Liza sat open-mouthed. There was no way she could identify the Mattie with this woman who promised eternal salvation to these people. And how creative she was with the water gimmick. Now Liza remembered her first teaching day when she, too, had offered magic. Instead of a water pitcher and Bible she had used a globe and Elson's Basic Reader. Liza had never thought Mattie particularly clever. But then, Liza had to admit, she had never paid much attention to her sister—she was just a stereotypical flirt, a conniving female who sold her body to the highest bidder without the least thought of sin or retribution. Liza examined this woman now, and though she recognized the showmanship, there was something else. Did Mattie really believe what she was saying?

The musician struck up the familiar hymn, "When the Roll is Called up Yonder" and the whole tent burst into animated song. Mattie stood with arms raised, face averted, hands holding up the open Bible as though she were offering a gift to heaven. The song ended and a lull crept over the tent as Mattie placed the open Bible on the speaker's stand. She began quietly, almost reverently: "Brothers and sisters, lemme tell you a beautiful story. 'Cept it ain't a story. It comes straight from that rock I been telling you about—the word of God. You'll find it right here in John, the fourth chapter beginning at the seventh verse. You kin read fer yourself when you git home. I ain't gonna read to you, and I kin read. I was taught at my Mama's knee. I'm gonna put it in down-to-earth talk. The kind of talk you hear under the tobacco sheds or in the cotton fields. I ain't got nothing aginst King James, but if our Lawd was here, he'd talk the way we talk." There was a loud amen coming from a corner. "You see, it was this way.

Jesus had been travelling a long way—all the way from Judea. Bout as fur I reckon as from here to Georgetown. Well, he was tired. Remember he got tired like you and me. Got thirsty. It so happened he was in a place called Samaria. Now the Jews kinda looked down on Samaritans—kinda like city fellows look down on the Neck. Or Yankees on the South. But praise the Lawd, Jesus don't look down on nobody." There was a loud applause. "Not even colored folks." There was no applause. "Well, Jesus was thirsty as I was saying. Mouth dry. Hot day. Been walking in the hot sun in the desert. Hotter than the Neck the Fourth of July worming tobacco. So he sit down by a well. Reckon it was kinda like our wells. Well, he wanted a drink the worst way. But he ain't got no bucket. Out of the blue here comes this Samaritan woman all diked up. She had a bucket. Right away Jesus asked her to give him a drink. Now that woman knowed how Jews felt about her people. Considered 'em dogs. They wouldn't eat or drink with 'em. She knowed he was a Jew by what he was wearing and his beard. Course she asked him why he'd ask her for a drink. Must be powerful thirsty to ask her, a Samaritan. Then Jesus said something downright strange to that woman. Told her if she knowed who she was a talking to, she would be asking him for a drink." Now she raised the pitcher slowly so that everyone could see it. "You know what kinda water he was talking about? He was talking 'bout living water, the kind where the well never grows dry, don't matter whether it rained in six months." Now her voice grew louder. "Brothers and sisters this kind of water won't never make you thirsty again. It's the kind where death won't never parch your lips. It's the kind of water, not black like Little Pee Dee water but clear and always cool. It's the kind of water that will be right under that boat when you cross over to Gloryland." Now the air was filled with amens and praises. Mattie now had to raise her voice to a scream. "And sinners, this water is free. You don't have to pay a red cent for it. Only thing you have to do is step down this aisle and fall on your knees and accept it. Jesus will forgive you no matter what you done. And brothers and sister I done plenty. Just like that Samaritan woman had done. She had five husbands and Jesus knowed it. Praise the Lawd, my cup runs over tonight. It's lipping full. I invite everyone of you sinners to drink with me." At that moment the piano struck up "There is a Fountain Filled with Blood." The tent shook with singing voices and running sinners, kneeling at the bench with Mattie standing with outstretched hands.

Liza gazed into her sister's eyes. She appeared transfixed, caught up in a world she had just set in motion. There was a strange glitter in her eyes that Liza could not identify. All she knew was that woman in front of her was no sister she had ever known—a woman who had power, who could bring young boys and old men to her feet, some of whom were even now jumping and shouting, "I'm saved. I done drunk from that pitcher." Now there was a general uproar—a hundred voices and waving arms. A young mother grabbed the pitcher and dumped the water on her nursing baby, who responded with a thin wail lost in the avalanche of praise.

Somehow Liza found her way unnoticed to her car. Her mouth was dry and her head throbbed. She eased the car out from between a mule hitched to a wagon and a stripped-down truck. A pale moon against a darkening sky tipped the long-leaf pines ahead as Liza turned right. She could still hear the voices, muted now, coming from the tent. She drove in a trance. The two globes of her lights picked up the dark ruts of the country road and the bright frightened eye of a rabbit as it skittered out of the path of the strange intruder. That was exactly how Liza felt. She had inadvertently stumbled into another world and discovered that she was an intruder. She was no less alienated from sister Mattie than she was from Omega. There were things she wanted to talk about to someone who could explain the difference between reality and illusion—who could tell her where three sisters were in proximity to truth—or was there truth at all but a mere illusion. Nora was too young to understand; Uncle John had been too cynical; Papa Gideon too simplistic, and Ted would have the same questions. She looked down at the ring, which even in darkness caught a ray of light. "Oh, my dear Charles," she whispered.

Jed and Martha were still on the front porch. Surprised to see her home so early, Jed remarked, "Home early. Ain't eight o'clock yet."

"No, no. I developed a headache. I think I'll turn in early. Please excuse me." She brushed by them hastily, knowing she was disappointing these good people burning with questions about what she would have to say about her sister.

Somewhere among visions of Mattie sprouting wings and flying skyward with a pitcher of water pouring a thin stream below, a gentle rap brought her up sharply.

"Who is it?"

"Liza, it's Mattie. I ain't seen you in so long. Missed you at the meeting." There was a softness in her voice almost like a child begging admittance after being bad.

"Come in. The door is unlocked." Don't let her think I'm her confessor, she prayed. Let her go to her God.

Mattie stood beside the bed in her white flowing dress that matched the curtains billowing in the night breeze. The long hair had escaped the pins holding it in buns and now fell below her shoulders—lighter than Liza's, but the dark eyes were identical. How odd that she had never noticed that another Brown had grandmother's eyes. Liza had the insane desire to say, "Look, Mattie, me and you got nigger eyes." Instead she bunched a pillow behind her back, drew up her knees under the sheet, and clasped them.

"God loves us both." The statement was as matter-of-fact as if she had said, "The sun rises tomorrow morning at six-forty-seven."

"Did you come just to tell me that, Mattie?" Her question was quizzical, just shy of amusement.

"I reckon it's as good a way to begin as any. I ain't the talker you is."

"You didn't seem to have any difficulty tonight, Mattie."

"I know. But you see, Liza, I opened my mouth and the Lord filled it. It won't me out there tonight. But it's me now. I'm awful glad to see you. How you been?"

Mattie suddenly sat down on the edge of the bed. Liza found herself moving over to give her room. Liza searched frantically for words which eluded her. The truth was Mattie had stymied her. In some queer way Liza realized that Mattie had taken charge, and so there was nothing else to do but wait for Mattie. What she next said startled her even more.

"Liza, I loved your Tom. Only man I ever knew good and gentle like. I woulda took him from you if I coulda. He made me leave after. It hurt me bad when he paid me. He didn't say so but I knew he was calling me a whore. I took the money 'cause I was mad. 'Sides, I needed it. You and me learned long time ago we had to make do. Tom wont your kind, but he worshipped you. I coulda loved him real like. All of me."

At last Liza found her voice. "What you are saying, Mattie, is I married Tom to get away from Papa and Jane. To some extent you are right. I tried to be a good wife. To my credit, Tom thought so, too—especially at the end."

"Liza, I ain't blaming you none. In your shoes I'd a done the same thing. Only there was no Tom for me. I got beatins, too. You didn't notice. You had to look out for Omega. She was so little." There was no rancor in her voice.

"I'm sorry, Mattie." Liza's hand reached out and found her sister's. It was the left hand. The moonlight caught the sparkle in the little diamond.

"I ain't never seen sich a pretty ring," Mattie said.

"You're the first person ever to tell me that. If you could see it clearly, Mattie, the diamond lies on top of a cross."

"I usta want fine jewlry. I wanted Mama's gold wedding band the worst way. I knowed you being the oldest you'd git it. I never had any real diamonds. Only dime store stuff. I don't wear none now. Don't want none. I'll git my jewlry someday. It ain't no doubt about that."

Liza moved over to the other side of the bed. She took a pillow and patted it. "Lie down, for awhile, Mattie. We're both tired. It won't be too long before morning."

CHAPTER THIRTY FOUR

OF TIME
AND THE RIVER

SUNDAY MORNING of the seventh of December 1941, Liza had risen early. Today would be a full one. Still there was time to light the logs in the fireplace in her bedroom and with a mug of coffee, generously laced with sugar and cream, to curl up in her flannel robe in her easy chair and read. She might doze between Donne's poetry or even a Mark Twain tale. Unless she had been completely absorbed the night before in a book she had not been able to finish before sleep overtook her, her custom was to twirl her revolving bookcase of

Edwardian vintage and scan familiar titles as well as new ones. Her fingers pulled out an old friend, Thomas à Kempis *The Imitation of Christ*. There was something so gentle yet compelling in this writer of the fifteenth century. His thoughts were not new: the key to inner peace is the denial of self and the whole-hearted love of God. His was a simple message; the problem was in following his admonition. Yet the forthright way he couched his counsel was comforting if still unattainable. So many times did she remember Charles's words, "I have no choice except to seek God." Now in her fiftieth year she felt no closer to that center which saints of the ages had described and found herself standing on the periphery. Blind acceptance without question remained a problem, but she had to admit that the easiness of circumstances in her life had lessened the need for that oneness with God which people like Thomas appeared to have achieved. Her sister Mattie—no happier human being Liza had ever known—had no doubt about where she stood with the Almighty. Papa Gideon, now an octogenarian, still retained his quiet, undemonstrative faith. Liza, however, pragmatist that she was, accepted Christianity on its orderliness and its benevolent teachings, reasoning that "to imitate Christ" was to find stability in one's life, and if society could adopt his approach, the world would be a pleasanter and safer place to live. The overwhelming joy of communion, which people like Mattie exhibited, Liza did not know. Still there was something in the soothing drops of rain on a tin roof or a dying sun discarding remnants of its last robes of glory. On rare occasions when she approached the altar rail, she experienced a kind of awe that went along with lighted candles, stained glass windows, and the beautiful words of the liturgy in the Prayer Book. These would bring her into deep contemplation of the unequivocal, unconditional love of "the man on the cross" for beings that had not yet been born. The years after her first communion with Charles, she had attended, for the most part, Brown Hill Baptist Church, but when automobiles made Episcopal churches more accessible, she and Nora would often make Sunday a kind of holiday where the two would attend Prince George in Georgetown. Along with Nora, in her sophomore year at the university, Liza had at last been confirmed at Trinity Episcopal in Columbia. The moment when the Bishop's hands had touched her head lightly should have been a profound experience. Liza, however, found herself wondering if this Apostolic Succession—the hands in confirmation reaching back to those of Christ's—had been broken in the Reformation as Roman Catholics insisted. Even so, it was a special time, which she had shared with her child. Omega had surprised them as she had at Josh's graduation. She was there after the service, having made the trip down from Chapel Hill. Another surprise was the afternoon when Omega announced her intention of pursuing a doctorate in English. She was interested in a new kind of literature—stream of consciousness—and introduced Liza to the complexity of Joyce's *Ulysses*, endless sentences without punctuation or capitalization. Their common literary interests had brought them back together, though that spontaneity of affection and openness had disappeared. Strangely enough, Liza shared a kind of warmth and understanding with Mattie, who could not have cared less whether her sister preferred the stodgy ceremony of Anglicanism or the fires of the Pentecostals. Today she would visit Our Saviour in Conway in Horry County, a distance of twenty some miles. The devotion would be Morning Prayer, short enough that she could then drive to Black River Church, where Mattie would be winding down her service with a last altar call inviting sinners to the mercy seat. Liza would sit quietly in the back of the church and would eventually be joined by Mattie with hugs and kisses. Mattie might then announce to all who cared to listen that here was her beautiful sister who, although she had never learned to shout or speak in tongues, would one day lead the praises when she reached the streets of glory paved with pure gold. Then they would go to her comfortable parsonage near-by and warm up the baked chicken or ham and vegetables that had been prepared the day before. Sunday was a holy day. Saturday was the day to do the work. Mattie, whose appetite for men had apparently been satisfied, was now content to mingle with her flock, who all adored Sister Mattie. Her checkered past made her the more endearing, because her changed life was living proof of the power of God. On the days when Liza visited, they dined alone, but today was spe-cial. Joey and Omega would join them for dinner, the midday meal in the South. Two years ago Mattie had rescued Joey from the sins of perdition in the flophouses in Charleston and worked her magic on him, finally getting him a steady if ill-paying job in the Morgan Lumber Company nearby. Joey was neither the vocal witness for Christ like Mattie nor the silent skeptic like Liza. His religion was to take no thought of tomorrow and if today held promise—*carpe diem*—seize the day. Again Omega brought surprises. The times when she and Joey had been together, there appeared an easiness and cama-raderie that neither Liza nor Mattie shared with their siblings. Liza smiled and thought to herself, "Life's little ironies." Now Liza read aloud from Thomas: "No creature is so little or so mean" (or so big Liza mentally injected) "as not to show forth and represent the goodness of God." With that thought Liza replaced the book on the shelf and went over to her chifforobe to take from the hanger the red wool suit with black velvet trim. Hats being fashionable and a must in any church, Liza chose the wide-brimmed black felt that accentuated her slim figure mounted on three inch heel shoes and matched the eyes that still flashed upon occasion. On recent Sundays a middle-aged lawyer who had set up practice in Conway after a messy divorce in Spartanburg had surveyed her appreciatively and had suggested three Sundays before that they might share dinner at the Town Grill. Liza had demurred graciously but thought that sometime she might investigate the interest registered in his gray intelligent eyes. But not today. The four Marion off-springs, children rising from dark waters of the past, would sit around a table and share food if not inner communion. What an odd assortment they were. All grown up, Mama, she thought, but no longer in rainbow colors.

The strains of the organ following the benediction had scarcely drifted up toward the beamed ceiling of Our Saviour when a tall figure in gray pin stripe blocked her exit from the pew. "Have you heard the news, Mrs. Brown?"

She raised her dark eyes, questioning. For the life of her she could not for the moment remember his name. He read the dilemma and said quickly, "Oh, I'm sorry. I'm Mark Highsmith. I just didn't know whether you had heard the radio report." There was gravity in his voice.

"No, I haven't." Liza found herself thinking she liked his voice and the wealth of gray hair perfectly groomed. Before she could assess other possible attributes, he broke in.

"Pearl Harbor was bombed this morning. There is no doubt. We are at war."

Before Liza's eyes flashed Tom in his uniform and the naked fear in his eyes, and Charles and Jess and the buddy that Jess couldn't save. Now there was Josh and Forest and all the other young men—and women, too. She could almost see her

Nora, full of that youthful enthusiasm to save the world, asserting her feminine role and fantasizing the glamour of it all. "Oh, no!" she whispered.

"I have a son in ROTC in his last year at Clemson." It was as if he were reading her thoughts. "I knew a long time that it was inevitable. I'm surprised it didn't happen sooner. Guess I'm one of those weak pacifists."

"Me, too." Liza confided. She reached out to steady herself on the oaken pew. What she said next shocked her. "Damn!." How dare she raise such a profane voice in this place and to a stranger.

"I know." He did not appear the least startled by the ferocity of her reaction. "Looks like we are determined to destroy ourselves." He opened the door to the pew and stood aside for her to pass. No other words passed between them, and Liza felt somewhat deprived that the conversation had ended so quickly.

As she opened the door to her Chevrolet, she turned back to see Mark Highsmith conversing with the robed lay reader who had conducted Morning Prayer. Both men's eyes turned on her. Liza knew that they were exchanging opinions of the woman who so brazenly expressed her radical ideas that maybe matched their own. Driving along the few miles to Mattie's house, Liza gripped the wheel and momentarily blinked her eyes to shut out the horrors of lives in trenches unprotected from falling bombs. Certainly the atrocities of Germany had to be stopped, but like the man who had broken the news to her, she abhorred war. The bids by Britain for American help had struck a certain accord. Charles's England was under daily fire; yet she could not be a part of those who waved the banners of war. She remembered how Jesus had wept over Jerusalem as he foresaw the destruction. Imitating him had nothing to do with waging war.

The bright sunny morning had sunk into a gray misty rain. The whir of her windshield wipers monotonously repeated, "Please God! Please God!" The quiet contentment of her life had been interrupted and once again she found herself calling upon Power, real or imaginary, to intervene. She feared not so much for her country but for the ones she loved who would be drawn into the conflict. She drove slowly. A group of teenage boys in the car behind her honked as they zipped by on their Sunday morning joy ride. Liza wondered how long before the terror of driving into enemy lines would replace their happy, carefree excursion. These were her thoughts as she paused in front of Mattie's church.

The doors were still closed and Liza didn't feel inclined to join the praising throng who, she thought, were unaware that a place like Pearl Harbor even existed. So she steered the car forward and turned into the circular driveway in front of the five-room shotgun house built by loving hands for their beloved Sister Mattie. From her clutch bag she drew out a silver compact engraved with the letters *EB*, a part of the memorabilia of her great grandmother. She dusted her nose lightly and was preparing to freshen the color of her lips when another car drew in front of her. Joey was at the wheel of Omega's Olds. They both waved just as the mist became a downpour, sending rivulets of water down the windshield. The rain turned her brother and sister in the car facing her into phantom figures closer to her mental images of them. She could not understand their latent closeness anymore than she could fathom the reason for nations to be driven apart until war thrust them into each other's arms on a battlefield.

The downpour ceased as suddenly as it had begun. Typical of Low Country weather, she thought. Would that the affairs between heads of state could change so swiftly and avert disaster. Each of them waited for Mattie, who ten minutes later was beckoning them into her house. The three, with hands over their heads to protect them from the drizzle, ascended the steps to the porch. "Lord, have mercy!" Mattie chortled. "Afraid of a little rain? Must be all you needing a fresh baptizing." With that she ushered her brother and sisters into the sitting room, the humbler name for the formal parlor in more ostentatious domains. A hodgepodge of nondescript furniture, no doubt donated by church members or bought at a second hand store for a few dollars, filled the room. On one wall behind the sofa was a large framed picture under glass of Leonardo da Vinci's *The Last Supper*. Two other pictures, the familiar head of a bearded Christ in sepia and *Praying Hands* completed the decorations on the blue walls. Joey flopped down on the sofa and yelled, "Mat, I'm hongry as a bear. Git the vittles on the table so these guts will stop growling. That stingy Mega wouldn't stop long enough to buy me a hot dog. Sho kin tell who raised her. Uncle Joe would squeeze a nickel 'till the pennies hollered." Omega stopped his speech with a playful slap on the cheek. He grinned, completely oblivious to the missing teeth making three gaps as though they had been targeted by a BB gun. Liza looked at her brother and saw Papa. He had the same boyish face, marred though with a jagged scar, and blue eyes and hair that needed cutting. A two-day's growth of beard gave evidence that Joey had traded a shave for an extra hour's sleep. Blond Omega in flannel trousers and a red pullover sweater pushed Joey's feet aside to make room for her to sit down. Liza followed Mattie into the kitchen to lend a helping hand. As they passed through the dining room, Liza noted that the table had been set for four and a few sprigs of pyracantha made a pleasing centerpiece. Not one of the four plates was of the same pattern and was quite at home with the unmatched straight chairs assembled around the table. Antiques and fine china don't of themselves bring warmth, Liza thought, and the little room had plenty of it, even though gray mist out the one window shrouded the pecan trees. Mattie wrapped one arm around Liza's waist and gave her a second hug. "Lemme git you a apron. Don't want you to spill gravy on that suit. Don't believe I seen it before. Did you order it from Sears or Montgomery Ward?"

"No, I picked it up at Tapps in Columbia. I was visiting Nora. She's finishing up pre-med courses at the university. She has already been accepted in medical school in Charleston for next fall."

"Gracious goodness, Liza," Mattie said as she tied the sash of a flouncy apron around Liza's waist. " Wouldn't our mama be downright bamboozled at how we all turned out? Me a preacher," she said proudly. "Mega one of them college profs; you a big land owner and writer, and now Nora gonna be a doctor. Even that no-good Joey," she said affectionately, "finally settling down. The bookkeeper at the lumber company told me Mr. Morgan gonna make him a foreman. That'll mean a raise. I wanta see him git the hots for some good Christian girl, git married, and have some younguns. Kinda wish I had had some. Got rid of 'em quick like. Ashamed of it. But God done forgot it. Me, I still git bad dreams. Wages of sin," she finished philosophically.

Liza decided now was the time to ask. "Mattie, you didn't get pregnant with Tom?"

"Yep. It was a boy. Only youngun I carried to the time. I woulda kep him, husband or no husband. Fact is, after Tom, I started turning my life around. Now look at me. Woman preacher of the largest Pentecostal church this side of the

Little Pee Dee." Even the news of the imminent war paled at this announcement. The inscrutable ways of God, Thomas à Kempis would have said, Liza mused.

Mattie was dishing out dessert, mounds of banana pudding—fruit and vanilla wafers snuggled in thick yellow custard. On each dish she plopped a healthy dollop of whipped cream. "Go slow on mine," Omega warned. "I must get off five pounds before Christmas. Fruit cake and apple pie are hard to resist. College won't be opening until after New Year. I plan to celebrate at Oak Grove. I want you all to come for Christmas dinner. Liza, bring Papa Gideon and Mama Minnie. Josh wouldn't think it was Christmas without them. He's bringing his new girlfriend. I haven't heard from Nora but know she'll be where her mama is. And by the way, Liza, I got a copy of the *WPA Guide for the Palmetto State*. I know you did the articles for the Low Country. They are quite beautiful," she added. "You must keep writing. A whole novel lies somewhere between the Little and the Great Pee Dee. You don't even have to fabricate the conflict among characters." Omega glanced briefly at the ring Liza was wearing on her right hand. "This time next year you might be at the top of the bestseller list," Omega finished as she took her spoon and pushed the whipped cream to one side of her dessert.

"I don't know what any one of us will be doing this time next year, Omega. Have you heard that Pearl Harbor was bombed early this morning?" Liza questioned.

"Where in the hell is Pearl Harbor?" Joey asked. "Never heard of a landing made outta pearl. Thought they was what rich women like you and Mega wear." Joey now turned his full attention to the last spoonful of his banana pudding and handed it to Mattie for a refill.

"Joey," Omega informed him, "Pearl Harbor is a port in

the Hawaiian Islands. Our navy's anchored there." She turned to Liza. "When did you hear?"

"At church. This means war. Next year this time people close won't be celebrating Christmas with us. I think your idea of a reunion at Oak Grove is a good idea. Nora and I will be there."

Mattie had moved quietly from the table and switched on the radio in the sitting room. Above the static they could hear the announcer in excited gasps describing the carnage of sailors in noisy slumber after a previous night of celebration and never waking as leaden missiles fell from the sky into American ships. Speech around the table had ceased. Liza crossed herself and Omega followed suit. Joey, not quite understanding the import of the news, moved his spoon around his still empty dessert dish. It was Mattie who broke the silence. "The Bible tells us that before the end of time there will be wars and rumors of wars. May be Judgment Day is a coming. Last time, God destroyed the earth in a flood. Promised next time it would be with fire. Might be the end of us all."

"It most certainly will be for numbers," Liza said solemnly as she rose and began taking empty plates into the kitchen.

"Mighty hard on Liza," Liza heard Joey say as she stacked the plates in a dishpan of sudsy water. "Done lost a husband in the war," Joey reflected.

"And someone even closer," Omega responded. Liza was pleased that there was no bitterness in her sister's voice.

Liza closed the door on Mark Highsmith and turned toward Uncle John's library. Mark's kiss still lingered on her lips, pleasant and warm and satisfying. She sat down in a swivel chair in front of a mechanical typewriter. A calendar with a beautiful view of Lake Grasmere was thumbtacked to the bookcase at her side. All the days had been crossed through April twenty-second. Shakespeare's birthday and death, Liza mused. The letter from Prentiss Hall publishers lay open on the desk.

April 1, 1943

Dear Mrs. Brown,

We are interested in your novel, *Beyond Two Rivers,* and would like to discuss certain revisions before publication. Could you possibly come to New York for a meeting with one of our editors? We shall be happy to defray the expenses of travel and hotel accommodations. We hope to hear from you soon.

Liza opened the hefty tome of typewriting papers and pulled out the prologue.

Spring comes early in the Deep South. No mountain snows trickle down to swell streams. Lakes do not clack under a thaw. Frigid days are few even in January, and winter's breath is little more than icy mists collapsing hours later under the gaze of Phoebus...